CHIMERA

Chimera

Published by Wavelength Books.

www.wavelengthbooks.com

ISBN: 978-0-9847738-5-5

Also available as an ebook:

eISBN: 978-0-9847738-4-8

Books by Sarah Stegall

Farside

Deadfall

(Research)

The Truth is Out There: The Official Guide to The X-Files

Trust No One: The Official Third Season Guide to The X-Files

I Want to Believe: The Official Fourth Season Guide to The X-Files

Maps by Wavelength Books.

CHIMERA

BY

SARAH STEGALL

wavelength
books

Wavelength Books

2012

Contents

Maps

Map of Canada

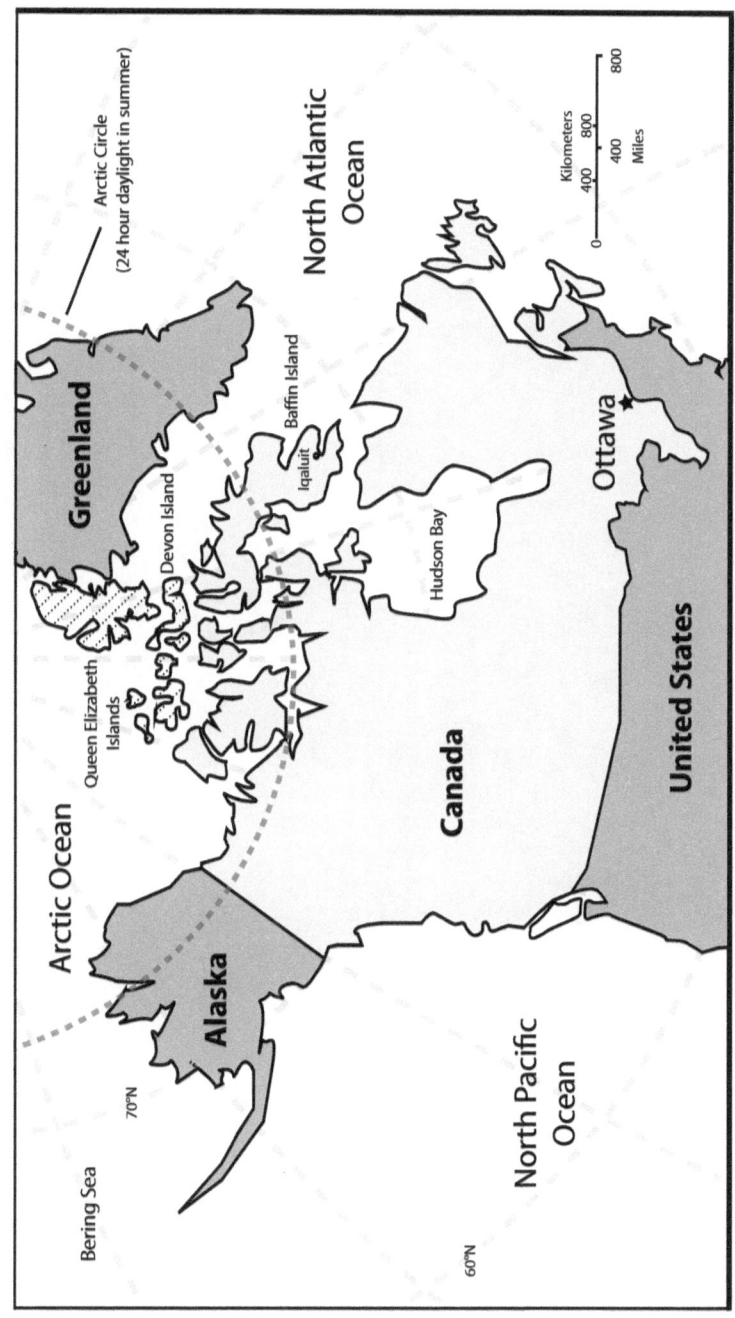

I - RESOLUTE BAY

Resolute Bay "Qausuittuq", Nunavut, Canada
74° 41'51" N, 94° 49' 56" W

Nick Tonarak slammed the socket wrench against the undercarriage of the all-terrain vehicle sitting on the blocks above him. "Dammit!" He scooted backwards on his mechanic's sled, sucking on his hand. He rolled out from under the ATV into the large, cold garage, staring up at the fluorescent lights.

A large white wolf wagged her tail as Nick emerged. She looked down at him, tongue lolling. A whine, and a cold nose was stuck in his ear.

"Stop it," he said. "I cut my hand with this cheap piece of *merde*. Get me the twenty millimeter socket wrench, will you?"

The wolf turned and padded across the concrete floor of the garage to a tool chest lying open on the floor. Neat and compact in her ivory fur, she looked wildly out of place in the cluttered garage. She nosed among the tools lying around the box, then looked back at Nick. She whined, and wagged her tail again.

In Nick's head, he heard her frustration. Her head came up and she looked at him intently. ::Which one?::

"The one with the green duct tape wrapped around the grip," Nick said.

The wolf pawed at the tools on the floor, found the green-handled one, and gently picked it up in her teeth. She trotted back with it and dropped it to the floor next to Nick.

"Thanks," he said, rubbing behind her ears. Grabbing the wrench, he scooted back under the ATV and attacked the stubborn plug again. Suddenly it gave way, and a thick jet of red-black fluid gushed out. It splashed on his jacket as he scrabbled for the collector pan. Positioning it under the flow, he backed out from under the ATV. When he was clear, he rolled off the mechanic's sled and sat up. In one hand he held the bleed plug.

"Stripped the threads. I hope we have another one." He turned the short screw-like plug over in his hand. The hand was callused and dark, with grease worked into the creases and fingernails. He grimaced; it would take hours of scrubbing to get the grease out of his hands before he could carve again. The oil tended to stain the delicate bone he worked with. He sucked on the bleeding scratch that ran across the back of his right hand.

Something thumped to the concrete floor beside him— the first aid kit. The wolf sat down on her haunches, tail wagging, grinning. ::Bandage::

Nick smiled. It softened his harsh features, whose wide cheekbones, high bridged nose and black eyebrows spoke of his Inuit heritage. His eyes met the wolf's in a companionable moment. "Thanks, kid. Too bad you can't stitch me up." He opened the kit and started sorting through it for alcohol swabs and a stick-on bandage.

The wolf licked his ear. ::Change the music? Please?::

Nick looked up. He was on eye level with the wolf, so he met her amber eyes squarely. Among real wolves, that would have been a challenge, but Amaruq had not been born or raised a wolf. "I thought you liked this song."

The wolf turned her head to look at the ancient CD player sitting on the work bench against the wall. It was playing a country and western tune. She growled once.

"Everybody's a critic," Nick said affectionately. He finished tending to his hand and shut the kit. "Admit it, you're a snob. Hank Williams isn't good enough for you?"

She barked again. ::Come on!::

"Okay, okay," Nick said, getting to his feet. He took a moment to stretch, extending his long arms high overhead. His sleeves slid down nearly to his elbows. At six feet, he was one of the tallest men in Resolute Bay, and it was hard to find clothes that fit. The local co-op tended to stock small and medium men's sizes. Nick thought briefly of his mother, how she had made clothes for him, working late in the light of the single oil lamp next to her chair. He shut that thought down. She was dead, and the grief was still too near the surface.

Nick flipped his long black braid over his shoulder and turned to the work bench.

2

"So what's it going to be?" he said, looking down at the wolf. Nick took out the current CD and sorted through the rack next to the player. "Rap? Hip-hop? Jazz?" he teased. He held up a battered CD case. "Or this bubblegum stuff?"

The wolf sat, ears flicking back and forth. ::That one!::

"Oh, man. Are you really going to make me listen to this crap?"

Another tail thump, and an excited yip.

Sighing, Nick stuck the CD in the player and hit PLAY.

As Justin Timberlake began singing, Amaruq barked happily and wagged her tail in time to the music. Suddenly her head swung towards the door. ::Mike::

The door to the outside opened, bringing with it a blast of cold wind and a large man wearing a parka and a knitted navy watch cap. He shut the door firmly behind him. "Hey, Nick," he said, pulling off gloves. "How's it coming?"

"Finishing the last fluid change."

"Good." Mike Thompson nodded, glancing at Amaruq. He was a large white man in his fifties, balding and bearded, with hard features chiseled by a lifetime of harsh weather. "I thought you were going to keep the dog out of here," he said.

"It's cold outside," Nick said.

Mike stared at him. "Yeah. We're above the Arctic Circle, Nick. Maybe you noticed."

Nick bit back a reply. He couldn't afford to rile his boss, not now. "She's no trouble. She stays out of the way."

Mike looked at the wolf and shook his head. "Dogs belong outside, Nick. You know that." A long pause. He shrugged. "If she messes, you clean it up."

::Stupid jerk::

Nick agreed with the wolf's unspoken thought, but said nothing. As Mike passed him, heading for the door that led from the garage into the co-op, Nick put out a hand to stop him. "Uh, can I ask a favor?"

Mike stopped, holding his gloves in one fist. "Yeah?"

Nick looked away, ashamed. "Um. I need another advance on my paycheck."

3

"Again? What happened to the last one?"

I shouldn't have to explain this, Nick thought. He cleared his throat. "You know Tom is sick. He needs more painkillers."

"Why don't he come in to see the doc?"

"He can't. Look, I'll work an extra week. For nothing. I just have to have the money now."

He met Mike's eyes, and saw reluctance warring with compassion. "I don't run no bank," Mike said.

"I know." Nick stood straight. "But I'm good for it."

There was a short silence. "Yeah, you are." Mike ran a hand through his thinning hair. "You know, you could do me a solid."

Nick waited. He felt Amaruq lean up against him in a silent show of support.

"I got that new crew rotation coming in for the NASA project up on Devon," Mike said. A corner of his thin-lipped mouth went up. "Annual migration of the ivory-tower peckerwoods," he said. Nick made himself smile; the joke was as old as dirt. "Anyway, I was gonna send Tom with them as bear guard and back-up mechanic. It don't look like he's gonna make it."

Tom would never hold a wrench again. Nick swallowed. "You want me to take his place."

Mike eyed him. "I was gonna ask Cheechoo to do it, but if you're available..."

Nick nodded shortly. This was a chance to earn money, not beg for it. "Yeah. I'm available."

"It'll be hard work," Mike warned. "You're stuck out there on the cold rock with a bunch of egotistical eggheads fighting academic battles they should have left at home. These guys will stab one another in the back just to get mentioned in the right journals."

Nick knew Mike didn't like the yearly influx of academics and engineers from down South who came up to the Arctic during the short summer for their research projects. He sneered at the professors and called them smarty-pants. Mike especially didn't like the NASA people from the US, who used the cold, deserted polar landscape to test their theories and their tools. Nick had met only one or two of the visitors, but thought they were nice enough.

"How long?"

"Six weeks," Mike said. "I can get Jimmy to show you the ropes—"

"I've been up there," Nick said. He remembered a summer spent with his laughing brother, hunting and teasing the tourists, the scientists. "Tom took me once."

"Okay, then." Mike tugged off his work gloves. "It'll be six weeks, if you feel you can handle it."

A whine made Nick look down.

::Let's go!::

"When do we leave?" he said.

Mike looked down at the wolf. "You can't take the dog."

"Why not?" Nick said instantly. A soft growl sounded; Nick pressed his foot on a nearby paw.

Mike looked at him incredulously. "In a plane? What are you going to do, pack fifty pounds of kibble a week? No, the dog stays home."

Nick opened his mouth to argue, but then an image popped into his mind's eye, an image he knew had not come from his own brain: Amaruq curled up behind a crate in the back of a Twin Otter airplane. "Whatever you say," he said.

Mike nodded. "Come on in when you're finished here. You need to sign some papers."

Nick nodded back. Mike went inside (blast of warm air washing Nick's face as the door opened and closed) and Nick was alone with Amaruq and Justin Timberlake. He looked down.

"You're going to get us both in trouble, Sis."

Amaruq thumped her tail and grinned.

Devon Ice Cap, Devon Island, Nunavut
75° 36' 44.14" N, 83° 48' 09.88" W

The Devon Ice Cap on Devon Island was a half-mile thick and three million years old, covering nearly five thousand square miles of the island. Every summer sizable chunks of it broke off the eastern edge into the Arctic Ocean, and every winter another layer of snow melted a year's worth of information about air and earth and time and change into its surface, building it up again. From space it was a giant splash of white against the brown-gray of the island; from the ground it was an endless plateau of shining ice, whose western face loomed high above the surrounding gravel plain.

But a hundred years of quickly warming climate had fissured the face of the ice cap, causing chunks of the ice cliff to crash to the ground. After millennia of darkness and cold, sunlight had finally reached into the interior, filtering through layer upon layer of ancient ice.

Three days ago the sunlight had touched the device frozen at the ice cap's base for the first time in thousands of years. It had blazed into life, melting a pocket under the ice cap, a rapidly expanding chamber dissolving out of the ice.

Hovering above the uneven floor of the ice cave, a perfect dodecahedron no larger than a man's fist spun silently. The dazzling point of light at its center was as brilliant as a star, and would have blinded anyone looking at it with unprotected eyes. It had been spinning, shimmering, gaining speed ever since the filtered sunlight had triggered it. Now, the air above it grew opaque, then dense, then cleared. A window opened in mid-air, a hole in reality that showed something beyond the ice cave. Anyone gazing through the window would have seen a distorted view of barren dunes, windswept rubble, and a sky the color of rust—a sky that held two scarlet moons. Red light from the floating window poured through, giving the ice-hollowed chamber a bloody tinge.

A shadow passed across the window, and then a gleaming sphere the color of mercury emerged through the window into the cave, hovering, faintly pulsing. Fog-like tendrils of gray and slate swirled inside it, concealing its interior. Slowly its color changed from silver to red, and heat waves shimmered around it. Water cascaded down the walls, froze, melted, refroze into a shining, solid waterfall. A hissing noise from the opposite wall, and a floor-to-ceiling crack opened up, becoming wider. As it widened, the sphere advanced into the hole, still pulsing red. The window, with its view of dunes and blasted rubble, remained suspended in the center of the ice cave.

The orb emerged from the fissure in the face of the ice cap into the brightly lit day at the top of the world, tendrils of frost curling around it. The orb's surface dimmed, shimmered down into white and gray, rendering it nearly invisible against the landscape of ice and rock. The sphere reshaped itself, becoming now a hovering rock, now a chunk of fallen ice before resuming its globular shape. A dim glow reached the surface of the silver, as though something was rising to the outside. Silently, it glided away from the glacier, heading north.

Half a kilometer from the ice cap, it crossed paths with a wolf, trotting across the rocky ground and carrying a bird in his mouth. When he saw the hovering sphere, he halted and crouched warily. A low growl rumbled in his throat. His snout went up, sniffing; he laid his ears back, wrinkling his nose at a smell he could not identify. The sphere circled him, and he turned with it, never letting it get behind him. The sphere re-formed itself into a rock, the bird, then a vague resemblance to the wolf, before returning to its chrome-marble shape. The wolf dropped the bird and barked once, warningly.

White light glowed from the lower half of the sphere, and a spear of light touched the wolf. He whimpered and fell over, foam at his mouth. He lay unmoving, while the sphere descended like a balloon leaking air. It hovered above his body, and a blue light shone down. The sphere moved slowly from nose to tail. The wolf's eyes rolled, showing white, and thin drool fell to the rocks beneath him. The sound he made was something between a whimper and a growl.

Then the sphere moved, twin blades snicking out on either side. It swooped once, there was a wet, ripping sound, and blood sprayed the underside of the sphere, disappearing instantly. There were tearing and sucking sounds. The sphere rose and flew on a beeline back to the ice cap, bearing a dripping burden beneath it.

"I thought you said this was midsummer." Sophia Abenezra stood in the doorway of the 727, looking out over the world's most northerly airport.

"It *is* midsummer," a voice said behind her. Jennifer Roth, her research partner, wrestled with her carry-on. "Watch out for ice."

Sophia gripped the railing, and the cold seeped through her lined glove. She hefted a knapsack on her shoulder; the layers of thermal underwear, sweater, and parka made her movements slow and clumsy. The wind stung her face. It teased the ends of her chin-length brown hair out from under her parka and whipped it into her eyes. With her gaze locked on her boots, she made it to the ground. She stepped aside for Jennifer and looked around.

Her first impression of Resolute Bay, Canada, was of gray. Every shade and tint of gray surrounded her, from the slush plowed into berms on the edge of the runway to the slate-colored rocks that made up the landscape. The town of Resolute Bay was a huddle of trailers and prefab housing; the occasional red or yellow paint job only emphasized the overall drabness of the landscape.

"And to think we could have spent this summer in Hawaii, studying volcanoes," Sophia said.

Her blonde friend, eyes hidden behind movie-star sunglasses, grinned. In a blatantly fake Russian accent, Jennifer said, "But Captain! This is the garden spot of Ceti Alpha Six!"

Sophia chuckled; in their undergraduate years they had bonded over cheesy dialogue from science fiction movies. *Star Trek II* proved to be a gold mine of catch phrases. "It's a good thing we don't have to rely on our genetically-engineered intellects to survive, then. This can't possibly be summertime; we've traveled through a time warp or something."

"This is picnic weather above the Arctic Circle. Thank God this is mid-summer, or we'd have no sunlight at all." Jennifer grabbed the handle of her pink roll-around. "Come on, I'm going inside."

Sophia squinted into the brilliant sunlight. Alaska had been cold, even in the summer, but it was nothing like this. There was no vegetation, nothing green in this world, only rock and ice and that freezing wind off the North Pole.

Flame and smoke, scorching heat across her back, the angry bite of fire along her ribs...

"Sophia? You okay?" Jennifer peered anxiously into Sophia's face.

"Just...remembering the fire." Sophia took deep gulps of the freezing air, so different from the searing-hot air she'd remembered.

"A flashback?" Jennifer's tone was sympathetic.

Sophia nodded. When would she be free of these memories? "I guess being back in the Arctic triggered something," she said, as neutrally as she could. She was a scientist. She could get past this.

"Well, think of it this way," Jennifer said practically. "There's damn little up here that will burn."

Sophia glanced around at the treeless landscape. *It didn't matter*, she thought. The fire was in her memory, its wake burned into her flesh. She could not dismiss it so easily.

"We should get inside out of this wind," Jennifer said. She tugged on Sophia's arm. "Come on."

Sophia followed Jennifer across the tarmac. This was Jennifer's second trip to the Haughton Crater Research Project, but only her first. It was so unlike any place she'd ever been—remote, forbidding, alien.

They halted to let an ATV towing a trailer full of baggage pass. Sophia spotted a berm of bulldozed rock at the edge of the field; she knelt down and started sorting through it. No matter what memory haunted her, she could always lose herself in this: the cool logic of stone. Dolomite, some granitic gneiss, some green schist—*ah*. Sophia picked up a rock the size of her fist, gray with veins of translucent white running through it. She reached inside her parka.

"Come on," Jennifer said impatiently. "I'm cold."

"Go ahead," Sophia said without looking up. Absorbed in her find, she no longer felt cold. She pulled on a lanyard, and it came out of her parka attached to a long black tube, thicker on the ends than on the middle. It had a sleek, deadly look to it.

Jennifer stared. "Why are you carrying a rifle scope?"

She smiled. "That's what it started out as. Remember Greg, back at the lab?"

"The microscope tech?"

"Yes. I got him to build it for me. We took an Austrian-made competition rifle sight, broke it down and rebuilt it with a series of double lenses. It's the only 1500x hand-held microscope in the world. Greg ground the lenses himself; he's patenting the design."

"And all that time, I thought you two were dating," Jennifer said.

Sophia felt her face warm. "Dating? No. Greg is gay. But he's anxious to get this field tested, so he made one for me." She put the scope to her eye and bent over the rock. "He gave it to me right before we left."

There it was, leaping into view: a thin green line meandering through the clear quartz vein in the rock. Sophia turned the knob—it had been designed for one-handed use—the view blurred, then sharpened. *Aha*, she thought with an inner smile. Just as she'd thought: *Nitrosomonas*. There, less than millimeter under the surface of the rock, life flourished in dead stone. Protected from the harsh dry cold of the environment by the quartz "window", a thread of green thrived, taking its energy from the sun, a foothold for life. It fascinated her, this tenacity, this vibrancy. No matter how dead the land might seem, life found a niche, a crevice. The sight of it never failed to thrill her, this hidden life tucked away in corners, in crannies, silent and alive no matter how grim the circumstances.

"I'm freezing," Jennifer said.

"I told you to go on without me," Sophia said. She turned the rock, seeking other signs of life. Was this what the first explorers would find on Mars? This hidden life?

"If I leave you here, you will stay here," Jennifer said impatiently. "I remember last time I left you; you spent the night next to a pond full of alligators."

"But there were concentrations of *Pelagibacter*—"

Jennifer reached down and jerked her arm. "Come on. There is a building over there with hot coffee in it, and we are going there. You can bring your little friend with you."

Reluctantly, Sophia stood. She debated whether to bring the rock along, then dropped it. There were literally thousands just like it within sight. She sighed. "Okay." She dropped the scope on its lanyard back down inside her parka, and winced when its cold metal hit her thermal shirt.

She followed Jennifer across the snow-swept landing strip to the low white building at the edge of the landing field. Even now in July, snow still lay on the ground, thicker in the shadows.

Falling into a bank of snow, rolling to put out the flames, smelling her own flesh burning...

No, she told herself. *She was not going there.* She had returned to the Arctic determined to make a new start, to leave those memories behind her. To leave Paul behind her.

The airport terminal was a battered white building sporting a "Welcome to the Top of the World" sign painted in bright red.

"Does every town above 66 degrees North have to have that slogan?" Jennifer asked. "Wasn't that the same slogan at that little town near Gates of the Arctic?"

Sophia winced inwardly. The very name reminded her of smoke and flame. "Yeah," she said in a voice full of broken glass.

Jennifer glanced at her. "Oh, Christ. I'm sorry, Soph. I didn't mean to bring up bad—"

"It's okay," Sophia said. "I wonder if they have any decent coffee here."

Sophia and Jennifer crowded into the "airlock" type entrance, waited until the outer door was closed, and then pushed through into the interior. An enormous stuffed polar

11

bear glared out of a glass case. Next to it, a computer display cycled through the current temperatures for Miami, London, Moscow and Resolute Bay. The Resolute Bay display told her it was just above freezing outside.

"Oh, that's just cruel," Jennifer said as the display flashed the current temperature on Maui: 80 degrees. "I swear it's as cold in this building as it is outside."

"Yeah, but it's a dry cold," Sophia said. "At least there's no wind. Who are those guys?" She nodded towards a group of people huddled around a thickset man in a fur cap. "They weren't on our plane, but they're all carrying equipment cases."

Jennifer snorted and tucked a strand of blonde hair back under her hood. She took off her sunglasses, revealing baby blue eyes and a makeup job so expert it had held up through the twenty-hour journey. "Martians. Their plane must have gotten in right before us."

"Those are the Mars researchers you were talking about? They look harmless enough." Sophia shifted her pack.

"So does poison ivy, until you step in it," Jennifer said acidly. "I met a bunch of them last summer, when I came here the first time. And they're not researchers. They're amateurs. To them, this is more like a vacation than a research project."

Sophia watched as the group chatted, laughed, and consulted several maps. Jennifer had told her about the rivalry between the NASA researchers in her own group, and their former partners in the Mars Habitat Project.

The "Martians", as NASA referred to them, were a privately funded research group of laymen and scientists, all of whom believed in a manned mission to the red planet. They had come up with their own funding and their own missions. They had even raised an experimental building at Haughton Crater, intended as a test of a Martian colony design.

Every summer, they arrived with a new team of eager volunteers to test their theories about how humans could live for extended periods on Mars. NASA's own Haughton Crater Research Project focused on the testing of robots and unmanned rovers, so the ideological battles could be fierce.

"Frankly, I don't see the problem," Sophia said. "They want to go to Mars. NASA wants to go to Mars. Why the big snit?"

Jennifer glared. "Because they're idiots, Soph. They want to spend billions to send one or two humans millions of miles to a dead planet, support them in an artificial environment for a year, then fly them home. For the same amount of money, we can send unmanned robotic missions to every planet in the solar system. Twice. They're not just dreamers, they're dreamers who keep telling the public the impossible is possible. And sucking up all the money."

Sophia wasn't sure she agreed with this but was too tired to argue. Jennifer was normally the friendliest woman in the world but got very defensive when the subject was funding for experimental research. Sophia understood: her own funding was shaky at the best of times. *Oh, what she could have done with more money...*

Sophia eventually found her equipment crate, her overnight bag, and her laptop case.

"Ready?" Jennifer said. "Let's go."

Outside, Sophia found herself leaning into the freezing wind, watching where she placed her feet. Walking down the gravel road, they passed small pre-fabricated houses, sheds, and several parked snowmobiles stranded on rocky beds. One square building sported a steeple and a white cross.

Jennifer grunted as her little rolling suitcase hung up on a stone. "I swear, elves come out in the winter and sharpen these rocks."

Ahead, a large green building with a huge dish antenna mounted on the side read "CO-OP". Framing the front door, two huge curving white objects reached nearly to the roof. Sophia said, "What the heck are those?"

"Whale jaw bones," Jennifer said. "That's our hotel, at least for now." The interior proved to be beige, crowded and blessedly warm. "Watch our stuff and I'll check us in," Jennifer said.

While Jennifer stood in line to get their room, Sophia looked around. The walls were decorated with murals of Inuit women and children done in a naïve style, with posters of frozen seas, pack ice and polar bears here and there. But for those, Sophia could have been anywhere in North America in the winter. Men and women in parkas, toques, sweaters and boots stood or sat, talking, fiddling with luggage. One couple in a corner was necking. Another man, grizzled and lean, had slumped into a corner and was asleep, head back and snoring.

She listened to snatches of conversation.

"...but his magnetic anomaly map is all wrong. When you do the quantitative analysis, it doesn't add up."

"...and the Russians are demanding more access even though Norway claims it as sovereign territory..."

"...unmanned Arctic drift station, but I told him we needed better monitoring..."

"...left the project to work for some damned oil exploration outfit. We really needed him to finish the survey of the Lowlands."

"...ordered those supplies ten weeks ago, where they hell are they?"

Sophia felt a little lost. What was a biologist like her doing in the midst of all these rock hounds and engineers? For a moment, she wondered if it had been smart to apply for her research permit up here at the top of the world. She could have been diving off the East Pacific Rise looking for shrimp that lived in boiling water, or even classifying new phyla in her lab at Berkeley. But no, she had to sign on with a bunch of space jocks, stuck at the top of the world in weather that made more sense in December than July. How did the people who lived here stand it? She couldn't even imagine what winter was like here, in total darkness for three months, in snow and ice and constant cold.

Restless, keeping one eye on their pile of bags, she sauntered over to a display case against one wall. Apparently it was a display of local arts and crafts. She noted a few watercolors, but most of the work consisted of carvings. The materials looked to be stone, but the lighter substances might be ivory or bone. She thought of the huge whale jaws framing the outside of this building. She was turning away, preoccupied, when her eye was caught by one figure at the back of the case. She leaned over for a better look.

A woman, sleek and round-faced, sat on a rock, looking away to her left. Her right arm lay across a large dog—or was it a wolf? But there was something about the wolf...Sophia peered closer. Was that a human face? Was that a hand, or a paw, or maybe something in between? She tilted her head one way and the other, trying to get a closer look.

"Sedna," said a man's voice. "She's a shape-changer."

Truelove Lowlands, Devon Island, Canada
75° 36′ 43.62″ N, 84° 2′ 27.65″ W (coordinates unreliable)

"I can't believe it. *Another* dead battery," Leo West said. In his bulky parka, with goggles and scarf hiding most of his face, he looked like a poorly dressed astronaut. He bent over the magnetometer he was assembling. "This is what, the third one?"

"They were brand new two weeks ago," his partner growled. Glenn Donovan was thin and dark-bearded, in his mid-thirties. He pushed his parka hood back and shoved his sunglasses up onto his balding head. He was intent on the GPS locator he held in one hand. "This thing's dead, too. Did you forget to recharge it?" He shook it irritably.

Leo straightened and pulled his goggles down. "It was working just fine right before we left the camp." He pulled off his gloves to make an adjustment to his instrument.

"Hey, guys." A young Inuit man in heavy parka, reversed ball cap and baggy jeans had been leaning against a granite outcropping. Now he straightened. "Something coming." He shifted the Remington 870 Express shotgun from his shoulder to his hands.

Glenn followed his gaze. "What is it, Joe? A polar bear?"

Both scientists stopped to scan their surroundings. Here in the Truelove Lowlands, at the northern edge of Devon Island, the normally lifeless rocky plateau gave way to a long, shallow valley cut by the Truelove River. Sheltered somewhat from the merciless winds off the Arctic ice sheet, it was an oasis.

The lowlands were cut by several small streams coming off the melting ice cap, sometimes coming together to form a muddy meadowland, sometimes diverging among hummocks of grass or outcrops of granite. Here, in the short but intense Arctic summer, the tundra meadows supported bears, foxes, and even musk oxen. Lush plant growth and acres of open water attracted insects, so the lowlands teemed with butterflies, moths, mosquitoes and the birds that preyed on them. In this season, bears that could not find food out on the rapidly thinning ice roved inland. But what had drawn Joe's attention was not a bear.

It was hard to see if you looked at it directly; Leo thought briefly of stargazing sessions with his father, when he was a boy. If you stared straight at a star, it disappeared into the darkness. But if you looked past it, or to the side, you could catch the glimmer of ancient light. In the same way, the object coming at them across the tundra was there, then not. A gleam of light speared through the clouds and struck it, so that it winked like broken glass. It was that wink that had caught his eye.

"What the hell is that?" Glenn said. He put up his gloved hand to shade his eyes.

Leo scowled. "A new toy from the NASA guys?"

Closer it came, resolving into a ball of chrome about the size of a basketball, bobbing two meters above the ground. Leo saw reflections of flowers, grass, rocks swirling across its mirrored surface.

"Some kind of mirror finish," Glenn said. "I thought they were working on a flying thing over at the research camp?"

"I've seen Vincent's gyro. This isn't it," Joe Palituq replied. "I don't like the look of this." Leo could see Joe's knuckles go white as his hands tightened on the rifle.

Leo didn't like it either; it put his back up. *Too much Syfy channel*, he thought to himself. *Chill.*

Glenn shrugged. "Probably the damn Martians. Amateurs. Hey, assholes! Hello!" He yelled, waving his arms.

"What are you doing?" Joe stepped back.

"You know they have a camera on that thing. They're just trying to mess with us. Very funny."

Joe stared at the approaching sphere. "Hey, don't. This is…I've never seen anything like it. And what's that smell?" He waved a hand in front of his face.

Glenn shrugged. "Fucking Martians. Get back to work. We have three hours to go before lunch. I'm going to switch out that battery one more time. You should be using the—"

"Look out!" Leo cringed as the sphere zoomed over his head, nearly braining him. He spun, keeping the sphere in sight as it slowed, circled the men, and came to rest above their heads, turning slowly. "Hey, you morons!" he yelled at the globe. "Watch how you're driving that thing! You nearly—"

The air around the globe shimmered, there was a silent white flash, and Glenn fell to his knees, then over on his back.

Leo swore and picked up a short red pole, part of the geo-radar assembly. "Hey! What the hell are you doing?" He swung the pole at the sphere. He missed, his momentum swinging him around in an arc like a batter missing a fastball. "This isn't funny!"

Joe brought the shotgun up in both hands, but didn't fire.

Leo saw his hesitation and yelled, "Shoot it!"

"Could be worth a lot of money," the young man said.

Leo could almost see his thoughts: what if this was some expensive instrument deployed by the researchers? How much trouble would a young Inuit man be in if he shot down a multi-million dollar NASA research project? Even if it was only a prank, he'd be the one in hot water.

Leo snarled and swung his pole again, and the pole bounced away before it even struck the surface. Still, the sphere bobbled, dipped, and then drifted closer, its silence both eerie and ominous. "Joe, help Glenn!" Out of the corner of his eye, he saw the boy hesitate, then run to where Glenn lay.

Gripping the pole in both hands, Leo circled to get the sun out of his eyes. The reflective surface showed Leo a distorted image of himself: eyes wide, mouth open, face flushed with anger. Was that a glow under the silver surface? *The Martians were up to some pretty sophisticated pranks,* he thought. But zapping Glenn with some kind of static electricity—not cool. Then the smell of ozone struck his nostrils and a tiny lightning bolt snapped out towards his hand. Leo stumbled backwards with a cry, dropping the pole. "Hey!"

Joe scrambled up, leveling the shotgun.

"Shoot the damned thing!" Leo yelled. "I don't care what it costs some egghead, this has gone too far!" When the boy hesitated, Leo said, "Go on!"

Joe brought the shotgun to his shoulder and fired. The three inch rifled slug bounced off some invisible shield around the silver ball. The ball rocked under the impact, but appeared unharmed. The swirls of silver under its surface hurt to look at. Joe pumped another shell into the chamber. Another flash of white light, and Joe doubled over, gasping. He fell face down and didn't move.

"Joe! Hey, Joe!" Leo lunged forward, slipped on a rock and sat down hard. Now the sphere drifted towards him. Fear trickled down his back as if someone had dropped an icicle down his collar.

"Joe! Glenn, get up, dammit! This is serious. I don't even think that thing is American. Maybe Russian or something. We gotta get out of here."

Silence greeted him; there wasn't so much as a twitch out of either man. *How had this nightmare unfolded so fast?* Leo thought.

"Glenn?"

The sphere hovered, drifted over to the still unassembled radar array. The glow near the surface of the mirror ball intensified, and a ray of blue light shot out; it looked to Leo as if the light *crawled* over the equipment. The sharp smell of ozone tickled his nose. Leo glanced over at Glenn. "Hey, buddy! Can you move at all?"

Glenn's eyes were open, staring. He did not blink. The sphere wafted towards him again, close enough that Leo could see his own terrified face reflected in it. As he opened his mouth, silver-white light glowed on the underside of the ball. Two black lines appeared, widened, lengthened. It took a moment for Leo to recognize them as some kind of thin-bladed extrusion from the sphere, as mirror-silver as the sphere itself. Distorted by the reflections off the convex surface of the globe, it was not clear that they were lengthening...until one touched Leo.

He yelped and rolled, terrified, scrambling to get away, but fetched up against the rock outcropping. He glanced to his left and right, but could see nothing but the long, low stretch of seamed rock. He scooted up into a sitting position. The orb was between Leo and the dropped pole. His right hand encountered something hard—a fist sized rock. Without thinking, he snatched it up and hurled it at the globe. It bounced off, but the globe jittered a bit, turned slightly.

"Go away!" Leo yelled. He glanced over at Glenn, whose empty eyes met Leo's.

He groped around for another rock, his eyes fixed on the hovering globe with its now extended blades. Or wings. Or whatever they were. Just as his hand closed over a rock, the surface of the globe shimmered. A sudden odor, chemical and alien, hit his sinuses. Heat soaked through Leo like hot water through tea. Suddenly his muscles burned then went numb, and he slumped against the rock in a sitting position. He fought to move but could only stare, unblinking, as the globe approached.

Closer and closer it came, the mirrored surface showing him his own distorted, slack face, eyes dull. He fought to move an arm, a finger, to no avail. The globe was within arm's reach now, and Leo could see the swirling, seething metallic patterns just under the surface, as if its interior were liquid. *Mercury?* he wondered.

One of the mirrored blades swept down the right side of his face, so lightly it was like a spider's touch. The light below the surface of the globe glowed and dimmed, glowed and dimmed, like a heartbeat.

Then the icy blade touched his neck and there was a tugging sensation and everything in his head went dark.

Sophia looked up from the display case. A short, red-haired man with wire-rimmed glasses stood next to her, hands on hips. His parka hood was thrown back, and his pale skin was raw with windburn.

"'Sedna'?" she asked.

He glanced into the case. "Goddess of the sea. There's a different version of the legend for every shaman in the North, but generally speaking she is supposed to rule over animals. That looks like the version where she thumbed her nose at her dad by marrying a dog."

"A dog?"

"The creator god, her father, kept trying to marry her off to various men, and she didn't like any of them. Dad threw her out, but the dog was faithful and brought her food so she would not starve. In some versions, he turns into a man at night. After a while she gave birth to a litter made up of dogs and humans. The humans became the ancestors of at least one tribe around here."

"Are you an anthropologist?"

"Nope, just an interested amateur." He smiled, blue eyes twinkling, and held out a hand. "I'm David Beringer."

She shook his hand, feeling awkward. "Of course. Doctor Beringer. You're the one who signed off on my application."

"Yes, but it was Doctor Skorjik who gave final approval. He was impressed with your research in extremophiles in the Aleut range. You really found microbial mats in thermal vents?"

She nodded, turning back towards her pile of luggage. "Some of them were living in waters as hot as 160 C. But I don't expect to find many hot springs up here in the Arctic."

Beringer grinned. "You might be surprised. The impact of the asteroid that formed the Crater punched so far through the Paleozoic marine sedimentary rocks that it hit the Precambrian basement. We've speculated for years that there may be some hot springs far to the east of the crater, maybe even under the ice cap. That's where you planned to go, right?"

His easy manner was appealing, and Sophia found herself relaxing. "Yes. My friend Jennifer and I have teamed up to test her remote-assay DNA mobile laboratory, while I'm—" She blinked. "Wait. I didn't even tell you my name. How do you know who I am?"

Beringer chuckled. "There are only three women coming to the Crater on this flight, and I know two of them personally. That means the one with the field sampling kit traveling with Jennifer Roth would be Sophia Abenezra."

"Ah. Of course. And you're the assistant director of geology?"

"Planetary sciences. I'm head of the mapping project for the Haughton Crater Research Project and environs, for NASA. Also in charge of bio research."

Sophia pushed her hair back from her forehead, wishing she'd had a chance to run a comb through it before meeting her supervisor. "So you'll be taking me out to the ice cap?"

Beringer's smile slipped a little, and he looked away. "No, that's the job of this guy here. Hey, Nick, you've got a fan." He turned, gestured, stepped aside, and a young man who had been facing the other direction turned and met her eyes.

Sophia actually heard the *click* in her head. Certainly she felt the warm flush that spiraled up from her center. His eyes met hers and she saw dark amber, the color of sunlight through beer. He had the wide cheekbones, straight black hair and copper skin of the Inuit, to be sure, but also long legs and a slightly different musculature. That much the biologist in her read. The woman in her read *shy* and *smart* and *sexy as hell* in one swift primal cataloguing.

Beringer was making introductions. "This is Nick Tonarak, our mechanic and local liaison for the Haughton Crater Research Project. By Canadian law, he has to accompany any outsiders over Inuit-owned land, and some of the area you've requested for your survey falls under that rubric."

Sophia caught herself staring and realized that the young

man was holding his hand out. Sophia shook it; his grip was firm and warm, but very brief. He snatched his hand back and stuck it in the pocket of his olive green snow pants. "Nice to meet you," she said.

He mumbled something and looked away. Beringer, amused, nudged him with an elbow. "Sophia was admiring your work here."

Sophia blinked. "Oh. You're the artist? You made the...the Sedna figurine?"

Nick shrugged, not meeting her eyes.

"It's very nice work," she said, wishing she knew more about art.

"You like her?" His voice was a mellow baritone; it almost sounded like a voice trained for radio.

"Yes." Sophia looked down at the little goddess and her dog. "Something about her. I don't know. But I like her."

Nick shrugged again. "You can have her."

Sophia's eyes widened. "What? No, I couldn't."

"You said you liked her."

"Well, yes, but it's valuable. I'd be robbing you—"

His shoulders hunched a little, as if he were bracing against a cold wind. "It's my work. I can do what I want with it. And I can always make another."

She wanted to protest again, but the note in his voice stopped her. *Proud*, she thought. "Then in that case, thank you very much. I...I'll take good care of her."

Beringer touched her arm. "Native tradition says you should give him something of equal value."

Sophia thought furiously. She didn't know what the art piece would be worth. Several hundred dollars? Over a thousand? What did she have that was worth four figures? Her car? Panic started to rise in her.

Nick snorted and said something, not in English. But she caught the tone of it, and the glare from Nick to Beringer. "Oh. You're pulling my leg," she said to Beringer. The older man grinned mischievously.

Nick answered. "You don't owe me anything if I say you

don't. And you don't." He opened the top of the case, tilting it up. He reached in and drew out the little statue. He turned it over in his hand, his thumb running along the smooth curve of the figurine's back. Then he held it out. "Take it."

Sophia for it. His hand was warm as he delivered the figure to her palm; that was why the statue itself felt warm. "Thank you," she said. *Inane.*

His eyes met hers for an instant; his expression was unreadable under the slant of coal-black eyebrows, the broad brow. His mouth was full but unsmiling, very serious. Sophia found herself wondering if he ever smiled.

Jennifer joined them, handing a card key to Sophia. "I've got our room. Hi, Dr. B." She shook hands, then grinned when Nick was introduced.

Beringer's expression grew serious. "Now that Dr. Roth is here, I'm afraid I've got bad news for you ladies. Your colleague, Dr. Greene, was airlifted to Iqaluit yesterday morning."

"Ike? He's okay?" Sophia said in alarm.

"Absolutely, it's just flu, but I'm afraid he won't really be seaworthy for at least two weeks. Canada Health won't give him a certificate allowing him to work up in this remote area until a week after that."

Sophia and Jennifer stared at one another. "Oh, hell," Jennifer said.

"That's not all the bad news." Beringer frowned. "Was Dr. Rivers aware that he had to fill out the paperwork for carrying a rifle, and get it approved *before* entering Canada with a weapon?"

"Uh..." Sophia thought hard. "He was in charge of all the paperwork. I assumed—"

"He has been detained at Ottawa customs for attempting to enter the country with an unauthorized weapon."

"Well, of course," Jennifer said. *"He* was bringing the bear gun. You told us about the bear situation—"

"I'm sorry," Beringer said. "But Dr. Rivers will have to get approval to bring the gun in, and that may take several weeks."

Sophia felt her stomach turn over. "So Jennifer and I are the only two members of the team?"

"Looks like it."

"I don't suppose we could come back in three weeks, when Ike is better, to do our field work?" Sophia asked.

Beringer shook his head. "Not a prayer. We're tightly scheduled as it is, and we had to turn down several proposals after we approved yours. It wouldn't be fair to let you take someone else's slot."

"Maybe we could switch with another team," Jennifer said.

"I doubt it," Beringer said. "This is a highly specialized research area, and most teams have already made other plans."

"You're saying we're shut down? But the Institute has already paid our fees, our expenses. We get a refund, right?"

Beringer looked embarrassed. "I'm afraid the money for your visit has already been spent on supplies and food. The contract states that your deposit is non-refundable."

Sophia jammed her hands into her parka. "We'll just have to manage without Ike and Andy somehow."

"I'm afraid Dr. Skorjik may insist that you abort your mission. You can stay in Resolute Bay tonight, of course, but I suggest you call your sponsors and tell them you're coming back on the next flight." He turned away.

"No!" The word erupted spontaneously from Sophia. All the preparation, all the scrimping and saving, the stress and anxiety of begging for a spot on the NASA schedule—it would all be for nothing. "Please! Dr. Beringer! At least let us talk to Dr. Skorjik! Give us a chance!"

Beringer shrugged. "I just can't see the logistics of it."

"Look, we only need one person in the lab prepping the analyzer," Sophia said. She looked at Jennifer.

"I built it," Jennifer said. "I can run it. No sweat."

"That leaves me to do the fieldwork, gather the samples," Sophia said. "We can get that much of the...the mission done. The rest we can forego." Although foregoing it, she thought, would waste a year of prep work. Still, it was better than going home empty handed.

Beringer narrowed his eyes. "Do you have a field rifle, Ms. Abenezra?"

"No, Doctor Rivers was bringing it, of course—"

Beringer shook his head. "You can't go into the field alone, Ms. Abenezra. And you can't go without a gun. You agreed to abide by our rules."

"Maybe I can borrow a gun—"

"I'll take her," said Nick.

Everyone looked at him. He stood with his arms crossed, his braid a black rope over his shoulder. His gaze was direct, challenging, and it was aimed at Beringer.

"You know the territory she's going? Truelove Lowlands?"

"I've hunted the Lowlands."

Sophia felt a wave of relief go through her. "Yes! Perfect. Dr. Beringer, it won't take more than a few days."

"You're supposed to be our backup mechanic," Beringer said to Nick.

"Got any breakdowns?"

"Well, no, not right now."

"Then I'd just be taking up food and space," Nick said. "Unless you'd prefer me sitting around playing cards with Jackie Qillaq and Matt Issaluk while these ladies fly home with nothing to show for their trip."

Jennifer stepped up to Beringer, almost right up against him. He took a step back, looking down at her with surprise. "We can do this, Dr. B," Jennifer said.

Beringer gave way with grace. "Okay, okay. Tonarak, if one of the ATVs breaks down while you're on this little expedition, I'm docking you a day's pay."

Nick said nothing, but his jaw clenched as the assistant director turned away. Sophia put a hand on his arm and he looked down at her.

"Thanks," she said. "I didn't know he'd dock your pay."

He smiled, and Sophia felt something inside do a slow roll. "Don't mention it," he said. "I'd much rather be out on the land than nursing some wreck of a machine back to life."

"We can't thank you enough," Jennifer said. Her bright gaze told Sophia just exactly how she would like to thank Nick. "This will mean all the difference to us."

His smile faltered, died in confusion. Nick looked away and thrust his hands deep in his pockets. "Meet you at the plane," he mumbled. "There's two groups ahead of you, so you can catch some sleep. Our flight leaves in 18 hours. Be on the tarmac early." He nodded at the women and walked away.

Jennifer nudged Sophia. "Flip you."

"What?"

"I'll flip a coin with you. Heads, you stay in the lab and I go tramping about the wilderness with a healthy, good looking young man to keep me warm."

"What?"

"Oh, come on," her friend said. Her tone grew serious. "Sophia, it's been years. Isn't it time you moved on? Since Paul—"

"No." Sophia felt her throat tighten. "No, not yet. Maybe never."

Jennifer laid a hand on her arm. "You're my best friend," she said. "And you know I'd never say anything to hurt you. But I hate to see you still grieving, still hung up. Paul wouldn't have wanted that."

Sophia felt her face go cold. "It's not about Paul."

Jennifer nodded and withdrew her hand. "Just as well, I guess. It'll do you good to get out, spend some time in the field."

"You sure you're okay staying back here?" Sophia chewed her lower lip.

"Sure. You know I'm happier with indoor toilets and electricity. And maybe there'll be a cute lab assistant I can toy with."

"Knowing you, there will be several, who will all throw themselves at your feet. How do you do it?"

Jennifer arched an eyebrow. "My dear, I *am* a biologist. Field sampling of the local specimens is just part of the job." She bent to pick over her luggage, checking to make sure all their carry-ons were present.

Clutching the little statue in her hand, Sophia gazed after Nick. She saw him slip between some parka-clad tourists carrying backpacks and thrust through the doors to the outside. There was something melancholy about the set of his shoulders. So quiet, and yet...she looked down.

The little sea goddess looked up at her, serene as the moon, a slight smile on her face, as if she knew a secret and wasn't telling.

Stupid. Stupid. Stupid. What the hell was wrong with him? Nick kicked at the snow piled outside the door to the terminal. He'd just given away the best piece he'd carved. What was he thinking? It could have sold for several hundred dollars, enough to keep Tom in medicine for awhile. Instead, he'd handed it off to someone he didn't even know, on some crazy impulse. Could he ask her for it back? *Unthinkable.*

As he cursed himself for a fool, he wondered why his stomach was jittery with excitement, the kind he got when he woke up on the morning of his birthday. He thought of her round face, soft brown hair, a wistful smile. She had big eyes, expressive. They reminded him of a baby seal, so vulnerable. *Which*, he thought, *was ridiculous. She was nothing like a seal.*

He could tell Beringer was none too pleased with his volunteering to escort her. Would he talk to Mike? Maybe get him replaced? There were plenty of men in Resolute Bay who would jump at the chance to earn that kind of money in a week.

He stopped cold, brought up sharply by one thought: he would be alone with this woman, in the outback, for several days. And nights. He felt a slow, hot tide flood through him and then ebb. *Unthinkable.*

But he was thinking about it. That smooth cheek, and the way she moved, light but athletic, like she had a body under that jacket that would—

Amaruq ran up, tail wagging. ::Can we go now?:: Then she sat down on her haunches and cocked her head. It was the same tilt to the head Nick remembered from years ago, when Amaruq had been a little girl. ::What's wrong, Brother?::

"Nothing," he muttered in Inuktitut. "Tourists. Let's get something to eat."

Amaruq snorted and wagged her tail in agreement. ::Pancakes?::

"Sure." What the hell. He'd spring for one last hot meal before jerky and tea for a week.

As he stepped away, headed for the cafe, Amaruq fell in behind him.

Resolute Bay, Nunavut, Canada
74° 41′ 51″ N, 94° 49′ 56″ W

Will Fraser stopped in the door of the Qausuittuq Cafe and scanned the diner. Crowded as usual, with tourists and locals alike. He caught Annie Etulu's eye where she stood by the register, got her nod of welcome. She came over with a coffee pot and cup and filled it without asking. "Hey, Constable. The usual?"

"You bet," Will said. She went away, passing Nick Tonarak and his dog coming in the door. Will nodded at Nick, got no response, and watched as the tall Inuit sat down at the counter. Amaruq flopped down beside him; no one commented on her presence.

Will savored his first cup of the day. He mused over Nick Tonarak; after four years in Resolute Bay, Will still knew next to nothing about the reclusive Tonarak clan. He tried to think about what to do about Johnny Itigaituk's liquor smuggling. He worried over the budget cuts to his department. He thought about the coughing sound he'd heard in the engine of his department's old trawler, and how much it would cost to get it fixed, and how much paperwork that would involve.

His train of thought was interrupted by the six trekkers in the next booth. Five men, one woman squeezed into the red faux-leather benches, laughing too long, talking too loud.

"They'll never believe it when I tell them," one man said in French.

"Then you must show them, not tell them," the woman said, also in French.

Fraser watched with some amusement as a man in a

bright blue parka reached into his pocket and brought out a shiny flask. The stranger made hardly any effort to hide his actions as he uncapped the flask and poured a clear liquid into his coffee. He passed it to the woman. She was short, wiry, with faded brown hair and the windburned cheeks of a veteran outdoorswoman.

The first man reached for the sugar shaker. "But Yves is an idiot. He would not know an uncut diamond if his life depended on it." He poured a long stream of sugar into his coffee.

"This is probably the first time one of your photo safaris ever paid for itself, let alone showed a profit," another man laughed. His long hair stuck out from under a woolen cap with the flag of France in red, white and blue knitted into the pattern. He was slurring his words a bit. "Here, let's have a look at them."

"No, Henri. It is not a good idea—" Blue Parka said.

"Oh, come on. Nobody here but us. I've never seen half a kilo of diamonds in my life. Show 'em off."

Unbelievable, thought Fraser. A little booze, a woman to boast in front of, and a foreign locale were all it took to turn some men into fools. Unless they started off that way. He sipped his coffee, watching over the rim of the cup. Sure enough, the first speaker took a plastic zip-lock bag out of an inner pocket. With "oohs" and "ahhs", his companions leaned forward.

Fraser eased out of the booth, catching Annie's eye behind the counter. The heavy set woman raised an eyebrow, nodded to him. She leaned forward and whispered to Nick. Very casually, Nick swung around on the stool to face out across the cafe, leaning against the counter. He raised his coffee mug to his lips. His gaze slid past Fraser, but the dog at his feet came to attention, staring at the booth full of tourists. Nick's free hand dropped to her head and she sat down again, but her gaze never left the tourists. Fraser reached for his wallet and stepped up to the edge of the table. He cleared his throat.

Six pairs of eyes flashed up to his, and there was a scurrying noise as hands scrabbled some dirty white rocks into a bag. "No need for that," he said in English. He showed them his RCMP badge. "Afraid I'll have to ask you to show me your identification and permits."

Blue Parka man swore obscenely in French.

In French, Fraser replied smoothly, "Monsieur, I speak French very well, and it is well for your sake that I do not, in fact, have a sister. Passports, please."

Muttering, the six displayed their passports, duly stamped. Their permits showed that they had been granted permission to hike the desolate reaches of Cornwallis Island, north of the town of Resolute Bay. He skimmed the permits, noting out of the corner of his eye the furtive movements of the man with the bag. Fraser's hand shot out and pinned the other's wrist to the table. "And this? What is this, Monsieur?" He raised the man's wrist, and the plastic baggie of rugged pebbles fell to the table top. Fraser snatched it up.

There was a long silence, as eyes met eyes around the table, and dropped.

"Monsieur is aware that it is not permitted to cross from Crown lands to Inuit-owned lands without permission? And that it is also illegal to carry away any minerals, artifacts or products of the land?"

"They're just rocks," Blue Parka said sullenly.

Fraser dumped the contents of the bag into his palm. They did look like roughened pebbles. But long experience showed him the clear spots where the matrix had rubbed away, the tell-tale natural shapes of uncut diamonds. "These pebbles are worth quite a lot on the open market. It is not permitted to mine diamonds on Inuit land without permission. Which makes you more than trespassers." He sent his gaze around the table, noting the guilty expressions. "It makes you diamond smugglers."

A small gasp from the woman. The leader spread his hands. "Constable, surely there is some innocent mistake. We were on the lands noted on our map. We may have wandered off a bit. Our compasses, as you know, are not reliable this close to the magnetic north pole."

Fraser poured the rocks back into the bag, sealed it, and

pulled a marker from his pocket. As six pairs of eyes watched, he wrote his name, the date and his service number on the bag. He held it up. "This is evidence of diamond smuggling. I have your passport numbers. And I have a local witness." He jerked his head towards Nick. Nick raised his mug, saluting the six. "So if I decide to press charges, the six of you will stand trial in a court of Nunavut. The government of Nunavut does not look kindly on foreigners coming here to steal native resources." He tucked the bag into an inner pocket of his jacket.

The woman began to sniffle and dab at her eyes. "Valentin, you fool."

"Constable, please—"

"We didn't mean any harm—"

Fraser held up a hand. "It will take me a couple of days to process this paperwork. I note that your plane leaves in three hours. Possibly by the time you leave Canada, my paperwork will be finished. Maybe not." He put his palms on the table and leaned forward. "But I would advise you, Messieurs and Madame, to get on that plane, go back to France, and Do. Not. Come. Back."

He stepped back, and the six poured out of the booth as if it were on fire. Blue Parka was the last one out. As he sidled past Fraser, Fraser put a hand on his chest. "Your flask, Monsieur."

Reluctantly, the Frenchman pulled out the chrome flask and handed it to Fraser.

"Thank you," Fraser said smoothly. "Liquor is strictly controlled in Nunavut. Unless you can show me a permit, this is contraband."

For a moment, the man went very still, and something ugly came into his eyes. Fraser reached up and unzipped his jacket. The halves parted, and the Smith & Wesson automatic on his hip was revealed. The big man's eyes flicked down to it, then up to Fraser's face. Blue Parka scowled, muttered something, and turned away. The six filed out of the cafe. As the door closed behind them, scattered applause sounded from a few locals. Fraser grinned and executed a half-bow.

Nick scooted off the stool and walked over. "Guess some folks never learn."

Fraser nodded him to a seat on the other side of the booth. Annie bustled over with a plate of eggs and toast for Will, pancakes and three eggs for Nick, and a side of pancakes for Amaruq which she put on the floor. Fraser ignored this breach of health regulations. "It's a variation of 'outsiders are idiots'. In this case, tourists who think they're smarter than local law."

Nick dug into the eggs. "What happens to the diamonds?"

Fraser eyed him, saw the frayed cuffs on his long sleeved sweater, the raveled collar of the T-shirt underneath. He knew the eggs had to cost a fortune, knew the Tonaraks didn't have much money. "Same as usual," he answered. "They go to the Crown. Official policy is that they are sold at auction, with the money going to Inuit education funds."

Nick gave him a sharp glance before reaching for the salt and pepper. "And unofficially?"

"Sold at auction and the proceeds go into the general fund," he said. "Same pot, different ladle."

"What's the going rate?"

Fraser squinted. "Not going into the diamond smuggling business, are you, Nick?"

He was treated to Nick's quick, white flash of a grin. "Nah, I'm into rubies. And Amaruq here favors black pearls."

Almost as if she understood, the dog thumped her tail once. She laid her head on Nick's knee.

Haughton Crater Research Project, Devon Island
75° 26′00″ N, 89° 51′00″ W

Dr. Martin Skorjik strode into the communications tent, ducking under the canvas flap. "Have Leo or Glenn called in yet?"

Verna Morris sat hunched in front of a monitor, rubbing her hands together between her knees. "Not a word." She was a burly blonde woman in her late thirties, with hair tucked up into a knitted wool cap of a particularly revolting shade of orange. "Last call-in was yesterday at 1022 hours."

"Have you radioed them?"

"Can't raise them," she said.

"Dead batteries, maybe?"

Verna sat back and crossed her arms, still staring at the monitor. "Dead batteries. Polar bear. Dysentery. Drunken brawl. Take your pick, Doc."

Skorjik frowned. He stood six feet two, with another inch added by his heavy hiking boots, so his head brushed the roof of the tent. The wind had blown his gray hair into a wild crown of spikes, which gave him a mad scientist look known by all his subordinates as the Doctor Frankenstein Haircut. His deeply tanned face and sharp blue eyes spoke of many weeks in the full sunlight and unforgiving winds of the Arctic.

As director of the Haughton Crater Research Project, he had logged more hours in this environment than anyone except the local Inuit. Now he shoved his glasses up onto his head and pinched his nose with one gloved hand. "What's your take on this? Are they just fooling around out there on the Lowlands and lost track of the time? Or are they really in trouble?"

"Dunno," she said shortly. She swept a hand at the computer monitors on the table in front of her. "I've tried the satellites, thinking maybe they could spot them. But the resolution is too low. I pulled the morning flyover image off the GOES East-West satellite at 0700 UTC. The Canadian-Arctic composite told me only that there is too much cloud cover to track two guys in a four-thousand square kilometer area at the top of the world, and that we have a mother of a storm moving in from the west in the next 24 hours. You sure NASA doesn't have the pull to ask for military grade high-res imaging? Infrared would punch right through that cloud cover."

"Come on, Verna. We've been through that before. First time I call in that favor and we find out two field researchers only overslept, NASA will write us off as crackpots. We'll never get access again, even when we really need it."

"Protocol says we have to alert the authorities, then," she reminded her boss. "I contacted Grace and Erlend; they're out collecting meteorites. But they're over at Cape Sparbo, too far to hop over and look for Leo and Glenn." She sighed. "You want to send an ATV to look for them?"

Skorjik thought. Prudence dictated that when a member of the team failed to report in as ordered, all hands should drop what they were doing and find them. And that had been exactly his reaction the first time this had happened, in the second year of the HCRP. After twelve hours of frantic searching, the re-tasked scientists of the Project had discovered their field researchers naked in a tent, oblivious as to the time or the necessity of reporting in.

The next time someone failed to report in, the "rescue" squad found four very surprised researchers, whose unfamiliarity with twenty-four hour daylight had caused them to lose track of time.

"Doc?" Verna's finger hovered over the SEND switch.

"Dammit, we don't have the manpower. I'd have to take someone off a research project, or drag the cook out of the kitchen and everyone would miss lunch. You just know those two guys have dropped the damned radio or some such," Skorjik said, scowling.

"Yeah. Probably." Verna shrugged, her big shoulders riding up and down under her pink parka. "But it's protocol."

"Okay. Tell you what, let me talk to the constable in Resolute Bay. Maybe he has somebody close by up here, a Ranger or someone, who can go looking for them."

Verna scooted over and Skorjik plumped down onto the upturned crate that served as a bench in front of the table full of monitors. Verna tuned the radio to the emergency frequency used in Nunavut, handed the mike to her boss, and sat back with her arms folded.

It took Skorjik three tries to raise the RCMP detachment in Resolute Bay. Finally he heard Constable Fraser's baritone. "Resolute Bay RCMP here. What is your emergency? Over."

"Constable, this is Martin Skorjik up at Haughton Crater. We have a couple of missing field researchers. They're twelve hours overdue to check in. Over."

"Acknowledged. Do you require search and rescue? Over."

Skorjik closed his eyes. If he said yes, and the researchers turned out to be larking about, relations with the RCMP would be strained. But if he said no, and they really were in trouble... Skorjik shook his head. Better he should be embarrassed by a maverick scientist with no understanding of field protocol, than have it on his head that one died on his watch. "Yes, Constable. We need some help. Over."

Verna let out a long sigh and stood up. As he filled Fraser in on the details of the missing men, Skorjik watched her walk over to the radio locker and open it, and begin hauling out walkie-talkies.

Cornwallis Island, Nunavut, Canada
74° 39′ 21.53″ N 93° 49′ 16.28″ W

Nick edged the eighteen-foot open boat around the floating chunks of ice bobbing in the water of the tiny inlet. They were heading up the meltwater creek that led to his home on Cornwallis Island.

This close to home, Nick could feel their voices in his head. Not as distinctly as Amaruq's, more like a faint, whispering echo of emotion. Even in the same room, it would never be more than that, not between the humans in the family. Only Amaruq had changed enough to be 'heard' intelligibly. The farther he got from his family, the more faintly he felt the echoes of them. *Which is why we tend not to get too far from one another,* Nick thought.

::Slow down!:: Beside him in the open boat, Amaruq braced her forelegs.

"Relax." Nick spun the wheel under one hand and slowed the throttle with the other. The ancient Lund Sirius' motor growled deep in its throat, as Nick brought his speed down to a slow walk. "I've been driving this boat all my life, and now you criticize?"

::You're as bad as Tom.::

"You cut me to the quick, Sis," he said, keeping his tone light. "*I* never flipped a boat in my life."

35

::Tom and I did. Fun.::

"Oh, for crying out loud," Nick said, annoyed. "Are you telling me Tom actually rolled this thing with you in it?"

::Teaching me to drive.::

Nick laughed. "Okay, you got me with that one. Hang on, the last turn is coming up."

The wolf braced herself, her fur ruffed up around her neck. Nick slowed, turning the wheel, watching for ice in the shadows. Sure enough, as he rounded the last corner, he spotted the blue-white gleam of ice below the rock. He adjusted the wheel delicately, anticipated the slight bump, and then straightened out of the turn into a narrow, turbulent inlet. The rocky sides sloping down to the water threw back echoes of the muttering 140 horsepower OMC engine. He cut the power and crept up to the battered dock.

Amaruq barked happily. ::Home!::

Uphill from the inlet lay a small cabin backed by a series of low gray hills. Like most houses in this part of the Arctic, it was an insulated prefabricated building raised above the permafrost on pilings. Windows glowed with lantern light. Beside him, Amaruq whined with anticipation; Nick agreed with that sentiment. He reached over and lifted the passenger seat, pulling boxes out of the insulated compartment underneath. Amaruq leaped down onto the dock, barking and wagging her tail, and bounded up the hill. She whined and pawed at the door of the cabin. It opened, and she leaped into the arms of a weathered man in his mid-fifties, sitting in a wheelchair.

::Daddy!!::

"Whoa! Slow down, girl!" he said, laughing as she licked his face. The man wore several plaid flannel shirts layered over a torso running a little to fat. A brown woolen blanket was tucked around his knees, and the tips of moccasin slippers peeked out from under the blanket. His thick black hair fell to his shoulders, with only a touch of gray at his temples. Nutjuitok Tonarak hugged the wolf to him with one hand, waving at Nick with the other. "Come in, son! Coffee's on."

Nick tied off the boat and picked up the stack of flat cartons; the aroma of warm pizza had his mouth watering. He climbed onto the dock and strode up the hill. He passed a battered ATV up on blocks and a dismantled engine of indeterminate make, then took the steps two at a time.

The door led directly into the mud room, a tiny area intended to insulate the rest of the house from sudden blasts of Arctic air every time the outer door was opened. Nick stomped off his boots and shed his parka, gloves and scarf before pulling open the door to the living room. Heat and laughter met him.

The room was almost unbearably hot, but Nick had expected that. It was some eight by ten meters, and served as the main living, dining and family room. On the walls hung trophies his father and brother had brought home from the hunt: walrus tusks, caribou antlers, a tanned sealskin. Some crooked drawings of houses and bears, now faded, were all that remained of Amaruq's elementary-school art classes. No curtains hung in the windows. After all, this far from the town there was no one to peek into them.

A kerosene heater dominated the west wall. Boxes and tools were stacked across from it, and a Nerf basketball hoop had been nailed to the wall. The east wall was taken up by a large bed, now covered in blankets and skins, and currently occupied by a large young man wrestling with a wolf. Amaruq's yips and squeals alternated with human curses and laughter.

Tom Tonarak had once had the same rangy build, wide shoulders and high cheekbones as his younger brother. His eyes were the same amber brown, his hair long and black. Once there had been something more relaxed, more boyish in his face, and his mouth had held laugh lines at the corners. He had looked like the easy-going young man he was.

No longer. His face was bloated, lopsided, and his hair had fallen out in patches, giving him a mangy appearance. Under the blankets, his body was twisted and lumpy, and even now his movements were jerky, uncoordinated as he wrestled with Amaruq. Last time Nick had been here, only two days ago,

Tom had been sitting in a chair. Now he could barely raise himself from the bed. Still, he was a strong young man; he finally got Amaruq in a headlock and thumped her with a fist. "Hey, knock it off! Have some respect, I'm a sick man!"

::Sick in the head!::

In response, Tom tickled Amaruq's side. The wolf yipped and wriggled. ::Stop!::

"You two, behave yourselves!" The man in the wheelchair rolled over, plucking the wolf from the young man's arms. She squirmed around until she could lick his face. "Down, or I'll put you out!" Nutjuitok said, but his affectionate tone belied his words.

Tom looked over at Nick. "Do I smell pizza?"

::Pizza!:: Amaruq launched herself out of the wheelchair, dancing around Nick. ::Pizzapizzapizza!!!::

Nick grinned. "It was all I could do to keep her from eating them on the way here," he said. He set the boxes down on a couple of crates shoved together in the center of the room, which served as a coffee table. He lifted the lid, and Tom leaned over, sniffing.

"God, that's fantastic. Dibs on the first one!"

Nick reached into the box. "The first slice?"

"Hah." Tom reached for the box. "The first pie!" His knotted fingers clutched at the box, slipped and the box fell to the floor. Pizza slices flipped and landed upside down on the wooden plywood floor.

"Dammit!" The sudden fury in Tom's voice froze everyone in place. Nick reached for the box, and Tom slapped his hand away. "I'll get it!" His fingers were bent and gnarled, as if arthritis had reshaped them into claws. Nor could he work them well; they slithered and groped along the smooth surface of the box, unable to find purchase. Amaruq whined and licked her brother's face, but he only scowled and cursed, his good mood gone.

Quietly, the old man rolled his wheelchair over and picked up the box. He set it on his lap and opened it, bent to retrieve the fallen slices. "Pepperoni and extra sausage!" he said in a mild voice. "You remembered. Thanks."

"How could I forget?" Nick said. He tried to keep his voice as normal as possible, coming as it did through a throat locked tight with tears and anger. "If I'd forgotten, Amaruq would have made me swim back for it."

The old man held out a slice of pizza to Tom. "You called dibs, son."

Tom looked at him, at Nick, with eyes full of anger and misery. "I'm not hungry any more." He turned painfully away, facing the wall. One crooked hand drew the blanket up around his head. Amaruq jumped up on the bed, turned around three times, and curled up in the crook formed by his knees under the blanket. Her tail curled over her nose and her eyes stared at them.

::Not hungry either.::

Nick's father reached down and picked up the pizza boxes, stacking them on his lap. "Just as well. I want to heat these up anyway." He jerked his head at Nick and turned his chair towards the other door, the one that led to the tiny kitchen. Nick followed him and closed the door. It was colder in the kitchen, away from the heat of the kerosene stove. The room was only big enough for a counter; the opposite wall held shelving on which boxes and cans of food were neatly stacked. Nutjuitok rolled to a small camp stove and busied himself firing it up.

"He's worse," Nick said flatly. He reached into his pocket and drew out the bottle of pills from the co-op. "I brought the painkillers."

"Won't help much now," Nutjuitok said. His seamed face was short and broad, his black eyes hooded by heavy eyelids. His Inuit ancestry showed in his heavy frame and big shoulders, his thick black hair. "It's mostly fever now. And convulsions."

Nick looked away, staring at the kitchen shelves, the knife rack, the bucket they used for a sink, anything to avoid his father's gaze. "Is there...is there anything I can do?"

Nutjuitok put the pizza on a tin plate, then placed it on the camp stove. "Not now. I think...I think it's gone too far. It's not going to stop."

Nick's stomach did a slow roll, hearing the fatalism in his father's voice. "Amaruq survived it."

His father tore paper towels off a roll. His short, jerky movements revealed the repressed anger and grief Nutjuitok refused to let his face show. "Your sister was eleven years old. She weighed, what, fifteen kilograms? Your brother is nearly thirty years old and weighs over four times as much. Far too much body mass to survive the Transformation."

Nick clenched a fist. "We need to get him out of here. Down to a real hospital. We can airlift him from Resolute Bay to Iqaluit."

"And then what?" The older man swung around in his wheelchair, his hands hard on the wheels. "No. He won't have it; I won't have it. You know what they'd do—isolation wards, quarantine, tests. Some PhD candidate would turn him into a science project and make his last days hell. And what do you think would happen to Amaruq? To you?"

"We've got rights. We'd be protected by—"

"*Rights?* We've only had our 'rights' in Nunavut for less than ten years; before that, the white men told us what our rights were and weren't. It's not much better now!" He clenched his jaw, and muscle rippled along bone. "Son, I won't risk your brother, your sister. Even if the government tried to protect us, what about other governments? Have you thought about that? Have you thought about what Russia or China would do to get their hands on Amaruq or Tom? Or even you? They'd do their damnedest to turn Amaruq or Tom into some kind of weapon, and they wouldn't care how they hurt them."

Nick looked down at his feet, sick at his stomach. He wanted to argue with his father, even though Inuit tradition forbade it. But he had the sinking feeling that told him his father was right. He hadn't thought about foreign intervention. It seemed so far outside the world he lived in.

Nutjuitok turned back, wrapping a dishcloth around his hand to lift the pizza onto a clean plate. "Take this to your brother and see if you can get him to eat it. He doesn't seem to keep anything down."

40

"Yes, Dad." Nick took the plate from his father. He met the old man's eyes. "I'll...I'll do whatever you and Tom say. I promise."

Nutjuitok nodded and waved him towards the main room. "You may have to hold it for him, but make him eat."

It took all of Nick's patience to persuade Tom to eat some pizza. He finally lifted his brother to a sitting position, propping him up with pillows. Nick was shocked to see how weak Tom was, to feel how hot and feverish his skin felt. Finally he wedged a slab of pizza between the almost-paws of his brother's hands. "See if you can keep from eating it all in one bite," he said jokingly.

Tom grimaced and bit into the pizza. Nick saw the canines, long and sharp, and the gaps where other teeth had been.

::He has lost his chewing teeth.:: Amaruq's voice said in his head. ::Hard to eat. I remember.::

Nick's stomach clenched. Tom's jaw was losing molars, re-making itself into the fanged mouth of a wolf. He looked down at Amaruq, who was gulping down—wolfing down—the greasy pizza Nick had put on the floor for her. She looked up, licking her muzzle, and her amber eyes met his. Nick knew Amaruq was thinking the same thing that he was: Death was coming for their brother.

Ice Cavern, Devon Island, Nunavut, Canada
75° 36' 44.14" N, 83° 48' 09.88" W

Leo opened his eyes and found himself staring into the snarling muzzle of a wolf. He felt curiously unaffected, as if what he saw was behind glass or in a movie. His vision blurred momentarily, and when he blinked, he realized that the wolf was dead. In fact, it was only a wolf head.

Leo felt suffocated; there was something wrong with his breathing. He tried to draw a deeper breath, but nothing happened. His head hurt and it was hard for him to see; either the light was very dim or he was indoors or maybe he was going blind. Everything looked red, as if the room were lit by a traf-

41

fic light stuck on STOP. His head felt stuffed with cotton. It wasn't so much that he hurt, as that he felt nothing at all. So much nothing, in fact, that he felt immediately uneasy. Why couldn't he move? Was he tied up? His inner ear told him he was upright, not lying down. His face felt cold but not dangerously so. Was he on a ventilator? More distressingly, why didn't that thought frighten him?

Leo blinked again to clear his vision. He was in a room made of glass, dimly lit by a suffuse red glow. No, he realized, it wasn't glass, it was ice. That must account for the cold and the numbness. Was he suffering from frostbite? Was this some innovative way to treat frostbite? Something hovered in the center of the room, a gray object he could not see around; a monitor screen? But why would a monitor screen show a night sky? He blinked again (why were his eyes so very dry?) and realized the "screen" was floating in mid-air. What was holding it up?

He remembered the sphere that had attacked him and Glenn. The thought of it scared him, but curiously his heart rate did not speed up or his breathing quicken. They must have him on some kind of drugs, tranquilizers maybe. Wherever he was, it smelled like crap. Didn't they clean this place? It was an odd, chemical reek, not like any hospital smell he remembered.

He opened his mouth to call out. No sound emerged, not even a wheeze. He tried to breathe more deeply, and the feeling of suffocation increased. His chest was not moving. He could not feel air moving in his throat. He tried again to yell for help, but there was no sound. His mouth worked, he could feel his teeth and his tongue, but no air moved in his throat or nose.

Panic welled in him, and he strained to look left and right out of the corners of his eyes, trying so hard that it hurt his eyes. All he could see was the sheen of ice, the flicker and glimmer of light on water, and heads. The wolf head stared back at him. It was set on a low bench, on top of some kind of collar. There were tubes and bulbous sacs attached to the underside. Leo squinted; there were other heads mounted on the bench. He recognized a bird head and what must be the head of a musk ox. All of them appeared to be dead trophies, as if from some hunter. This could not be a hospital; no hospital kept trophy heads around.

What frightened Leo now, on a really deep level, was his realization that the bench was floating without visible means of support. It reminded him of the silver sphere, and he felt a sudden stab of panic. But even that stab felt dry and weak, as if he were too exhausted or enervated to really react.

Leo took in as many details as he could. The walls and floor were irregularly shaped, as if they had melted haphazardly in some sudden heat. He could see slick, icy spots characteristic of re-frozen meltwater. He could hear a trickle somewhere, and surmised that something was melting. Leo became aware that the room was lined in ice. Or maybe made of ice? His mouth got even drier. There was only one place on Devon Island with enough ice to melt a room of this size: the ice cap itself. But where was he? How had he gotten here? Who had brought him?

He tried again to call for help; again, he could make no sound. He strained to turn his head, and found he could move a fraction of an inch to the left or right. But that was enough to change the angle of reflection from the opposite wall. The sheen of meltwater over ice turned it into a funhouse mirror, distorted and warped. He squinted again, trying to focus.

Then the image across from him resolved, and he realized what he was seeing, and his mouth gaped in a silent, useless scream. The mirror wall showed his head, sitting on a collar full of some liquid, with tubes and bulbous sacs dangling below it.

There was no body below his head.

Cornwallis Island, Nunavut, Canada
74° 39′ 21.53″ N 93° 49′ 16.28″ W

Nick lay in the upper bunk of his old room, staring at the ceiling. It was hardly larger than a closet, opening off the main room. Its only real luxury was its lack of a window, so it was dark and easy to sleep in. But Nick could not find peace in sleep yet.

Once he had shared this room with Tom, and it was still crowded with their boyhood collections: bird feathers, harpoon points, leather projects. On one tiny fold-down bench lay Nick's tools and a half-finished carving of a seal mother and baby. One wall held a photograph of Tom in a hockey uniform, posing with his teammates from high school. His easy grin dominated the picture, outshining the shy smiles of the others. Cocky, smart, strong, Tom had always been more popular than Nick, even among those who looked askance on the entire Tonarak clan.

Murmurs from the front room, a soft groan from Tom. His father's low voice, murmuring words of comfort. Useless, useless. There was nothing anyone could do. Nick thought about radioing the Resolute Bay medical center, even asking the military for a medevac. But his father was right: there was too much at risk, and nothing to gain. Emotionally and physically exhausted, he fell into an uneasy sleep.

Surrounded by the singing of the younger units, the Whole floated in space, within the bubble of the vessel that had been its home for many Divisions. Within the vast consciousness that was its mind, there were individual minds and memories, but each one was open to all its siblings. Every thought was shared, every memory, every skill. Some units used some skills, some used others, to keep the vast colony on course and well maintained. No matter what an individual's task was, however, the bond of mutuality was maintained. To Separate was painful, to Join bliss itself. United in harmony, the Whole abode in peace.

Nick shook himself awake, his fingers clutched on his blanket. Lying in the dim quiet, he forced himself to take deep breaths. When his breathing returned to normal, he swung himself down off the top bunk and padded into the main room in his socks.

Nutjuitok sat next to Tom's bed, asleep in his wheelchair. Tom tossed and moaned, feverish, eyes shut. It seemed to Nick that even in the short time he'd been asleep, Tom had lost weight and even some hair.

As he entered, Amaruq lifted her head and looked at him.

She was still curled on Tom's bed, but her tail thumped once in greeting.

::You okay?::

"I had the dream again," Nick muttered. "You know the one."

::Yes. I know.:: She put her head on her paws.

Nutjuitok snorted awake. His first glance was to Tom, and he put a hand on his son's forehead. "His fever's worse," he said in a low voice. Nick heard the despair in it.

"Dad, we have to take him to a doctor."

The older man swung towards him. "What do you think they can do, son? None of those doctors have ever seen anything like this." He stopped and rubbed his eyes. "Enough. We've talked this to death. And I haven't asked about you. How are you, Nick?"

Nick sat down on a crate, his hands between his knees. "Mike offered me a job with the NASA people. It's good pay. I'll be gone a week, maybe two up on Devon Island."

"That's good," his father said. "You're a good worker. They'll keep you on."

Nick drew a deep breath. He felt reluctant to bring this up in the face of Tom's dire situation, but he needed to talk to someone. "I...something happened. I don't know..." He glanced over at Amaruq, but she was asleep, with her tail over her nose. This wasn't really the time to talk to his father about his troubles. "Never mind."

Nutjuitok leaned forward, the hard planes of his face harsh in the low light. "Tell me, son. I'd love to talk about something other than Tom's sickness."

Nick gripped his knees. "Dad, when did you...know... about Mom?"

The old man blinked. Whatever he'd braced himself for, this wasn't it. "About your mother? You mean when she had the—"

"No, not that." Nick swallowed. Everything in this family came back to the same subject—the family curse. "I mean, when did you know you... she was the one you wanted."

A slow smile spread across his father's face. "When I met her. Are you saying you've met some girl—"

"No. Forget it." Nick rubbed his face in his hands, partly to hide his hot blush. "It's...I just saw someone I... she was..." He stopped, took a deep breath. "I just met this...this visitor. She's nice. Real nice. And pretty. And when she talked to me, there was something special..." He trailed off, looking at the lump of bedclothes that was his brother. *Who was he kidding?* Nobody in his family could pretend to have a normal social life. "Forget it. If she knew..."

His father nodded. "I know." He patted Nick's hand. "But you have to have faith. Some day you'll find a woman who will...understand. Your mother understood. Or tried to." He stopped and swallowed.

Tuva's suicide hung between them like some miasma of plague for a moment.

The old man gripped the wheels of the chair until his knuckles turned white. "Your mother loved you. She loved all of us. She just couldn't take what happened to N—to your sister." At the last moment, his father stopped himself from saying the name. Nick's sister wasn't dead, but the taboo against mentioning the names of the departed applied anyway.

He continued slowly. "I want you to remember, son. She loved us. She...she loved me. I never thought I'd find a woman who did. But I did. And ..." His mouth grew firm, took on the look Nick remembered from hunts and outings, times when his father had faced a difficult truth. "Remember that wolves mate for life." His eyes burned into his son's. "Choose carefully."

Then Nutjuitok shook his head and turned his wheelchair. "Come on, I have something for you."

Nick followed him across the room to the east wall, where most of the hunting equipment was stored. Nutjuitok had taken pride, before the accident that crippled him, in hunting for his family. He liked the old ways of harpoon and fishing spear, of trap and line. But he was not so much of a traditionalist that he neglected modern methods. He brought down from a shelf a leather rifle case and laid it on his lap.

"Dad..." Nick said, understanding. "I can't—"

"You must, son," his father said. "There's no one else. Tom will never hold it again, and I can't use it with these wheels."

Nick swallowed. "Dad, you don't have to do this."

"You said you are going to Tadjun," the old man said. Tadjun was the Inuktitut name for Devon Island. "You'll need this." He unzipped the soft leather case, revealing the vintage rifle. The Lee-Enfield 4 Mark I was a veteran of the Second World War, a bolt-action repeating rifle whose stock had been repaired with glue and duct tape more than once. For all the developments in modern weaponry, this venerable weapon had proven its ability to withstand Arctic conditions over the years. Nutjuitok handed him a box of special soft-point .303 British cartridges along with the gun. "You're the only one of us now who can use it, and the bears will be hungry this summer. The ice has thinned too fast. You'll need to protect yourself."

Nick knew what he meant; with global warming came a shorter and shorter ice season, so that the polar bears who usually travelled far out on sea ice to hunt seals were now con-fined to land, where they turned to easier game: men. Unafraid of anything, they were as likely to roam through a town look-ing for a stray toddler as they were to hunt seals along the dry coast. Like all Inuit, Nick had been trained from birth to avoid them, but sometimes it was necessary to shoot one. One took no chances with a *nanuq* weighing nearly half a ton.

Reluctantly, Nick took the rifle in his hand. The smooth wood was warm against his hand. He remembered seal hunts when he was a boy, laughing and running between his father and his brother, his pride at bringing home the seal, knowing they would eat well for weeks because of his good aim, his skills. "Thanks," he said. "I'll take good care of it."

He felt something nose his hand and looked down.

::Hunting?:: Amaruq's tail thumped.

"You'll take her with you," Nutjuitok said. It was not a question.

"I don't have to go," Nick said. "I should stay here with you." He glanced over at Tom, who lay back against the cushions, his eyes closed, his face gray with exhaustion and sheened with sweat.

"I can take care of my own son," the older man said. His voice held the bark of authority, not to be discounted in Inuit culture.

Nick swallowed. He glanced down at Amaruq. "Better finish your pizza, Sis. There won't be much on Devon Island."

As she bounced off to devour the leftovers, Nick stared at his brother and wondered if he would ever see him alive again. His stomach hurt thinking about it. He should stay. He should.

"I wish things were not this way," the older man said in Inuktitut. "I wanted you to go to school, to study..." He swallowed, holding back tears Nick knew he would consider unmanly. "Your mother wanted it. She said you were the smart one. She was right. If things had been different..."

Nick felt the old ache of disappointment and set it aside. "I should be here with you," he said. "I should be with the family."

"We need the money, son. There's no one else to work for it, and the government check is not enough." He was silent a moment, jaw working. Nick knew how much his father hated taking money from others. "There's no one but us," he said in a low voice.

Nick tasted bitterness. Of course his father was right—the very curse that forced them to live apart from others also meant they were shut out of the community, estranged from the close-knit villagers who might otherwise have been generous with food and money. But there was no use thinking about that. It had always been this way. The Tonarak clan stood alone. And now, they all depended on him.

Nutjuitok met his eyes, and silently shook his head. "Go," he said.

And Nick knew he would.

Queen Elizabeth Islands

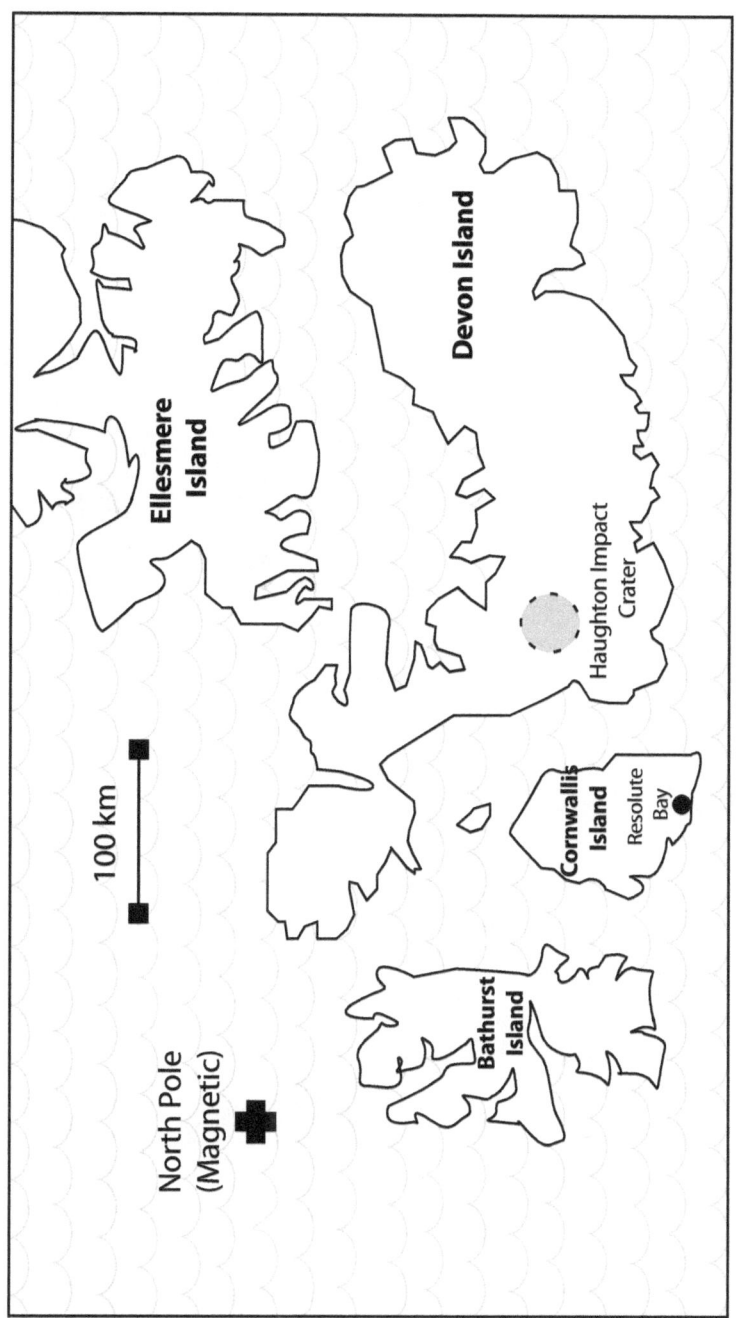

II - DEVON ISLAND

Resolute Bay, Nunavut, Canada
74° 41′51″ N, 94° 49′ 56″ W

The small plane warming up on the tarmac had seen better days. Sophia eyed it with suspicion, noting the peeling paint, the mismatched colors on the fuselage and door. The de Haviland Twin Otter DHC-6 sat on three fat tires, its twin engines mounted on wings that were flush with the roof of the plane. Nominally green and yellow, there were scrapes, dings and dents all over the wings and body. A fold-down stairway hung under the rear door, and she saw one parka-clad man handing bags up to another.

She looked again. The man receiving the bags was the one who had given her the carving now in her pocket. Nick? Was that his name? He turned, reaching down for a duffel bag, and caught her look. He hesitated and their gazes locked for a second, before he ducked back into the plane.

A row of fuel drums were lined up, waiting to be loaded. A tiny frisson of anxiety went through her as she thought about flying with a load of flammable liquids on board.

Sophia heard a bark, turned, and froze. A large white wolf stood only a few feet away, staring at her. It was white, almost blending into the snowbank behind it, and its tail was up and curled over its back. Sophia stared back at it, alarmed. Did wolves simply roam freely through this Arctic town?

"Amaruq! Come here!" Sophia turned and saw Nick hop out of the small plane. His parka fell open, showing off the tight T-shirt over worn jeans. The wolf bounded over to him, jumping up and licking at him just like a dog. Sophia, who had summered for several years in Alaska, was sure it was not a dog. *Maybe it's a wolf/dog cross*, she thought. Still, it was very large for a dog...

"Sophia!" Jennifer strode up, pulling her rolling suitcase and carrying a paper bag.

"Give you a hand with that?"

"Sure," Jennifer said. A nap had restored her clear complexion and put a bounce back in her step. She handed the paper bag to Sophia. "Hang on to these for your life."

Sophia peeked inside. The sweet smell hit her like heaven in one breath. "Donuts?"

"Shh! Don't say it so loud, we'll get mugged."

The two of them helped Nick and the other man stuff and push suitcases and bags into the rear of the plane. Sophia noticed that he worked fast, with the assurance of long practice. When he turned to answer a question, she saw the black braid that hung down his back. She caught Jennifer looking at her looking at Nick, and flushed at her friend's merry wink.

"All aboard, folks," a cheery voice announced. Their pilot, a rotund man (but they were all rotund in parkas and jackets) with olive skin and a black mustache, sauntered around the tail of the plane. "Everyone going to Devon Island, get on board now. We're leaving."

"Wait!" A stocky man in a green jacket ran across the landing strip. He carried a long rifle case over a shoulder, and a backpack in one hand.

"Hey, Will," Nick's deep voice greeted him. Sophia looked up; he was hanging halfway out the door, extending a hand.

"Nick," the new man acknowledged. He tossed the backpack; Nick plucked it out of the air and stood aside for him. The man climbed on board and then Nick was leaning down from the doorway, holding out his hand.

"You're the last one," he said.

She grasped his hand, felt his strong grip as he hauled her aboard. "Thanks."

He said nothing, but dogged the hatch behind her. She caught a whiff of him—an outdoorsy smell of wood smoke and engine oil. As she entered, the smell hit her: wet laundry and stale coffee. And the smell of kerosene.

Oil and kerosene and the flames licking along the ceiling, the screams...

Gritting her teeth, Sophia pushed the remembrance away. The interior was stuffed as full as a sausage. On the right side, the passengers were crammed into six rows of double seats. All the seats on the left side had been removed to leave space for cargo: boxes, crates, luggage, instrument boxes, even a guitar case. The rear of the plane was just as jammed, and she found herself squeezed between a huge pile of luggage and Nick.

Nick called past her. "Hey, Pete, we're ready back here." He looked down at her. "Better grab a seat."

Sophia heard the engines cough to life. Nick shoved past her and grabbed three duffel bags out of the last two seats.

"Hey!" A man in a blue toque scowled from further up. "Those are mine!" Nick ignored him and tossed the duffels into the back of the plane, where they landed on a couple of ice chests and then slid off onto the floor. Sophia heard a muffled yelp and peered over the mountain of bags.

Curled on the floor of the plane was the big white wolf/dog. Her eyes met the dog's, and Sophia was shocked when one closed and opened again. Had the dog just *winked* at her? The tail thumped and the dog made a low, whining sound, almost as if it were saying, "Please." Sophia saw that one of the bags had landed on a paw. She leaned down and shifted it off the dog's paw. A warm tongue shot out and licked her hand.

"Well, if you are a wolf, you have nice manners," she said. Another tail thump. She straightened, turned, and found Nick standing right behind her, looking at her. "What? Is this your dog?"

He raised a hand to silence her and darted a glance over his shoulder. No one was looking their way, and at that moment Pete the pilot revved the big Pratt & Whitney. Sophia had to lean forward to hear Nick. "Her name is Amaruq," he said. It sounded to Sophia's ears like 'Amma-rook'. "And she's not supposed to be here." His breath ghosted against her cheek, warm and intimate.

She leaned towards him to answer over the roar of the engines. "I won't tell."

This close, she could see a piercing in his ear for an earring, and she wondered what kind of earring he might wear. He was tall enough that his shoulders blocked her view of the rest of the compartment, so for a moment it felt as if they were alone in the plane. Then the craft lurched forward, Sophia swayed, and he caught her upper arms. "Come on and sit down," he said.

The only seats left were the two he had cleared at the end of the row. He gestured for her to take the window seat and slid in next to her. Sophia fiddled with seat belt buckles and other adjustments, and then there was a lurch under her stomach. The plane started forward, taxiing down the runway. She felt her stomach jitter.

A crackle, then the pilot's voice from a tiny speaker overhead. "Settle down, everyone. This is the Admiral speaking." Good natured jibes met this. Pete continued unperturbed. "I have only two requests. Please fasten your seat belts, and keep the screaming to a minimum. It disturbs my nap. We're off now."

With that, the plane jerked forward, swayed, and flung itself into the air. Sophia clutched the armrest. Instead, she found herself hanging onto Nick's arm. "Oh, sorry."

His eyes flicked down to her, and something curled at the corner of his mouth. "Don't worry about it," he said. "Pete can fly a tractor if he has to."

The newcomer who had come aboard at the last moment was seated in front of them. He turned around, bright blue eyes staring over the seat. Ignoring the "Fasten Seat Belts" sign, he unbuckled and stepped into the aisle. He leaned across Nick.

"Hi. I'm Will Fraser," he said, holding out a hand. "Constable, Royal Canadian Mounted Police." Sophia took in his fur hat with a badge pinned to the front, his heavy jacket and boots. Under the jacket he wore a gray shirt and a navy tie. The bulge under the coat told her he was armed.

She shook his hand. "Sophia Abenezra, biologist. What, no red tunic?"

He smiled. "Only for the Queen, I'm afraid. For regular duty, we put away the fancy costumes." His voice was low, well modulated. Nick rose quietly and stepped to the rear of the plane. Fraser slid into the empty seat. "Your first time in the Arctic?"

"No." *Don't talk about it. Don't remember it. Leave it behind.* Sophia glanced down and saw the handgun in his belt holster. "What's a Mountie going to do on Devon Island?"

"Your head man called in a missing persons report last night."

Ahead of them, David Beringer turned around, looking concerned. "Who's missing?"

"A couple of geologists." Fraser dug a notebook out of his jacket pocket. "A Dr. Donovan and a Dr. West."

Others were turning around, and as the plane leveled out the noise of the engines fell to a background noise. "Glenn and Leo are missing?" one woman asked.

"You know them?" Fraser asked.

"Yeah," the woman said, frowning. "They're not amateurs. This is their third season."

David Beringer leaned forward. "I hope it's not a bear attack."

Sophia heard a snick and looked over her shoulder. Nick sat behind her on the floor, propped against the pile of baggage, with a shotgun balanced across his knees. Next to it was the gun case Constable Fraser had brought aboard. She recognized the weapon as the standard bear gun in wild country, a shotgun that fired lead slugs nearly three inches long, heavy enough to stop a bear in its tracks at close range.

Fraser was looking at her. "Ever seen one, ma'am?"

"I carried one for three summers in Alaska," she said. "Pretty heavy. Are you shooting sabots or Buckhammers?"

Fraser smiled, and she saw that he was missing a side tooth. It gave him an approachable look. "Bucks. I see you know your bear guns."

She shrugged. "I go to a lot of wild places. Bears don't scare me as much as sharks." She heard a deep chuckle and turned around. Nick's grin was wide and white. "What?"

Fraser answered for him. "You haven't met our bears." He slewed around on his seat, putting his back to Sophia. He let his hands dangle between his knees as he watched Nick examine the gun. "I notice that we've got an extra passenger on board."

Nick went very still, his eyes boring into Fraser's. Sophia looked from one man to another.

"She's probably breathing fuel fumes back there," Fraser said. "That can't be good for her. Why don't you let her come on out?"

Before Nick could move or speak, Amaruq's head popped up behind him. She saw Fraser, and leaped over the mound of baggage, slipping past Nick. She put her head on Fraser's knee.

He patted her head. "Good girl. I saw that you arrived with her this morning, but didn't see her later. And Nick, you don't go anywhere without this dog." He ruffled her ears. "So I figured she was on board."

"You got a problem with it?" Nick's tone was light, but Sophia could sense the tension in him.

"Far from it," Fraser said. He scratched Amaruq behind the ears. Her eyes closed in canine bliss. "I may need to draft her. And you."

"Hey, what's that dog doing here!" Beringer said sharply. Others turned around in their seats again. "We didn't authorize it at the Project!"

From further up the aisle, Jennifer Roth's eyes met Sophia's, flicked to Fraser, back to Sophia. A knowing smile and a raised eyebrow told Sophia that her new friend was jumping to all the wrong conclusions.

Fraser held up a conciliatory hand. "Don't worry about Amaruq, Dr. Beringer. She's here on official business." Beringer continued to scowl, but said nothing as Fraser turned back to Nick. "Which is true, because I may need to conscript both of you."

"We're supposed to be babysitting the geeks," Nick said.

Sophia frowned. *A geek, was she?*

"There are two men out on the Island who may be lost, or hurt, or dead," Fraser said, lowering his voice. "I will find them, one way or another. But it would be easier and faster if you and your dog cooperated."

Amaruq lifted her head, turned and looked at Nick. The man stared back, almost as if he were conversing with the creature. Then he shrugged. "I'll talk to Dr. Beringer about it. Usual rates?"

Fraser laughed and stood up, returning to his seat. "A bag of dog food and a large pepperoni pizza? You're on, mate."

Amaruq barked, causing every head in the cabin to turn back to stare at her. She wagged her tail, looking from Fraser to Nick.

"Well, that settles it," Fraser said. "The brains of the outfit have spoken."

Nick sat in the seat next to Sophia's. "Fine, but how am I going to eat all that dog food?"

Ice Cavern, Devon Island, Nunavut, Canada
75° 36′ 44.14″ N, 83° 48′ 09.88″ W

If Leo had had a stomach, he'd have thrown up.

Leo had screamed silently until madness threatened, had wept tears that gathered in the corner of his mouth and then dripped off his beard onto the floor, joining the tiny meltwater stream that trickled away to his right. No one had answered. Nothing had changed, except the light, and the scene depicted in the central sphere. That had changed slowly, showing dawn creeping across the barren, broken landscape shown. But the dawn revealed only stretches of black sand, lumps of red rock, and a sky that was not the blue of Earth but a rosy pink from some other world. When the second sun rose, Leo tried to scream, but again no sound came out. Without a larynx, he could make no sound but the harsh rasping of breath in his sinuses. And the smell—he gagged.

He had experimented, rolling his eyes, opening and closing his mouth. All those actions had been reflected back at him, along with the absolute void below his neck. In his ears, he heard a faint susurration, not the steady pound of a heartbeat but more like the passing of fluid through a pipe. In fact, the bulbs and tubes below his neck, reflected in the ice of the opposite wall, looked very much like organic constructs, he thought. Like veins and arteries, maybe.

He had prayed to every god he'd ever heard of. He had held his non-breath, willing himself to die. He felt insanity creeping in, a black tide of despair and horror; the thought of giving in to it was almost worse than death. To lose his reason, to lose himself, was almost as bad as losing his body. And that thought by itself started another cycle of panic.

Now he watched as the blood-tinged hue of the light bouncing off the walls slowly faded to purple, then brightened again to a ghostly blue. Around him, the collection of heads threw shadows across the icy walls. From them, he deduced that the source of the blue glow was near the floor. He stared at the heads: wolf, several birds, a seal. Like him, all had bulbs and tubes below the racks on which the heads sat. Horrified, he saw the seal's eyes slowly close and then re-open. It was alive! And yet it, too, consisted only of a head. Could it, did it feel the same fear Leo did? Was it aware of its fate?

I'm a trophy, Leo thought. *A head-hunter of some kind, some sick twisted monster, has taken my head.* How could that be? How could anyone live after losing his head? He racked his memory, thinking of old wives tales about guillotined heads that moved, about people revived after being pronounced dead. He thought about all the Frankenstein movies he had seen.

Slowly, the dread engulfing him gave way to an even more powerful emotion—rage. Who had done this? Why? And where was the rest of him?

Movement to his right. Leo's eyes shot to the side of their orbits, straining to see. Slowly the silver sphere drifted into the cavern, silent as thought. Terror surged through his mind, but the sensation was curiously muted. *Of course*, Leo thought. *No adrenaline glands, no adrenaline surge.* Something like hysteria trickled through his head. He watched the silver globe with the intensity of a mouse watching a cat. It drifted from one head to another across the chamber.

The sphere stopped in front of the seal. A pulsing red glow rose to its surface, and Leo felt heat wash over his face. The seal's fur twitched as the creature roused, its eyes rolling. A wisp of smoke rose from its fur, and Leo smelled burning hair. The mouth opened, showing sharp teeth, but no sound came out. The sphere flashed for a tenth of a second, surprising Leo and leaving blue dots dancing before his eyes. The seal's head twitched as if shaken by an invisible hand, and the tubes and bulbs below it swung heavily. A long red line appeared in the animal's forehead, and then widened into a crack. Leo realized the seal's skull was being opened while it was still alive. Beams of light played over the exposed brain, as the seal's eyes dulled, closed in death. A liquid spatter, and Leo saw brain leaking, spilling over the rack to the floor.

What do you want? he screamed silently as the sphere turned from the dead seal. *What do you want from me?*

Slowly the sphere revolved, traversed the room languidly, playing a beam of white, then blue light over the wolf, the birds, the other heads. None of them responded, being truly dead.

With cold dread, Leo watched the approach of the sphere, and saw it stop in front of him. He closed his eyes, held his breath as the light played over his face. Then he felt heat and something loud, and knew things could, indeed, get worse.

Haughton Crater Research Project, Devon Island
75° 26′ 00″ N, 89° 51′ 00″ W

The little plane had been so cocooned by cloud cover that when they fell out of the clouds at five thousand feet, Sophia gasped. The ground rushed up like a brown blanket being thrown aloft. A cross wind caught the plane and the entire craft shuddered.

The smash, the explosion, the fire—

The plane gave a little bump and hitch, and she found herself clinging to Nick again. She glanced up and caught his expression—not amusement, as she'd expected, but sympathy. He put his hand on hers for a moment, then drew it away.

"Almost there," he said in a low voice.

Constable Fraser was strapping himself into his seat, but

turned around. "You can see the Fortress from here. See that massif, sticking up to the east?"

Sophia swallowed and made herself look out of her window. In the midst of an otherwise featureless gray-brown plain, what looked like the remains of twin castle towers rose into the air. "Is that a ruin of some kind?"

For the first time, Fraser's seat mate roused. "Ruin? Hardly." The face that peeked over the seat back was weathered from many years of outdoor exposure. "Hello, I'm Roddy Mevasp," he said, blinking through round black-rimmed glasses. "That's a rock. One hell of a big rock. It was ejected from the crater when the meteor hit. It's called the Fortress."

Suddenly the landscape below her seemed to resolve, and she realized that what had looked like a faraway scene was only a few dozen feet below the plane. The featureless plain had deceived her eye. Sophia drew her breath in sharply, even as the plane banked, straightened, and turned towards the giant rock.

"We're going to hit it!"

"No, it's only—" Nick started.

But Sophia clutched his hand tight in hers, shutting him off, her eyes shut tight. *Fire and smoke, the screaming the screaming the screaming—*

"It's okay," Nick murmured. "We're landing now."

She kept her eyes squeezed tight, tried to control her breathing. The plane dipped, yawed a little, and then thumped down on a hard packed gravel runway, bumping to a stop. Sophia opened her eyes. Seat belts clicked open, conversation rose, and now the plane was even more crowded as people stood, grabbing duffel bags and carry-ons. She released Nick's hand, noticing a bandage on the back of it.

Sophia drew a deep breath. Nick leaned across to fiddle with the window shade, shielding her from view, and turned his face to hers. It brought his eyes within inches of hers, and she saw the depths of them, warm and brown. "You okay? You need a moment?"

She was grateful and embarrassed at the same time. "I'm just not used to small planes," she said.

"It's okay," he said. "You can sit here for a while, but put your hood up. Here." Gently, he tugged the hood of her parka up around her face. "It'll get colder after we open the door." He turned and leaned forward to speak to Constable Fraser, a move which, she noticed, continued to block the sight of her from other passengers. Sophia appreciated his tact, and realized he must have a keen sense of privacy.

Out of the window, Sophia saw a repeat of Resolute Bay: a gray, cheerless landscape in beige and slate. Her view of the horizon was obscured by a thin drift of fog. As the plane emptied, she caught a glimpse of a conical structure on a distant hilltop, then a distant view of brightly colored tents.

The passengers' eagerness to depart made it easy for her to remain in her seat, watching the chaos. Nick stepped to the rear hatch, opened it, and let down the stairs. Amaruq, disdaining steps, made it to the ground in one bound. Nick stood by the door, helping passengers out, then started handing out bags and duffels. Fraser helped him, chatting with some of the researchers he knew.

Jennifer plopped down in the seat Nick had vacated. "Whoof!" she said. "What a landing! I don't know whether to kiss the pilot or slap him."

"Oh, I'm up for either one, miss," said a cheerful voice. They looked up to see Pete the pilot threading his way down the aisle, zipping up his parka. He stopped when he reached their row. "What'll it be?" He threw his arms wide in a gesture of welcome.

Jennifer laughed. "Let's see what the return flight's like."

"Oh, now, who's to say it'll be me on the flight back? When are you leaving?" His expression was hopeful.

"Pete, for God's sake leave the women alone and come help us unload this fuel," Fraser called out. He and Nick were wrestling a fifty-gallon drum that sloshed.

"Oh, it's a sad day," Pete said mournfully. "But I'll practice up for the return trip," he said. "You'll never forget your first northern kiss." He winked at Jennifer and slid by.

"I'd probably freeze right to his lips," she said, hugging

herself. "Grab your gear, Soph. Time to go."

Sophia stood, found that her legs had stopped shaking, and threaded her way through the crowded aisle. Nick's hand was warm on hers as he handed her down to the ground. She took her duffel bag from him and turned to survey the camp. It lay about four hundred yards away, but with no vegetation to block the view, it was stark, barren, naked under the gray sky. Like the rest of this part of the world, they sat in the middle of utter desolation.

The buildings were flimsy, intended for only temporary use, but they were as shabby and weather-beaten as if they'd stood for a long time. A huddle of Quonset huts and prefab buildings clustered around a central core. No one had bothered to paint them.

"Makes the Sonoran desert look like a freakin' oasis," Jennifer said beside her. She unfolded her sunglasses and slipped them on. Hand on hip, she surveyed the gravel airstrip, the rock-strewn ground that undulated to a far horizon, unbroken by any hint of vegetation. She shaded her eyes with her hand. "Is that the rim of the crater?"

David Beringer took a heavy box out of Nick's hands and set it down. "Yes. The crater rim itself is part of Inuit-owned land, so we camp out here. The Martians managed to get permission to build on the rim." His tone was sour. "Of course, that gives them a spectacular view." His manner indicated that mere viewing was something only tourists came for, not real scientists.

"It must be something to see," Sophia said.

"I'll take you on a tour, if you like," Nick's voice said behind her. She turned, looked up at him.

"Uh. Sure, that'd be great," she said. "How far is it?"

A corner of his mouth turned up, and she saw what might be a dimple. "Farther than you'd want to walk just for a casual view. Doc, can we take an ATV?"

Beringer nodded, looking off towards the camp. An ATV pulling a makeshift trailer, followed by two others, approached. "Sure, as soon as we get this stuff unloaded. But Jerry won't be waiting supper on you guys, so don't be late getting back."

Sophia turned to Jennifer. "How about it?"

"You go ahead. I want to set up the analyzer as soon as I can, and check it out. That last hundred miles was the roughest yet." Jennifer went to stand beside the crate holding the precious machine.

Nick stooped to lift some boxes. "I'll have to help load this stuff, then we can go. Wait here." He strode away, the dog at his heels.

While Nick and the other men loaded up the ATV's trailer with luggage, Sophia stared up at the noisy sky, where wind roared and clouds scudded. She felt lost in time, with none of her usual indicators to tell her whether it was early evening or just after midnight. On the western horizon, the sun kissed the rim of the world; it looked like sunset, but she knew that could be deceptive. *Life here was deceptive,* she thought. Like what looked like a dead rock, which on closer inspection held living cells. *Life can find a foothold anywhere,* she thought.

Except in fire…

Mars Habitat Project, Devon Island, Nunavut
75° 25′ 52.61″ N, 89° 51′ 00″ W

The muffled roar of an all-terrain vehicle met Sophia's ear. Nick drove up on a bright red Kawasaki ATV, with Amaruq sitting placidly on the seat behind him. "Hop on," he said.

"Are you sure this is okay?"

"I have to take these up to the Habitat anyway; you're on the way." He nodded at a couple of boxes lashed to the front of the vehicle. He muttered something in Inuktitut to the dog, who jumped off and trotted away.

Sophia climbed onto the saddle of the ATV, fitting her front against Nick's broad back. She wrapped her arms around his waist. His parka rubbed against her cheek; she felt a little awkward at the close contact but he said nothing. He released the brake and they rolled. Jennifer waved as they passed, a smirk on her face.

Their route took them through the sprawling outpost, past

tent labs and a slew of fifty-gallon barrels huddled together under tarps. In a minute they were out of the camp and rolling along a path that wound towards the horizon. It followed a bundle of tubes that snaked across the plain. She pointed at them.

"Comm lines," Nick said over his shoulder. The engine was unmuffled, so he had to shout. He shifted, and Sophia felt his muscles move against her. "They have their own power supply up there, but use the base camp's satellite dish for communications."

The trail wound around past the huge massif she had seen coming in. Sunlight carved shadows and fissures into its craggy surface; on the summit she saw satellite dishes of various sizes and a radio tower. Perched on the edge was an odd pile of rocks: two stacked columns bridged by a long, flat one, with another column on top of that. The whole effect was that of a squat human figure, juxtaposed against the 21st century technology arrayed behind it. The ATV rode past the Fortress, and then the rock formation was between them and the sun and Sophia was in shadow for the first time that day.

She shivered, and felt Nick hesitate. "You okay?" he shouted over his shoulder.

"Fine," she said, eating wind. "How far is the Habitat?"

He mumbled something she didn't catch, and then the ATV dipped sharply downward. She clutched at Nick, earning a grunt in return, as the vehicle ran down a slope to a wide gulch with water at the bottom. A rock dam held back part of the trickle of snowmelt, and a white plastic box at the water's edge growled. A fat hose led away, back towards the camp.

"Lowell Canal. That's the water pump," Nick shouted as the ATV splashed across downstream of the dam. "Water supply for the camp comes from here."

Sophia thought of all the microbes that lived even in this polar desert, and decided to ask Dr. Beringer about the camp's filtration system as soon as possible. Then the ATV was climbing back out of the gully at a steep angle. She gasped and clutched at Nick again, and felt his silent chuckle under her palms.

The vehicle rounded a curve and Nick braked to a stop in front of a towering structure that looked like it might be an actual house from Mars. Sophia got off, stretched her legs, and stared up at the Mars Experimental Habitat. Thirty feet tall and twenty-five feet in diameter, it looked like nothing so much as a giant oil filter with a diamond-shaped window in the middle. One vertical half of the building was painted white and the other a stark black. Plywood steps led up to a door that looked like a hatch from a submarine. Sophia pushed back her parka hood, and the wind ruffled her hair, a cold caress.

"Anyone home?" she called.

"It'll take them a few minutes. They're supposed to pretend they're going through an airlock, so there's a delay," Nick said. He unstrapped the boxes from the front of the ATV.

Sophia turned in a slow circle. Above them, layered clouds in gray and white scudded at different speeds along a ceiling so low Sophia felt claustrophobic. Back the way they had come, the sun lay on the western horizon, sending long golden rays of light under the edge of the clouds, striking across the landscape. The rays picked out the Fortress, a hill here, a shadowed gully there. A shadow drifted across the distant camp, where the colorful tents stood out like specks of confetti on the barren ground.

Nick came to stand beside her. "We're still working on the landscaping," he said. "What do you think?"

She smiled up at him. "Maybe some moss, a little lichen. I think you've got the makings of a spectacular rock garden here."

He turned around, and she did too, and then she was looking into the bowl of the crater. Sophia drew in her breath.

Thirteen miles from rim to rim, the Haughton Crater was a shallow basin filled with grey rock and sunlight. From where she and Nick stood, the slope fell at a steep pitch for hundreds of yards, maybe half a mile. The floor of the crater was seamed with cracks that ran out of sight; here and there patches of snow clung to gray, crumbling slopes. It was a landscape out of a lunar nightmare, an endless plain rimmed with dark brown ridges.

"They told us in school that the meteor was about two kilometers wide," Nick said. "There used to be a lake in the center, but it's been gone for several million years." He looked at her. "You here to study meteors or something?"

"No, I'm a biologist. I study life forms that live in rocks," she said. "It's the kind of life we might find on Mars or other planets."

He raised one of those black-bar eyebrows. "Most of the visitors up here are geologists," he said.

Sophia felt the warmth in that gaze. *Not now,* she thought. *Not so soon after Paul.* She turned away and stopped, puzzled. "What's that?"

Further along the ridgetop path lay a cairn. Stones had been piled into the image of a crude human figure with outstretched arms. Nick led her over to it. "We call it an *inunnguaq,* but you white folks call it an *inuksuk.* They go back to prehistoric times on these islands."

She reached out a hand but did not touch it. "I saw one of these on top of the Fortress. What's it for?"

Nick bent and picked up a pebble, turned it over in his hands. "Landmarks, navigation aids, memorials." He tossed the pebble and watched it roll down the slope into the crater. "Some of them are thousands of years old."

"How old is this one?"

A smile curled in the corner of his mouth. "About seven years old. Tom, my brother—" He stopped for a moment, gazing off across the crater. He cleared his throat. "He works here some summers. He says the guys down in the camp put it up a few years back as a memorial to one of their astronaut friends who died on the *Challenger.*"

Sophia looked at the pile of stones, a marker shaped by ancient native traditions of the land, established to commemorate a man who had wanted to explore other worlds. "You know, this is a very odd place I've come to."

She looked up in time to catch his grin, and found herself grinning back. It transformed his face; behind the mask of impassivity lay a sense of fun. Something warm stole over her as his eyes met hers. "Yeah, it is," he said. "But we like it."

Sophia looked away quickly, quashing the bubble of excitement in her stomach. Her gaze lit on a patch of green that stood out against the pervasive gray-brown. "What's that?"

She stepped closer and saw that it was a group of low-growing plants, no higher than the instep of her boot. They grew in a circular pattern, and someone had ringed them with rocks. A tiny hand-lettered sign read. "DEVON ISLAND NATIONAL FOREST. PLEASE DO NOT STEP ON OUR TREES."

Nick chuckled. "Arctic willow," he said in response to her look. "They grow about a millimeter a year. Those are some of the tallest trees on the island." She smiled.

Behind them, she heard thumps and bangs. Sophia and Nick looked towards the Habitat. The oval door slowly opened outward, and a man in a spacesuit emerged.

Nick raised his hand. "We come in peace, white man," he said. "And we bring beads."

Ice Cave, Devon Island, Nunavut, Canada
75° 36' 44.14" N, 83° 48' 09.88" W

Pain shot through Leo's body. Even though he knew he no longer had a body, he felt it lance into him. *Phantom pain,* he thought. Tears rolled down his cheeks, his harsh breath rasped through his voiceless mouth, but he could not scream.

What do you want? What do you want? he screamed silently at the sphere.

It hung before him, an occasional wash of light crossing its surface. The light changed to blue and washed across his face, and then the pain came spiking through him.

He remembered. Fever, and the ache deep in the bone. He'd had influenza a few years ago, and remembered the chills and hot flashes, the wracking pain in all his joints, the sharp headache. Was that it? He had the flu?—

Suddenly he was awash in cool, wet peace. He could almost feel water gliding past his skin, smell the green smell of an algae-laden pond. He was back in the stock tank behind his grandfather's barn in Idaho, when he was a boy. Mud squished between his toes—

Sadness swept through him, soaking him in despair. He was at the funeral, smelling the stale flowers, the over-perfumed women in tight dresses and wide hats who told him his mother had gone to a better place. How could it be better to be someplace away from him? Was it his fault she was dead? Had he done something wrong, to make the cancer come back? He wept—

He leaned back in the dentist's chair, watching the clock crawl. The pain jabbing into his jaw was like a red-hot ice pick. Dr. Mackey had promised to fit him in between patients, and now Leo waited for the anesthetic to take effect. His tooth hurt like hell—

Leo snapped back out of memory to the present; his tooth hurt like hell. His whole jaw throbbed. In fact, it felt hot. Suddenly something burned the inside of his mouth and he gasped.

The sphere dropped, hovered, and Leo felt his jaw lock. He couldn't close it! His mouth gaped open, as it had that day at the dentist's. A beam of light lanced into his open mouth, and his tooth felt very hot. He smelled something burning, and felt blood pouring out of his mouth. Then pain lanced through his jaw, something popped, and the pain fell to a dull ache.

A molar fell out of his mouth; a beam of white light shot out and the tooth halted in mid-air. The metal surface of the old-fashioned filling gleamed. Light played over it, changed color. A long moment passed.

The molar dropped to the ground. Before Leo's eyes, the sphere changed color, became a mirror, a ball of ice, a ball of mist...There was an eye-crossing moment when the opposite wall seemed to bend around the image of the sphere.

And then the sphere disappeared.

Mars Habitat Project, Devon Island, Nunavut
75° 25′ 52.61″ N, 89° 51′ 00″ W

It wasn't a real spacesuit. Nick watched with some amusement as the man (he could see a beard through the plastic helmet) struggled through the Mars Habitat hatch and down the steps. Finally he shut the hatch and turned with a wave.

"Oh, hi," Sophia said. "Do you mind if we look around?"

The space-suited man tapped his helmet.

"I don't think he can hear you," Nick said.

The space-suited man walked over, boots crunching on gravel. Nick could see that the makeshift spacesuit was a modified white coverall with a modified motorcycle helmet and a large backpack. The boots, however, were ordinary Arctic issue, with the coverall tucked in. Nick saw a chunky white man, balding, with glasses perched on a big nose, behind the faceplate. He thought the guy looked like he was dressed for Halloween.

"Hey," Nick said. Nick saw the space suited man's lips moving and grabbed the walkie-talkie from the ATV. "Hi. I'm Nick. I brought the mail and a couple of boxes up from the airstrip."

"Bob Courtenay," the spaceman said. "Project director. You didn't happen to bring an extra video cable with you? We need another HDMI. Trouble with the satellite feed."

"No, sorry. I can ask around."

"Thanks." Bob turned to Sophia. "Hi. Welcome to Mars Lite."

Sophia shook hands with the spaceman. The spacesuit's gloves, Nick noted, came right out of an online mountaineering catalog.

He handed Sophia the walkie-talkie. "I've got some stuff to unload." *Time to fade into the landscape again*, he thought.

While the two chatted, Nick pulled more boxes off the ATV and stacked them next to the hatch door. He suspected that, regardless of the protocols the Martians had established for their project, someone would sneak out without a "spacesuit" and gather them in when he was gone.

Part of him wanted to laugh at the silliness of grown men and women pretending to be on a Mars base, with space suits, "EVAs", and delays built into their transmissions. Another part of him longed to see another world, anything beyond the bleak horizons in front of him. Then he thought of Tom and Amaruq, and he shut down that thought. Finished, he leaned back against the wall of the habitat and watched his passenger talking to the spaceman.

Fine bones, was his first thought. The artist in him appreciated those high cheekbones, that fine brow. She talked with her hands, animated, now and then pushing her hood back as she spoke into the walkie-talkie. The spaceman towered over her small form, but her energy and liveliness made them equal. *She's a spark*, he thought. *A man could catch fire.* He shook himself, straightened.

"We need to get back," he said.

Sophia looked up, disappointment on her face. "Oh. I wanted to see inside the Habitat."

Nick shrugged. "Sure. We've got 'til sundown."

Sophia nodded, then caught herself. "Oh, very funny," she said. "Sundown's not until late August."

"You catch on quick," Nick said, pushing away from the wall of the Habitat.

"This is not my first stint in the Arctic," she reminded him, annoyed. Then she paled a little. "Although I was in Alaska, below the 24-hour daylight line."

Nick shrugged and looked at Bob. "Do we have to do the 'airlock' thing?"

"It's part of the protocol."

"It's okay," Sophia said. "We'll follow whatever procedures you've set up."

Nick could tell she was excited by the novelty of the idea. Part of him wanted to remind these two that the Inuit had invented "airlocks" long before white men did, that their igloos were usually built with a door and tunnel arrangement to keep cold air out and warm air in. But what was the point?

Bob led them around to the entrance. "Um. There's really only room for one person wearing a spacesuit at a time," he said. "I'll go first, and then you two come after. When the light goes from red to green, you can open the inner door."

"Right." Sophia handed the walkie-talkie to Nick, who put it on his belt.

They watched as Bob climbed into the hatch, fighting the bulky suit all the way. "I hope they have bigger doors on Mars," Sophia murmured.

Nick looked down on her, liking the way the sun lit her hair. "You really think you'll go to Mars?"

"Not me." She shoved her hands into her pockets, looking off into the blue-gray distance. "And maybe no one in my lifetime. But someday. And then, all this will have been important. Even if it seems a little...ridiculous...now."

He felt his face go hot. She had picked up on his amusement, even though he'd tried to hide it. "Well ...," he said, clearing his throat.

She looked up at him, honest eyes meeting his. "I know. It seems a little silly. And when I first read about it, back in California, it seemed so...childish. But here ..." She swept an arm out to take in the bleak landscape, the winds, the scudding clouds. "Now it seems more real, more possible. As if we really were on Mars."

Nick frowned. "But we're *not* on Mars," he said. This was his home. To have it compared to a nearly airless desert seemed insulting. *She's a stranger,* he said to himself. *She would never understand this land. White people...*

Part of him, a part which had been feeling closer to this woman than he ever expected, backed away from this... othering.

"I think we can go through now," Sophia said. She tugged open the door. Nick climbed in after her and shut the door behind them. *It was a tight fit, all right,* he thought. They stood chest to chest in the tiny fake "airlock", both of them self-conscious.

They said nothing, watching the light bulbs over the inner door closely. Nick could feel her chest rising and falling against his as she breathed, could smell her shampoo, or something. He felt a little dizzy and wondered if they really were pumping air into this closet-sized room. Then the light winked to green. Nick reached past Sophia and opened the door. They stumbled through and found themselves in the Mars habitat.

The room was about twenty-five feet in diameter, round as a hoop. The shape reminded Nick of a really large igloo, the kind his ancestors might have built for a gathering. Otherwise, it looked like nothing so much as a round, cluttered garage. Flimsy plywood partitions divided it in quarters. "Spacesuits" hung on pegs beside the door, and several helmets were lined up on a folding table underneath. A plastic box held heavy work boots; tools were piled in a corner.

Sophia stepped past him, turned a corner and gasped, hand to her mouth. Then she laughed, and Nick felt himself grow several years younger hearing it. He stopped next to her and grinned. This area had been fitted out with a shower, and someone had posed a blow-up green alien doll, with staring eyes and a bulbous head, peering out of the tiny cabinet.

"My first real Martian," Sophia laughed. Nick smiled back at her. He watched her explore the rest of the first level: chemical toilet, racks, shelves, tool lockers. Nick had expected it to be warmer in here, out of the wind. He stepped forward and felt the floor give slightly under his feet. Eyes narrowed, he inspected the joint where the floor met the wall. It was out of alignment. He dropped to one knee, probing. Just as he'd thought: the annual freeze/thaw cycle had warped both the floor and the wall which, he further noted, was not even insulated. Cold air flowed in against his hand. He felt a flicker of contempt for such shoddy work, then shook it off. None of his business.

"Hey, you guys!" Courtenay shouted from above. "You gonna hang out there all day? Come on up!"

Sophia had found the ladder and was halfway up. "Permission to come aboard, Captain!" she called.

"Granted!" Courtenay's voice answered. He climbed up after Sophia, noting where the ladder needed mending.

The upper room was divided off into sleeping quarters, leaving a half-circle for cooking, working and socializing. Sophia went immediately to the diamond-shaped window and stood looking out over the crater. Nick had to admit it was a spectacular view. He wondered if she even saw the crack that ran through the lower half of the window. Since the pressure inside the Habitat was the same as outside, it was only an annoyance. But on Mars, the lack of air pressure outside would have blown the window, venting the air inside the Habitat and killing everyone.

If this had really been Mars, he thought, *all these people would be dead.* Did they care? Did they write this off as unimportant? It would be like them, he mused. A bunch of white men from Southern lands, men who had never lived through a winter in the Arctic, could afford to be nonchalant about insulation, about cracks in their walls and windows. Nick thought that perhaps he was the only person in this Habitat who was truly suited for life on Mars.

Courtenay hovered near Sophia, pointing out their workstations, the kitchen with its hot plate and microwave. Nick inspected the wiring, shook his head. Really, it was a miracle they hadn't set fire to themselves. While Courtenay droned on about mission parameters and living conditions, Nick looked at the fuse box. He quietly re-aligned some wires, noted a fuse that needed replacing.

"What are you doing?"

He turned to find Courtenay staring at him with a hostile expression. "Uh. Your thirty-amp fuse is out. You should replace it. And your wires here, they're crossed. I moved—"

"Don't do that," Courtenay said. "We're supposed to handle all repairs ourselves." His tone said what his words did not: no Indian could possibly be competent in electrical matters, he was an outsider, not welcome.

Nick shrugged. He caught sight of Sophia staring at him, felt himself grow cold all over. Did she, too, see him as interfer-

73

ing, superfluous? Something thick and hot flooded his throat; he turned away, making his movements slow and casual.

Nick stood with his back to the others, staring out of the window. It occurred to him that here, among all these white people, with their education and money, from another world, he was more of an alien than any creature from Mars. Then he thought of the people he'd grown up with in Resolute Bay, people who shunned his family for reasons they could not put into words, out of instinct and vague whispered memory. He thought of his brother, changing into something not human only a few miles from here.

Truly, Nick thought, *not all aliens came from Mars.*

Haughton Crater Research Project, Devon Island
75° 26′ 00″ N, 89° 51′ 00″ W

The ride back to the research station took Sophia and Nick over fist-sized rocks and corrugated ground. It was too cold and windy for conversation, but she was aware of his solid chest and back as she wrapped her arms around him.

He swung into a wide circle around the camp and stopped at a large beige tent on the southern side. Three of the buildings were the usual prefabricated structures she'd seen in Resolute, but the rest were tents large enough to hold offices and labs.

Straddling the ATV, he helped her off the four-wheeler. "I have to put this away and check in with the camp manager," he said. His eyes met hers, deep and dark. "If I'm going to lead you out tomorrow, we have to talk about your plans. I'll come back later, after you've eaten."

"Thanks."

With a nod, he roared off just as Jennifer walked up. Her eyes followed Nick's retreating figure. "Nice ride?"

"Yeah. I met a Martian. You all set up?"

"Not yet, but I found the ladies' room. I've seen better facilities by the road in Mexico."

"Picky, picky," Sophia said. "At least there aren't any tarantulas."

"Bears are better?" Jennifer grinned. "I've set your laptop up in here, but I'm still unpacking. Give me a hand?"

"Right. How much longer until we eat? I'm starving."

Jennifer raised her eyebrow in imitation of Mr. Spock. "If we go 'by the book', hours could seem like days..."

"*Star Trek* again?" Sophia rolled her eyes and ducked into the tent ahead of her.

It was crowded below the low ceiling. Despite the presence of several large space heaters, the people inside wore parkas and hats. Crude tables lined the walls to either side, with laptops laid side by side. Workers sat on upended crates or other handy substitutes, pecking away at keyboards in fingerless gloves. One or two looked up as Sophia and Jennifer entered, but most continued with their work. Banners from various institutes hung on the walls: Sophia recognized MIT, the Canadian Space Agency, a Russian technical institute, and of course the NASA flag.

A canvas wall with a slit entrance divided the tent into two spaces; as they entered, David Beringer emerged. "I thought you'd like a spot in our medical tent," Beringer said. "We already have microscopes set up in a special heated area."

Jennifer brightened. "Oh, excellent!"

"Right, then. I'll show it to you." He ducked back through, taking Jennifer with him.

Sophia found her laptop on the long table against the side of the tent, and sat down on an upended box. The man next to her, sporting what she was coming to view as the usual Arctic beard, shifted and then glanced over. He stuck out a gloved hand. "Mel Brunner. Planetary geology."

She shook his hand. "Sophia Abenezra. I'm out here researching extremophiles."

"Cool. You met Ted yet?"

"Ted?"

"Ted Meyers. Our onsite sawbones." The big man scratched his nose. "He's out here testing some remote surgical equipment, but xenobiology is his hobby. Might be fun to talk to."

"Thanks, uh, Mel."

"Don't mention it. I've got to get back to this report."

"Right."

None of the other scientists in the tent had so much as glanced up at them during the conversation. Sophia found a power strip, plugged in her laptop and powered it up. She checked her email, sent off a synopsis of their trip and an explanation of Dr. Rivers' absence to her sponsoring institute in Berkeley, and shut it down again. She rubbed her eyes. "Hey, Mel? Where can I lock this up?"

He looked at her out of startled blue eyes. "Lock it up? Oh. You don't need to worry about that. There are only thirty people onsite, and we all know one another. No one will take your laptop. I leave mine here all the time."

"Oh. Thanks."

She ducked through the interior doorway to find Jennifer and Nick busy at a table. The air smelled of formaldehyde and doughnuts. Like the rest of the research tent, this area was set up with tables along the canvas walls, workstations crowded together side by side. Narrow strips of fluorescent lights added their harsh glare to the ambient sunlight seeping through the canvas walls. An open shipping crate on the floor told Sophia that Jennifer had started unpacking her lab equipment.

"Hey," Jennifer said as Sophia entered. "Do you know where I put the backup thermocouple for this thing?"

"Probably in your roll-around," she said.

Nick knelt to gather packing peanuts and other trash into the open crate. The bandage across the back of his hand fell onto the nearby table; he ignored it.

Jennifer held up a cable. "Soph, I need you to plug this into the power strip while I plug the other one into the back. Nick, maybe you could find my pink suitcase? The one with the wheels?"

Nick nodded, picked up the empty crate, and ducked through the doorway. Sophia moved in to help her friend set up. Next to the sleek white plastic housings of the microscopes, analyzers and other medical equipment in the tent, Jennifer's home-built box of dark plastic glued and thumb-screwed together looked amateurish. Yet Sophia knew that it held some of the most advanced DNA analysis tools ever devised. She'd watched Jennifer design, build and test it many times over the past three years. Sophia reached for the cable end. "I still think we should call it the Roth Analyzer," she said.

"Bullshit," Jennifer said, plugging a USB cord into a socket. "It's the SlimeMaster. I'm gonna trademark that name." She straightened and pushed her hair out of her eyes, glancing over Sophia's shoulder. "So," she said, lowering her voice. "What do you think?"

"I think it should be 'slime Mistress', but that sounds like a bad sci-fi movie."

"There is no such thing as a bad sci-fi movie. No, I meant about yonder long, dark and intense."

Sophia blinked. "Oh. You mean Nick? What about him?"

"Oh, come on. Don't tell me you're not going to hit that!" Jennifer reached for a zip-lock bag, one of many into which she had ruthlessly organized her many cables and connectors. "He's got eyes for you, that's for sure. He's hardly looked at me," she said, in a fake tone of offense.

"Then he's blind," Sophia joked. Her friend's attraction to men, and theirs for her, was almost legendary. "No other explanation. Anyway, he's all yours."

Jennifer snorted. "Like I'd have a chance. He's going to be with you, remember? Just the two of you, on a long romantic walk over the tundra – "

"Permafrost."

"—under the Northern lights—"

"Which don't shine in 24-hour daylight."

"—alone in a polar paradise. You know that the best way to keep warm—"

"Stop it." Sophia heard the tension in her voice, and didn't try to hide it.

Jennifer put a hand on Sophia's shoulder. "Okay, you know I'm kidding. Mostly. Look, Soph, I don't mean to rush you. But you know Paul would not have wanted you to take vows of celibacy just because he's gone."

Sophia slowly closed her hand in a fist, then released it. "I thought I could come back to this. Maybe I was wrong."

Jennifer pulled up a stool and sat. "Back to the Arctic, you mean?"

Sophia nodded, not looking at her friend. "I thought after all these years, after going to Mexico and Hawaii, I could come back to this. I thought I could put it behind me." She swallowed, fighting tears. "But it's almost like he's here again. Almost as if I could turn around and see him, hear his voice."

Jennifer took Sophia's hands in hers, and her voice was gentle. "You're still in love with him."

"I don't know. I just don't know."

"Then maybe you need a fresh start. Maybe you need a new man to—"

"I am not interested in Nick," Sophia said. "He's just a...a guide. He's a babysitter."

"Yeah, but a damn cute one," Jennifer said. "And you could definitely do worse in this crowd. You know what they say about the social scene up here? For a woman, the odds are good, but the goods are odd. You're lucky: Nick's got the looks, and by what I see, the inclination. Oh, hi."

Jennifer's bright tone warned her. Sophia looked over her shoulder to see Nick standing in the doorway, the pink rollaway suitcase in his arms, a strange look on his face. Next to him, Amaruq sat with tongue lolling. *Oh, God, how much of that did he hear?* Sophia wondered.

"Thanks for finding it," Jennifer said, taking the rollaway from Nick. She did not appear at all embarrassed at possibly being overheard. Sophia, however, felt hot and uncomfortable.

"Cook says dinner's ready," Nick said. His voice sounded a little hoarse. He did not look at Sophia. "Better come before it's all gone."

"Just a minute," Jennifer said. She opened the rollaway, which revealed itself to be fitted with a myriad little shelves and racks, each containing a sample case. She plucked two from their nests and reached for a capture swab. Popping open the top one-handed, she squatted down on the floor. "Here, girl!" She gestured at Amaruq.

"What are you doing?" Nick said suspiciously.

"Hey, she's a pretty girl," Jennifer said in what Sophia recognized as her talking-to-animals voice.

Curious, the dog walked forward, head down, ears alert. Jennifer ran a hand across her head, scratched behind her ears. "Yeah, you're a good girl. Wanna treat?"

She held up her hand, and Sophia saw she had a section of doughnut in it. The dog watched her hand, tail wagging, then sat down and raised her paw. "Aw, you've got beautiful manners," Jennifer said. "Open up!"

She held the treat over the dog's head, and Amaruq opened her jaw. Quickly Jennifer ran the surface of the cotton-tipped swab over her tongue. Quick as a flash, Amaruq jumped backwards, shaking her head.

"Hey!" Nick said, and took a step into the room. "Knock it off!"

But Jennifer was holding out the doughnut piece, and Amaruq took it delicately from her fingers. She swallowed it in one bite, tail wagging, as Jennifer pulled the cap to the end of the swab. It sealed itself and she turned away to label it.

"What the hell?" Nick reached for her hand, then stopped. "What did you do to her?"

"Just taking a DNA swab," Jennifer said, concentrating on her writing. "I'll be doing the two other dogs I've seen in camp. Are there any others?"

Sophia saw the scowl deepening on Nick's face. "She needs as many samples from the area as possible, to weed out any background contamination," she explained. "If I come back with a sample that, for example, one of the dogs peed on, she can filter out its DNA. That way we can test the ability of the SlimeMaster to pinpoint a species."

"SlimeMaster?"

"Uh. Working title," Sophia said hastily.

"You didn't ask her permission," Nick said, still frowning. "I don't know that I like you doing this."

Jennifer looked up in surprise. "Asked her permission?"

"I meant my permission," Nick said. "And you don't have it." He stepped forward, hand outstretched. "Give it to me."

Slowly, Jennifer handed him the swab. "Is there a reason you don't want me to have your dog's DNA? Trust me, I'm not going to clone her or anything."

"*Clone* her?" Nick looked startled. He stared down at the dog, who stared back at him.

"Look, it's just baseline stuff. I'm also gathering DNA from all the personnel onsite. You, for example." She picked up another clean capture swab in its plastic housing, and took a step forward.

Nick backed up, and Amaruq laid her ears back warningly. "No way," he said, holding up his hands. "Don't come near me with that."

"It's just a cheek swab. It won't hurt."

Sophia laid a hand on her friend's arm. "Jennifer. I think Nick has privacy issues with this."

Jennifer shrugged. "Okay. But if Sophia collects any samples from some place you've peed, let her know, will you?"

A ghost of a smile came and went on Nick's lips as he glanced at Sophia. "Deal. Look, ah, if we're late to the mess tent there won't be anything left..."

"Gotcha," Jennifer said. She smiled at him, then nodded to Amaruq. "Thanks for being a good sport, girl."

Amaruq thumped her tail once, cocking her head to one side. Sophia helped her friend pack away her samples, then they were shrugging into their parkas. Sophia finished first, but as Nick turned to lead them out, she caught his hand. "Let me look at that."

His hand was large and warm in hers; she turned it over, feeling calluses, feeling strength in it. The long scratch across the back had started bleeding. "You cut yourself carving?"

He shook his head, looking away. He started to pull his hand back. "It's nothing. Don't worry about it."

Jennifer said, "I've seen scratches smaller than that cost a guy his hand. Have you had your tetanus shots? Sophia, here's an alcohol swab."

Nick hissed as Sophia dabbed at the cut. She leaned in to blow on it to dry, and he took a step back, bringing her with him. She glanced up and met his eyes. "Relax," she said. "If this goes wrong, you have nothing to worry about. Jennifer has a lot of experience with amputations."

His eyes widened, then slitted. "Ah, I'll probably just let Amaruq lick it. Dog saliva helps them heal their wounds."

Jennifer pulled on her gloves. "Good way to lose a hand, that," she said cheerfully. "The enzymes in dog saliva only work on dog wounds. Besides, you know where that tongue has been?"

Sophia repressed a grin. "And on that note, let's go to dinner."

Haughton Crater Research Project, Devon Island
75° 26' 00" N, 89° 51' 00" W

The mess tent was noisy and hot. Like most of the other semi-permanent structures, it was a huge tent stretched over a wooden frame, held down by guy wires to anchor it against the wind. The walls gusted in and out as Sophia, Jennifer and Nick pushed their way in. Flags from a dozen space agencies, universities and research institutes hung on the walls, and fluorescent lighting strips hung from the high rooftree threw a harsh light over the assembled scientists. Most of the room inside the tent was taken up by a large table, formed by shoving together several folding tables. About twenty people were laughing, talking, and eating in the type of academic din Sophia associated with every dining hall in every dorm she'd ever lived in.

"Dr. Roth!" David Beringer waved from the other side of the tent. He motioned towards an empty space on the bench next to him.

Nick moved away, sliding along one wall, heading for the rear of the tent. The kitchen took up the back third; steam obscured most of it but Sophia could see a round Inuit woman stirring something on a stove. Nick greeted her in Inuktitut but she turned away from him.

Sophia squeezed in between Jennifer and a man with the usual beard and toque of the northern male researcher.

"Hi," he said, a grin splitting his black beard. "Caribou meatloaf today. Don't miss it." He waved a spoon at her. "Did you bring flatware?"

Sophia blinked. "Excuse me?"

"The rules say if you don't bring your own, you have to eat with your fingers," said a skinny, redheaded man across the table. He waved a pair of pencils, held like chopsticks, in the air. "Improvisation allowed, of course."

When the heaping plate of meatloaf and macaroni arrived (with plastic forks), Sophia dug in, ravenous. Years of field experience had taught her not to count calories, at least not in the way most people did. The extreme environment of a polar ecology put a tremendous strain on the body's resources. Just to maintain normal body temperature required twice the calories of a day spent in San Francisco or Kansas City. She had cleaned her plate and was contemplating seconds when David Beringer cleared his throat and banged on the table.

Conversations wound down, heads turning to him. "I'd like to take a moment to welcome our two newest team members," he said, introducing Sophia and Jennifer. "Dr. Roth's field experiments are in biological assay; perhaps you'd like to explain it?"

Applause, and a few wolf whistles, greeted the little blonde as she stood. As always, Sophia wondered how her friend always managed to look well-turned out even in extreme conditions. Jennifer's shoulder-length hair bloomed golden even in the harsh lighting, and her frank, open countenance highlighted her bonny blue eyes. Having shed her parka, Jennifer's lush figure showed very well in her tight blue sweater and figure-hugging ski pants.

"Hi. Uh, what we're trying to do is verify our earlier tests in extreme environments. We've designed—"

"You designed," Sophia said. "I'm just the flunky who grabs samples for you."

A low chuckle went around the tent.

"We have designed a portable DNA lab. It takes samples brought back by a remote exploration device such as a robot, assays the specimens, and performs basic DNA analysis."

"How can you perform any analysis on such a small sample?" The question came from a handsome man in the middle of the table—mid thirties, with black hair and fair skin. Unlike most of the men on the research station, he was clean shaven. "Ted Meyers," he introduced himself. "I'm the camp doctor. Dr. Roth, how fast are we talking about? Soil samples are notoriously difficult to culture, because they contain so many different organisms."

"Correct," Jennifer said.

Sophia noted the blank looks from the others at the table. *These are geologists,* she reminded herself. She cleared her throat. "The device is specifically designed to compare, eliminate and isolate different organisms. That is to say, the device can multiply even a tiny sample of DNA in a matter of hours into a large enough sample for rigorous testing."

Taking up the thread, Jennifer continued. "We've built in multiple extraction technologies, both ARDRA and RISA. Sub-unit ribosomal DNA genes are amplified from each sample before PCR amplification."

"Intriguing," he said. His dark eyes flashed at Jennifer. "I assume this is the new lab-on-a-chip technology we've all been hearing about."

"Hardly new," Jennifer said, twinkling at him. "It's been around awhile."

Meyers twinkled back. His coworkers exchanged glances. "But surely the sheer volume must affect the bacterial diversity analysis."

Jennifer warmed to her subject, her expression serious. "The real test of the process is the comparison algorithm. We've spent the last few years assembling a basic database of essential sequences, anticipating that any actual extraterrestrial finds would be analogous."

David Beringer stood up. "That sounds fascinating, Doctor, but I think we'd better save the technical details."

Jennifer looked around at the politely bored faces, flushed. "Of course. I get carried away."

"We all do," Meyers said, flashing her a warm look. "Hey, David, can we book her for an after-dinner slideshow?"

"Oh," Jennifer said. "Well, in a couple of days, perhaps—"

"That's fine," David said. He put an avuncular hand on Jennifer's shoulder and she sat. "And now, we've got a special celebration ..."

The lights flickered, dimmed, and then everyone was standing. Sophia struggled to her feet just as the group burst into a chorus of "Happy Birthday". Sophia watched as the cook brought a huge sheet cake out to the table. It was decorated with a picture of the solar system and a fat candle. She watched as the cake was passed to an older woman with gray-blonde hair, a weathered face and a sheepish grin. Sophia noted all of this in passing; her gaze was riveted on the flame flickering on the cake. She was all too aware of the canvas billowing in and out around the assembly, of the shriek of wind. Her skin felt clammy.

Fire. The crackle of flames. Screams...

Sophia leaned over to her friend. "Stuffy in here," she said. "Going out for air."

Jennifer, eyes on Meyers, nodded. Sophia pushed past her and hurried out the door.

Devon Island Research Station, Truelove Lowlands, 75° 35'2.20″ N, 84° 6'14.04″ W (coordinates unreliable)

"Coming up on the research station, mate," said Pete.

Fraser leaned to his right, looking down through the cockpit at the expanse below. Devon Island showed him its usual barren rock face, of tumbled gorges, cracks and pits, rolling hills topped by the occasional bench of hard rock outcropping. "You could lose a battalion in that," he said.

"That you could," said Pete. He switched the enormous hunk of chewing gum from one cheek to the other. "If those NASA johnnies have gotten themselves lost, it'll be a damn job to find 'em." He adjusted his headphones, then touched the controls of the Twin Otter. It banked south, then back to the east.

Abruptly, the ground below bloomed with dark green patches that grew larger and larger as they progressed east, until finally the ground for miles was a landscape of hummocky grass, meadows and meandering streams.

Fraser shook his head. "Gets me every time. It's like we just travelled two hundred miles to the south."

"Aye," Pete agreed. "But without the trees. What I never understood is, why 'Truelove'? Looks like a pretty barren place for love." He cackled to himself.

"Named after a ship," Fraser said. He reached behind him to his pack and brought out his field glasses. "One of Sir John Franklin's supply ships, I think."

"Franklin? The explorer guy?" Pete sounded awed.

"Yes." Fraser leaned forward. "Take us down along the river valley."

"Right," Pete replied. The little plane banked right, dipped.

Fraser felt his stomach lurch as the landscape swung under him. He was aware of the delicacy of thin aluminum wings in the wind off the top of the world. He focused on the ground skimming by underneath. Shrub, hummock, rock. A low marshy area blooming with fern and horsetail, species dating back to the age of the dinosaurs. A long rill of uplifted gravel that used to be a beach. And then, cutting through the green, a winding gleam of swift water.

"There," Fraser said. "The Truelove River."

"I see it," Pete said, already banking further. "Dropping to five hundred meters," he said. "Reducing air speed." The engine's high note changed as he throttled down. "You want to run an expanding square search, right?" An expanding square search was a box-shaped spiral that wound its way outward from the last known location of a victim.

"Right," Fraser said, his glasses glued to his face. Below, the shiny thread of glacial meltwater wound back and forth across the flat plain, flanked by steep gravel banks. He tore his gaze away long enough to check his notes. "You have the GPS coordinates?"

"That I do, mate," Pete responded. He glanced up at the GPS readout. "Almost there. Want me to set down?"

"Find 'em first," Fraser said. He stuck to protocol, not voicing the fear in the back of his mind. He hoped he would find the men alive. So often, he did not. There were so many things that could kill even experienced Arctic trekkers, let alone a pair of relative newbies with their heads in their academic clouds.

"Coming up on coordinates," Pete announced. He reduced his air speed even further, slowing the craft. "Cross-winds," he said as the plane was buffeted.

The GPS locator beeped. Fraser glanced up. He'd already programmed Leo and Glenn's last known coordinates in as a waypoint; the GPS told him they had arrived at it. He leaned to his right again.

The Truelove River Valley snaked off to his left; below was the twisted rivulet of some unnamed tributary. Fraser stared, looking for anything out of the ordinary: the sudden white patch of a scraped encampment, the remains of a campfire, a tent. He saw no sign of human habitation. "Can we go any lower?"

"We can try. If we wind up crashing, you're carrying me back."

"If we crash, the government won't pay you," Fraser said, glasses up again.

"Harsh," Pete said.

Fraser scanned the world below. Even with high magnification, all he saw was brush, grass, water and rock. Movement caught his eye and his heart lurched, but it was only a hare bounding off into the rocks. The ground wheeled as Pete circled slowly.

"No sign of 'em?" Pete asked, eyes on his altimeter.

"Nothing," Fraser said.

"Maybe they got lost. Could the river have swept them away?"

Fraser looked at the map in his lap. "They weren't on the river, they were above it, or so they said. I can't even find a trail through the mud or snow."

"Might be we need dogs on this," Pete suggested.

Fraser silently agreed.

Haughton Crater Research Project, Devon Island
75° 26′ 00″ N, 89° 51′ 00″ W

Outside the mess tent, the wind was louder, sharper and much colder. She slipped her hands into her pockets and took a deep breath. The wind smelled fresh and frigid, with a hint of salt tang. *Air fresh off the Arctic Ocean,* she thought. The coldest ocean in the world.

I should not have come here, Sophia thought. She'd thought she was ready for it all again—the cold, the fires inside tents, the smell of kerosene. She wasn't. It brought back that awful day, a day she'd lived through and others had not, one that had scarred body and soul. *I should have gone to the Great Salt Lake,* she thought. Or back to Yellowstone. Someplace hot, someplace where nothing would remind her of Alaska. Or Paul.

Movement at the edge of sight; she turned and Nick Tonarak was standing in front of her, within arm's reach. His parka hood was up around his face, framing it, giving him a look out of some old photograph of the 19th century explorers.

"You're a quiet one," she said. "You totally snuck up on me." Something nudged her knee; the dog. Sophia dropped to eye level with the dog. "Hey, there." She offered a hand to be sniffed, then slowly reached for the dog's ears. The white dog closed her eyes as Sophia scratched behind them. "She sure looks a lot like an Arctic wolf," she said. Sophia looked carefully at the dog—she had the lean, rangy look of a wolf, the close set eyes, the deep fur.

"Yeah, she's probably got some wolf in her," Nick said. Sophia was struck once again by the deep timbre of his voice. "I have to keep an eye on her during hunting season, or some trigger-happy hunter from down south might shoot her."

Laughter floated out of the tent. Sophia stood, just in time to catch his wistful look at the tent. "There's birthday cake." She tilted her head towards the tent door.

He shrugged, and she saw that closed-down look come into his face. "I don't like crowds," he said. "You headed for your tent?"

"I don't know. I guess. Where do I set up?"

"Already done."

She blinked. "Oh. Thanks."

"Not me. Beringer told the guys in the motor pool to set you up."

Sophia remembered the moment in the research tent, and looked away. "Look, what I said earlier, I didn't mean anything by it. I...Jennifer has a habit of teasing me about...She doesn't mean..." Horrified, Sophia made herself shut up. She was only making it worse. She stopped in front of the research tent. "I...I guess I better grab my laptop."

Nick turned away, saying nothing, and entered the research tent. Amaruq nosed under the flap and followed him inside. Sophia ducked in after her. Nick pulled a crate forward and sat down on it, unzipping his parka. Under it, he wore a cable knit sweater. "We need to talk about where you're going tomorrow," he said. He reached into his pocket and brought out a laminated map. "I'm not exactly sure what you're looking for out there."

"Bacteria," Sophia said. "They're called 'extremophiles', because they live in extreme environments, like boiling water or acid springs. I've studied them in volcanic springs and deserts where the temperature exceeds 110 degrees Fahrenheit."

He looked at her. "Acid springs?"

"There are some really beautiful blue-green algae living in acidic waters at Yellowstone that look almost turquoise," she said. "And right here on Devon Island there are cryptendoliths all around you."

He blinked. "Crypt..."

"I'll show you." Sophia stood and strode back out through the tent flap. Amaruq followed her out, ears forward. The light was weaker now, filtered through a light fog gathering in the west, where Sophia knew the land met the frigid sea. Rocks were piled all around the base of the tent to form a foundation and hold it down. She picked through them for a moment until she found one with a streak of translucent quartz. Perfect.

She pushed back into the warmth of the tent, Amaruq crowding in behind her. Nick was hunched over the map. He looked up when she came in and set the rock down. "See the vein of quartz there?" she pointed to it.

"Yeah."

She pulled out her lanyard with the scope attached.

"What's that?" Nick said.

She explained the instrument; he turned it over in agile fingers. "Good workmanship," he said.

She reached across him and turned on a reading lamp clipped to the table. The action brought their faces close together. A muscle jumped in his jaw and he leaned back. She placed the rock under the light. "Take a look at the vein."

He stared through the scope at the chunk of rock. "A line of green rock."

"That's not rock. That's an endolith. It's an organism that colonizes the inside of rocks. This one is green because it's chlorophyll based; it hides behind that seam of translucent quartz. The light from the sun can reach it, but it's protected from cold, predators, everything. The vein of quartz actually turns this rock into a kind of miniature greenhouse."

Nick stared at her, then at the rock. "What does it do?"

"Do?"

"Does it eat other stuff? How does it grow?"

He was close enough for her to see flecks of gold in his eyes. Most of all, she saw his eager expression. Most men zoned out when she talked about her work, but Nick was interested. "We don't really know. Some cells seem to divide only once every hundred years or so, which means they can survive whole ice ages in a single rock."

"And you think you'll find these on Mars?"

"If we find anything this complex on Mars, I'll be astonished," she said. "But it's possible."

He picked up the rock and turned it over in his hand. "It doesn't move around? It doesn't leave the rock where it is now?

What does it do?" Amaruq nosed his hand, he held the rock so she could sniff it. She licked it, sat down, cocked her head at Sophia.

"It doesn't have to *do* anything," Sophia said. "All it has to do is live. That's meaning enough, in a universe this cold." She stuck her hands in her parka. "I think about how cold and violent it is out there in space, with cosmic rays and solar winds and radiation. And here on this planet, this warm, wet little planet, life is so stubborn it even lives in rocks—" She bit her lip. "It doesn't have to mean anything more than that it is."

He said nothing, but put the rock down. Sophia remembered that he was a carver, that to him a rock was material to be shaped, lifeless and inert. *Like everyone else,* she thought, *he didn't understand.*

"I'm not just looking in rocks," she said. It occurred to her that his silence might be embarrassment; for all she knew, he hadn't even finished high school, and had no idea what she was talking about. "I need mostly water samples, lichen, mud and so forth. My main focus is what's living in the ice."

He nodded. "Then it sounds as if the bed of a river is the fastest, easiest place to get samples."

"Exactly." Sophia ran her finger along a sinuous line on the map. "This would be the Truelove River?"

Nick leaned in for a closer look. One long brown finger tapped the contour lines. "Yeah. It winds through the Lowlands for quite a bit after it emerges from the ice cap. How much collecting are you doing along there?" On the floor at his feet, Amaruq circled three times and settled down into a round bundle of fur.

"A couple hundred samples, but that's all. I had hoped to walk the raised beaches along the north shore, but it looks like we won't have time. So let's focus on the lowlands, the river and the ice cap."

"We're taking ATVs?" Nick sat back, shoving his hands in his pockets.

She shook her head. "I'd rather not. I'll be stopping every few yards, sorry, meters anyway, to collect samples. We may as well walk the whole way."

He nodded. "Shouldn't take us more than two days to get to the ice, then." He glanced over at her. "Unless you're a really slow walker."

"I can cover about ten miles a day over rough ground," she said. "This is not my first field trip. It's not even my first in the Arctic." Sophia heard the edge in her voice, but Nick wasn't paying attention. His gaze swept back and forth over the map, measuring. Golden light played along his high cheekbones. When he sat back, she caught a whiff of him: diesel, leather, and something wild, something like the smell of the wind outside. "So what do you suggest?"

"Two days, about ten miles a day. We stick to the river as much as possible."

Sophia was aware of another conversation taking place, on a non-verbal level. She'd felt it before: a man/woman vibe that filled up the tent, that made her acutely aware of his nearness, the size of his shoulders, his warm presence in this close space. She made herself concentrate on the map.

"After the first day, we can cut across the plateau here, where the river takes a deep bend to the south, then join up with the river again; that will save us about five miles."

"Agreed," Nick said. "It will also take us to those scientists' last known location, so we'll probably find Will Fraser there or nearby. We can check in with him, maybe send some samples back to base with him. We'll get to the ice cap by the second day." He folded the map and smiled at her. "Also, there's a bonus for you."

"What's that?"

He pointed to a tiny dot on the map. "A hot spring, about five miles before you reach the foot of the ice cap. You say your critters live in hot water. Might be some, uh, extremophiles in that. It feeds into the river."

"A hot spring? I didn't think there was any hydrothermal activity—" She stopped. "I mean, any hot springs—"

He gave her a hard look. "I know what 'hydrothermal' means," he said.

Sophia felt her face getting hot. "Sorry. Most of the people I talk to don't."

"You don't have to talk down to me, just because I'm an Indian."

She stared at him. "That's not fair."

Jaw muscles rippled and he looked away. "I don't have a college education, so you college guys think we're all idiots. But what you don't realize is that I have nothing to do all winter but hunt, surf the Internet and read. So don't assume I know nothing." He looked at her with a challenge in his eyes. "I know that the eastern side of this island is made up of metamorphic basement rocks from Precambrian sediments dating into the Cambrian and Ordovician eras. And that the ice cap is melting at the rate of two meters a year. I'm not ignorant." At his tone, Amaruq came awake and sat up. Her ears flattened as she stared at Sophia with round amber eyes.

"If I've given that impression, I apologize. But this is a two way street, you know. You don't know me very well. You're making a lot of assumptions—such as the idea that I'm a slow walker just because I don't live here. I've been hiking, diving and trekking most of my life; I can pull my weight and I'm not a whiner. What's more, I don't enjoy being cast in the role of arrogant white oppressor any more than you like being treated like...like Tonto."

His eyes were dark, staring at her. Then something in his face relaxed, and he smiled a little. "Okay, Kemosabe. Start over?"

She nodded. "Let's grant that I know something about back-country hiking, and you know something about geology. Deal?"

Amaruq thumped her tail. Sophia looked at her. "You, too. Deal?"

Amaruq barked and wagged her tail. Sophia laughed. "I swear sometimes I think she understands what we're saying."

Nick reached down and put a hand on the dog's back.

She turned and licked his hand. "Sometimes I think so, too." He folded the map. "I'll take you to your tent now. I'll go talk to Pete, the pilot. He'll be flying us over to the Lowlands in about six hours, so you should get some sleep."

Sophia left the rock sitting on the table and followed him out into the windy light. It took only a minute or so to cross the camp, and then they were out on the bare gravel of the plateau. Ahead of them the ground rose and fell in gentle waves, marked by fist-sized lumps of rock and shadows where snow lingered. As they walked, the day grew darker, grayer; some mechanical racket ahead of them grew louder. Sophia looked to the west; the sun was low on the horizon but was fast disappearing behind a bank of grey fog.

"Sets in about this time every day," Nick said. The wind gusted, blowing the braid over his shoulder. Amaruq lifted her nose into the wind, whirled and raced off. Nick looked after her. "Chasing a hare, I think."

They came to a broad, flat area dotted about with colorful tents, each one firmly staked against wind. The bright yellows, blues, reds and oranges stood out against the gray landscape like lollipops on a dirt mound. Nick led her to the edge of the camp; the motor sound grew louder as they approached. She spotted her gray-green tent set up on the edge of the encampment next to Jennifer's yellow one. Less than twenty feet away, a generator the size of a refrigerator roared away.

Nick leaned close to her ear. "Tradition. Newbies always have to be next to the generator."

Nice, she thought. *Put a bunch of professors in the wilderness, and they turn into frat boys, complete with hazing traditions.* A touch on her arm, she looked down. Nick was holding out some round pill-sized pieces of foam—ear plugs. She stuck one in each ear. They blocked about half the sound, a blessed relief. She put the others in her pocket to give to Jennifer later.

Nick turned and gestured angrily. Sophia glanced over to see Amaruq squatting next to her tent. The dog finished her business and trotted over with what Sophia swore was a look of mischief. Nick nodded goodbye, and strode off.

Sophia found her tent in good order, except for one thing: whoever had set it up had left her camp stove inside. She fumbled, almost dropped it in her haste to set it outside her tent. As she ducked back in, reaching for the zipper, she caught sight of Nick Tonarak and his dog, walking back to the camp headquarters. Silhouetted against the fog-shrouded sun, his figure was tall, broad-shouldered, proud. And somehow lonely.

Haughton Crater Research Project, Devon Island
75° 26′ 00″ N, 89° 51′ 00″ W

Nick walked right through the camp and out the other side, walking west towards the fog-shrouded horizon. The wind off the Arctic ice cap had died down a little; the smell of sea air hung heavy in the wet air. Amaruq trotted beside him, nose to the ground. Nick walked past some broken boulders, and then the camp was out of sight. He perched on the edge of a boulder, staring into the distance. Before them, the gray-brown plain rolled on and on towards the distant sea, broken here and there by outcroppings, but otherwise blank and featureless.

::You okay?:: Amaruq sat on her haunches.

Nick looked down at his hands. Oil stains and grit darkened them here and there. He wished for his tools, a stone, something to keep his hands busy and his mind quiet. "Tired, I guess, Sis," he said. For once, he was glad she could not hear his thoughts the way he could hear hers.

Distantly, a long, ululating howl spun up into the air. Amaruq sprang to her feet, nose high. ::Wolf!:: There was an eager note to her inner voice that hurt him to hear.

"Go on," he said. "Just be back before we leave."

She dashed forward, then stopped as another long howl sounded, farther away this time. Amaruq sat, uncertainly. He waited for her to answer them, to run to join the pack now hunting across the broken hills to the northwest. As always, Nick wondered if she would not come back this time.

Amaruq lifted her nose, and a long, moaning wail broke

from her. Nick felt shivers go down his neck, and listened for an answer.

There was none.

After a while, Amaruq turned and trotted past him, headed back to camp. Her tail and ears were low, and she avoided his look. But he felt the pain in her, felt the rejection eating at her. Her own kind—if indeed they were her kind—shunned her. Nick ached to follow her, to comfort her, but knew she wanted to be alone right now.

For a while, Nick sat, throwing pebbles, testing them in his hand for weight and shape and carving prospects. He kept thinking about the little Sedna figure, about how it had looked in Sophia's hand. He didn't understand why he had given it to her. He didn't understand why he was drawn to her.

Should he make a move? Ask her out? He didn't know how Southerners did these things. He had never been South, had no knowledge of that world except what came over the Internet or television. But he wondered if maybe they could go for a walk, share a cup of coffee.

He didn't know how to do this. Probably he should do nothing.

He gazed out over the empty lands, marked only by broken rock, ice and patches of snow. He thought about how the wolf pack had reacted to Amaruq's overture. Grim-faced, he closed his fist over a rock until its sharp edges pressed into his palm. A dark look came into his eyes, and he threw the rock down.

Better to keep his distance, he thought. He stood and started back for the camp. He would do his job. And he would keep his thoughts about her to himself. He would hold them inside, secret even from Amaruq.

Devon Island Research Station, Truelove Lowlands, 75° 35′2.20″ N, 84° 6′14.04″ W (coordinates unreliable)

The little plane bucked slightly as it met minor turbulence over the Lowlands.

"I'm not picking up anything on the emergency channel," Pete noted. Many hikers carried emergency beacons that would signal their location to rescuers. They were required on all Project sponsored traverses. "Could it have fallen in water, shorted out?"

"I don't know." Fraser sighed. "Well, we'll start from the waypoint and work our way out in an expanding square," he said. "We'll take it out to a ten kilomet—"

The sudden beeping of the GPS locator on the cabin roof interrupted him. He glanced at it, saw Pete frowning.

"What's wrong with this bugger?" Pete muttered. He reached up and tapped the housing, then thumped it. On the readout, a set of numbers Fraser didn't recognize flickered, went dark, flickered back, with the seconds readout running down.

"I don't recognize those coordinates," Fraser said. "Is it receiving a signal from the beacon?"

Pete shook his head. "This is tuned to the GPS satellite feed over Northern Canada." He thumped the housing again. "Must be on the fritz."

Fraser was staring at the numbers. "Twenty-five degrees north? Where the hell is that?" He pulled the laminated quick reference card out of a holder on the dash.

Pete banked the plane again, nosed into the wind. "And?"

Fraser stared at him, blinking. "Florida. The GPS says we're just off the beach at Miami."

Pete let out a short laugh. "Damn. And here am I without my surfboard. Well, we know where we are, mate, and it's not frickin' Miami. Want me to come about again?"

Fraser stared down through the window, an uneasy feeling washing over him. No camp. No men. No equipment. There was no sign a human had crossed this territory at all. The GPS was, unaccountably, not working right. What if the coordinates Glenn and Leo had radioed in had been wrong?

They might be anywhere.

"Let's go back," he said heavily. "We need more men. And more equipment."

As Pete banked away, heading west, the ground dropped away below him. Fraser stared at it, thinking.

It was a hell of a place to be lost.

Haughton Crater Research Project, Devon Island
75° 26′ 00″ N, 89° 51′ 00″ W

The research tent was colder than the mess tent. After dinner and birthday cake, Jennifer had elected to finish her prep work before Sophia took off tomorrow. *Whenever 'tomorrow' was in a place where the sun never set,* she thought. Checking her database carefully against her protocols, Jennifer sighed. Still not enough human DNA samples. She needed that baseline to prove that Sophia's field samples were uncontaminated by humans. Contaminated samples would skew her results, which were aimed at proving life existed—or didn't—on another planet.

She stood, leaning backwards to work a crick out of her back. She could use some coffee right now. A steaming vanilla latte, maybe with cinnamon. And her chances of that were remote to slim. She thought longingly of her lab back in Berkeley, where she had smuggled in an espresso maker to hide behind the refrigerators. On long nights of analysis and data crunching, it had been her best friend.

A beep on her laptop told her the tests were finished. She checked the diagnostics, smiled and patted the SlimeMaster's black plastic hood. "That's my good girl," she said. "Prepped and ready to go."

She checked her watch; just enough time to run some test samples and tweak the database before dinner. A breeze bellied the canvas tent wall inward; she glanced up and saw the silhouette of someone passing on the other side. *Damned Arctic,* she thought. Her watch told her it was bedtime; the daylight told her it was early afternoon. She hated jet lag, but Arctic lag was worse. She wouldn't feel right again until she got back to where night followed day.

Jennifer's manicured fingers sorted quickly through the

rack of labeled reagents, picking out ligase buffers, oligo mixes, and PCR primer. She pulled gloves from a box and snapped them on, wishing someone could invent surgical gloves with insulation. She blew on her fingers to warm them, and set to work.

Proteobacteria, subclasses alpha and gamma. The *Bacillus–Clostridium* group; the order *Actinomycetales; Desulfuromonas acetoxidans*. Familiar cultures, all of them. Jennifer thought of them fondly as research assistants. She started PCR reproduction on all of her index cultures, and turned to the samples she had collected so far.

Too bad I couldn't hang on to Amaruq's swab, she thought. She liked dogs. It would be interesting to see what breed this one was. Reaching past a rack of test tubes, she knocked a manual to the floor. When she bent to pick it up, she saw several white hairs scattered on the floor.

Well, well, she thought. Scooping them up with tweezers, she slid them into a plastic bag and sealed it. "Looks like I've got some samples after all."

She stood up to put the dog hairs away. In the packing litter at the end of her lab table lay a used adhesive bandage. Dried blood smeared the inside. *Where had that come from?* She thought back, remembered handing Sophia a bandage for Nick.

Nick. A slow smile crossed her face. Of course. He'd discarded this bandage, or it had fallen off. Either way, she didn't need his consent to use something he'd thrown away. She picked it up in her gloved hand and turned to her processing area. She wanted to get a good head start on his DNA.

Devon Island

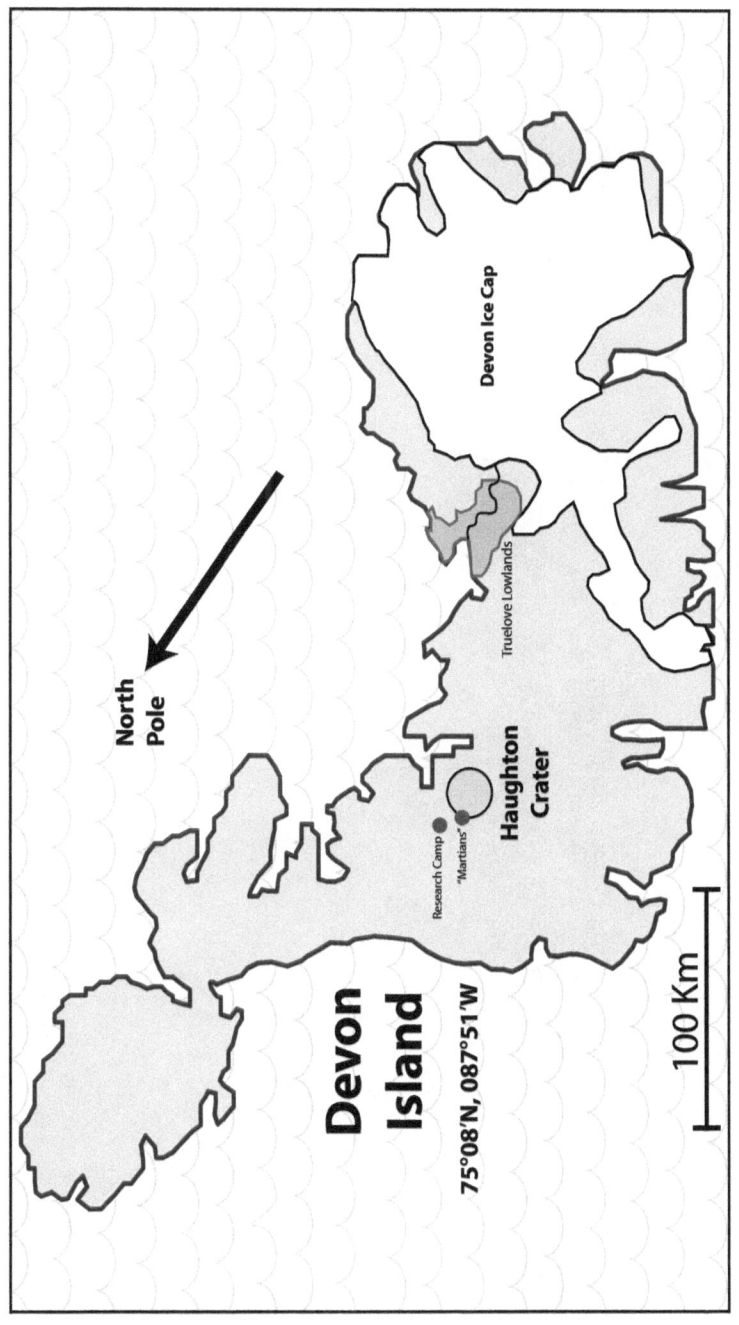

Devon Ice Cap

Truelove Lowlands

Haughton Crater

Research Camp

"Martians"

North Pole

Devon
Island

75°08'N, 087°51'W

100 Km

III - THE TRUELOVE LOWLANDS

Devon Island Research Station, Truelove Lowlands, Nunavut
75° 40′ 36.27″ N, 84° 35′ 05.33″ W

The roar of the airplane died away and left Nick and Sophia standing on the rubble beach of north Devon Island. The sun was nothing but a diffuse glow behind wispy grey fog. The wind off the sea ice whipped around Sophia's parka hood; she pulled it tight around her face with cold fingers. She drew in a long, deep breath, smelling ice and wet rock and ocean.

Nick bent to hoist a backpack to his shoulder. He tucked a box of rations under his arm and looked back at Sophia.

"I'm coming," Sophia said.

He nodded and turned away, striding on long legs across the barren gravel.

Amaruq barked happily and dashed off across the scree to a pair of dilapidated blue Quonset hut a few yards away.

Sophia struggled into her heavy backpack and bent over to pick up a cardboard box of food. She almost overbalanced and staggered a couple of steps before she could straighten. The merciless wind cut at her exposed cheeks. When she was steady, she huffed over to the blue hut.

A 2 x 8 wooden plank leaned against one of the double doors. Why lock a door on a deserted island? And from the outside? Anyone could lift the bar and come in. Then she crossed the threshold and knew the answer. She wrinkled her nose at the smell.

"Pew!"

"Foxes got in," Nick's voice told her. Movement in the distance, and then light; he had forced open a window stuck with ice and grime. Amaruq circled the baseboard of the hut, sniffing. Sophia stood blinking, waiting for her eyes to adjust.

Dim light showed her a room shaped like half a tin can buried in the ground. It was about twice as long as it was wide. The hut was aligned east to west in a futile effort to reduce the draught of the constant wind. Tables, work benches, and shelves crowded north side. The lower shelves were a mess of gnawed boxes and spilled sacks of staples like oatmeal and powdered milk. Someone had left some canned goods on an upper shelf, which had frozen, burst, and spewed their brown contents across the shelf. A stack of empty five-gallon water jugs climbed one wall. On the south side, a boxy oil heater jutted out into the room. Sophia deposited her box of goods on a cleared space on a table, next to Nick's box.

"Home sweet home," she said to herself.

Nick was working at another window. "Better than a tent in the wind," he said.

"I wasn't criticizing." She shrugged out of her backpack and let it thump to the floor. While Nick struggled with the stubborn windows, she explored the hut. It smelled of mildew and kerosene, with a taint of rotten meat. The far end of the hut boasted a window (now open) and two sets of bunk beds. One of the bunk beds sagged so badly she was sure it could not bear anyone's weight. The lower bunk was crammed with the large plastic tubs used to store non-perishables in the Arctic. She pried the top off of one and found blankets.

"Is it okay if we use these?" she said.

Nick was at the door. He nodded and ducked out. Amaruq followed him. The wind caught the door and banged it shut.

The lower bunk bed was covered with a tarp. She hauled it off and found rodent turds scattered all over it. Something had chewed a hole the size of her hand in the mattress. Still, it was out of the wind and she could sleep in her sleeping bag on top of it. It was bound to be warmer than a tent in the wind, as Nick had said. She wondered why he was so short with her. Had she said something to irritate him? She pulled the tarps off the bunks, shook them out, and folded them neatly on the spare bunk.

As she unpacked her sleeping bag and rolled it out, she heard a thump and some banging noises from outside. After a few minutes Nick came back inside, ducking as he entered. The door had not been built for tall men. Amaruq was not with him. He went straight for the tool box and began rummaging in it.

"You want the top or bottom bunk?" she asked him.

He looked startled. "Bunk?"

She gestured at the beds. "I'd rather have the bottom, but I'll take the top if you want to be closer to the floor."

"I was going to sleep in the shed."

She blinked. "Why?"

He seemed at a loss for words. "I thought...it just seemed right."

She realized he was embarrassed. It was almost funny. "Well, suit yourself. But I think it would be warmer in here."

After a moment, he shrugged. "Yeah. I'll take the top. Easier for me to get up there."

"True," she said, and smiled. He did not smile back. "I was going to start some supper. Do you have any preferences?"

He fiddled with a socket wrench on the work bench. "Whatever. It would be better to use the stuff in the cans."

She knew that. The weight of canned goods almost never justified carrying them on one's back. She'd learned that on her first hike into high country when she was ten, but Nick was determined to treat her like a complete novice.

"Spaghetti, then," she said. "You like spaghetti?"

He shrugged. "It's okay." He took pliers out of the tool box and stuck them in his pocket. Without a word he went out and closed the door.

Sophia investigated the small kitchen. The electric stove did not have power yet. There were plates and cups and cutlery, though, and a bar of soap to wash dishes. She set out her cans of spaghetti sauce and her packet of pasta, most of which was broken into two inch pieces. No running water. She picked up the largest cook-pot she had and ducked through the door to fetch some water.

The grey clouds overhead were so low she almost felt she could reach up and touch them. She thought their bellies would feel soft and cold and fuzzy. The wind stung her eyes; she held up a hand to shield them and looked around.

The camp sat between the shoreline and a short, sharp cliff. There was no grass, no lichen, no living thing to be seen between the grey sky and the gunmetal sea except for a wheeling bird high overhead. A white shape ghosted along the shoreline—Amaruq, hunting birds. Arctic loons and gulls squawked and squealed, wheeling into the sky in outrage at this intrusion. Sophia looked around and saw a small shed behind the Quonset. The door was propped open with a rock. She heard a metallic ring from inside it as Nick dropped a tool.

Small rivulets of meltwater trickled down the cliff behind the camp and fanned out across the rocky shore. The ground was broken up by grassy hummocks crowned with tough, weathered grass. A white musk ox skull was propped against one. She walked to the nearest one, but it was only half an inch deep, not enough to fill the cook pot. She walked on, her boots scrunching over the gravel. Still too shallow. She crossed tire ruts and wondered how old they were; in these latitudes, the marks of man lasted for many years.

The next rivulet was light grey, laden with silt from the plateau above. She'd heard stories about how milky meltwater could give you digestive cramps, so she skipped that one. She came to the top of a slope, and spotted a tiny but promising streamlet at the bottom. Careful of where she put her feet on the steep descent, she crunched her way down into the narrow defile. She knelt by the water and tugged her glove off with her teeth.

Something cold and wet hit her ear. Sophia gasped. "Dammit, dog!"

Amaruq whined and thumped her tail. She circled around Sophia, then put her head down and butted her. Sophia fell sideways onto sharp rocks the size of her fist. The cook pot fell from her hand. "What the hell is wrong with you?" She batted at the dog. "Get away!"

Amaruq butted her again, nudging her back the way she had come.

"I don't want to play," Sophia said with exasperation. She

104

scrambled up onto her knees and reached for the pot. "Go away!"

Amaruq circled to her other side, barked sharply and grabbed Sophia's sleeve between her teeth.

"Stop that!" Sophia swiped at her with her free hand, but the dog backed away, ears down, pulling at her sleeve. "You'll rip that! Stop!" Was the dog crazy? A slight chill went down her back. Sophia wondered if the dog had rabies. Had she gone feral? Right now, Amaruq looked more like a wolf than a dog.

Amaruq let go of her sleeve, barked, wagged her tail, and wheeled to looked upslope. Sophia heard skittering noises and turned around. Nick was almost falling down the incline, the rifle cradled in one arm, the other waving for balance. He fetched up at her feet, swaying, breathing fast. "What are you doing?" he demanded.

She held up the cook pot. "Getting water. What's wrong?"

Nick scanned the ravine, the stream, the ridge above them as he answered. "Don't ever do that again."

Sophia frowned and dipped the pot into the tiny stream. Icy water drifted over her hand as she held it down, filling it. "Don't do what again?"

"Don't go off without telling me. And don't go off where I can't see you. In fact, don't go off without me, period." His voice was harsh.

The presence of the gun registered. Sophia sat back on her heels, hefting the dripping pot out of the water. "Why? You think there are polar bears around here?"

Amaruq barked and Nick nodded. *It was weird how closely dog and man echoed one another,* Sophia thought. "That's right," he said. He shifted from one foot to another, keeping an eye on the horizon. "This time of year they hunt along shorelines. Are you finished?"

She got heavily to her feet. "Yeah. But we'll need more water than this."

He made no move to take the pot from her, but jerked his head at the slope. "If you see anything moving at ground level, tell me." He brought the gun down so that he was holding it in both hands. "Amaruq, you go ahead."

Amaruq took off up the slope, powerful hindquarters propelling her up the sliding rocks faster than Sophia could manage. She had to place her feet carefully, mindful of the full pot of water slopping back and forth. She'd be lucky to get back with half as much as she'd collected, she thought.

Nothing ambushed them in the short trek back. Far out on the ice, she saw shapes humping from one place to another: seals out on the ice. As they neared the Quonset hut, Sophia heard a muted racket from the shed; the generator was up and running.

"You got it started already?" she said.

"Not hard to do," Nick said grudgingly.

She opened the door and stepped inside.

The smell hit her, and in the blink of any eye she was back in a nightmare she had thought long behind her...

The stink of burning oil, the roar of flames, the smoke as thick as a blanket, the soot choking her nostrils, the high pitched scream-ing, the air searing her lungs...

She dropped the pot and heard it splash, felt cold wetness on her lower legs but she didn't care. She turned to run and cannoned into Nick. He had been carrying the rifle in both hands; now its hard metal barrel smashed into her chest. All her air went away as it had when the flames came and ate all the air and she was crying and falling, falling, trying to breathe.

Then she was caught in strong arms and lowered to the ground and something warm and wet was licking her cheek. She fought to make her lungs expand, but it was as if her body had forgotten how to work them. Nick's face swam into view, his eyes alarmed, his hair falling towards her face as he said something she could not hear. The suffocating feeling dragged at her lungs, she felt the panic rising.

Then her brain rebooted her autonomic system and she drew in a long, ragged gasp of air. Wonderful air. Sweet air. Cold air that set her to coughing, and the coughing reminded her of *smoke and flames and the smell of roast pork.*

Sophia rolled away from Nick and vomited. Amaruq

danced backward, her ears swiveling back and forth with curiosity.

"What's wrong?" She could hear Nick now. He sounded equal parts worried and angry.

She waved a hand at him to shut him up, and took in a long breath. *Relax. Breathe. It's just a memory. Nothing is wrong. Nothing is on fire.* Slowly she pushed herself to her knees. Nick caught her under the elbow and helped her to her feet. She felt a wave of shame and could not look at him.

"Just...I fell," she said. Her mouth tasted of bile. She spat and spat again. She looked at the door of the shelter, standing open. *You have to go back in. You have to. Nothing is on fire.*

Sophia clenched her fist and stepped toward the door. Something wet and warm on her hand. She looked down and saw Amaruq licking her hand, a reassuring gesture. She met the dog's amber eyes and smiled. Amaruq wagged her tail and then turned and went into the hut, as if scouting for her. Sophia paused on the threshold only a fraction of a minute, and then stepped in.

The smell was stronger now—burning kerosene—but she pushed it away from her mind. It was just the heater. In front of her, Amaruq shook her head and sneezed. Sophia laughed shakily. "Yeah, me too."

Nick was behind her, a hand out as if to steady her. "Are you all right? Do you need to lie down?"

Sophia shook her head. The cook pot was a lost cause, rolling on the floor. She leaned on the shelf to her left. "I need to brush my teeth. Right now." Her knees chose that moment to take a time-out and she slid down to the floor.

He set down the gun and stepped past her. He strode to his pack and retrieved the filled water bottle. He grabbed a cup from the counter, his eyes on her, and splashed some water into the cup. He knelt in front of her and held it out. Beside him, Amaruq stood looking at her, head cocked to one side.

Sophia took the cup in shaky hands, rinsed her mouth and spat. "Thanks."

Amaruq turned and trotted over to Sophia's pack. She sniffed it all over. Nick saw her, stood, and followed her. As Amaruq pawed at the very side pocket where Sophia kept her personal toiletries, Nick unzipped it and fished out her toothbrush and toothpaste. He brought them to her and set his water bottle down next to her. "If you're sick, I can radio the plane. They can come back and get you."

She shook her head, embarrassed. "I'll be all right in a minute. Thank you. Please... leave me alone." It came out more abrupt than she wanted, but he didn't seem offended.

Nick got to his feet. "There's a stream on the other side of the camp, away from where you were looking for water. I'll bring us back a gallon or two, and then we can have some tea." He picked up one of the empty five-gallon plastic jugs and reached for the rifle.

"Tea would be good."

"Come on, girl," Nick said, and Amaruq trotted at his heels.

The frigid air swirled and the door closed and there she was, closed in with the smell and the heat again. Gritting her teeth, Sophia climbed to her feet. She was not going to fall apart. This was just nerves. Nerves, and physical exhaustion, and a memory burned into her soul that would not go away. She glared at the boxy heater in the center of the room as if it was a personal enemy.

While she waited for Nick, she brushed her teeth and went through the food stores. She found the usual stock of non-perishable items packed into lemming- and fox-proof boxes: freeze dried jerky, boxes and boxes of mac-and-cheese, crackers, rice, beans, milk powder, salt and sugar. And a large square tin containing tea bags. At the back she found a treasure—cocoa powder.

She had set out the cups and tea bags when the door opened, bringing with it the smell of cold rain and a blast of frigid air. Nick came through with the filled water jug on one shoulder. He set it down and turned to close the door.

"Snow coming," he said. "Temperature might drop a little." He turned to face her, his face neutral. "You okay?"

She nodded, still mortified. "I don't want to talk about it. It won't happen again."

He said nothing, but propped the gun in the corner nearest the door and went from window to window, shutting them. He took one of the tarps from the sagging bunk and shook it out. He draped it over nails driven into the lintel above the door to act as insulation against drafts. Despite the heater, the air was still cold enough for her to see her breath. Nevertheless, she pulled off her gloves while she opened the spaghetti sauce cans and found her tiny packet of herbs.

Nick collected all the burst cans and stacked them near the door. At some point he shed his parka; she turned around and found him in a close-fitting dark green wool sweater and hiking pants. He hung his parka near the heater, found a broom and swept the floor, brushing straw and dust and fox droppings into a corner. Amaruq was very interested at first in the fox droppings, then yawned and sat down.

The room was warming, although it still stank. Sophia peeled out of her parka and hung it next to Nick's. That left her with a dark blue wool sweater over silk thermal underwear, but the air still felt very nippy. She left her wool cap on her head.

Sophia set the cook pot on the electric stove. She happened to glance around just in time to see a curious exchange. The dog was staring at Nick's back. In mid-sweep, Nick stopped, looked around, and met Amaruq's eyes. He set the broom aside and went over to the bunk beds. He found a blanket and folded it up on the floor. Amaruq sniffed it, stepped onto it, turned around three times, and curled up on it. Her bushy tail flicked across her nose and she closed her eyes. Nick went back to sweeping.

"She's really got you well trained," Sophia said. How had Nick known Amaruq was looking at him? It was as if he was reacting to a call from her. Weird.

Nick smiled. His teeth were very white and even. "Yeah. Her bark is my command." His tone was affectionate. He finished with one swipe and set the broom aside.

The water was boiling. Sophia dumped the pasta in and

waited for it to boil again. She caught herself yawning for the third time in as many minutes. "What time is it?" she asked.

Nick looked at her curiously, then rummaged in his backpack. He flipped open a GPS locator and looked at the display. "Two fifteen," he said. He closed the case. "In the morning."

Sophia stared at him. "Get *out*."

Nick nodded at the windows, glowing with the same dim light they'd shown since their arrival. "Sun's down a little, but not much."

Sophia shook her head. "I may never get used to twenty-four hour sunlight," she said.

"It'll be easier if you don't worry about clocks," he said. "They just mess up your head. Listen to your body and it will tell you when to eat and sleep."

"My body is telling me this pasta is done," she said lightly. She dumped the cans of spaghetti sauce into the pasta and set it back on the stove. When she opened her herb packet, the aroma of basil and oregano suffused the dry air, counteracting the stink of oil. She smiled to herself, remembering her sunny windowsill back home, her pots of green herbs. She missed the green, up here in this gray land. She wondered how someone like Nick could stand to be without it, month after month. *Well, he probably didn't miss what he'd never had,* she thought. She stirred the herbs into the pasta and sauce. "You want to set the table?"

Nick looked at the several folding tables stacked against the wall. To get to them, he would have had to shift several heavy packing crates. He reached over and hauled a packing crate in front of the bunk.

"This'll do." He sat down on the lower bunk and unlaced his heavy boots. "Smells good." The boot hit the floor, and he reached up to unbraid and shake out his hair.

Sophia found herself fascinated by the change in him; his hair was a black waterfall, shining in the light. "What does your body tell you to do in constant daylight?" She dished the spaghetti mixture out onto plastic plates. "Besides surfing the Internet and reading geology."

110

"Depends." The other boot hit the floor with a thump. "Hunt. Fish." He looked up at her. "Take scientists on hikes." He paused, looked away. "We sing a lot."

"Sing? Really?"

He pulled some thick socks out of his pack and started pulling them on over the socks he was wearing. "Yeah. Old Inuit custom. Before we had TV, we'd sing or tell stories all winter. We slept a lot."

"So what do you sing?"

She expected him to start listing songs, maybe comment on some artist or band. Instead, he started humming, a warm baritone that reverberated around the room. She turned in surprise.

"The Dixie Chicks?"

"'Wide Open Spaces'. It felt right."

"Wouldn't have thought you'd be into country and western," she said.

"I like the way country music tells stories. Kind of like the songs we used to make up before white people came."

"You made up stories about cowboys and pick-up trucks?"

"No. But we sang about loneliness and heartache and a good dog."

The dog thumped her tail, jaws open, ears up. Sophia thought she looked like she was laughing.

"Everybody's a critic," Nick said. He bent over and scratched behind her ears.

Sophia watched him, then smiled and sang, "You showed me the way/in your own delightful way..."

"...Into the night/of the following day," he sang. He grinned. "A Kit Marlin fan. Nice."

"Stands to reason," she said. "He's Canadian."

Nick shrugged. "More surprising that you're a fan. Isn't country music considered kind of low-class in universities?"

Her eyes narrowed. "I'm a member of a certain group, so I must share all the characteristics of that group?" She turned back to the stove. "I'll be sure to restrict my singing to classical music or urban despair from now on."

She heard him stand, take two steps to the door, then stop. She didn't care; let him stomp out. She simmered with annoyance.

Then he was standing beside her, hands in his jeans pockets. "Sorry. That was a nasty thing to say."

"Yeah, it was," she said. She scraped spaghetti sauce onto the heap of pasta. "Why are you being such a dick to me?"

She looked up in time to see his eyes go wide. She had surprised him.

He looked very young. His mouth opened, closed. Then he shrugged. "Sorry. Look, we've got a long trip ahead. No reason to be snapping at one another. Start over, Doc?"

"Okay, Nick. Maybe we should stick to singing. And call me Sophia." She smiled and handed him a plate. He took it and sat on the bunk. She filled her plate, looked around, and found nowhere else to sit.

"Don't be a hog," she said. He scooted over to make room, and Sophia squeezed in beside him on the edge of the lower bunk, the plate steaming in her hands. They were so close their shoulders touched.

He started forking the food into his mouth. "This is good."

"Thanks." Sophia ate more slowly, feeling fatigue settle into her bones. Nearly three o'clock in the morning, but the light outside looked like early afternoon. Her internal clock was off. She had been up and working almost non-stop for... twenty hours? She blinked.

They ate silently. The oil heater chuffed to itself. Amaruq came to sit in front of Nick, staring at him and his plate of food. Nick ignored her.

Nick finished eating first. There was a comfortable silence as Sophia washed dishes and Nick spent a few minutes honing a belt knife. He took their packs apart, sorting the contents neatly on a work bench. When she had dried the dishes and put them back on their shelf, she turned to help him. He looked on with amusement as she laid out her field kit.

"How many of those do you need?" he asked as she shook out a bagful of small capped vials.

"A hundred, if I'm lucky. I don't expect to get another chance at this, so I want to get as many data points as possible." She took out the field scope, held it up to the light, polished a lens.

"How much would one of those cost?" Nick asked.

She held it out to him. "No idea. It's a one-off."

He held it up to his eye, looking through it at his hand. "Huh," he said. "I don't think it's working. Just a bunch of brown dots."

She took the scope away, put it to her eye and leaned in. She took his hand in hers and leaned close. "Yeah, you've got it on 1000x magnification," she said. "You're looking at *Staphylococcus epidermis*." She released his hand and straightened. "Those are the bacteria on your skin."

"I just washed my hands!" he said.

She smiled. "Which is why I'm not also seeing *Bacteroides fragilis*, *Bifidobacterium bifidus* or even *Acinetobacter johnsonii*."

He snorted. "Now you're just showing off."

"You bet." She put the cap on the scope carefully and looped its lanyard around her neck. "I don't get to show off that much. Anyway, relax. Humans have been walking around full of bacteria for millions of years. We're used to it by now."

"You mean, we have this crap on us all the time?"

"Sure. It's a symbiotic relationship. That's where—" She caught his look, hesitated, smiled. "Okay, I guess you know what a symbiotic relationship is—two species living in harmony. Anyway, there's some speculation that some of our own internal organs are symbiotes that were originally different organisms."

Nick blinked. "Different organisms? Like...parasites?"

Sophia shrugged. "I guess that's one thing you could call them. Not really accurate. In any case, whatever our livers started out as, they're part of us now." She turned away, fussing with her pack. "You're carrying the gun, of course?"

"Of course."

She rolled a spare pair of socks to tuck into a corner of her pack. "Then you should know that I know how to handle one, and I've shot game before. If you need me to do any guarding, I can."

"Good to know." He tugged at a lacing, tightening down his pack.

She poured the last of the hot water into the tea cups and dried the pot. As he finished packing, she handed him a mug of tea and the sugar bowl. She sipped her tea and watched him ladle several spoonfuls of sugar into the tea. Despite his sweet tooth, she mused, he had very white teeth. And then wondered why she was thinking about his teeth.

Nick stood and stretched, gulping down the last of the tea. "I'm going to bed."

She nodded, drew a deep breath. She should have raised this issue earlier, but she hadn't found a way to do it. "Do we need the heater?"

He looked at her with surprise. "Uh. Yeah."

"Why? I mean, tomorrow night we'll be sleeping in tents on the ground, in the cold. Why not just rely on the sleeping bags tonight?" *Please don't make me explain, she thought.*

He looked at Amaruq, as if the dog had made a noise. Sophia frowned. *What was it with that dog?* Nick looked at the bunks, at the sleeping bags, at her. Then he looked at the heater. He said nothing, but stepped across the room and turned off the oil heater.

Something in her middle relaxed, as if she'd been clenching a fist. "Thanks," she said.

He said nothing, but turned away and pulled the dark green sweater off over his head. Underneath it, his patched thermal shirt clung to the muscles of his back as he rolled the sweater up. He ran his fingers through his hair, reached up to the rail of the bunk bed. One powerful pull-up, and he was in the top bunk. She heard the rustle of his sleeping bag.

Feeling a little self-conscious, she wriggled out of her blue sweater and spread it over the foot of her sleeping bag. The air was already cooling now that the heater was off. *Not much insulation in this hut,* she thought. She yawned as she tugged off her boots. Amaruq had curled up on her blanket and watched this process with interest. Sophia slid into the sleeping bag and zipped it shut.

"Sleep well...Sophia," Nick said above her. "We leave at first light."

She was almost asleep before she realized he had made a joke.

Haughton Crater Research Project, Devon Island
75° 26′ 00″ N, 89° 51′ 00″ W

Will Fraser pushed open the door of the Haughton Crater Research Project headquarters and clung to it as the wind tried to bang it against the outer wall. He tugged it closed, already feeling the warmth of the interior washing over him. The headquarters of the research camp was the only 'permanent' building on the site, a pre-fabricated structure with square walls, real doors, and a sloping roof. After the constant drone of the wind, the sudden quiet was almost unnerving. Fraser resisted the urge to whisper.

The building was divided into two sections; the front part was taken up with a desk, a fax machine, and several stacks of file boxes. Fraser pushed on through the door to the back half without knocking. This room was lined with charts and maps. A battered door set on sawhorses served as a desk, and Dr. Martin Skorjik sat behind it typing on a laptop. Stacked in a corner were survey stakes, tripods, and a walking stick. The room smelled of peppermint from a dish of candies on Skorjik's makeshift desk.

"I see you're still working in the Taj Mahal," Fraser said.

"Constable." Dr. Skorjik nodded. "Still no luck?"

Fraser pulled off his gloves and parka and sat down without invitation.

"Couldn't find any sign of them at all."

Skorjik rose, his lean windburned face showing nothing of his anxiety. "Coffee?"

"I won't say no. Pete is refueling now. We can go up again in an hour, but I'm not sure where to look."

Skorjik set the coffee in front of Fraser. "Verna is dead certain the coordinates she gave you were the ones they radioed in."

Fraser sipped carefully. "How much experience did those guys have with GPS equipment?"

"This was their fifth survey, including one they did in Alaska two years ago. They know their GPS."

Fraser nodded. "Then it has to be some kind of interference," he muttered.

Skorjik looked a question.

"When we were out over the Lowlands, our GPS malfunctioned." Fraser explained the odd readings the GPS had generated. "As soon as we got back within two miles of the Crater, everything went back to normal. Right now the GPS on Pete's plane is working. Have you had any reports of interference from other teams in the field?"

Skorjik shook his head. "Never. And we rely absolutely on GPS, as you know. If the satellite feed is somehow corrupted, we're toast."

"If the feed was screwed up, it would have stayed screwed up all the way home," Fraser pointed out. "Any chance of natural interference? Rocks with uranium or something?"

A tiny smile curled in the corner of Skorjik's mouth. "We have thirty of the top geologists on this *planet* here, Constable. If there was anything in those rocks causing it to jam a GPS signal, we'd know about it. Whole careers would be built on it."

Fraser set his cup down. "You said it. That's just what I'm afraid of—jamming."

Skorjik blinked. "I was joking. There's nothing in those rocks—"

"What about something man-made, maybe something criminal? I caught a bunch of tourists in Resolute trying to go home with pockets full of diamonds. You know how that goes."

Skorjik made a disgusted face. "Yes, I know. Vultures. I assure you, none of our people are involved in smuggling."

"Are you sure? You've got complete strangers cycling in and out of here all summer long, some of them never to be seen again. Can you vouch for every one of them?"

Skorjik glared back at him. "These are men and women of impeccable credentials. This program is one of the most competitive programs in the world. We vet every one of our applicants through academic, institutional and governmental agencies—"

"Including criminal databases?"

Skorjik blinked. "Well, no. But these people come to us from NASA, from the Canadian Space Agency, through respected institutions like Berkeley and Stanford and MIT. I can't believe they'd risk everything for something like this."

Fraser leaned back, hearing the flimsy chair creak under him. "Nice to know that everyone in this camp values his academic reputation higher than diamonds, Doctor."

Skorjik was silent. Fraser laid one ankle on his knee, sipping his coffee. "Let me suggest something to you, Dr. Skorjik. Let me suggest that something has gone very wrong out there in the Lowlands. Let me suggest that either your missing scientists went missing deliberately, or someone made them go missing. And that person or persons is jamming some electronic transmissions to cover their tracks."

Skorjik was silent a moment, his jaw working. "Constable, are you familiar with the principle of Occam's razor?"

"No."

"It's a principle that says given competing theories, you should accept the one requiring the fewest assumptions. It's a guiding principle of scientific research and, I thought, of police work. In short, when I hear hoofbeats, I think horses, not zebras." He leaned forward, tapping an impatient finger on his cluttered desktop. "Glenn and Leo are lost out there, Constable. Their GPS failed, for some reason we don't understand. It doesn't really matter why it failed; what matters is that they may be lost, hurt, hungry, cold and tired. If so, they don't have long. We have to find them soon. I will not, will not have two men die on my watch. If I have to go out and look for them myself, I will." He leaned back. "But I did rather think that was your job."

Unperturbed, Fraser picked up his cup and sipped the black brew again. *Why did professors always have the worst coffee?* he thought. "I'll hold you to that, Doc," he said. "When Pete finishes refueling and I get a sandwich inside me, I'll be up in the air looking for them again. But if we still don't find them, I'm going to need men. I'll need all your men. All your ATVs. I'll for damn sure need all your Inuit guards, the ones who know this land. If you're serious about this search, that's what it will take."

Skorjik paled during this. Fraser could see the conflict in his head, could imagine the shock and turmoil at the prospect of interrupting the work of thirty irascible and focused geniuses. But the older man merely bit his lip a moment.

"You'll have it," he said.

"Most of all," Fraser said. "I'll need the dogs."

Skorjik nodded. "Of course. But I have to tell you, none of them are trained in tracking, search or rescue. They're just pets."

Fraser raised an eyebrow. "One of them is more than that. I want Tonarak's dog. She's a hunter."

Skorjik scratched his head. "Tonarak? The new mechanic?"

"I've known Nick for years. He and his brother hunt all over these islands. And the dog goes with them. If there's a hunter in this pack of 'pets', she'll be the one."

"But he already left this morning with Dr. Abenezra."

Fraser's jaw clenched. "Call him back."

"I can't leave Dr. Abenezra out there alone."

"Bring them both back."

"And cancel all her work?" Skorjik leaned forward on his elbows. "Look, they're already going to be crossing the area you want to search. If I called them back, you'd have to turn around and fly Tonarak back anyway."

Fraser stood. "I'm going to call him. He took the dog and a gun, right?"

"Of course."

Fraser shrugged into his parka. "I want to see the itinerary they filed. And I'm going to tell Nick to be careful. There may be more than polar bears out in the Lowlands."

Truelove Lowlands, Devon Island, Nunavut
75° 36′ 21.18″ N, 83° 29′ 00.44″ W

Nick woke to the sound of wind, howling around the edges of the hut. He lay for a moment, savoring the warmth of the sleeping bag. The wind told him this would probably be the last warm moments of his day. Lying in the bunk, he performed his morning self-check: hands, arms, face, feet and legs. No extra hair or bumps anywhere. No fever. No aches, no strange feelings or itchy patches of skin. He was still normal. Still human. For today, anyway.

::Coffee:: He heard the thump-thump of Amaruq's tail.

"Coffee will just make you hyper all day," he said.

A rustling sound below him. "Say what?"

He leaned over the edge of the bunk bed and looked down. Below him, Sophia's dark hair was spread over the sleeping bag; her face was rosy from sleep. She looked young and pretty, and something inside Nick Tonarak went all wobbly for a moment. Then he swung his feet over the edge and dropped lightly to the floor. "I'm going to fire up the heater," he said. "Okay with you?"

"I...I guess."

He heard the doubt in her voice and wondered what she had against warmth.

She yawned and stretched. "What time is it?"

"Daytime," he answered, kneeling to open the control box on the heater. Her constant need to know what the clock said amused him. Was she afraid of losing daylight, in a place where the sun didn't set until August?

Sophia was not a morning person, he could tell. She stumbled about the hut, rubbing her eyes. She dragged on two sweaters and a pair of hiking pants over thermal underwear. When she finally got to the point of pulling on her boots, he took one of them out of her hands and swapped it with the other.

"Can't walk far with your boots switched," he said.

"Oh. Okay. Thanks."

When the water boiled, he made tea (over Amaruq's silent objections) and oatmeal. He passed Sophia a bowl. She poked a spoon in it. "What's this?"

"Old Inuit recipe. Dates and raisins in oatmeal."

"Yeah, I remember flying over that date palm plantation on the way in."

He grinned at her. "That would be the one next to the grape arbors, right?"

She smiled, and he noticed a dimple at the corner of her mouth. He hadn't seen that before. He turned away. *Down, boy,* he told himself. He shoveled hot oatmeal into his mouth, burning his tongue.

He climbed into his outdoor gear and picked up the rifle. "Weather check," he said. "You'll have plenty of time for..." He nodded towards the chemical toilet in the corner.

She followed his look, nodded without comment. Nick swung out the door with Amaruq on his heels.

The weather would be unreliable today. He lifted his nose into the wind, sorting out the cold scents of sea, ice, and rock. The breeze played with his hair, snapping it across his face one moment and then streaming it out behind him the next. His eyes slitted as he scanned the horizon—what he could see of it. A grey fog bank hung off the north shore, hiding Ellesmere Island twenty kilometers away. Shredded clouds skittered overhead on a north-south orientation, which told him high winds and snow were on the way. He debated whether to wait for better weather, then decided they could always just pitch camp if necessary. Not for the first time, he wished Tom was there to advise him.

Amaruq yipped and dashed into a jumble of rocks. There was a scuffle, and her tail waved like a plume for a moment. Then she emerged, trotting back to him with an Arctic hare in her jaws. She dropped it at his feet and sat down, grinning.

He rubbed her ears. "Congratulations."

::All mine:: she bragged.

He grinned. "Bon appetit, *cherie*."

::Coffee::

"Maybe later," he said.

Amaruq bent her head to worry at the hare. ::I like her.::

"Then why did you kill it?"

::Silly. Not this. The girl. I like her.::

"Sophia?" Nick liked the sound of her name in his mouth. He felt a slow heat circle outward from his center.

::You like her, too.:: Amaruq sat back on her haunches, licking her chops. She cocked her head, thumped her tail. ::She likes you, Brother.::

"What is this, high school?" Nick muttered, feeling his face go hot. "You think I should pass her a note between classes? Ask her to the summer dance?" He heard the bitterness creeping into his voice, but couldn't stop it. He had no chance with a woman like Sophia, even if Amaruq was right. She'd be here, at most, a couple of weeks. Then she would fly away again, never to return. And she'd completely forget the likes of him. He remembered her words all too clearly: *He's just a guide. He's a babysitter.*

::She looks at you when you're not looking. You do the same. I'm not stupid.::

"No, *nukka*, you're not." Nick used the Inuktitut term for little sister, remembering that Amaruq had always been a good judge of character. The smile faded. "But she's not for me," he said.

::Why not?::

His sister's fierce loyalty warmed a cold place inside of him, even though he knew he was kidding himself. Still, he found himself stuck with the sight of Sophia's face when he handed her the carving, the look of fear when they landed on Devon Island, her easy smile with her friend Jennifer. He thought about how friendly she had been with Amaruq, how her hand had felt on his when she tended his cut.

"I wish..." he muttered. He shifted from one foot to another, restless. "If there was any way..."

::Tell her.:: Amaruq sniffed at her hare, nosed it over. ::She likes you. I can tell. When you're around, she smells different.::

"Whoa. Too much information, Sis," he said, but smiled again. "Keep your girl-secrets to yourself."

::Not a girl-secret.:: Amaruq sank her teeth into the hare. ::Wolf-secret. She likes you. Trust me. Do you want any of this or not?::

"No, thanks," he said. "Enjoy yourself."

Leaving her to tear the hare apart, Nick walked down towards the shore, the rifle cradled in his elbow. *Could Amaruq be right?* Could Sophia really see him as anything more than a guide, something more than mobile equipment out here? He felt something flutter, felt something tighten, and his face grew even hotter. He thought of her soft hands, thought of them on him, and abruptly turned to face into the icy wind off the polar cap.

Down, boy.

He kept a lookout for movement; in this white-on-grey landscape, he could miss a polar bear. A few years ago, the beach would have been invisible under a thick cover of ice stretching most of the way to Ellesmere Island. Today it was open water all the way to the fog. Seals and other game would be far out in the sound, too far to hunt from land. The bears would be hungry.

When his boots hit wet sand, he stopped and turned, looking back at the island. Against the magnificent and oversized landscape, the man-made buildings looked small and shabby. Rocks the size of trucks lay in jumbled piles at the base of the cliff, where erosion and time had abandoned them. No trees, no grass softened the stark and empty contours. To his left, the eastern shore wandered out of sight into distant fog, the even expanse cut by innumerable small, shallow rivulets bearing melt water from the million-year old ice to the sea.

It was a landscape of inexorability, harsh yet beautiful in its own stark way. It had shaped his people, was still shaping them. It was hard to believe that now men, far to the South who had never seen this landscape, were re-shaping it even now.

Whatever the reason for the warming of his world, Nick knew it was not something men could control. As always, they would have to adapt. Or die.

Two hours later, Nick turned and looked back at the same camp. This time he was far down the eastern coast, about to turn a corner that would take it out of sight. The pack on his shoulders was heavy but well balanced; experience had taught him that he could carry most loads as long as the weight was evenly distributed between hip and shoulder. Beside him, Amaruq wore a doggie backpack with extra batteries, dog food, and her water bowl. She turned to see what he was looking at, whuffed her non-interest, and loped onward to catch up with Sophia.

Sophia trudged onward with a slow but tireless pace. Her pack was small, but she carried a ditty bag full of empty plastic sample vials banging on her hip. She stopped every half hour to take soil and water samples; once she knelt and scraped lichen from a rock into a vial. Nick had tried to hurry her along, then tried slowing down to keep pace with her shorter legs. But even when she sped up, she eventually slowed to her more comfortable pace. Nick had to admit she was covering ground steadily, but he worried about the weather. Since they'd left the research camp, the wind had grown sharper and colder.

It was good hiking terrain, flat along the shoreline. Nick noted the sanderlings playing in the surging tide, the occasional glimpse of bright orange or yellow lichen on a rock near the water. Canada geese in a long line honked overhead, flying to nesting grounds on Ellesmere Island across the water. The sand gave good footing, and the tide was far enough out to give them a wide margin to walk. Nick skirted a wind-carved ice boulder stranded at the high-tide mark.

They neared the Truelove Lowlands. Here the land sheltered small valleys from the incessant wind. Tiny patches of long grass poked through fog-colored rocks. As he rounded a rock pile, he heard the happy trickle of a meltwater stream. Sophia squatted beside it, cupping her hand in the water. Amaruq sat beside her, head up, nose in the wind, on alert for bears. Nick loosened the straps of his pack harness enough to kneel beside her.

"Best water in the world," Sophia said. "This morning, and for a million mornings before that, it was ice. Tomorrow it will be part of the north Atlantic current, winding down past Greenland to the Banks. This water is connected to all the waters of the world." She reached into her pack and took out a plastic sample vial. She dipped it into the water, capped it. Then she reached into her shirt and drew out her field scope on a lanyard. She held the vial up to the sun and gazed through the scope at it.

"Hmm."

Nick squatted down, watching her, her total concentration. "What do you see?"

"*Pseudomonas. Bacillus.* Some *Cytophagae.*" She lowered the scope. "Pretty much what I've been finding all morning." She took a marker out of her shirt pocket, checked her wristwatch, and scribbled on the vial. "What's our GPS location?"

He read the coordinates off to her. "How many more of those are you going to need?"

She shrugged, copying the coordinates onto the label. "As many as possible. Jennifer needs to lay in a good baseline for her tests."

Nick said nothing. He felt the delicate touch of snow and looked up. White spiraled out of the sky at him. He let it drift across his face a moment.

"Should we make camp?" Sophia asked.

"Not unless you want to. This will start and stop all day."

She nodded and slipped the vial into a zippered pocket that now bulged with a dozen other samples. He helped her to her feet and helped tighten her straps. He felt her slim, quick fingers at his waist, cinching his straps, then she was turning away. "The shore starts narrowing here," she said over her shoulder. "This looks as good a place as any to start inland. What do you think?"

"Sounds good."

Sophia followed the tiny rivulet up the narrow ravine it had cut through the ancient soil. Nick scrambled after her, alert to catch her if she fell. When he caught himself watching her rear end as she negotiated a pile of rocks, he looked away. He found Amaruq looking at him; he told himself he imagined her laughter in his head.

A short but intense scramble brought them to open ground dotted with rocks and cut by tiny streams. The distant cliffs of the upland plateau and ice sheet were shrouded in creeping grey fog; snow whirled in the distance. Tufts of grass, outcrops of lichen and moss, and the occasional wild flower broke the monotony of gray and brown. Sophia stopped, her hand lifted to shield her eyes. Nick followed the direction of her gaze. Several dark dots moseyed over the tundra, a few hundred yards away.

"Musk ox," she said.

"Five, maybe six," he agreed. "Just be sure not to drink downstream from them."

"Right," she said. She shifted from one foot to the other, still looking at the huge animals. "Is it safe to approach them? This isn't mating season, is it? I mean, wouldn't the males be more dangerous then?"

"Those guys might flirt around a bit right now, but they're not going to get serious until August," Nick said, smiling down at her. "I thought you were a biologist."

She smiled back. "I don't usually pay much attention to anything large enough to see without a scope."

He shifted the burden on his shoulders. He didn't like the sound the wind made now, a low keen across barren rock. "Let's go on."

Sophia splashed across the shallow stream. Soon they were crossing flat, marshy ground. The way was wide enough that Nick walked beside Sophia, matching strides. Amaruq ranged ahead, swerving back and forth across their path, nose down. Now and then a flurry of snow swirled around them, or the wind kicked into high gear and hooted at them. Otherwise, though, it was as balmy a summer day as the Arctic ever enjoyed.

The Truelove Lowlands were a mosaic of marshes, lakes, and raised gravel beds. This kind of wetland was extremely rare in Nick's world, so a visit to it was always something to look forward to. Here, unlike his home island, there were outcrops of tiny plants, open fresh water, and plenty of game: musk ox, lemming, hares, even wolves. By Arctic standards it was an oasis.

The ground became muddier, until it was sucking at their boots with every step. It made walking much more tiring. At the same time, the fog was closing in. Fat snowflakes fell, at first a few, then more thickly, confirming Nick's worst fears.

Sophia was ahead of him, entering data into a PDA as she walked. Amaruq ranged off to Nick's left, nose to the ground. He caught thoughts of ravens and lemming nests from her, heard a snatch of Justin Timberlake from her mind.

His only warning was a sharp cry, cut off, and the sound of gravel sliding. Amaruq's head came up and around, then in a white flash she was past him, racing into the dark grey swirl of fog.

::Nick!:: He caught Amaruq's warning just before he would have stepped over the cliff. He pulled back just in time, and stood swaying on the edge of an abyss. Below his feet, the ground sheered off in great undercut bluffs, with the river tumbling below. The drop wasn't far, but it ended in rocks as sharp as fangs. A fresh gash at the edge showed where something had gone over.

"Sophia!" he called, his heart hammering.

"Here!" came a voice from the abyss.

Nick dropped to his knees and leaned over the edge, feeling the friable ground crumble. "Where are—oh. Hang on!"

"Okay," came the dry answer.

Nick peered over the edge. Below, Sophia hung by her hands, clutching an outcropping of rock. The cliff fell away below her, wind buffeting her against the rock face. Her boots dangled over thin air. Nick could see blood and scrapes on her hands where she had scrabbled for a hold. She looked up at him, strain showing in her pale face.

Nick tore at the buckles of his pack, flung it from him, threw himself flat on the ground. He crawled forward, testing his ground, until his chest met the rim. Dirt slid away out from under him, to vanish in the fog rising from the river. "Can you reach my hand?" he said, extending his arm.

Fingers brushed his, barely touching. "Not...quite..." He heard the strain in her voice. Her left hand was all that was holding her, and he could see her knuckles whitening. How long could she support her full weight, and her pack, with her hands alone?

"Can you dump your pack?"

"No," she said. "Caught against the face of the rock." She grunted. "No footholds, either."

Nick inched forward, eyes on the broken rock at the edge of the ledge. "Try again," he said.

Something tugged at his belt; he looked over and saw that Amaruq had sunk her teeth into the leather, planted her legs to anchor him.

::Gotcha:: she said. ::Won't let go.::

Nick stretched his arm as far as it would go, his eyes on Sophia's hair, her upturned face. He saw fear in her expression, but determination as well. "You can do it," he said quietly. "Take your time. Don't rush."

Her right hand came up, her fingers on the rock outcropping slipped, caught. His stomach lurched. She caught the outcropping with both hands again, her mouth a grim line. Below her, rocks bounced and ricocheted into the jumble below.

"Okay," he said. "We got one shot at this. On the count of three, you have to swing your arm up, reaching for my hand. Can you do that?"

"I'll try." Her voice trembled a little, but he heard resolution in it.

Carefully, Nick bent forward, wary of the crumbling surface beneath him. Pebbles trickled away, one bouncing off of Sophia's shoulder. He dug his fingers into the soil, took a deep breath, let it out slowly, and reached down as far as he could with his right hand. "One...two...three!"

She lunged upward with her right hand, and he felt her palm slap into his. He tightened his hand, then felt her gasp as her left hand slid off its hold. Her weight, pack and all, hung from his right shoulder. Nick let go of the earth with his left hand, swung it down. Her hand met his, grabbed tight. Nick grunted with the effort of holding her; his shoulders and biceps screamed.

"Can you...climb up and over me?" he grunted.

"I don't know." Her hand clutched at his sleeve. Nick could hear her breath coming harsh and ragged as she pulled, pulled. It was no use. She wasn't strong enough to haul herself and the pack up.

Her weight was pulling him over the cliff edge, an inch at a time. He felt Amaruq's tremble as she fought to anchor him, felt himself slip. "Okay," he said. His voice came out as a ragged croak, his chest crushed against the earth. "I'm going to back up. Hold tight."

"Okay," she said. Her voice was flat, terrified, but she wasn't panicking. Not yet, he thought.

"Amaruq, pull me," he said in Inuktitut.

::Can't!::

"You have to. Come on!"

A tug, then a stronger one. Nick felt his forward slide stop, reverse. His forearms and shoulders screaming, he worked his knee against the hard ground, scooting himself backward. Left knee, right. Amaruq's paws scrabbled for purchase as she hit a slick patch, and Nick waited until she found better purchase. It seemed to take hours, and Nick was sure his arms were being pulled from his sockets. The strain was making his arms numb; he feared that his hands would lose their grip.

::Slipping!:: Amaruq's voice held panic. He heard a whine.

"You can do it, Sis," he said in Inuktitut. Even so, he knew the wolf would never be able to drag him and Sophia off the

128

cliff's edge. And his strength was going fast.

He had to risk it all on one strong heave. "One try," he said to Amaruq. "Give it all you have."

::On three.::

He heard her countdown in his mind, and then yanked backwards with all his might, thigh muscles contorting, back muscles shrieking in protest. A scraping sound, pain in his neck, but he hauled her over the lip of the cliff. Then he was falling sideways onto the ground with Sophia's weight on him, crushing the breath out of him, her hands on his wrists in a death grip.

They lay for a long moment, panting, as he stared at the racing gray clouds overhead and thought about the long fall he'd barely missed.

She raised her face from his shoulder, stared into his eyes. "God."

"I get that a lot," he said. "But you can call me Nick, just the same."

"Thank you," she said, not smiling.

Her face was very close to his, her mouth right above him, her breath on his lips. *Irresistible.* His blood thundered through him, he felt his stomach drop out from under him just as it had when he realized she'd gone over the cliff.

"You're welcome, Sophia," he whispered. And kissed her. Just a brush of lip to lip, a fleeting touch soft as mist, enough to feel the warmth and softness of her mouth.

She closed her eyes, but didn't respond otherwise.

Flushed, he eased out from under her and got to his feet, well back from the edge of the cliff. Nick stretched his aching arms, rotating his shoulders. *Was she angry?*

::I was scared.:: Amaruq thrust a wet nose into his ear and he bent, draped a complaining arm over her neck.

"Thanks," he whispered into her fur. She licked his face.

Sophia sat up slowly, looking away from the cliff edge, away from him.

"It's whiting out," Nick said. "Too dangerous to walk. Let's have some tea and get our bearings."

"Not here," Sophia said.

"No," he agreed. He got wearily to his feet. This time she let him help her up, and stood swaying a moment. He steadied her, hands on her shoulders.

She looked up at him out of somber eyes. "You could have gone right over with me," she said. "But you didn't even hesitate."

He was tired, and he'd been afraid for her, and he felt a little reckless. So he touched her cheek, drew it down to her chin softly. "All part of the service," he said. "Although I do have to add a surcharge."

"Okay if I run a tab?"

He smiled. "Sure." *No tears, no hysteria. She didn't look tough, but she had steel in her,* he thought. Her skin had felt like cool velvet on his fingers. He picked up his pack and strode out, careful of his ground. Sophia followed him.

Veils of fog drifted over the land, obscuring the view ahead. The rock pavement gave way to gravel and sharp rocks the size of his fist. Hummocks of gravel and weed rippled over the open ground away from the cliff edge. After a few minutes, he found a heap of jumbled granite with a flattened top. He climbed up and ditched his pack, helped Sophia loosen her straps and then lifted the pack off her shoulders. Amaruq followed and lay down, facing into the fog.

Sophia squatted on the bedroll tied to the end of her pack and put her head on her arms. As Nick took off his pack and swiftly set up his little camp stove, she picked up a broken hunk of stone. When Nick had the flame sheltered from the wind and had set a pot of water on to boil, he sat back to watch her.

After a few minutes, she raised her head and gave a wobbly smile. "I hope that's the biggest adventure I have out here," she said.

"Me, too." Nick plucked the tea bag out of the water. His hand trembled; he felt exhaustion, and the aftershock of their close brush, creeping through his limbs.

She stared off into the swirl of snow and fog, where distant shapes of musk ox moved. He poured tea into a plastic cup and handed it to her. Their hands met.

Amaruq nosed at Nick's hand. ::Sugar::

"Bad for you," Nick said affectionately. He rummaged in his backpack and came up with some jerky. "Try this."

The wolf lay down and gnawed on it. Her coat sparkled with snowflakes. Nick caught some of her thoughts—hares, the smell of oxen, a fox lair half a kilometer to the west. A memory of a mystery story drifted through her mind and he smiled. She'd always loved Nancy Drew.

"I think I owe your dog a biscuit." Sophia blew on her tea to cool it.

Amaruq's tail thumped but she didn't raise her head.

"You didn't panic. That was good." Nick felt his cheeks grow warm.

The silence grew between them, both shy and intimate. Those few moments on the edge of the cliff had changed something between them, Nick thought. He wasn't sure what, but she seemed both ill at ease with him, and drawn to him. He understood it, because he felt the same.

Sophia cleared her throat. "So. Where are we and how far do we have to go?"

Nick considered a moment, calculating how far they'd walked. "We can cut across this plateau," he said. "When the snow lifts a little. It will cut about five kilometers off. But it's going to be a lot windier up here. Maybe you should put some rocks in your backpack, to keep from blowing over a cliff."

"Or I'll tie myself to you," she said.

Amaruq stood, her nose in the wind, ears forward. She growled a warning, low and ominous.

"What is it?" Sophia asked.

Nick ignored her as he came to his feet. "Go," he murmured to the wolf, and Amaruq shot off into the mist.

Sophia stood up, peering into the white-out. "A bear?"

He shook his head, tension in every line. "Wolf."

Jennifer bent over the keyboard, fingers dancing. Now and then she stuck her hands under her armpits to warm them up. *Damn*, she thought. Her breath steamed in the frosty air.

Outside, the wind whipped through the camp, slamming against the canvas walls of the tent. It bellied inward, making the electrical cords draped over rods and struts rattle. Jennifer blew on her fingers.

"Anyone home?"

She turned just as Ted Meyers poked his head through the slit door. "Hi. Come on in," she said. She gave him her best smile.

He stepped through, his gaze sweeping around the crowded research area. "You didn't bring much as much equipment as I expected," he said.

"That's the idea. If we ever send the SlimeMaster here to Mars, it needs to be a minimal payload." She patted the black box on the table. As if in answer, it beeped, and a green LED on the front panel began blinking. Jennifer frowned. "Oh. That was fast."

"Something wrong?" Meyers stepped closer. Jennifer was conscious of his slender, wiry frame next to hers, the heat from his body.

"No," she said. "I'm just running a baseline analysis on some local samples. I use them to screen out contaminants in the field specimens that my partner brings back." She opened up a new window on her laptop. "Now it's telling me that it's found a match."

"Well, sure," Meyers said. He leaned over her, one hand on the table, looking over her shoulder at the screen. "That makes sense. Whoever you've got there is all over camp."

"Not that kind of match." She jabbed at the keyboard, glowering. "Damn. Glitch of some sort."

"Really?"

His breath on her neck distracted her. But Jennifer shook

132

it off, concentrating. "I'm showing a match between two samples in the database. Two mammalian samples. What the hell?"

Meyers straightened, his gaze intense. "I don't understand."

She slid onto the packing crate she was using for a stool, used the mouse to highlight two areas on the screen. "How much do you know about DNA?"

"Some," he said. He stared at the screen. "That's an electrophoresis gel. But I don't recognize this method."

"It's called sequencing by hybridization. I'm testing it to see if we can speed up the analysis of unknowns, at least sort unknown samples by major factors like size, acid arrays, and so forth. The SlimeMaster isolates and labels a sequence with a fluorescent tag and compares it to an array of known sequences. I was putting together that array using background DNA from the area here."

"Sure," he said. "You don't want your sample to show a mix of dirt and dung as a single organism."

"Right. This method analyzes the 'hybrid' and isolates various spots on the array. That way I can identify the sequence inside the DNA sequence, so to speak."

Meyers blinked. "I may have to take your word on this. Are you sure it will work?"

Jennifer sighed. "I thought it would. It's a strong theory. But this is showing me something very strange."

He peered at the screen, leaning close. Jennifer smelled mint. "Uh. Those two sequences look pretty similar."

"Normally, I'd say they came from siblings. You know that brothers and sisters share half of the same genes."

"Sure. They come from the same two parents." He straightened, still looking at the screen. "But we don't have any siblings in camp."

"Oh, it's weirder than that," Jennifer said. She pointed at the labels generated by the program.

Meyers eyes widened. "Whoa. Different *species?* Major glitch!"

"Human and canine," Jennifer mused. "It has to be contamination. But that's just what the algorithm is looking for."

"Human? Crossed with canine? That's impossible."

Jennifer frowned. "I know. Damn. I just ran the diagnostics and calibration routines. The analyzer checked out. Twice."

"Okay," Ted said. "Let's assume your SlimeMaster is right. What could explain this kind of...hybridization? You don't think...I mean, bestiality is—"

Jennifer shook her head. "No. Not what you're thinking. This is not hybridization. The program would have flagged that." She drummed her fingers on the table, staring down at the softly winking LEDs on the SlimeMaster. "I think...it's chimerism."

"What-ism?"

She looked up, staring somewhere beyond him. "A chimera. Named after the ancient Greek myth of an animal made up of parts of other animals. Body of a lion with the head of a goat, tail of a snake, that sort of thing."

"Like a hybrid, then."

"No. A hybrid is what you get when you cross a horse and a donkey and get a mule. That's a cross of two species, and the chromosomes are the same throughout the organism. If you took a single cell from a mule you could theoretically grow it into a new mule. A chimera is made up of individual cells from two different species, each with its own nucleus containing its own separate chromosomes. The genes aren't mixed. Your liver may have one set of genes, your blood cells another."

Ted picked up the printout and stared at it. "So if I took a cell from the man or the dog, and tried to grow it, what would happen?"

"It would depend on what cell you picked. If you picked the right cell from the guy, you'd grow a human being; if you picked a different one, you'd grow, I don't know, I guess you'd grow a dog."

"This is...really weird. Is it even possible?" he said.

"Chimerism is a well-known phenomenon, but not like this, not between species. There are instances of humans, for example, who have incorporated DNA from an absorbed twin. Or mice mothers who have retained fetal cells from earlier pregnancies, which show up as separate DNA on analysis."

"So they get, what, a liver with a different DNA signature or whatever?"

"More or less. But in those cases, we're talking about incorporating human DNA from another source. Something like this...wait. Wait a minute."

Ted smiled, watching her fingers dance over the keys. "Delighted."

She paid him no mind, focused on the files she was calling up. "There," she said, leaning back and pointing at the screen. "Yeah. Homeobox genes."

Ted blinked. "What?" He laughed. "Take pity on me, Jennifer. I'm just a lowly MD."

"Oh." She laughed. "I get caught up, I forget. How much do you know about human development?"

"Will this be on the test?" he asked.

She shot him a surprised look. "Oh, no. Sorry. Look, you know we all come with a full set of human genes, with human DNA, right?"

"So my crib sheet told me in Anatomy 101."

"And every cell can, potentially, grow into a full human being, right?" Jennifer's expression was earnest, focused.

"Right." Ted half-smiled.

"But what tells the cell, the chromosomes, to build an arm or a leg or a liver?"

"Ahhh..."

She pointed to a blue cluster in the DNA spiral. "The DNA needs a master plan, a blueprint. This DNA sequence, and others like it, tells the body whether to grow another leg or form a human being with three eyes."

Ted blinked. "So, theoretically, you could manipulate the sequence? Make the expression of the organism look different."

"Nothing 'theoretical' about it," Jennifer said. "Since the 1980s, people have been fiddling with HOX genes, as they're called." She touched a key, and window opened with an image in it. Ted's eyes widened in surprise.

"Is that real?" The image showed an extreme close up of a common fruit fly. But this fruit fly had legs growing where

135

its eyes should have been. Repelled, Ted leaned away. "That's...
disturbing. But what does it have to do with your findings?"

Jennifer felt her cheeks grow cold. "If this is not a glitch,
if it's real..." She swallowed. "There's something in this camp
that carries genes from two different species."

"So what?" Ted laid a hand on her arm. "Hey, it's weird,
but not dangerous, right? I know enough about human anatomy to know there are all kinds of mutations that don't hurt
people. A shorter nose, smaller ears, a heart on the right side
of the chest instead of the left."

Jennifer's hand under his became a fist. "You don't understand. These are homeobox genes. They control somatic—" At
his look, she shook her head impatiently. "They control what
the organism develops into."

"But nobody out here is *developing*," Ted said. "Everybody in camp is a grown-up, not a child or an adolescent." He
turned her on her stool so he could look into her eyes. "I think
you're tired and need a break. Come on, I'll take you over to
the mess tent. The coffee pot's on twenty-four hours a—"

Jennifer's eyes went wide as the full implications hit her.
"Oh God."

"What?"

She stared past him. "We change, all the time. Not just
from child to adult, but every hour. Cells die, get replaced,
right?"

"Sure. And you need coff—"

"And what controls the replacement of those cells?"

"Um."

"The HOX genes." Jennifer clutched his arm in both
hands. "Oh, God. Wolf. And human. Amaruq...and Sophia's
out there alone with Nick!"

Truelove Lowlands, Devon Island, Nunavut
75° 36′ 21.18″ N, 83° 29′ 00.44″ W

Nick was a dark blur in the fog ahead of Sophia, leaping
the gravel humps and stepping over high rocks she had to
climb over. She heard faint yipping sounds from the dog, but

the fog made echoes all around her. Or else, she thought, she really was surrounded by wolves.

The memory of that moment when there had been nothing but air beneath her feet was enough to keep her eyes on the ground, to test every step before she put her full weight on it. Focused as she was, she nearly fell over Nick. He knelt over something on the ground, and as she came up he held up his arm. She halted in her tracks and gasped.

The wolf lay on its side, all four legs sticking out stiffly. There was no head. The neck ended in a clean edge.

"No blood anywhere." Nick laid a hand on the hide, to check the body temperature. He flinched and rocked backwards. "It shocked me!"

Amaruq bared her teeth in a growl. ::Bad. Get away!::

Nick shook his stinging hand and squatted on his heels. "Check the area," he told Amaruq in a low voice.

With a low-pitched growl, Amaruq wheeled and trotted away, nose to the ground.

Sophia leaned over him. "What happened to it? A bear?"

Nick shook his head, wishing she had stayed behind. He didn't like the look of this, not one bit. "Not a bear. A bear would have torn it up more."

"Looks like scavengers got the head."

"No wounds. No bite or claw marks." Nick unslung the rifle from his shoulder. Holding it by the stock, he nudged the headless body. "Something's wrong here."

A ripple ran from neck to tail, just under the hide.

Nick jumped backwards. "What the hell was that?"

The ripple subsided. The wolf corpse lay still. Nick inhaled deeply—no smell of decay. What had happened to this animal?

"Insects?" Sophia said. "Could be *Calliphoridae* larvae, maybe *Silphidae*. Probably *Thanatophilus lapponicus* larvae burrowing under the skin." She glanced up at him. "Sorry. Blowflies, carrion beetles." Even as she said it, she realized that the smell assaulting her sinuses was not the reek of biological decay, but something different. Something not natural.

"Yeah. But where are they?" Nick slid the muzzle of the rifle under the wolf, tipping it back a few inches. "No egg casings. No maggots. Not a single insect. There's no snow under the body, and it's been snowing since yesterday." He pulled his rifle back. Again the skin of the wolf rippled, as if he had disturbed the surface of a pond. "This wolf has been dead more than a day, but nothing has scavenged it."

Sophia gazed about. "You're right. Maybe the carrion eaters just haven't found the carcass yet?"

Nick said nothing. Sophia took out her digital camera and began taking a series of shots, working her way in a circle around the body to get pictures of it from all sides. "Could it be frozen? Maybe that's why there's no blood."

Amaruq trotted up and sat down across from Nick, well back from the carcass. She cocked her head; Sophia watched as the man and dog stared at one another.

"Come with me," Nick said to Sophia. "Don't touch the carcass." Nick stepped around the wolf. Without a sound, Amaruq turned and led them ten feet north, to the scattered bones of medium sized bird. He bent and picked up a bone, sniffed it. The delicate bone had tooth marks on it.

Sophia looked from the bird to the wolf. "Something attacked both the bird and the wolf? I don't get it."

Nick straightened and looked around, scanning the entire horizon. "It's a ptarmigan, what we call *aqiggiq*. Favorite prey of the Arctic wolf, like that one." He shifted the rifle, cradling it in both arms. "I figure the wolf was carrying it, and something got the wolf."

"Some*thing?*"

He looked over at her. "Someone, I mean. But there's no sign of a pack or a bear, no sign of any predators. Maybe it was a human hunter."

She frowned, watching Amaruq circle and sniff. "I thought hunting was forbidden in the Lowlands."

"It is. Doesn't mean it doesn't happen, though."

She nodded, scanning the fog-shrouded horizon. "Poachers," she said. It was not a question.

"Maybe," Nick said. "Some guys will do anything for a trophy to brag about back home." He slung the rifle on his shoulder. "We've got to call this in," he said finally. He gestured at Amaruq to follow, and turned back towards their rest stop.

"I don't like this. Don't be surprised if we get an order to abort this trip."

Sophia looked at him in dismay. "But I've come so far!" she blurted out. She looked from the wolf to Nick and back again. "It's only poachers. Do you really think they'd attack us?"

"Not us, no," he said quietly. He nodded to Amaruq, padding along, nose to the ground, tail in the air. "*She's* a different matter. I'm not looking to see her hide stretched in front of some rich man's fire."

Sophia nodded sympathetically. "Of course. I understand."

Nothing had been disturbed at the rock outcropping, and Nick found his radio in his pack where he expected. Linking up with base camp was another story. Static crackled and hissed as he fiddled with the settings.

"Battery OK?" Sophia asked.

"It was new when we left the research station. Maybe a solar flare?"

Finally he reached Verna.

"What's up, Nick? Over." Verna said.

"I've got a dead wolf here," he said. "Missing the head, probably taken by some hunter. You guys might want to report it to Fraser. Over."

"Yeah, well, he's still out looking for Glenn and Leo," Verna said laconically. "I'll let him know when he reports in. What's your twenty? Over."

Nick read off his GPS coordinates. "Have you heard anything about poachers, hunters, anything? Over."

"Nothing about poachers," Verna replied. "We've got a NOAA satellite image telling us we've got the mother of all summer storms headed our way. ETA noon tomorrow. Over."

"Shit," Nick said under his breath. "Are we still green for this traverse? Over."

There was a long pause. Sophia braced for bad news.

"Nick, you're still good to go as long as you feel you have full field capability," Verna said finally. "Martin says it's your call."

Nick took a deep breath. "Actually, it's your call," he said to Sophia. "With Fraser in the area, I don't think we'll have much trouble from poachers. The smart ones are monitoring law enforcement frequencies anyway, and the dumb ones won't be able to track us."

"I want to go on," Sophia said. "We can cut the schedule if you want, maybe spend only half a day on the ice cap."

Nick nodded. "No need. We'll stick to the plan." He keyed the transceiver again. "Base, we're going ahead. Next check-in will be two hours. You'll let Fraser know about the kill? Over."

"Roger that, Nick. You two have a good day, and give Amaruq a kiss. Base out."

"Mobile out," Nick said. He switched off the transceiver to save the battery. "So we go on," he said.

"And the wolf carcass?"

He shrugged. "Leave it."

She stared off into the fog in the direction of the body. "So it decays *in situ*. I kind of wish I could come back next spring and see what ecosystem sprouts there."

"Wolfbane?" he joked.

She smiled, and Nick turned away and busied himself adjusting the straps of his pack. When he turned back, she was staring thoughtfully at the carcass, a plastic vial in her hand.

"Don't," he said.

She looked at him. "Yeah, I agree. Much as I'd love to get a sample of wolf DNA for Jennifer, I'd just as soon not touch that thing." Her eyes flicked to Amaruq.

He shifted his feet. "We've already lost an hour, so we'd better get going."

Sophia nodded and followed him into the fog, Amaruq scouting ahead. The fog closed behind her, hiding the headless carcass. *There had to be some explanation for that*, Sophia thought. She tried to tell herself that it was predation, that some human hunter had taken a trophy head. But if so, why

140

was there no blood? And what was that odd ripple under its hide?

Whatever had happened to the wolf, it was not natural.

Haughton Crater Research Project, Devon Island, Nunavut
75° 26' 00" N, 89° 51' 00" W

Will Fraser stormed out of the base headquarters, jamming his hands into his gloves. "Dammit, you should have stopped him!"

Martin Skorjik followed him, zipping up his parka. "Nick was hired as a guard. Dr. Abenezra had permission to go. What was I supposed to do? Arrest him?"

"You're his boss! You could fire him if you have to!"

"If I fired Nick Tonarak, then I couldn't tell him what to do, could I?" Skorjik stopped, waved at a passing bulky figure. "David! Come here!"

David Beringer lumbered over. "Hey, Martin. Will. I was just on my way—"

"I need you to gather everyone in the mess tent," Skorjik said. "Call in any teams that have left within the last fifteen minutes."

"But—"

"Now, if you please," Skorjik said. His words were polite, his tone was not. Beringer nodded and walked away.

Fraser was staring out at the eastern horizon. Skorjik followed his gaze. "Oh, no. Not a chance."

Fraser continued to stare at the Habitat. "I need all the manpower I can get, Skorjik. This is serious. They've been missing for—"

"I know how long they've been gone," Skorjik snapped. His eyes were slitted both in anger and against the sharp wind. "And I don't think having Tonarak—or his dog—searching hundreds of square kilometers by themselves would make a difference. Nor would calling in those...simpletons on the hill. I'm telling you, it's time to call in the Marines."

Fraser snorted. *Americans*, he thought. *It always came down to the military with them.* "You should have done that earlier; now we can't wait. Every hour counts."

"Constable, these are amateurs! None of us is trained in search and rescue!"

Fraser fixed him with a glare. "Are they, or are they not, in your own words, 'the most knowledgeable people on earth' when it comes to this island?"

Skorjik glared back. "Yes. They know the geology, the ecology, the plant community better than anyone. That's not the same as looking for lost, possibly injured men!"

Fraser looked at him coldly. "Professor, is this not *exactly* the kind of emergency explorers would face on Mars? Is this not *exactly* the kind of thing they would have to do—drop their research and form search teams? NASA may be good, but not even they can send Marines to Mars. Here or there, your people will have to do what they have to do."

Skorjik ran his hand through his spiky hair. "These are not astronauts, Constable. You're as likely to get these guys killed as to rescue Leo and Glenn. Please, call for help. If you do, I...I'll help you all I can."

Fraser looked at him, then shrugged. "I'll put in a call for Rangers. They may not be able to get here inside twenty-four hours, but it's the best I can do."

"Thanks," Skorjik said.

"I'll need all your ATVs and all your weapons."

In the mess tent, people milled about or sat huddled over mugs of tea and coffee. They all looked up as Fraser entered behind Skorjik. Skorjik held up his hand for silence, but before he could speak, Fraser stepped in front of him. "You all know the situation. Two men have been missing for several days. We are conducting air searches, to no avail so far. So now I need boots on the ground, covering every ravine, every valley, every spot we can't see from the air. I need all of you."

A surprised murmur went around the tent, followed by rumbles of dissent. A pale redheaded man raised his hand. "Officer, some of us have vital work we're in the middle of—"

"Which you'll return to all the sooner, when we find your

missing colleagues. Now I'll need teams of two each, armed at all times, carrying walkie-talkies. Dr. Skorjik, can you find us a map? I'll need to know which of you fine scientists has been where, so that the teams can cover ground that's already familiar."

As he watched the men and women sort themselves into teams and begin plotting their strategy, Fraser accepted a mug of tea from the silent cook. He thought about Nick Tonarak's report of a dead wolf, of possible poachers. He thought about diamond hunters who might stop at nothing. He wondered if any of these scientists had any idea how dangerous it was out there. He needed them, he knew every minute counted now, but still he wondered: was he sending them into danger?

Truelove Lowlands, Devon Island, Nunavut
75° 36′ 21.18″ N, 83° 29′ 00.44″ W

Nick led Sophia down off the plateau back to the riverbed. The way was easier, if foggier. Soon, the fog grew so thick Nick could hardly see the ground. He felt uneasy as they continued, stopping regularly to allow Sophia to take samples of soil and water. The wind tugged at his pack when he turned broadside to it, flipped his braids into his eyes, stung his unprotected cheeks. It was an unrelenting force, hammering down from the Arctic ice cap, icy and inhuman.

"Time to camp," he said. *Better to quit too early than too late,* he thought, *when they'd both be too exhausted to put up the tents.* He glanced around. They had come to a halt in a defile that blocked some of the wind. "Look around for a good spot. Up out of the riverbed, but sheltered."

"Right." Sophia set her feet doggedly on the steep slope. Nick scrambled up after her, keeping one eye on her ascent. If she fell, he wanted to be able to catch her. He'd had enough disasters for one day.

Sophia reached a shelf of gravel carved out by some ancient flood. She walked to and fro, her head down, staring at the ground. Amaruq nosed at her hand, then bounded upslope into a scatter of rocks. Nick was debating the attractions of a gravel-filled depression versus a slightly sloped but dry talus, when he heard Sophia call him. He walked over.

She pointed to a raised bed of rocks that formed a V shape pointed north, below which lay a level area free of large rocks. "How about this?"

Nick shook his head. "Can't tent here," he said. "That's a protected Ancestor site. We can't disturb it."

She stared at the bare rocks, some of them covered with lichen. He could almost hear her thoughts.

"I know," he said. "Doesn't look like much. But sometimes sites like this are all we have of our ancestors." A sudden gust whirled sand at him and he blinked.

She swallowed, nodded. Her eyes squinted at him against the wind. "So where?"

He nodded to his left. "That ledge will do." Nick shrugged out of his pack. "I'll set up the tents."

"I can do it," she said stubbornly. "You aren't my servant."

Nick shrugged and turned to his own pack. As he was unlacing the top flap the wind caught the lacing string and whipped it painfully across his cheek. He snarled at it and wrestled the ground tarp out of the top of his pack. Wind gusted at him and he fought to keep it from becoming a sail.

Sophia cried out. Nick turned just in time to see a mass of gray-green plastic take wing, like a poorly made kite.

"My tent!" Sophia dashed after it, but the wind had already lofted it beyond her reach. The tent flap was open; the wind filled the interior like a balloon, and propelled it even higher. Nick sprinted after her and the tent, with Amaruq running beside him, barking. The tent swerved, careened out over the edge of the gravel shelf above the rushing water. Nick stumbled and his right knee came down on broken rock. He grunted and struggled to his feet.

Sophia scrambled down the slope, sliding in the loose gravel. The tent swept across the water, flattened itself on a boulder; she splashed in after it and sank to her thighs. Nick limped after them both. The wind gusted again, lifting the tent off the boulder, lofting it into the air. Sophia slogged across the water, floundering when it came to her waist, and finally stumbling out onto the opposite bank. She ran, leaping up now and then to snatch at the dancing tent. Every time, it eluded her. She splashed down in a shallow pond, drenching herself.

Then a burst of wind slammed the tent into an outcrop of ice-shattered rock, and even at that distance Nick could hear the rip of nylon. The tent flapped helplessly against the sharp rocks, slicing itself to ribbons. By the time Nick caught up with Sophia, she was soaking wet, kneeling and trying to unwind the shredded tent from the rocks it had tangled in.

"It's ruined," she gasped as he reached her. She was shivering, her fingers white with cold as she picked at the pieces of nylon and webbing.

He caught her hand. "Leave it," he said. "You're soaked. You need to get changed. Right now. Come on."

"But—"

"Now." He caught her under the arms and hauled her bodily to her feet. His knee spiked with pain and he stumbled, and then she was turning and was in his arms. For a moment they stood locked together, swaying. Then she backed out of his embrace and turned away. "Come on," he said roughly.

She followed him back to where they'd left their packs. Nick thought of a dozen things to say, starting with a lecture on unpacking in a high wind and ending with another sermon on polar bear safety, but said nothing. She was miserable enough. And they were down to only one tent.

When they reached the packs, Nick made Sophia sit in the lee of a rocky outcrop. Heedless of any concerns for privacy, he rummaged through her pack, pulling out sweaters and hats. He thrust them at her. "Here, put these on."

"Don't look."

He scowled. "This is no time for modesty." But she clutched the sweaters close to her chest, eyes full of misery. "Fine," he muttered, turning his back.

While she changed, he turned away to unsling the rifle

from his pack. He checked the load, facing away from her. Down here in the river wale, there was less chance of running into the big bears, but he was taking no chances.

"I'm d-done," Sophia said.

He turned. She was now wearing two sweaters and her parka, and had jammed her knit hat down onto her head. But he could see her shivering from ten feet away. He debated—set up the tent first, or get a fire going to warm her up? Another gust of icy wind decided him. Without a better windbreak, his camp stove would never light.

"Help me set up the tent," he said. He braced himself for some argument about sharing the tent, about propriety, whatever.

But she only nodded, and helped him unpack his hunting tent. He noticed that she kept a death grip on the fabric, never letting go with more than one hand. They soon had it standing, anchored with piles of rocks along the edges and inside the tent. He threw their packs inside and gestured for her to follow. Sophia crawled in and he came in after her.

The tent had originally been orange, but over the years had faded to a sunny yellow. The light filtering through turned everything to gold, and made the interior look warmer than it really was. Sophia huddled against her pack as he sat in the entrance. He pulled out his camp stove and started to set it up.

"No!"

He glanced at her in surprise. She was shivering, but her eyes were alert and afraid. She was staring at the stove.

"What? You need something hot to drink. Hand me the tea."

She shook her head. "No fires in the t-tent. Too d-dangerous."

Nick frowned. "I've done this for years. Don't worry. I know what I'm doing."

She shook her head so violently her hair flopped into her face. "If you start that thing in here, I'm going out."

What kind of politically-correct rule of Southern wisdom was he breaking now? He didn't care. "Fine," he snapped. "When you freeze your fingers off, don't cry to me." He picked up the stove, reached through the flap, and set it outside.

Sophia turned away. "Thanks." Her voice was rough. She shivered as she unlaced the sleeping bag tied to her pack. Nick helped her roll it out. Without speaking, she climbed in and zipped it tight.

"You should eat something," he said. Despite his annoyance, he felt nervous. He'd been on hikes before where an amateur got hurt, and the trip back was always a mess.

She said nothing. Nick brought out his dry-camp supplies: jerky, cheese, crackers, chocolate bars. He handed some of them to Sophia and they disappeared into the sleeping bag. Faint crunching noises came from inside.

"I'm going after your tent," he said. "Amaruq will stay here. If she barks, there's a polar bear around. I'm leaving you the rifle."

She said nothing and he put his parka back on and left the tent.

The wind carried the smell of snow now, and the swirls of white reduced visibility to a kilometer or less. Nick took careful note of every outcrop, every pool or boulder he passed as he made his way back to the tent-killing outcrop. By the time he'd found it, his knee was a steady ache and his head hurt from squinting into the fog.

The tent, when he reached it, was a dead loss. Nick gathered what he could, wadded it into a ball, and stuck it into his pockets. Useless as it was, he would not leave it here to trash up the landscape.

Amaruq greeted him when he returned. He took off her pack, and fed her. He checked the rocks holding down the tent, piled on a few more, then hunched down over the stove, sheltering it from the wind with his body. It took him only a few minutes to get the flame going. Amaruq came over and sat beside his pack, sniffing, tongue lolling.

::Candy::

"Only if you promise to brush your teeth afterwards,"

Nick said. He was careful to speak in Inuktitut, in case Sophia heard him.

::Hah hah. Funny.::

"Find me some big rocks."

Nick put water on to boil, watching the shadows creep sideways towards the east. The sun would not actually set, but it did get lower on the horizon. He thought about the woman in the tent and her patience and her (now wounded) pride, and most of all her liveliness and her smile. He wondered about her odd fears, but he was glad he had given her the carving. When the water boiled, he shook powder into it and soon had some hot-and-sour soup steaming in a cup.

Gently he pushed aside the tent flap and eased inside. "Hey," he called.

There was no answer, so he nudged the lower end of the bag. He had to nudge it harder before Sophia stirred, and two bright eyes peered at him over the edge of the bag. "What?"

He held up the soup. "You need to drink something warm," he said.

"I'm n-not hungry."

"I don't care. Eat."

After a pause, she sat up, pulling the bag almost to her shoulders. "Thanks," she said as he handed her the plastic bowl. She blew on the soup, watching him. "What about you?"

"Got other chores first," he said. He turned to leave, paused. "If we can't have the stove in here, do you object to heated rocks?"

She shook her head. As he bent to leave, she said, "I'm sorry," in a low voice. "About the tent. It was...clumsy of me."

Nick didn't know how to answer that. He went out and found Amaruq waiting for him.

::Fat rocks up above. Candy?::

"Later."

Nick followed her up the slope to the top of the river bank. Here the fog had lifted a little, enough to show him that they were at the edge of the Truelove Lowlands. To the north, the land cut down and was protected by the short cliff he stood on. To the south, all vegetation disappeared, and the landscape disappeared into the fog, a flat expanse of rocks, gravel and scree. Amaruq led him to an outcropping, where he spent a few minutes kicking and pulling. When he had several pounds of fist-sized rocks, he carried them back to camp.

The wind had picked up, and his camp stove had blown out. Nick patiently re-lit it and put the rocks into the largest pan he had and waited for them to heat.

Amaruq stuck her nose in his ear. ::Candy!::

"Greedy," he shot back, but pulled a plastic bag from his pack. He opened it and shook out a handful of gumdrops. He watched her devour them, thinking about the little sister he'd had once, the one with the merry laugh and the sweet tooth. Amaruq lay down next to him, licking her chops. Nick rested a hand on her head.

When they were in physical contact like this, Nick could sense her thoughts even more clearly. Now he eavesdropped on a casual interplay of images: hares, birds, a gravel patch that smelled of musk ox urine. As she drifted towards sleep, her thoughts became less ordered, less focused on words, until she was awash in the memory of scents, of thoughts Nick could hardly comprehend.

Except for one: loneliness. His heart ached as he felt the core of sadness in his sister's thoughts, the sense of isolation. She was not a human and not a wolf, unwelcome and feared in either camp. He could sense her longing to run free with other four-footed hunters, but also felt her repulsion at their primitive minds. He caught an echo of a memory of her fourth-grade reading class, when she had won a spelling bee. And as she finally succumbed to sleep, one image came clear: their mother, smiling and humming a lullaby.

Nick sat staring at the dancing flame. No point dwelling on what could not be changed. He made himself think of more immediate problems. Were there poachers on the island? The dead wolf would seem to say so. The head had been severed cleanly, like someone taking a trophy. Yet there were no other signs of human presence in the area, certainly none of the trash and trampling he associated with illegal hunters. He knew there were plenty of men, red and white, who treated the hunting laws with contempt, and thought it was their right to hunt any time and any place it suited them. But an Inuit would never have taken only the head. Never have wasted all that meat. It's not our way.

Nick stood and retrieved the radio from his pack. Aware that Sophia was sleeping, he strode out of earshot and called base camp.

"Hey, Nick," Verna's voice said. "You guys missed the peach cobbler. Over."

"You're a mean person, Verna. Did you find your missing guys yet? Over."

"Not a word. You see any sign of them? Over."

"No, sorry. Listen, should we come back in? I think there's poachers in the area and I've got a civilian here. Over."

"Will Fraser is organizing search parties. He's even making noises about using dogs. Wants your dog, specially. Over."

Nick's hand tightened on the radio. "Does he want us to come in? Over."

"He hasn't said so. But if you've got any reason to think you're in danger, come on back. Over."

"Has anyone else sighted any carcasses, any sign of hunters? Over."

"Not so far. Over."

Nick thought about it. Maybe he was jumping the gun. Not only had he seen no sign of other humans around, neither had Amaruq. If there had been any scent of humans out here, she'd have caught it long ago. He keyed the transceiver. "I'll wait until we've slept. We've already made camp." He read off the GPS coordinates, frowning at the flickering screen. "I'll call in again in eight hours. Over."

"Copy that," Verna said. "You guys sleep tight. Base out."

He signed off, turned off the radio. He hadn't mentioned the fact that he'd be sharing a tent with Sophia. No need to, he thought. There would be gossip enough. Southerners could be amazingly prudish. His own people accepted nudity more easily than people who lived in much warmer climates. In an environment where propriety could get you frozen to death overnight, people were more accepting of mixed-sex sleeping arrangements.

Or so he rationalized it to himself. He thought about her, thought about her body solid and warm against his when he pulled her back from the cliff, thought about his mouth on hers. What was it about this woman?

He ached for her. For connection. Like Amaruq, he was outcast and lonely.

No point in whining about it, he could almost hear his father say. Balling his fists in his pockets, he stalked back to the tent. While he waited for the rocks to heat, he pulled his hunting knife out of his boot and checked the edge. Nick turned off the flame and rolled the hot rocks onto the ground. Careful not to burn his fingers, he slid them into two socks. He repacked the camp stove and put it away, then pulled a plastic bag from a side pocket of his pack.

Amaruq woke instantly. ::Pepperoni?::

Nick offered her some and she took it delicately from his hand. He finished his share and then crept into the tent.

"Hey?" he said softly

There was no sound from the lump that was Sophia's sleeping bag. He knelt next to her head. Her hair fanned over the ivory curve of her cheek; it fluttered with her breath. He laid the wrapped hot rocks on the foot of her bag. They would add just enough heat to keep her feet comfortable.

As quietly as possible, he shed his boots, pants, parka and top sweater. Clad only in his thermal long johns, he slid into his own bag. Amaruq slipped into the tent and Nick fastened it behind her. She curled up on the foot of his bag, looked from him to Sophia, and her tongue lolled.

::Cozy. Double up?::

"Shut up," he muttered, and lay down. It took him a long time to sleep. And when he slept, he dreamed.

Against a background of cold, bright stars, the Whole hung balanced and complete, in harmony with every member, conscious of its perfect unity. How long this state continued, it was impossible to tell, for time is measured in events and no events worthy of notice interrupted the perfect integrity of consciousness that was the vast living entity of cells. But gradually an unease set in, an awareness of Other, of some anomaly that could not be integrated. In its normal progress, the Whole had encountered another entity – another life form. This happened occasionally, and the response was the same: assimilation. Gently, with care for the Other's unique qualities, the fusion began. DNA sequences were analyzed, broken, merged, re-formed with utmost care. The Other became the Self, and peace was restored. And now there were new delights to share.

IV - THE INVADER

Truelove Lowlands, Devon Island, Nunavut
75° 36′ 21.18″ N, 83° 59′00.44″ W

The wolf lay as before, headless and still. No insects, no scavengers approached. The fur rippled with movement under the skin, but it was not the work of maggots or worms. Wind occasionally ruffled the wolf's fur, but nothing else touched it.

A light rain began to fall, as much snow as rain, scudding along before a frigid breeze that promised more snow soon. An Arctic tern flitted down to the ground beside the wolf but took off again, frantic to get away from something it did not understand.

A hole in the rain approached from the south, a void where the misty droplets did not enter, merely collecting on a convex surface before rolling off. The void drifted closer, coming to a stop above the wolf. The void turned opaque, then mirror-silver, and the sphere lowered to hover over the carcass.

From the severed neck and the anus, a flood of silver poured forth, pooling on the ground, then turned, flowing uphill to meet in the halfway point of the body. A blue light shot forth from the hovering globe, flickered over the pool. The silver stream coalesced, thickened, and then rose, shaping itself into the perfect replica of a wolf—tiny, but whole. Then it dissolved, pooled, reformed into the image of a truncated rifle.

Again it collapsed, again the blue light flickered. This time the silver formed a tiny image of a woman, a portrait of Sophia. This was followed by a man with long hair—Nick. The silver rippled, dissolved, stirred itself and rose to form an image of Amaruq. But the image was distorted, as though two images had been morphed together—a young girl, and a wolf.

The tiny sculpture collapsed, the pool formed itself into a perfect sphere, the echo of its larger twin. The blue light turned red, then the large globe descended, touched the surface of the smaller sphere. The two flowed together, like two blobs of mercury joining.

The sphere rose, no larger than before, and again took up its station above the wolf.

The shining mirror surface turned the color of molten lava, the flaming red of liquid glass. A pulse, another, and then there was a twenty-foot circle of ash where there had been wolf, brush, and rock. Another intense flash, and the circle bubbled and sank, forming a perfectly round depression a foot deep. Smoke twisted up until it met the rain, which dispersed it.

The sphere moved away, slowly returning to silver. It hovered, drifted, hovered until it came to a stretch of bare ground. There in the dirt were several perfect paw prints, next to the boot prints of a man and a woman. Dipping, the sphere lowered until it was only inches above the paw prints. It threw out waves of light and heat, then a red blast that reduced the ground to fused glass.

Rising, the sphere flew northwest, on a direct heading for Haughton Crater.

Truelove Lowlands, Devon Island, Nunavut
75° 36′ 21.18″ N, 83° 29′ 00.44″ W

Nick woke wrapped around Sophia. In sleep, she had rolled to face him, and now lay in his arms. Her lashes were fine and dark along her round cheek, her body rose and fell with her steady breathing. He could feel the contours of her, molded against him through their sleeping bags. The light filtering through the yellow walls of the tent warmed her skin. Her mouth was parted, her lips soft and red. *Irresistible*, he thought.

She opened her eyes, and looked up at him, her eyes dark and wide. There was a long, humming moment between them, and then she turned her head away and he sat up and his face got warm.

He cleared his throat. "Hey," he said. *Stupid, stupid...*

Amaruq chose that moment to walk between them. She licked Sophia's face.

Sophia smiled, but pushed the wolf away. The sleeping bag slid down. Her thermal shirt had ridden up in the night, and Nick saw a patch of rough skin spreading across her torso like branching coral. Drawn and puckered, it extended under her armpit. She caught his look and tugged her shirt down.

"I...uh, I'm sorry," Nick said, not quite sure what he was apologizing for. The embrace? The look? "Is it a rash? Can I get you something?"

She looked down, and her hair fell forward, shielding her face. Amaruq lay down across Sophia's sleeping bag, offering comfort. Sophia stroked her head. "They're burn scars," she said in a low voice. "I...I was in a fire." Her unease was palpable.

"You don't have to tell me anything," he said hastily.

She met his eyes, and hers were troubled. "You had to sleep cold, without a heater, twice now because of me. So you have a right to know." She took a deep breath, and focused in the distance.

"Four years ago, my fiancé Paul and I were in Alaska studying extremophiles in volcanic environments. There were five of us in the research group. We were staying in a remote cabin, miles from the nearest ranger camp. It...it was heated with a stove just like the one back at the research station."

Her fingers knotted into themselves. Nick looked down and saw that his fingers were twined together as well.

"One night, the stove caught fire. I woke up and the cabin was filled with smoke and...screaming. The door was in flames, and when we tried to open it, I fell. My sweater caught fire." She stopped, swallowing. Amaruq's tail thumped, and her head came to rest on Sophia's lap. "Paul broke the window over our bed and pushed me out into a snowbank. He said he was going back for the others, but he didn't...he didn't make it out. None of them did."

"I'm sorry," Nick said. He remembered how she had clutched her clothing to her chest, insisting he turn his back. *Not modesty,* he thought. *Scars. And maybe shame.*

She bent over, arms hugging herself, rocking. "I lay there for hours, until the smoke drew a spotter plane and the forestry guys arrived. I spent three months in the hospital..." She drew up her knees, put her face on them, and Nick heard a muffled sob. "The smell...I can't forget the *smell.*"

He reached out and took her hand. "I'm so sorry," he said quietly. "It must have been a terrible thing. But you survived. I'm...I'm glad."

She nodded, unable to speak. Slowly, her hand turned upward under his, until their palms met. His fingers wove themselves with hers, offering comfort and warmth and understanding. Outside, a sudden gust of wind pounded the tent, making the walls wobble and flap, but the two sat unmoving, a stillness between them no wind could affect.

"Usually I can cope, but being back in the Arctic, smelling the smells again, dealing with fire in the tent, it's hard. I guess it all came back to me. But I'd appreciate it if...if you didn't tell the rest, back there..." Her head tilted in the vague direction of the crater camp. "Jennifer knows, but nobody else."

"I won't tell anyone," Nick said. His eyes met Amaruq's; he was good at keeping secrets. He cleared his throat. "How about some breakfast?" he said.

She nodded without speaking. He unzipped his sleeping bag, and wriggled into his pants inside the bag. It was a skill he'd mastered long ago, but he was aware of her presence and that made him clumsy. He shrugged into a sweater. "I'm going down for water," he said, reaching for the tent flap. "I'll leave the gun here, all right?"

"I'll be fine," she said in a monotone. "And...I'm sorry."

"No reason to be," he said. "What happened was terrible, but it wasn't your fault. And as for heating the tent, well, I've slept cold most of my life."

He ducked out of the tent and into the maw of morning. Amaruq pushed out after him. She nudged him, leaning against his knee.

::Sad::

"Yeah," he said. The day was off to a foggy start; he could hardly see the stream below them.

::Like I said, she likes you.::

Startled, he glanced down. "Why do you say that?"

::Wouldn't have told you about the fire otherwise.:: Amaruq trotted off, nose to the ground.

Nick stood and watched her, surprised at her insight. But then, Amaruq had always been wise when it came to people. He stamped his feet into his boots. A warm, strange feeling stole into him. Sophia had trusted him with a secret. He could not remember the last time a non-family member had done that. If ever.

Cold, wet wind tossed his long hair in his face, obscuring his vision of Amaruq disappearing into the mist. He paid no attention. Something was happening inside him he didn't understand. He'd never experienced it. It scared him a lot.

But he liked it.

Haughton Crater Research Project, Devon Island, Nunavut
75° 26′ 00″ N, 89° 51′ 00″ W

"It's a mistake, Dr. Roth."

The communications tent was deserted except for Jennifer and Dr. Skorjik. Weak sunlight filtered through the billowing tent walls lent a sepia tone to the scene, as if Jennifer had walked into another century. Skorjik had rather pointedly placed himself between Jennifer and the radio transceiver.

"No, it's not, Dr. Skorjik." Jennifer clutched the computer printout in one hand and put a conciliatory smile on her face. "I ran every test three times, adhering to the strictest pro-tocols, protocols which have ensured the integrity of countless similar analyses. I'm telling you, as a geneticist, I am finding evidence of something very strange here."

Skorjik took off his glasses, pinched his nose between thumb and forefinger. "I'm sure you believe that, Dr. Roth. A mistake usually looks very strange. Your samples were contaminated—"

"I took steps to eliminate that—"

He overrode her, raising his voice. "And any competent independent analysis will prove that. In the meantime, I really cannot allow you to be using our comms for personal communications, not while we've got a search and rescue operation ongoing in the field."

"But Sophia needs to know. And I have to ask Nick—"

He lowered his hand, stared out of red-rimmed eyes at her. "Ask him what? If he's part wolf? Or dog or whatever? Ask him if his dog is part human? If he didn't laugh himself to death, the rest of this camp would. And they'd all be laughing at you. At me. At this operation." He swung a hand, taking in the entire research station. "We're precarious enough out here, small enough, remote enough, on limited funding—I can't even tell you what hoops I have to jump through every year to keep us going, keep the money coming in. And then for you to try something like this, a prank of some sort—"

"It's not a prank!"

"It damn well better be," Skorjik snapped. "Because if it's not a prank, I have to conclude that you don't know how to run a DNA comparison competently, and will report such to your sponsors at the University."

Jennifer glared, but held her tongue. There was no arguing with him in this mood, and confrontation was not her forte anyway. There would be some other way to contact Sophia. In the meantime, his words had stung her just enough to have her doubt her own work. So she nodded shortly, angrily to Skorjik and pushed past him out of the comms tent.

She strode into the medical tent, bumping past Ted Meyers. He grabbed her arm as she pushed him aside. "Hey! What's up? You look, ah..."

She glared at him. "Skorjik won't let me call Sophia and Nick." She shook the computer printout in his face. "I know what I'm doing, I'm not incompetent!"

"Of course not. Sit down. Here, let me see. Why were you trying to call your partner?"

"To warn her!"

"About what?"

Jennifer plopped down onto a stool. "About Amaruq. And Nick. And this." She shook the printout.

Ted looked sideways at her. "What exactly do you think the danger is? That one of them is a...a werewolf?"

The word hung in the air between them. Jennifer heard the mockery in Skorjik's voice, could imagine what would happen to her career if rumor got back to the University. "Not really," she said, knowing it was a lie.

Ted sat on the stool opposite her. "Look, even if there is some weird kind of genetic architecture here, are you sure it's dangerous? I mean, if this guy Nick was violent or unstable, would they have hired him on?"

He sounded so reasonable, so sure. Jennifer wanted to agree. But that would mean rejecting the data in front of her. That's the one thing she would not do, she told herself.

She held up the paper. "This is not a lie, Ted." She braced herself for his contempt, for sarcasm.

Instead, he shrugged. "Okay. Tell you what. Skorjik and Fraser are grabbing everyone for search teams. How about you and me team up, and we go find your friend? I can check out a rifle and see if there's an ATV available."

Jennifer sat up straight. "You believe me?"

"I believe you're scared for your friend," he said. "But I'm afraid we're going to miss the movie I came in here to invite you to."

Knowing he supported her, Jennifer relaxed. "Movie?"

"Yeah," he said. His eyes were warm, interested. "Long-standing camp tradition; every evening one of the camp managers shows an old sci-fi movie in the mess tent. We eat popcorn and hot dogs. I think tonight it's *Queen of Outer Space*, always good for a giggle. With all the teams out searching, we'd pretty much have the place to ourselves." He reached for her hand. "Too bad. It would have been fun. Maybe when we get back?"

"I don't know," she said warily.

Meyers reached up to trail a finger across Jennifer's cheek. "Look, I won't beat around the bush. You interest me. You haven't shoved me on my ass yet, so I gotta hope you're interested. I asked around, and you're not married or living with. Me, neither. So why not get acquainted, see where it goes?"

Jennifer liked Ted's smile, his humor and his smarts. And if he got handsy she could just slip away. *"Queen of Outer Space,* huh? The one with Zsa Zsa Gabor?"

He grinned. "In emeralds and high heels."

"Will there will be mockery?"

"Mockery, lampooning, Bronx cheers. Brutal disrespect of the cinematic art."

"Dahlink," Jennifer drawled in her best Zsa Zsa imitation. "Ve *must* see zis movie."

He grinned even wider. "I'll bribe the camp manager. So it's a date? After we find your friend?"

"Sure."

Ted stood. "Okay. Meet you at the garage in half an hour?"

"Make it forty five minutes," Jennifer said. "If we're going out on a long traverse, I need to change."

"Pearls?" Ted grinned.

"Long johns," Jennifer said.

"Ah." Ted smiled. "Arctic lingerie."

Truelove Lowlands, Devon Island, Nunavut
75° 36′21.18″ N, 83° 29′ 00.44″ W

Will Fraser held on stoically as he jounced in the passenger seat behind Lonnie Makivik. The ATV crested the hill and roared down the slope, its motor loud even over the wind. The wind whipped into his face hard enough to draw tears, but he said nothing. Lonnie swerved expertly around boulders, followed steep gravel trails with ease; Fraser knew the boy had been driving ATVs since he was tall enough to reach the pedals, with skill that put the Mountie's to shame.

Which was fine with Will. He wasn't that keen on "sports" that involved engines. He leaned forward. "How much farther?" he shouted into the boy's ear.

As if the gods had heard his answer, they crested another hill and Lonnie stopped, allowing Fraser an uninterrupted view.

The Truelove Lowlands spread out below them in a vast mosaic of dark green hummocks interspersed with asphalt-colored rocks. Above them, dirty cotton clouds skulked across the sky, threatening snow as the temperature dropped. Lonnie leaned over to scrape frost off the GPS unit. "Almost there," he said. "I don't see any sign of a camp."

Fraser accepted this with calm. Sometime in the last few hours some inner deadline had passed, and he now believed this was a recovery operation, not a rescue. He knew, deep in his gut, that the men he sought were dead. But it wouldn't do to let the troops know. They weren't used to death, to violent death, he thought. Except for the Inuit.

Lonnie scrambled the bike down the hillside, sliding on chunky gravel, slewing on the unstable slope. Then they were at the bottom, and a mud bog opened up ahead of them. The Inuit boy rolled to a stop. He tapped his GPS. "You getting a signal, boss?" His head turned; Will spotted several silver rings in the boy's earlobe.

Will glanced at the GPS wrist unit he'd borrowed from Skorjik. A twinge of envy went through him; he'd love to have one of his own. Maybe next payday... "Eh, I'm seeing the last known coordinates, minus thirty meters or so. Let's go, mate."

Lonnie shrugged and the ATV jerked forward, then settled into a long, slow crawl that took them up over hummocks of saw grass and down the frozen other side. Fraser turned his head left and right, searching.

"Wait!" He tapped Lonnie's shoulder. "Over to the left!"

It stood out of the rough and tumble landscape like a slab of marble in a rockslide: a smooth bowl carved from the earth—or melted into it. Twenty feet in diameter, with buzzards circling warily overhead.

Lonnie braked to a stop several meters away. "I don't like that, Constable."

"I don't either. Stay here."

Wary of his cramped limbs, Fraser climbed off the passenger seat and flipped the catch off his holster. Hand on the grip of his weapon, he circled warily, approaching the crater. But it was only what it had looked like at first: a circular dip in the ground, perfectly round, featureless.

Except for the charred grass at the edge. When he was on the other side of the depression, facing Lonnie, he plucked the radio from his belt, keying in his mic.

"Haughton Crater, this is Fraser. Do you read? Over."

Static. He tried again, got more static. A buzzing sound made him check his wrist unit; the GPS readout was flashing, cycling through numbers, blinking.

"What the hell?" he muttered. He remembered the GPS unit in the plane going haywire when he and Pete flew over. He keyed the radio again. "Haughton, do you read? This is Fraser. Over."

Static again. A chill that had nothing to do with the clouds and wind settled on Fraser. He reached into a zippered pocket, brought out a digital camera. He walked the perimeter of the depression again, taking pictures.

"What is it?" Lonnie said as he reached the ATV. The boy was still on the machine, hunched over, hands gripping the handlebars as if poised for flight. "Something the scientists at the crater did?"

"Might be," Fraser said. He glanced at the sky, smelled snow on the wind. "Maybe something else. I can't raise the base. Can you?"

The boy shook his head. "Nothing but squawk," he said, using the slang for static. "And I don't like the sound of this motor."

As he spoke, the idling engine gave a hiccup, a cough, then settled back to an unsteady idle.

Something interfering with GPS, thought Fraser. Something jamming radio. Something interfering with engines.

"Let's circle around," he said. "I need to see what's on the other side. Then we need to go back to camp. I want to talk to Skorjik."

He climbed back on, settled in. Lonnie gunned the motor, turned in a wide arc, and started around the depression.

Fraser thought about secret experiments, government black ops, space technology. Could be this was just some accident no one wanted to report. But he was dead certain these were the GPS coordinates Nick had called in when he reported the dead wolf.

And Nick had said nothing about a melted pool of glass.

Haughton Crater Research Project, Devon Island, Nunavut
75° 26′ 00″ N, 89° 51′ 00″ W

Jennifer shoved her arms into her parka, working it on over the three sweaters she'd pulled on. With the lined snow pants and heavy boots, she felt more like a statue than a woman. She grunted as she bent over to rummage for her knitted cap. Sitting in a tent, even an insulated and heated one, would be a cold business. Then again, she might have Ted Meyers to warm up with...

A hunched shadow passed across her tent wall, backlit by the tepid sun. Jennifer jumped as something scratched at her tent flap. "Who is it?"

"Eliza Bartell," came the answer. "Can I come in?"

"Don't let the wind—uh, okay." Jennifer's reluctant invitation was cut short as a large, bundled-up figure shoved its way through the opening, knelt down and tied the flap behind her.

"Thanks," said a voice from the depths of modern outerwear. Jennifer watched in amusement as scarves were unwound, caps were pulled off, and a pair of gloves were removed, jammed into pockets. A reddened hand was offered her. "I think we met at breakfast the other day, but hello again."

Jennifer shook her hand briefly; it was cold. "I'm not sure..."

The last scarf was unwound, and a tumble of dark curls fell across her shoulders. Bright blue eyes, ruddy Slavic cheeks, chapped lips curved in a smile. "I'm really sorry to butt in like this, but I heard you messing about in here. I need a favor."

Jennifer blinked. *People are certainly direct in the Arctic,* she thought. "What, er, can I do for you?"

Eliza nodded towards the far wall. "I'm in the red tent, two rows over. My research partner is Debbie Warner. You know, the black-haired girl with the military haircut?"

Jennifer smiled, racking her memory. No luck.

"Well, it's like this." Eliza settled herself on the foot of Jennifer's sleeping bag, apparently for life. "You'll have noticed there aren't a lot of women up here. Mostly guys. And while I'm no prude, I don't like to sleep with strange men, even if there's no, you know, fooling around."

Jennifer felt her smile slip. *Nut job*, she thought. *One in every crowd.* "Um. I can see your point," she said. She noted that Eliza was between her and the door. Not good.

Eliza was clearly one of those oblivious people who never noticed the reactions they caused in others. "So I'm sharing tents with Debbie, and mostly that's okay 'cause our schedules are staggered. You know, when I'm up and working, she's sacked out." She stopped, with a bright look on her face that told Jennifer she was waiting for an answer.

"Ah. Yes, I see. But I'm not quite sure—"

"The trouble is, I'm coming off a twelve hour traverse out across the Von Braun Planitia. And I only had a cat nap before that. So I'm wasted. I crawl into my tent and Oh. My. God." She waved the air in front of her face. "I just about pass out. I don't know what that woman was eating, but it was toxic."

Jennifer narrowed her gaze. "You mean Debbie? Your tent mate?"

Eliza looked at her, wide eyed. "Of course. Like I said, usually one of us is working and the other is asleep. *No problemo.* But this time she was zonked, coming off a fourteen hour stretch in the lab, and as far as I can tell, eating ten pounds of beans beforehand."

The light began to dawn, so to speak. "Oh dear."

Eliza cocked an eyebrow. "Yeah. Oh dear. I'm telling you, it's as much as my life is worth to light a match within ten feet of that tent." She glanced around the tent, her gaze coming to rest on the empty space next to Jennifer's sleeping bag. "So. Since you're the only other girl in the tent city, and your tent mate is out, I was wondering if I could bunk here for a few hours, at least until the effects of those beans wear off."

Jennifer hesitated. She didn't know this woman, and they were far from civilization in a place with few or no cops. She ran through a quick list in her head; there were supplies here in her tent but nothing she couldn't take with her. She saw that the pink roll-around case lay open next to her bed. "Okay," she said, reaching for it. She zipped it shut. "I'm going out for a couple of hours."

"Oh, thanks," Eliza said. "Trust me, I'm going to be snoring in five minutes. Two minutes. I really appreciate this."

Jennifer pulled on her boots but left them unlaced, then pushed out of the door. She stuck a hand back in for the pink case. "Okay, then. I'll wake you when we get back."

"Thanks!" came a muffled reply. "I owe you one!"

Jennifer leaned in to catch the tent flap tie. She spotted a bit of white in the corner of the tent; some of the sample swabs had fallen out of her case. She thought about going back in for them, then shrugged. She already had the DNA tagged and logged into the database; the original sampling swabs were just trash now. She fastened the tent flap, picked up the handle of the rolling case, and strode away, stumbling a little over her laces.

She wondered what favor she could ask of Eliza Bartell in return.

Truelove Lowlands, Devon Island, Nunavut
75° 36′ 43.62″ N, 84° 02′ 27.65″ W

While Sophia filled the canteens at the river, Nick tried to raise Haughton Crater, without success. He frowned at the readout on the radio; how had the battery gotten so low so swiftly? *They must be old*, he thought. He squatted down to cook breakfast for his charge.

Amaruq was gone, but as he finished stirring hot water into the instant oatmeal, he heard a long, low howl a few yards away, on the other side of a rise. It was answered moments later from far away, a lilting howl that carried on the air for miles.

Nick smiled sadly to himself. Other girls her age had email; all Amaruq had was the cold comfort of an occasional exchange with animals. Animals that would have killed her as an outsider. *Caught between two worlds*, he thought.

165

He glanced at the tent, remembered waking with Sophia in his arms. He and she were from different worlds, too different to mesh. Like his sister, he could take only cold comfort from an occasional brief contact, and then move on. To linger, to bond with an outsider, was to risk disaster. And yet his father had done it. Nick and Amaruq's mother had been an outsider. But that, he remembered with a twist in his gut, had ended badly.

Sophia squatted beside him, reaching for the oatmeal. "I'll clean up, if you like," she said. "You can take down the tent."

"Deal." Nick sat beside her cross-legged, spooning hot cereal. Despite everything he told himself, he felt close to her. Comfortable with her. He understood her fear, her shame, her memories that haunted her. Memories haunted him, too.

Half an hour into the morning trek, Nick and Sophia left the Truelove Lowlands behind for good. The fog came and went, fickle and cold, as they walked up the banks of the narrowing Truelove River.

The sky darkened as it filled with low-lying clouds, and the temperature seemed to drop with every step. Behind him, Sophia tramped doggedly, calling a halt every now and then to collect a few drops of water or a lichen scraping off a rock. "Getting anything good?" he asked.

She shrugged. "Some spores, maybe even some thermophiles like *Fimicutes*. We still don't know why some bacteria thrive in Arctic cold and some don't."

"If you're finished," he said. "We should get on. We've got about five more hours ahead of us, depending on how many samples you get."

She hesitated. "Jennifer asked for lots of samples for her tests," she said. "But I guess I've got all I need of the water samples. I could use some rock and tundra samples."

Nick looked upstream, where the river disappeared into the mist. "The river takes a U-turn to the south right about here and then bends back to this course," he said. "This is where we planned to climb out anyway, and we can cut across the U to the other side and save some time."

"And look for Constable Fraser's missing guys," she said.

"I remember." She tucked her sample vials carefully back into her equipment pocket.

Amaruq, who had been loping ahead of them up the stream, now came trotting back. ::Lunch.::

"Not yet," Nick said to her, not thinking.

"Someday you'll have to tell me more about this...dog," she said. She lifted her pack onto her back. "She's very unusual."

"Unique," Nick said. Then he shut up. He strode to the bank, dug in a toe of his boot, and started up the gravel scree. It was steep and had a tendency to slide. He told himself he should have found a better spot to climb out, but his mind was on the woman and how she had felt in his arms. *Dammit*, he thought. *Focus. Do your job.*

In a few minutes he was standing on the upper plateau, gazing out across the barren highlands of Devon Island. He heard Sophia scrambling up the slope, heard her slide, and then recover. He fought the urge to go help her. *She was strong*, he told himself. *Small but strong, inside and out.* He pushed thoughts of her out of his head and looked at their course.

From here to the base of the ice cap was about seven kilometers by line of sight, although walking it would take half again that distance. The fog hung over the cold ground like a lost ghost, drifting here and there aimlessly. Overhead the clouds shrouded the sun so closely it was not even a white spot in the sky. Before him stretched a rocky plain strewn with boulders, rocks, gravel and shards; there was no vegetation, no trees, nothing to block the wind as it screamed down on him now out of the northwest.

He heard Sophia come to a stop behind him. "It really does look like a lunar desert."

"Yeah," he agreed. "Except for things like the air and the fog and the wind and the snow and the rain and—"

"Funny," she said wryly. "I get it. But you have to admit, it's a little...barren."

"Barren?" He put an expression of surprise on his face. "And you an ecologist? I am shocked, *shocked* to hear that there is no life here."

"*Casablanca?* Really? You're going to quote Claude Rains at me? Not fair." She hefted her pack. "Let's go. If I don't find some *cyanobacteria* colonies, I'll never be able to face Jen."

Nick stopped to retie a bootlace. Amaruq sat down next to him and scratched her head with a back paw. ::Tell her.::

Nick stared at Amaruq.

"About what?" he whispered.

::Me. Tom. Us.::

Nick was astonished. Tell Sophia about their secret? Break the seal of silence that had lain over his family for generations? Not likely. What was Amaruq thinking?

When they'd gone about five kilometers, Nick called a halt. "Lunch," he sang out.

Sophia slumped to the ground. "I am so lost."

"That's too bad," Nick said. "'Cause I was following you." When she looked up in alarm, he grinned. "Oh, you're too easy."

She smiled. "Such a comedian. You've probably been here a hundred times."

"Nope," he said. He unlatched the catch on his backpack line and let it slide to the ground. "I don't even know if anyone has ever been here before."

"So we are boldly going where no man has gone before?"

"Man, woman or dog. Do you want peanut butter or tuna for lunch?"

Nick propped his and Sophia's packs against one another to form a windbreak, and settled down next to her. They shared a companionable lunch of peanut butter, crackers, chocolate bars and cold water. This close, he could feel her thigh against his, warm and solid, and he took a quiet pleasure in it.

::Going shopping.:: Amaruq trotted off, nose to the ground, tail high. Nick caught a fleeting mental image of a plover nest full of downy fledglings, as she faded into the mist.

"Not to criticize your cooking," Sophia said. "But I am so craving a hamburger right now."

"Yeah, I heard about you California types," he said. At her look, he crooked an eyebrow. "Health nuts."

She laughed. "Says you. What's your comfort food?"

"Seal steak," he said. "Side of crisps, a couple of cold beers."

"Crisps? Oh, you mean chips."

"No, chips are what you call French fries."

"Are not. Chips are thin, crackly, loaded with fat. Fries are fat, soft, and loaded with fat."

"And you Yanks eat them with ketchup. Yuck."

She laughed. "And lots of salt."

"See? Health nuts."

"You really eat seal?"

He braced himself for a lecture. "Yeah. Out here, it's the most abundant meat aside from fish."

"I've never tried it," she said pensively. She licked peanut butter off her cracker. He watched her tongue. "Would they have any at the co-op back in Resolute Bay?"

"We have a cache full of frozen seal steaks at home," he said. "My brother and I—" He stopped, bit his lip, went on. "When you get back to Resolute Bay, I'd be happy to cook one for you." He thought swiftly; he couldn't bring her to his house, not at all. "I'll bring it to the co-op, grill some up for you. And your friend," he added as an afterthought.

She looked up at him, surprised. "Really? That's...that would be very nice of you."

He hadn't realized he'd been holding his breath. "No trouble at all. I'm afraid the wine list is a little short, though," he said. "You'll have to make do with tea."

"I can't return the invitation," she said. "Unless you let me buy you breakfast or something in Resolute Bay."

His heart thudded slow in his chest. How long was she going to stay in Resolute Bay? "It's a deal," he said. He'd just stopped himself from saying *date*. "Where to after this?" he asked. "I mean, when you get back?"

She waved a cracker. "Oh, it'll take me a year just to catalogue and analyze anything I bring back. Then there are tests, DNA sequencing, toxicity studies—"

A burst of furious barking. ::Run! Get away!:: Amaruq exploded out of the mist, ears flat, tail low, running hard.

Nick came to his feet in one move, reaching for the rifle.

169

"What?"

Amaruq lunged at Nick, butting his knee with her head. ::Dead man with no head. Like wolf. Go!::

Haughton Crater Research Project, Devon Island, Nunavut
75° 26′ 00″ N, 89° 51′ 00″ W

Ted Meyers kicked at the ATV's tire. "Damn."

"Is it out of gas?" Jennifer sat in the passenger seat, squeezed in with Ted's medical kit and her own backpack. She glanced back towards the research camp, fifty yards away. The motor pool was separated from the rest of the camp, to reduce the danger of fire and noise pollution. The camp was now nearly deserted, with so many people out searching.

"No, I checked the tank. I think there's something wrong with the ignition."

"Probably why it's still here. I thought it was a little too lucky for us to find an ATV still in camp." Jennifer fought down her worry. "Did you check with Verna about Sophia?"

"Verna says Nick is three hours overdue for a radio check."

Jennifer swallowed. She thought about the canine DNA she'd found in Nick's blood sample. She thought about a master gene sequence that could re-design a human body based on that canine DNA. She wondered if it could spontaneously kick in. And what would happen to her friend, if Nick suddenly became...something else? "Hurry!" she said.

"I don't know what the hell is wrong with this thing. And none of the mechanics are in camp." Ted kicked the tire again. "I can radio for someone to come back." He didn't sound like he believed it.

Jennifer climbed off the ATV. "Well, if I can build a SlimeMaster, maybe I can fix a busted electrical system. How do you get this engine cover off?"

Truelove Lowlands, Devon Island, Nunavut
75° 36′ 43.62″ N, 84° 02′ 27.65″ W

Sophia struggled to her feet. "What's wrong?"

"Amaruq says there's a dead man out there with no head," he said. "If you can, carry my pack so I can use the rifle if we need—" He saw her face and stopped dead.

"Amaruq *says?*" Sophia stared at him. "How—?"

Nick cursed himself for a foolish mistake, but there was no time to explain now. "Then stay here—" he began.

"Not a chance," she said.

"Dammit!" There was no help for it. "Keep behind me but stay alert. In this fog, we may not be able to see anything until it's on us."

Tendrils of gray fog curled and folded in cold breezes, revealing and then concealing the rocky ground. Amaruq trotted a few feet in front of Nick, arguing the entire way.

::Go back! This is a bad idea, Brother!::

"We have to check it out," Nick said in Inuktitut. It was one thing for poachers to take a wolf illegally, but if they were stupid, desperate, or vicious enough to attack another human being, then he and Sophia were in grave danger. He racked back the bolt of the Lee-Enfield to verify that he had a full clip loaded. He shut it and gripped the rifle, telling himself to relax. Out of the corner of his eye, he saw Sophia struggling to carry his backpack as well as hers.

They broke through the fog into a clear space. Amaruq stopped, her legs stiff, tail down and low signaling fear. Nick halted, unsure what he was seeing.

One man lay on his side on the ground, eyes open, staring at nothing. Next to him was a box and a set of scientific instruments Nick could not identify. Further away, Nick saw another body, a young Inuit man, sprawled face down. But what drew his gaze—and Sophia's, who drew up short next to him with a gasp—was the headless body sitting propped against a rock outcropping. Up to the neck, the body looked like an ordinary Arctic explorer—boots, snow pants, several layers of shirts under an open parka. But above the neck, there was nothing.

"There's not even any blood," he said.

Amaruq growled low in her throat, head lowered and

fangs exposed as she looked from corpse to corpse. ::Let's go, Nick!::

"Who could have done this?" Sophia said, her hand at her throat. "Why?"

"I don't know," Nick said. He noticed that they were both keeping their voices low. He looked around, but within fifteen feet everything disappeared into the all-pervasive cloud of fog. "I've never seen anything like this."

Sophia glanced at the closest body. "These two both have their...heads. Could they be alive?"

Nick stepped over to the man and stared down at him. He crouched down and reached out a hand to seek a pulse, but stopped at Amaruq's warning bark. Remembering the shock he'd gotten from the wolf, Nick frog-walked back one step and gingerly touched the man's head with the barrel of the rifle.

A silver stream poured from the man's eyes and ears, erupting from his mouth in a slow fountain. Before Nick could react, the silver stream had engulfed the lower end of the muzzle.

::Drop it!:: Amaruq leaped backwards.

The silver stream flowed up the rifle barrel, encasing it in a slimy silver film. Wisps of smoke spiraled up from it. Reluctant to abandon his weapon, held it by the wooden stock, but the silver tide climbed inexorably.

"Don't let it touch you!" Sophia cried, and tugged on his shoulder. "Nick!"

Nick dropped the rifle. Already the end of the muzzle was blurred, its hard steel outline softening. More silver poured out of the corpse and onto the rifle, now climbing all the way to the stock. Within mere seconds, all of the metal in the weapon was covered in silver—and was dissolving, leaving only the wooden parts.

"What the hell is that stuff?" Nick whispered.

"Some kind of...acid?" Sophia said.

Nick stood up and stepped in front of Sophia, herding her back a step. She went to her knees, unslung her pack and started rummaging in it. She came up with a sample vial.

"Put this down near the silver stuff," she said.

"Are you kidding?"

"Then I'll do it," she said, and stepped forward over the backpacks.

Nick grabbed her hand. "No way. Leave it alone."

"We need to know what it is. Maybe it's toxic."

"All the more reason to stay away from it."

She glared up at him. "And if it is, we're already exposed. Better to find out what it is so we can warn others. I'll be careful."

She jerked free of his hand and knelt. Uncapping the vial, she rolled it across the flat ground until it came to rest against the rifle barrel. Instantly, the silver liquid flowed into it and around it. But instead of dissolving it as it had the rifle, it withdrew, as if it were being sucked away, leaving only a drop or two inside.

"As if it didn't like plastic," Nick said.

"*Like?* It's not alive, Nick," Sophia said. "Hand me those gloves."

Nick handed her a pair of vinyl gloves and she pulled them on. She picked up a rock and nudged the plastic cap into place. Finally, using one rock to hold the vial down and another to push with, she snapped the cap into place. Already the silver material inside had darkened to an iron-gray blob. Tugging another empty vial out of her pocket, she gingerly repeated the collection process until she had two vials with samples of the silver.

"I have never seen anything like this before," she said. She picked up the vials.

"Don't!" he warned, but she stood, the vials cradled in her hand. Nick felt as tense as a drawn bowstring, eyes riveted on the vials. "Dammit, Sophia! It *melted* my rifle! What will it do to your hand?"

She turned to him, held out the samples. "It feels cool, actually. And it's not affecting the plastic at all." She examined the vial, musing aloud. "It melted metal, but not wood. It doesn't affect plastic. Both wood and plastic are organic, metal is not. Yet whatever this stuff is, it's been inside that corpse but it hasn't melted it, so probably—"

Amaruq barked frenziedly. ::Look out!::

Nick spun and saw a slow tide of silver emerging from the neck of the decapitated man. "Holy shit! Amaruq, get back!"

Nick grabbed Sophia and drew her close, backing away from the bodies. They watched in horror as the silver stream met up with the stream from the prone corpse. The two streams merged, bubbled, and then began to re-form.

"What the hell?"

In seconds, the blob had become a small silver cube, then a cone, then a perfect sphere the size of a baseball. Then the sphere dimpled, collapsed, and became a concave surface. It swiveled, back and forth. To Nick, it looked like a tiny antenna dish; with a shock he realized *it was hunting them.*

"Get behind the rock," he said. "Hurry!"

Catching Sophia's hand in his, he lunged for the rock outcropping. Sophia stumbled, recovered, and leaped over it with him. He caught her in both arms just as the dish's bowl-like face faced them. He felt a wash of warmth, as though sunlight had passed across his leg, and then they landed behind the rock outcropping. Nick saw a flash of white and Amaruq piled in next to him. They all ducked down as if sheltering from a cold wind. Nick curled himself around Sophia, shielding her with his body.

A sharp buzzing sound, the smell of ozone. Then all was quiet, save for the song of the wind.

"Stay down," Nick whispered. He peeked over the top of the rock. He was no more than a foot above the terminated neck of the headless corpse; he noted that, like the dead wolf, it had not started to decay at all. But that was all he could see—the corpses, the abandoned equipment.

He crouched back down again. "The silver stuff is all gone."

"Back inside the bodies?" Sophia's voice shook.

"I don't know. Stay here. I'm going to—"

Amaruq alerted, her mind filling Nick's with fear.

She caught his hand. "Be careful!"

He squeezed her hand in his. "I will."

Nick drew his boot knife, wondering even as he did so what good it could do him. Still, he held it tightly as he stepped around the outcropping. He stopped, sniffed, listened, then stepped forward again. By slow degrees, he circled the bodies. Finally, he straightened.

"I think you can come out," he said. "But don't touch anything."

Sophia and Amaruq came out from behind the rock on opposite sides. Amaruq backed away from the bodies and sat on her haunches. ::Bad, Brother. We should go now.::

"We need to call for help," Sophia said.

"No kidding. I don't see any silver on our packs, do you?"

"No."

"Okay, let me use those gloves."

Without a word, Sophia stripped off her vinyl gloves and handed them to Nick. He stuffed his hands into them, reached into his pack carefully. There was no sign of any foreign substance. He drew out the radio. "We'd better ask Fraser to come with ATVs," he said. "Or maybe even—" He stopped. The radio had not responded. He shook the radio, turned it on and off.

"Is the battery dead?"

"I'll use the batteries from the GPS receiver." But it, too, failed to respond. He glanced at Sophia. "You got any electronics on you?"

"A digital watch. A thermometer...oh." She sat back on her heels, concern on her face. "They're both dead, too."

Nick's expression was grim. "Funny coincidence, wouldn't you say?" They both looked at the discarded equipment packs beside the dead men.

Sophia knelt and checked her magnetometer and her PDA. Nick leaned over the body of the young Inuit. "He's got an iPod," Nick said. "It's dead. And his shotgun is melted like mine was."

She sat back on her heels. "Not one single electronic device in our packs is working."

Both of them turned to look at the spot where the silver dish had stood only moments before. "The dish?" Sophia asked. "Could it have done something to jam all the electronics? But that's..." She trailed off thoughtfully.

Amaruq growled, and Nick stood. She was facing away from the camp, towards the north, nose in the breeze. And this time the tone of her warning was clear.

::Nanuq!::

Nick no longer cared if Sophia heard him talking to his sister. "Are you sure?" He stared into the fog.

Amaruq yipped once. ::Two hundred meters north and coming. Tracking our scent.::

"Shit," Nick muttered.

Sophia stared from Nick to the wolf. "What now?"

Nick scowled. "We've lost our rifle, our radio and our navigation. And there's a polar bear tracking us."

Haughton Impact Crater, Devon Island, Nunavut
75° 22′ N, 89° 41′ W

Just below the rim of Haughton Crater, David Beringer halted, puffing from the effort of climbing. He couldn't take long; it was imperative he get back across the rim before his absence was discovered. He wiped sweat from his brow. He wasn't used to this kind of climbing.

He shivered. "Someone walking over my grave," he muttered to himself. He glanced around—of course he was alone. He'd chosen this spot carefully; he knew no one could see him from the Habitat. Still, he felt as if someone was watching him. He knew Skorjik and Fraser and the others were busy organizing the rescue parties; if anyone caught him out here, they'd assume he was looking for Leo and Glenn.

Unless they looked in his pack. Then it would all be over for him but the shouting.

He hefted the backpack, feeling a twinge along his lower back. No matter, he thought. From now on, he'd be able to buy any rock he wanted, even a lunar sample. Because the rocks on his back were the key to his future. The raw diamonds looked like dull grey and brown pebbles, but his geologist's eye had identified them immediately. He smiled to himself; it wasn't just that he was rich now—or would be as soon as he got back to California.

He'd confirmed his pet theory: meteor impacts were good candidates to find kimberlite pipes, the matrix that produced diamond deposits, ejected from their deep birthplaces by the force of the strike. Three years ago, he'd spotted the tell-tale yellow weathering of kimberlite in a survey photograph, but said nothing. Three hours ago, he'd found the spray of kimberlite, the dull brown pebbles buried in that matrix like chocolate chips in cookie dough. One of them was the size of his thumb, and when cut and polished, well, who knew what a diamond that size would bring? Enough to fund his lab and his research for the rest of a very pampered life.

Almost home. He leaned forward into the slope, grunting as his toes dug into the slippery gravel. Something flashed in the corner of his eye and he spun.

Was that something in the air? Beringer squinted.

Then laughed softly to himself. Of course. A Mylar balloon. Probably one of the search parties or research teams had used it to mark a location, and it had torn loose. He watched as it drifted closer. *Yes, of course,* he thought. *A balloon.*

Yet he felt uneasy as it approached. Could it be some kind of surveillance camera? He shifted his stance, facing the sphere so that his pack was hidden.

The balloon spun, hovered, lowered, came closer. It occurred to Beringer that it was moving against a brisk wind.

"What the hell is that?" he said. He shifted slightly to the left, easing away from the ball, but it followed quickly, keeping station on his right with no visible effort.

"Must be ball lightning or something," Beringer muttered. He stepped northwest, heading up towards the Habitat.

And then it was in front of him, and Beringer jerked to a stop, his breath coming short. Was this a kind of camera? Was Fraser checking up on him?

"What do you want?" Beringer yelled, feeling hot and close

now in the parka. A wash of light—blue, then red—whisked over the globe; faintly he smelled something burning.

Beringer turned away and clawed his way up the steep slope with feet and hands. Out of the corner of his eye, he saw the globe easily keeping pace with him. *What was it?*

He paused just below the rim. A few meters away, along the curve of the crater ridge, the Habitat loomed.

Beringer glanced over at the globe. His stomach clenched. It was definitely keeping steady in a fast breeze; there was no way it was a balloon. *Some kind of robot. Maybe a scaning device? Worse, a camera?* He glanced over at the Habitat. *Must belong to them.* He'd have known about it if it came in with the NASA project.

Beringer suddenly jumped up, reaching for the sphere. It moved easily upward, farther than he could reach. He fell heavily, slipped when a rock rolled under his foot.

"God dammit, what are you?" he muttered.

Beringer pulled a digital camera from his parka and held it up. The globe held steady as he snapped off a few shots. He'd show Skorjik the photos later, after the excitement over the missing men had died down. He could tell the boss he'd spotted the thing while looking for Leo and Glenn, and find out who owned it. Then he'd find out if it had pictures of him in a place he wasn't supposed to be. He stepped to the left, took another photograph.

The globe approached. Beringer backed away, tottering on the edge of the slope he'd just climbed. Sweat broke out on his brow. The globe stopped, lofted upward to the level of his head. This close, Beringer could see clouds swirling inside it, like smoke inside a brandy snifter.

Without warning, it changed from silver to red.

"What—?"

Snap!

A spark of lightning stabbed out at Beringer. It caught him full in the face, knocking him backward. He fell onto his back, but the heavy backpack full of diamonds forced him onto his side.

He gasped, gasped again—somehow he could not draw

breath. He wanted to claw at his throat, but his limbs did not answer. The globe hung motionless, until Beringer's struggles slowed and stopped. When he lay inert, eyes glassy and open, the globe descended. It passed over the length of his body, shining a blue light along his torso. In the globe, the swirling clouds briefly formed the images of Nick and Amaruq, then an image of Beringer's face.

Then the light died and the sphere lofted up and away. Behind it, the breeze ruffled the hair of the dead scientist, worried a loose strap on the backpack full of diamonds that lay beside him.

Truelove Lowlands, Devon Island, Nunavut
75° 36' 43.62" N, 84° 02' 27.65" W

Top speed of a polar bear was nearly twenty miles an hour, Nick thought. Top speed of a human was forty, but only if the human was Usain Bolt. And Sophia didn't look like she could run that fast.

Nick scrambled down the embankment above the river, then turned to give Sophia a hand. She scooted down, gravel rattling all the way down with her. She landed on her feet, turning to look back up the slope.

"Do you think it will follow us?"

"Depends." Nick saw Amaruq questing back and forth on the embankment above, nose in the air. "If he can, he'll scavenge the bodies."

Sophia paled. "Oh. Yes, of course."

Nick winced. "I'm sorry. They were friends of yours?"

She shook her head. "No, I didn't know them. It just seems...to be eaten by a bear..." She smiled, but it was wobbly. "I know, I'm a biologist, it's what animals do. But personally..." She shuddered.

Nick wanted to pull her into his arms, to comfort her, as small and scared as she was. Instead, he stuck his hands in his pockets. "See what you've got left."

A search turned up a bear banger with two cartridges, four

energy bars, some of Sophia's sample tubes and her statuette of Sedna. When Nick saw it, he felt something hot curl in his center. "You brought that?"

"I...I didn't want to lose it," she said, not looking at him.

It was valuable to her. Knowing that made him feel warm. He watched as she stuck it back in her pocket. "Too bad I didn't carve an aarnguaq," he said. At her look, he said. "A charm. I think you call them amulets. To help in hunting."

She glanced up at the top of the embankment, where Amaruq had stopped pacing and stood staring back the way they had come. "Do your people have any that ward off bears?"

"Yeah." Nick held up the bear-banger. "Ever used one of these?"

"No."

"It's basically a really big firecracker. I'll show you." He bent his head to hers, bringing the banger close. The bear deterrent looked like a shotgun shell stuck onto the end of a ball point pen. "Point this end. Punch this trigger. Make sure it lands between you and the bear. If it lands on the other side of the bear, it will run towards you and you'd better be fast."

"Or at least faster than you," she said. Again the shaky smile. "You take it," she said, thrusting the bear banger at him.

"I've got this," he said, reaching into his boot. The eight-inch blade of his hunting knife gleamed.

She said nothing, but her mouth made a grim line. They both knew the knife would be meaningless against a polar bear. Sophia looked into his eyes, then away, nodding.

She's scared, but trying not to show it, Nick thought. He couldn't help but admire that. Above them, Amaruq barked, turned, and bounded down the slope.

::*Nanuq* coming:: she said. Her eyes stared into Nick's. ::And I can *hear* him, Brother.::

Nick stared at her. "You can hear him?" he said in Inuktitut. He knew what she meant: that she could hear the bear's thoughts. Which meant that it was no ordinary bear. "He's... like us?"

::Not sure. Bear thoughts only. Coming fast.::

Sophia was looking from him to Amaruq with a puzzled expression on her face. "What?"

Nick turned and scanned the river valley. "That bear didn't stop for lunch," he said. The Truelove River had scoured its way through several layers of rock down to a ribbon canyon. There was barely a foot of gravel on either side of the rushing water. "We're going to get wet," Nick said.

Sophia stared up at the embankment, as if she expected the white bear to appear at any moment. "Can we outrun it?"

"Depends." Nick wished he'd brought two guns. He gauged the width of the river, the speed, the hidden rocks and rapids. "Our best spot is about thirty meters upstream. We can cross there."

Sophia nodded. "Yes, of course. Crossing water—"

"Won't help much," Nick said. "Bears can smell a seal a kilometer away. But it might confuse him a few minutes."

::Hurry!:: Amaruq danced in front of them, dashing upstream and then back repeatedly. ::Come on!::

Nick let Sophia lead the way, following Amaruq as he dropped back, scanning the rear. And he used more than ears and eyes; he strained, with that part of his mind that could "hear" his sister, for hints of an alien mind. His heart pounded. There had been rumors in the family, hints of stories that went far back before white men came, that said some branches of the family suffered from a *different* curse. Yet in all the generations of hunters in Nick's family, he'd never heard of anyone coming across a bear whose thoughts could be heard. This was a first.

Ahead of him, Sophia had stopped. Amaruq put a paw in the water, nose to the surface. "I think she wants us to cross here," Sophia said.

"Go slow," he said, raising his voice above the roar of the river. "Don't cross your feet. Shuffle if you have to, and watch for rocks under the water. They'll turn under your feet."

Sophia nodded and stepped into the stream. She gasped. "C-cold!"

"Yeah," Nick said. He braced himself and stepped in behind her, slightly downstream. If she slipped, he could catch her. The water was not just cold, it was deadly. *Barely above freezing*, Nick thought. "Don't slow down," he cautioned. "But don't get careless, either. You don't want to fall and get wet all over."

Unable to speak for her chattering teeth, Sophia nodded and continued forward. The water rushed past their ankles, then calves. The deeper into the stream they got, the more Nick worried. There could be holes, sudden drop-offs hidden under the surface. Or broken rocks sharp enough to cut through boot leather. The water rose and he found himself gasping from the cold, his body in shock. Sophia stumbled and he caught her elbow.

"Just a few more feet," he said.

Sophia took another step, stumbled again and nearly went down. Nick caught her, supporting her with both arms. Amaruq had reached the other side and now shook herself vigorously, throwing water all over. "Come on," Nick said. He took her weight in his arms. "Another step."

She took it, and the one after that, and in a few more they were splashing out of the river, chilled to the bone. Nick wished they had time to sit down, take off their boots and wring out their socks, but he knew better. Sophia hugged herself and stamped her feet to warm them. "N-now what?"

Nick stared back across the river. White fog drifted lower in the sky, blotting out the way they had come—but was that movement in the mist? Something large and white, tracking them? "Let's go," he said shortly. "And try not to make any noise." Even over the thunder of the river, he knew a polar bear could hear them.

Sophia caught his sleeve, pulled him down close to her face. "Where are we headed?"

Her eyes were large and full of fear, but he could see her determined mouth. She wasn't giving in to her fear. "Remember the hot spring I told you about?" When she nodded, he said, "I think it's about two kilometers south, above the river. We might be able to lose him there."

"L-lose him? H-how?"

"It stinks. Really, really bad," he said. "Nanuq might not like the smell. Or it might confuse him."

She blinked. "Sulfur. Of course." She turned, boots squelching, and set off up the narrow gravel beach between the river and the high bank beside it. Amaruq loped on ahead, tail up, nose down.

Nick lingered a moment, staring back into the mist creeping closer. Was that just a swirl of fog, an eddy born of breezes and sunlight? Even more important, was that a whisper of dark hunger, hovering at the edge of consciousness? His fingers itched for his rifle. If they were cornered, was there any weapon he could use? Against a hungry, nine hundred pound predator with claws and teeth as long as his hand—probably not. Not successfully, anyway. He turned and strode after Sophia.

Nick felt himself slipping into the hunter's mind, the combination of intense focus and heightened awareness of his surroundings that characterized every hunt with his father and brother. His eyes constantly checked the sky, the river, the wind; he cast a glance back over his shoulder every few strides, seeing the fog closing in behind them. He could neither see nor hear anything, yet he knew the bear was back there, as certainly as the sun was above the fog. He searched his memory of the few times he and Tom had run across bears. He had hunted *nanuq* before, but had never been hunted by one, alone and unarmed. What would be his best course if the bear caught them?

Suddenly his nose caught the stink of sulfur ahead. The spring was near. Amaruq, in the lead, stopped and looked back at him. Sophia halted while Nick caught up. To the right, a notch in the bank climbed steeply upward, cut by a trickle of yellow water no wider than his hand. Amaruq sneezed, shook her head, sneezed again.

::Stinks!::

"Have you seen the bear?" Sophia asked.

"Not a sign. Doesn't mean it's not there." He looked up at the steep climb. "Can you make it all right?"

"Yes."

"Go on ahead. I'll be a few minutes."

She looked scared. "You're not coming?"

Nick shook his head. "I'll be right behind. Something I want to do first, something that might scare him a bit. Go on. If he gets past me, remember the banger."

Amaruq circled impatiently. ::Go!::

Sophia started up. The angle was so acute she had to use hands and feet, as if climbing a ladder. Nick watched as she reached a ledge, pulled herself over, and disappeared. He looked down at his sister. "Stay with her."

::No. Stay with you.::

"Go on!" he said sternly. "She needs help, I don't. Make sure she gets to the spring."

::Want to stay.:: Amaruq's tail sank. She whined.

"No, Sis. I need you stay with her," Nick said. "Please."

After a moment, the wolf turned and began scrambling up the ravine.

When the others were gone, Nick stood peering back at the fog. Still no sign, yet now at the edges of his mind a faint whisper, an echo of an echo of an echo of some vast, dark hunger, of a relentless focus on food. He had felt something like it when Amaruq was hunting, but this was not Amaruq. Could it be an echo of Tom? But Tom was far away, and sick.

Nick dropped to one knee, hands in the water, searching. Arctic winters were the best knife makers in the world, breaking hard rock into sharp splinters every season. The cold numbed his hands, so he alternated left and right, allowing one to warm while the other felt around in the freezing water...ah, there. His hand closed carefully around a flake of stone and he drew it out of the water. It was perfect, a leaf-shaped flake of white-gray quartz, shattered by the sub-zero temperatures of the North. It was as long as his hand, blunt on one side.

Nick searched further and found a river-sculpted cobble the size of his fist. With one eye on the backtrail, he sat cross-legged on the thin strip of shore. Propping the quartz flake on his knee, he brought the cobble down on the blunt edge with

184

one sharp, calculated blow. It struck hard, snapping off the blunt surface to produce a gleaming, sharp edge.

Nick rose to his feet. He had a spear point. What he needed was a spear shaft. In these lands, where trees did not grow, the only available material was either driftwood or bone, and he had neither. But he had his knife, and a spear point, and his wits. Maybe that would be enough.

::*Hungry*::

Nick tensed. That was not Amaruq's "voice" in his head. From downstream, he could hear a distant chuffing sound—a bear, running. He was out of time.

A quick glance up the ravine showed no sign of the girl or Amaruq. He stepped across the sulfurous rivulet and walked upstream, keeping his attention on the fog behind him. *Draw him upstream, away from her. Once he crosses the sulfur, he'll lose her scent.* To one side, the river bank rose above his head in a steep, rocky cliff. On the other side, the river churned, milk white with icy meltwater and grit.

And then it was there, looming out of the mist like a white nightmare. Nick felt his heart lurch. *Nine hundred kilos at least*, he thought. And hungry. He could see its ribs. It had the frame of a much larger bear, one that should weigh twelve hundred kilos or more. *Maybe that will give me an edge*, he thought. *Maybe it will be weak.*

The bear had not yet sighted him; although polar bears had good eyesight, they relied primarily on scent to track prey. This one slowed as it approached the sulfur-bearing water. It stopped, snorted, shook its head just as Amaruq had. Nick held very still, only ten meters away.

::*Hunger. Confusion*::

Nick shuddered inwardly at the touch of its mind. He fought a surge of panic: could this creature possibly be...a distant relative? Inuit culture taught that all animals were related, but this was a closer link than he wanted. The bear's thoughts were sharp, non-verbal, focused on the scent. Nick felt impressions he could give no name to, but one thing was clear: the bear had found Sophia's scent under the sulfur mask.

"Damn," Nick muttered. She was alone, and unarmed. He could not let the bear follow her.

Even as the bear stepped forward, turning to climb the ravine, Nick moved.

"Hey! *Nanuq!*" he cried in Inuktitut. He waved his arms and stepped backward.

Instantly the bear swung to face him, black eyes burning in its white face. Nose in the air, it stepped forward, one paw splashing into the tiny stream. The bear recoiled, then stepped over the palm-wide trickle and advanced on Nick.

Nick stepped backwards, slowly, keeping his eyes on the bear. *Don't run don't run don't run,* he thought. He gripped the knife in one hand, the spear point in the other. The bear grunted, nose up, weaving his head back and forth.

Nick felt rock at his back. At this point, the river bank came right down into the water. On his left, the wall was a sheer cliff rising over his head. His only choice was to step to his right, into the rushing white water of the river. He eased slowly towards it, sinking one foot and then another into the water.

The bear took another step forward. Powerful muscles rippled under the hunched shoulders. On the faint breeze, Nick caught the smell of bear: rank, animal. Its tiny eyes followed him as he stepped into the water.

How deep was the water here? Nick knew some rivers carved holes in their beds, pools beloved of spawning char and trout. He shivered as the cold water climbed above his boots. Another step, slow and careful. Another.

The bear swung around and Nick knew it was thinking about the scent behind it, the smell of the woman and the wolf who had climbed the notch. Nick could sense the animal's hesitation, its desire to follow easy meat.

Nick yelled and kicked at the water. The bear's great head swung back to him but otherwise it didn't move. "Come on, Nanuq!" he yelled. "Look at me!" As he shouted, he stepped sideways again, and this time his boot slipped. He felt himself stumbling even as the great beast lumbered forward, charging.

Flying into a headwind, the silver sphere lofted over the top of the crater rim and hung motionless, two hundred feet north of the Habitat. Rain curtained the lower slopes, hiding the camp below, drumming against the exterior of the Habitat. The sphere drifted slowly towards the Habitat, dipping down and then over a scuff mark on the ground, a hand-sized patch of snow hiding in the shadow of a rock.

The diamond-shaped window of the Habitat glowed warm yellow, the only sign of life in the gray landscape. Above, lowering clouds threatened to turn the downfall from rain to sleet, to snow. The sphere approached the Habitat, rose into the air.

Inside the Habitat, the crew crowded around a table, deep in discussion. Bob Courtenay leaned over the men, while others scooted forward on crates and suitcases. If any of them had looked out of the window, he would have seen the silver moon-shape of the hovering object, would have perhaps seen the pulsing glow of its scanning light.

"They can't order us to search for those guys," one man said. "We're volunteers here, we don't answer to NASA."

"Hey, shut the door, man," one of the engineers said. His lower half was encased in a white "space suit" coverall, rolled down around his waist.

At the wall-mounted counter in the tiny kitchen, a sandy haired man scowled as he peeked into an empty carafe.

"How come we get the most sophisticated technology in the world out here in this wilderness, but we can't get decent coffee?" He shook the carafe, as though that would magically produce coffee where coffee was not.

No one glanced out of the window, no one saw the faint red blush across the silver surface come and go, no one saw it change to silver and then fade.

But more than one man felt a quick shudder of ice down his spine, a faint queasiness, an ache in shoulder and joint. No one said anything. This was the Arctic, this was man country. A passing draft of cold air was nothing. Or should be nothing.

Courtenay glanced at his watch and touched the young engineer on the shoulder. "We need to suit up and get going. I've got the list of teams here."

"But we're not trained for this!"

"Pretend you're on Mars, Bayless. Would you refuse a search and rescue mission on Mars?" Courtenay snapped. "Let's go."

Grumbling, Bayless shoved one arm into a sleeve of the fake space suit, then another.

Outside, the orb circled the Habitat, drifted down towards the bottom, sending its light scan under the structure.

From the sheeting rain, a bark, then a furious growl. A large dog crawled out of a crate next to the Habitat, tail down, ears flat in challenge. As the orb circled it, the dog turned to keep the ball in view.

A ripple crossed the gleaming surface of the orb, then another. The dog flattened herself belly-down, intimidated but not surrendering. A flash of white, and the dog yipped loudly and fell over. She twitched, then she was still, eyes fixed, dead.

For a moment, the sphere hung motionless, then drifted down. Hovering an inch from the surface of the carcass, it moved from one end to another. Its shape changed from round to dog to a tiny head of a wolf that looked like Amaruq, then re-formed into a solid globe. It centered itself over the motionless open jaws, dropped lower.

The outer door of the Habitat banged open, bounced against the wall, and flipped almost shut again, hitting a man wedging his way through the hatch.

Silent as thought, the orb zoomed upward fifteen feet.

"Damn this thing!" Bayless struggled with the undersized doorframe, trying to make sure the suit didn't hang up on a nail or something. "Shit, it's cold!"

The suit was windproof but uninsulated, and Bayless hadn't bothered to put on his thermals. So the cold bit through him like a knife made of ice. If he had glanced up he would have seen the globe sitting as motionless as the moon above the Habitat. Another man pushed through behind him.

Once free of the door, Bayless shook himself all over. The suit settled a bit, cold where it touched his skin. He caught sight of a shape on the ground.

"What the hell? Maisie?" Bayless knelt beside the dead dog. "Maisie? Dog? What happened?" Bayless poked at the dog gingerly, turned her over. There were no marks on her.

The second man bent over her, his nose going red in the chill wind. "Poor girl. Guess it was too cold for her after all."

Ignoring the 20-minute-delay protocol, Bayless keyed his transceiver through the mic key on his wrist pad. "Guys, Maisie's out here dead."

A jumble of noise, then Courtenay: "Say again?"

"Reporting a carcass just outside the hatch. It's Maisie. I don't see any marks on her. Probably froze to death."

"After three trips up here? She's used to this climate." Courtenay's voice shook a little. "We'll be out in a minute."

"Ten-four. Out."

As he bent over the dog again, the orb above him revolved, slowed, and stopped.

Bayless shuddered, stood, looked around. He looked east, out over the crater, where veils of grey rain swept along the vast distant bowl. North, into the very teeth of the wind, then west, where the sun lay on the rim of the world, a white spot burning behind the mist of clouds. *Something, something out there, something watching,* he thought. His whole skin itched, his head ached.

"Probably catching something from the last SOB to use this freakin' suit," he mumbled to himself.

The second man patted the dead dog affectionately, sadly.

Above them, the hovering orb turned a dead black matte that sucked in every ray of light, and then disappeared. In its place was a void in the air where rain hit as if striking an invisible balloon.

The void moved off silently, into the fierce north wind, slanting down and unseen away from the Habitat, heading for the research camp below.

Sophia pelted up the rocky slope; the thread of water had shrunk to a dribble that steamed as it fell over pebbles. Grey crusts of hardened mineral deposits coated the stream bed. Sophia's nose wrinkled at the smell.

"Sulfur for sure," she muttered. Behind her, the voice of the river had hushed to a distant murmur. She strained to hear Nick behind her, but heard nothing. In a moment, she had climbed up and over the rim of a shallow bowl and stopped, coughing in the mineral stink. Amaruq scrambled past her, tail stiff.

Sophia looked around and her stomach sank. The cul-de-sac sat like a cup in the side of the cliff. Here, the dolomite cap lay exposed above a seam of sandstone, and where the two met, steaming water bubbled from the earth. Collecting in a trio of pools which dropped from one level to another, they showed rims of acid yellow and gray. In the crusts she saw the blue tinge of thermoacidophiles, bacteria that lived in sulfuric hot springs. She recognized *Hydrogenobaculum* and *Aquifica-ceae* species. If she lived, Sophia thought, she would definitely have to get some samples.

Where was Nick? He should have been right behind her. She glanced at the dog, and found that she was standing with her tail down, hackles raised, staring back down the slope. The dog circled, looking up at her, dashing back the way they had come and then coming back to her. Clearly, the animal was torn between staying with her and rejoining her master.

"Go ahead," she said. The dog shot off the way they had come, rattling pebbles as she dashed back down the slope.

Sophia moved closer to the spring and held her hands over the steam rising from it. Fear curled in the pit of her stomach.

Where was Nick? Should she go back to him?

Suddenly, she heard the roar of an angry bear.

Nick struggled to stay upright, and felt an icy calm settle over him as the bear charged. He thought *it's been a good life* and hoped the bear wouldn't go after Sophia after it had killed him. He clutched the knife in his right hand, prepared to get in at least one blow before the bear killed him.

"Goodbye, Sis," he murmured to himself, knowing she could not hear him. And then the bear was on him in a spray of freezing water, its roar filling his head, and Nick braced for the impact—

The bear fell. An icy wave swamped Nick. He choked, got his feet under him, and got his head clear of the water. The great animal struggled to its feet. He knew immediately what had happened: the bear had stepped into one of the holes gouged in the riverbed by the furious water. It was getting to its feet now, shaking its head. It was so close Nick could have reached out and touched its head.

If I can get it in the eye..., Nick thought.

A white ball of fury leaped off the cliff over Nick's head, and slammed into the bear from above. Amaruq landed on the bear's hindquarters and sank her fangs in. With a roar of outrage, the bear spun, swinging a huge paw. Holding on with her teeth, Amaruq snarled a feral challenge. When the bear turned, Amaruq leaped away, slicing a long red gash in the bear's flank.

"Amaruq!" He sprang forward, his knife raised high. But the furious tangle of claws and fangs in front of him made it impossible for him to get a clear shot.

Amaruq snarled, she howled at the bear. Miraculously, she managed to duck and weave and somersault fast enough that the bear's swift strikes did not connect. Each time the bear lunged at her, she retreated, drawing the bear away from Nick. The bear took a step, then another, snarling. One paw came down on a sharp stone and the bear staggered. Amaruq darted in and slashed her fangs across the bear's muzzle.

::*Kill!*:: Nick heard the bear's wordless emotions in his head. An ear-shattering roar burst from the animal, and it charged. Amaruq dodged, landing in the water with a splash. Nick saw her paddling to stay afloat.

"Hang on, Amaruq!" he yelled. Taking aim, he threw the spear point at the bear's rear. It smacked into the red gash Amaruq had already carved in his flank. The bear swung to face Nick, snarling. Blood ran down on either side of its ripped muzzle. Nick saw its teeth, as long as his fingers, as it bellowed a challenge. Its shoulders hunched for a charge.

White smoke shot from the top of the cliff to the riverbank.

BANG! The banger went off right below the bear's muzzle, with an explosion loud enough to make Nick's head ring. Caught in the confines of the steep river valley, the echoes boomed until it sounded as if a cannon had gone off. The bear reared, roaring, spun and dropped to all fours. It loped downstream, splashing heedlessly through the icy water, and disappeared into the mist.

Truelove Lowlands, Devon Island, Nunavut
75° 36′ 43.62″ N, 84° 02′ 27.65″ W

Sophia heard pebbles rattling and knew someone or something was climbing the slope. Nick's head appeared in the gap, looking around for her.

"Up here!"

He scrambled up to the ledge above the river. His face was pinched, anxious as he reached the spring. "Are you all right?"

"Yes, I'm fi—"

He grabbed her, hauling her against his chest. She was smothered in a tight embrace, her face pressed into him. She felt him trembling as she let her arms slowly circle his waist.

"That was...very brave," he said, his voice rumbling in his chest. "And very stupid. You could have been hurt."

"He was below me. I had a good shot. He was going to—"

Nick's mouth devoured hers, full of urgency and demand and fear and possession. Sophia felt her cheeks go hot, then the wave of heat flowed all over her and she was kissing him back, tasting him.

He released her mouth, only to pull her against him again.

"This is such a cliché," Sophia gasped.

"I know," he gasped, and kissed her again, harder.

There was nothing in the world now but the two of them, and the realization of how close they had come to losing one another, and the realization of what that meant. He tasted of salt; his mouth was warm and the heat that rose in her said yes. He started to pull away but she pressed him, opening her mouth under his, sharing a promise.

She felt his reaction: surprise and delight and caution, and something deeper and richer than that, hovering. She pulled him closer, and the kiss deepened to something softer, slower, more intimate. Then he stepped back, letting her go, and she saw the distance come back into his face, the knowledge that they were from different worlds.

Sophia didn't want that distance. The wind moaned about them and the grey sky loomed over them. It felt as if they were the only people in the world.

"If that bear had killed us, no one would have ever known what happened," she said. "No one would have even found our bones." Her throat felt tight; it was hard to speak. "Nick..." She swallowed painfully. "I...I'm glad you were with me. If I have to die out here, I'm glad it's with you."

"We didn't die," he said reasonably. "Sophia, I ..."

Then there was a yip beside them and they sprang apart like guilty teenagers. Sophia looked down.

Amaruq, bloody, tail wagging, sat at their feet.

Haughton Crater Research Project, Devon Island, Nunavut
75° 26′ 00″ N, 89° 51′ 00″ W

When the orb came to the generators chugging away near the massif, it stopped. Bobbing up and down, it pulsed light over the generator, which sputtered. The sphere floated away, following the electrical cables that snaked across the ground;

193

as it moved off the generators recovered, hummed again.

Rain hissed around it as the invisible ball glided along a foot above the cables. When the cables branched it hovered a moment, then chose one and followed it, up over a rise, down another, around a rock. It turned silver again, like a glass globe hanging in mid-air. Tt changed shape briefly from dog to wolf to bird; for one fleeting moment Leo's face, mouth agape, played across its surface. Then it returned to invisibility mode and moved through the rain.

The first thing it came to was the tent city. Slowly it circled the nearest dome, a faded green tent now zipped tight. Snoring noises. A gleam of light, then the sphere moved on. The next tent emitted fainter sounds—music. The sphere stopped, pulsed slowly in various shades of blue, then moved on. One by one, it examined every tent. Most of them were deserted.

Near the edge of the tent city, the globe came to Jennifer and Sophia's tent. Elaine Bartell's rhythmic snores could be heard outside the tent. The sphere circled the tent as usual; when it came to a corner far from the tent flap, it paused. The glowed silver as it descended almost all the way to the ground. There, where Amaruq had urinated, it shone a focused blue beam onto the ground, all around it. An image of Amaruq formed in the swirling interior.

A red beam of light shot from the globe's underside. A smell of burnt plastic, and one corner of the tent burned away. The snores were louder now. Just inside the hole, several cotton swabs stained with blood lay discarded in the corner. The blue light played over them. The inner surface of the globe swirled, and images passed across it: Nick, his rifle, his bootprint, as the orb at last identified its quarry.

Instantly, the globe turned fiery red. It shot straight up, then arced over the tent until it hovered dead center above it. Against the overcast, it hung like a firebrand, a torch, for one brief moment. Then it flared, and Elaine Bartell's snores cut off in mid-breath. The nylon fabric flared into bright flame.

The globe hovered a moment. There was no sound, no outcry from the surrounding tents. The globe's fiery color faded to matte black, then faded out altogether until it was once more invisible. It moved slowly off towards the main camp and headquarters.

Behind it, the fire built, and the wind picked up flaming sparks. They swirled in a manic dance, landing on tents, backpacks, a can of stove oil. The wind eddied, fanning the flames, sending a shower of sparks back towards the canvas shelters of the Haughton Crater Research Project camp.

Truelove Lowlands, Devon Island, Nunavut
75° 38′ 13.47″ N, 83° 49′ 21.46″ W

"Amaruq!" Nick dropped to his knees and grabbed Amaruq. He buried his face in her neck, almost sick with relief. She whined and licked his ear, tail thumping.

::I'm fine, Brother. You?::

He sat on his heels, holding her head between his hands. He touched his forehead to hers. "I was so afraid for you."

::I kicked that bear's butt.:: In physical contact, Nick heard her voice in his head clearly.

"Damn right you did," he muttered. "Are you hurt?" He ran his hands over her, feeling for broken bones. When he touched her right shoulder, she yelped and sprang away. "Sorry! Ooh. Yeah, looks like *nanuq* landed at least one punch. Careful, now. Careful." Talking in a soothing voice, he checked Amaruq for more injuries. She had a couple of superficial lacerations and some bruised ribs. Otherwise she was unharmed.

"You'll be limping a while, but I don't think that shoulder's broken." He hugged her again, gently. "Thank you," he whispered.

::You kissed her.:: Amaruq's voice in his head was a mix of curiosity, laughter and self-satisfaction.

Yes, he had, Nick thought. He felt his face heating up. *What had that been all about? What was he going to say to her?*

He found Sophia at the edge of the cul-de-sac, peering down over the ledge where the water trickled over the edge. She had pulled her hood up and was hugging herself.

"Hey," he said, coming to a halt.

She didn't look at him. "Is your…dog all right?"

"Uh. Yeah. Hurt her shoulder some."

She turned to look at the dog, lapping water at the base of the melting ice. "She saved our lives. When we get back, I'm buying her a steak."

Nick smiled. "Okay. But she prefers pepperoni pizza."

Her eyes flicked up to meet his, then away. "What now?" He wasn't sure but what that question covered more than one topic.

He took in a long breath, looking at the lowering sky. It had darkened in the last few minutes, with fat clouds coming together to roof them in. The wind on his cheek carried the wet smell of rain. "We could try going back for our stuff."

She shook her head violently. "No! The bear—"

::No!:: Amaruq barked in his head.

"Yeah, probably not a good idea" he agreed. "Amaruq chased the bear downstream, so we go upstream."

Her eyes met his now, wide with surprise. "Upstream? But aren't we going back to camp? We have to! All my samples are gone, our equipment…"

"I know. And yeah, we're going back. We'll just have to go back a different way." He stared off into the distance, recalling the map in his head. "I've never hunted this close to the ice cap, but from what I remember from the map, there's a high ridge to the west of the river about two kilometers upstream. We can climb the ridge, turn north again, hike over dry land to the Crater. It's actually faster going back that way, since we won't have to take samples."

"You're sure?" She was hugging herself again. Her voice still held a tremor.

Knowing he was probably making a mistake, Nick nevertheless slid his arm along her shoulder and turned her into his embrace. "We'll be all right," he said.

She went very still, and then he felt her relax against him and he felt warm inside. "We don't have a map. We don't even have a compass."

"Remember what I told you about the musk oxen?"

She nodded; he felt it against his chest.

"There's musk oxen on the other side of the ridge. They'll point us north, and we'll angle off to the left." He put more confidence into his voice than he felt. No point panicking her.

She laughed shortly. "What the hell. We're on an island," she said. "How lost can we get?"

He should let go. He should. Nick didn't want to. He just wanted to stand here awhile, holding her, sheltering her from the wind, smelling her hair (shampoo with undertones of sulfur) and feeling the rise and fall of her breathing.

But she was right. They had no shelter, no food, nothing. Even in high summer, that could mean death in the high Arctic. Nick pulled her hood up around her face, letting his hands rest a moment on either side of her head.

He struggled for words, but none came. He wasn't used to dealing with emotions, not when the day was always filled with questions of eating and hunting and shelter and survival. But this moment felt as important to him, maybe more important, than any other in his life. And he could find nothing to say. Or too much to say.

Amaruq barked. She had climbed the dolomite ridge above them, turned back to wait for him. Her wagging tail showed her impatience.

::Come on!::

"We'd better go," Sophia said.

He let her go and stepped back. "On up the ridge," he said. "No more than an hour's walk, then over the ridge to the plateau. It's all downhill to the crater from there."

She nodded without speaking and set out.

Nick lingered behind, sniffing the wind, watching her walk away. He felt odd, out of sorts.

A memory came to him—firelight, his father's hands patiently showing him the small parts of the rifle, laid out on a tanned hide, sorting them. His father showing him how they fit together. Laughter from Tom when he put them together backwards, a jigsaw puzzle of iron and fire that came out wrong.

He felt like that now, as if some parts of him had been left out, or put together wrong.

The wind shifted, bringing an acrid scent that came and went quickly. He swung into the wind, squinting along their back trail. No bear, no. Something...Nick realized his hand was clutching around an invisible rifle stock. He felt exposed up here, naked in the wind against the sky. Yet he could see nothing, smell nothing following them. *She's got me off balanced, confused,* he thought. He turned his back on the Truelove River valley and trudged upwards.

They hiked upward along the western bank of the river, and they were now several dozen meters higher than the hot spring. The ridge was only twenty meters or so above them, and the wind blasting over it from the northwest dropped its load of rain on them now in an icy spray. Tumbled rocks and boulders made the slope into an obstacle course of rockslides and breakdown. The clouds had darkened to a slate gray, giving the day a dark overcast. He caught up with Sophia just as she topped the ridge, and stopped beside her as she halted with a cry of disappointment.

Below them, instead of the empty plain he expected, a lake stretched shining and implacable to the horizon.

Haughton Crater

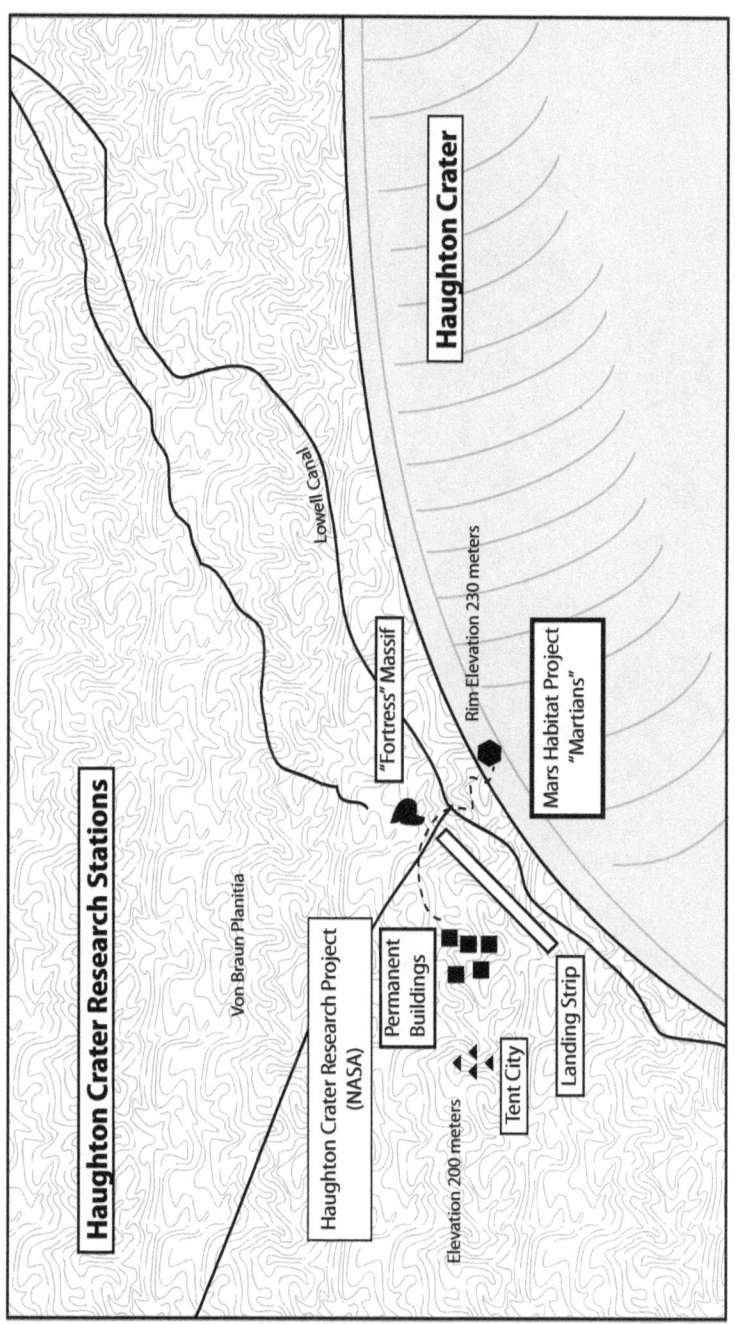

Haughton Crater

Haughton Crater

Rim Elevation 230 meters

Lowell Canal

"Fortress" Massif

Mars Habitat Project "Martians"

Haughton Crater Research Stations

Von Braun Planitia

Haughton Crater Research Project (NASA)

Permanent Buildings

Tent City

Landing Strip

Elevation 200 meters

V - UNDER SIEGE

Jennifer bent over the engine of the ATV, a voltmeter in one hand. "I think the battery's not being charged," she said.

"Would it be faster to replace the battery or to fix the charging system?" Ted asked.

"Maybe both," Jennifer said. "There's corrosion on these terminals, which could mean—" A hot ember landed on her hand. "Ow!" Snatching her hand back, she glanced upward. Sparks swirled overhead against the gray sky. "What?"

Ted spun around and looked back toward the camp. "Oh, my God!"

Flames roared twenty feet in the air above half the tents in camp, and the other half were already smoldering. Even as they watched, small figures ran to and fro with fire extinguishers and buckets. Distant shouts of "Fire!" reached them.

"What the hell?" Jennifer dropped the voltmeter. "Oh, no! The lab tent!" She dashed off towards it.

"Wait!" Ted called, right behind her. "It's too late!"

Years of work. Her only working prototype. Her samples. Jennifer ran to the burning tent as if her child were inside it.

The roof was afire, but the walls had not yet caught. Jennifer burst into the tent, arms above her head. Inside it was as hot as an oven, and smoke swirled in dark patterns throughout. She looked around for a fire extinguisher. She found it mounted on a central pole of the tent. She pulled it down, jerked the pin out of the safety lock, and pointed it overhead. A faint squirt of white mist came from the nozzle, not enough to squelch a cigar.

"Jennifer!" Ted thrust his way into the tent.

"Dammit!" she cried. The roof was sagging, raining embers into the tent. She glanced around at the lab equipment, and noted with extreme clarity the presence of half a dozen flammable compounds. It was hopeless, she realized. Slamming her laptop shut, she tucked it under one arm. How to get the SlimeMaster out? she wondered.

"We have to get out!" Ted grabbed her arm.

Jennifer pulled away and shoved her laptop at him. "Take it! I have to get the SlimeMaster!"

"No time! The whole camp is on fire!" He lunged at her, his face desperate.

But she dodged his grasp and flung both arms around the bulky analyzer. "There's no time! Leave it!"

"No!" she blazed at him. "I'm not leaving without it."

With a *pop* a support gave way, and the roof between them and the door collapsed. Ted ducked, shielding himself from the cascade of sparks with one upraised arm. "Jennifer! Please!"

"The cables!"

Cursing, he reached past her, yanking randomly at the power cords, comm cables, and assorted wires. Jennifer staggered backwards with the analyzer in her arms as the power cord pulled free of its socket. "Let's go!"

But where would they go? The door was a rectangle of flame. Ted darted past her, sweeping glassware off the tables to smash on the floor. Heat scorched Jennifer, swirling smoke choked her as she stumbled after him. "Where are you going?"

He turned, a dissecting scalpel in his hand. In the firelight it winked gold along a wicked edge. His eyes shone at her. "Stay low, and follow me!"

Ted pushed aside benches and makeshift tables as he forced a way to the back of the tent. Above them, the roof shimmered, long strips tearing loose to dangle down like flaming party decorations. Jennifer felt the fire scorching her back, heard glassware breaking—from heat or impact, she could not tell. Her eyes streamed with tears, and the smoke was dense and thick now, but she followed Ted's red parka through the darkness.

A ripping sound, the sound of Ted cursing, more ripping. A line of light appeared before her, then Ted's form struggling to force it wider. He hacked and tore at the rip-resistant fabric with the scalpel, slicing it along the rear seam. She heard shouting again, heard the hiss of water on flame, and then Ted turned to her, beckoning. "Come on!"

She let him tug her into the opening, and then realized his arms were empty. "The laptop!"

"Damn the laptop! Come on!"

He was right, she thought. *It was only a computer.*

Only her life work.

She shoved the SlimeMaster into Ted's arms. "Hold this!" And before he could reply, she ducked back into the burning tent.

An inferno of heat and smoke; she could hardly breathe and her eyes were streaming so badly she could hardly see. *Where was it?*

"Jennifer!" Ted called. She ignored him. *Where was it?* He'd had it when...there it was. Lying on the floor, the bright white casing shone. She scooped it up and darted back out of the opening Ted had cut, straight into his arms.

"Jennifer! What the hell were you thinking?" he shouted into her hair. The laptop made a hard rectangle between them. He stepped back, holding her upper arms. "Don't you ever do anything that stupid again!"

"Doc!" a cry came from their left. "Hey, Doc! We need you! There's a guy hurt over here!"

Ted looked over, nodded, then looked back at Jennifer. "Damn," he said softly. Then he turned, jogging towards a knot of people huddled around a writhing form on the ground.

Jennifer stood clutching the laptop, the SlimeMaster at her feet. Around her, every building and tent in the camp was on fire. Shouting crews with fire extinguishers fought a losing battle against fire and wind and dry air. Perversely, the rain-heavy clouds overhead held onto their moisture; no rain fell to help the firefighters. Smoke drifted, fog swirled.

She heard shouting, turned, and narrowly missed being run down by an ATV. It screeched to a stop, and Will Fraser leaped off, running towards a burning tent. His driver straddled the machine, staring around at the burning tents. He looked at Jennifer.

"What happened?"

She had no answer for him.

❄

Returning to the giant massif above the airstrip, the orb hovered above a forest of masts, antennae, dishes. It pulsed slowly through silver and red and blue. The smoke pouring from the burned camp wreathed around it, but had no effect. The orb dipped, circling the array. Briefly it followed the heavy cable emerging from the array, down the side of the massif to the floor of the plain. Then it zoomed straight up, zipped over to the masts, and hung motionless for a moment.

The orb turned red, and fire-bolts slammed into the satellite dish. It buckled, sliding off its foundation, then toppling over the side of the massif to crash to the ground below. The orb continued firing, first at the masts then at the finer antennae, until nothing was left but a twisted mass of half-burned rods and wires.

Hovering inches above the surface of the rock, the orb changed briefly, shaping itself into a wolf, then the image of Leo West's head, then Nick's face. Finally it smoothed itself into a chromed ball again, lifted itself into the air, and floated away, leaving the only transmitter on Devon Island in ruins.

Haughton Crater Research Project, Devon Island, Nunavut
75° 26′ 00″ N, 89° 51′ 00″ W

The smoke stank of burned plastic and gasoline, swirling black and thick around the huddled group. Grimed, exhausted faces sat in a ring around a burning pile of wreckage. Several of them sported bandages; some had only light clothing and shivered in the biting wind.

Martin Skorjik was the only man standing; from somewhere he had rescued a clipboard and was jotting on it. His hair was singed short and a red scorch mark stood out on one cheek. He looked up as Will Fraser stalked up, his face black with soot. "Any more?"

Fraser shook his head. Someone held out a coffee mug with water and he drank it down in three gulps. "No more survivors."

Skorjik's mouth made a grim line. "Five dead then. God." His face looked bleak. He looked around. "Anyone not accounted for?"

"No one can find Eliza Bartell," a bearded man with a German accent said. "And Dr. Beringer is missing."

"Of course we haven't heard back from the search teams in the field. Thank God they weren't here." Fraser held out the mug for more water.

A sputtering roar heralded the arrival of two men in the fake spacesuits of the Habitat. The ATVs rolled to a stop and one man climbed off. Behind him an ominously quiet bundle was strapped to the carrying platform.

Bob Courtenay walked up, his expression sober.

"Sorry to tell you this, Skorjik," he said. He gestured at the ATV. "We found David Beringer's body on the rim, about fifty meters down on the other side. One of our guys spotted it."

Skorjik stared. "David? What was he doing on the Rim? Did he fall?"

Courtenay's face got a closed look and he turned to Fraser. "Ah, actually, Constable, I think you need to examine his pack." He shut his jaw and shook his head. "I won't say any more. Except to say that no, he didn't fall."

"I'll take a look. Have your man take the body over to where Dr. Meyers is working," Fraser said. He met Courtenay's look, and nodded curtly.

"I don't understand this," Skorjik said, looking from one to another.

Courtenay sighed. "Let's focus on your people right now, Martin. We've got your wounded up at the Hab, in the crew quarters. I've got two guys filling a ten gallon tank at the river, so we can get you some water in an hour or so. What else can we do?"

Skorjik rubbed a burned patch of skin on the back of his hand. "I guess we need to figure out a way to get these people off the island."

"Do we have communications?" Fraser asked.

Skorjik shook his head. "The fire took out the comms

tent. And Verna—" He stopped, choking up. They'd found her body in the burned remains of the tent, her hand clutching the transmitter.

"I heard her," one man said, his teeth chattering with cold. "She was s-sending an SOS. She w-wouldn't come out when I yelled at her—"

"If she sent it, and someone heard it, then we'll be seeing search-and-rescue Rangers pretty soon," Fraser said. "Our own field teams should have heard it, at least."

Skorjik shook his head. "We can't raise the other end of the camp, let alone the other half of this island."

"What the hell happened?" one man demanded. He was a tall black man wearing a pair of glasses with one lens cracked right across. "Was this an accident? Some sort of terrorist attack?"

"Attack?" another voice asked.

"First two men go missing, then something about a dead wolf and poachers." The black man scowled at Fraser. "Now the whole place burns down around us. This is not what I signed on for."

"Verna didn't sign on for it, either," Skorjik said. He turned to Fraser. "Constable, what do you suggest we do?"

Fraser rubbed a hand over his face; it came away black with soot. "We've got injured people, and no place to get out of the weather. For now, the only shelter around here is the Mars Habitat."

Courtenay looked surprised. "Of course. We're at your disposal," he said. "But we are already pretty crowded up there. I don't know how many we can fit in."

"We'll do what we can," Fraser said. He looked sternly at Courtenay. "And I'm sorry, Doctor, but you'll have to abandon your 'protocols' for now. We can't have twenty-minute artificial delays in communications."

Courtenay drew himself up, looking as dignified as his round figure would permit. "Naturally. Er, our cook for the day is making stew. He can bring it down, or we can bring everyone up to the Hab..."

Fraser nodded. "We'll work out the details. For now, I want everyone to gather whatever you can that can be used for sleeping, eating or wearing. We're going to stuff that Habitat like a tuna can."

Jennifer watched the Habitat scientists lay the wrapped body of David Beringer at the end of a row of bodies. They climbed on their ATV, nodded somberly at her, and drove away.

"I'm glad Sophia wasn't here," Jennifer said. She and Ted had spent hours working on burn victims. Now she poured water over her hands, rinsing off as much blood as she could. Beside her, Ted lay flat on the ground, one arm over his eyes.

"We're lucky a lot of people were out looking for Leo and Glenn," he said.

Jennifer thought of Sophia, of the fire that had scarred her body and her soul. *This would have driven her mad,* Jennifer thought.

"I could use a beer," Ted said.

"Me, too. But all we have is water."

"That works." He held out a hand, eyes still closed, and she put the canteen into it.

She shook water off her hands. "What now?"

He sat up to drink. He glanced over at the body on the ground, wrapped in a half-burned parka. "I don't know. I've never had to deal with a death up here." Exhausted, he rested his elbows on his knees and covered his face. "We lost so many."

"You saved two," she said, and laid a hand on his shoulder. He said nothing, but laid a hand on hers.

The scuffle of boots on gravel, and Fraser walked up. "Doc?"

Ted rose to his feet, moving slowly. "Someone else hurt?"

"No, thank God. And thank you, for the work you did." Fraser held out a hand.

Ted shook it slowly. "Didn't do much. Wasn't much I could do."

"Still, it made a difference. We're all grateful to you. I'm afraid now I have to ask you to do a little more."

"Whatever I can do."

Fraser looked over at the body on the ground, and the one beyond it. And the one beyond that. "For legal reasons, we need to bag their personal effects. And I'm sorry if this seems disrespectful, but we need to write their names on their foreheads, so there's no problem identifying them later. I'll need a witness while I do this; will you help me?"

"Sure. But what do we do with the bodies? We can't just leave them here."

Fraser shrugged. "Nothing we can do now. In this climate, they'll mummify before they rot, and law enforcement will be here well before then. All we can do is guard them from scavengers until they can be flown out."

"Right. I'll get you those effects."

"After that, we're all moving up to the Hab," Fraser said. "You eat and get some sleep." He walked toward the line of silent bodies.

Jennifer laid a hand on Ted's arm. "You're tired. Sit. I'll do this."

"But—"

"Don't argue," she said. "You've done what you can, now I'll do what I can."

She turned, but he caught her hand. "You've done a lot. Thanks."

Jennifer shrugged. "I brought water and handed you things. Big deal. But this, I can do. Sit down."

Fraser looked up as she approached, pulling a notebook and pen out of a pocket. "I'm sorry I have to ask you to do this," he said. "The law requires two witnesses to identify the bodies."

"I'm okay. My hands are already dirty, so I'll go through the pockets and you can take the notes."

"If you want." Fraser's look was sympathetic.

She forced herself not to look at their faces. It was important not to look at their faces, because the bleak, slack expressions made her want to cry and throw up at the same time. The fire-blackened parts were different—they didn't even look human, so they didn't bother her. But the faces, those had been human, and some of them had laughed with her at breakfast. So she turned her face away as she went through pockets, making tidy little piles of wallets, PDAs, pocket change, keys.

"I'm really sorry," she whispered to each one. As her last act with the dead, she wrote their last names on their cold foreheads.

David Beringer was the last. There was no mark on him, only open eyes staring and blank. She didn't know what had killed him, but she hoped the end had been quick. The men who left him had dropped his backpack next to him.

"Should I go through this, too?" she asked Fraser.

"I need a complete inventory," he said.

Jennifer nodded. At least it would be scientific stuff, she told herself. Nothing personal. She pulled out a heavy plastic bag full of pebbles. "He was a geologist," she said to Fraser. "Always picking up rocks."

"Let me see that," Fraser said sharply. He held out a hand.

Jennifer put the bag in his hand, and he turned it round, held it up to the light. "I'll be damned," he muttered.

"What?"

He looked at her. "Have you ever seen raw diamonds?"

"Diamonds?"

He held out the bag. "I've busted enough smugglers to know kimberlite when I see it, and those are diamonds fresh from the matrix." He turned to look at the rim of the crater. "So that's what he was doing out there."

"So that's … illegal? Gathering diamonds?"

His gaze met hers, angry. "Hell, yes. And he knew that." Fraser stared down at the body of the geologist. "He knew it, and tried this anyway."

Jennifer felt sad to think the genial older man had had this secret. "I guess you never know about people."

"I have to confiscate these," Fraser said. "See what else is in his pack."

The rest of the pack was innocuous: a pick, some granite samples, water and a first aid kit. Jennifer set aside the backpack and went through his pockets, finding only scribbled notes on scraps of paper, some loose screws, a pocket-sized wrench. Then her hand came out with the digital camera. She turned it on, wondering what he'd photographed in his last hours.

A blurry marble, centered in the frame, backed by fog, cloud, and yes, she could see the ground below it. *What the heck was this?*

Cornwallis Island, Nunavut, Canada
74° 39′ 21.53″ N 93° 49′ 16.28″ W

After the last tortured gasp had died away to silence, the old man sat in his wheelchair, gazing down on his first-born. What remained of him was distorted, twisted. Tom Tonarak, in his last hours, had been racked with the spasms and convulsions of an accelerated growth surge: his arms had lengthened and narrowed, his legs and spine tried desperately to keep up. Worst and most painful had been the changes to his face, as it tried to assume the proportions of wolf-kind, tried to make a muzzle out of a flat primate face. Tom had been blind the last two days of his life, but his biggest fight had just been breathing. Between the lungs that grew too large for his ribcage, and the nasal passages trying to develop canine characteristics, he had been reduced to gasping deep gulps for air, like a drowning man.

All his father could do was to hold his hand, and weep. Now the hand, which in Tom's final hours had grown thick, sharp fingernails like claws, grew cold and clammy. The tears rolled down Nujuitok's face. "I'm sorry, son," he whispered. "So, so sorry. I wish it had been me."

He wiped his face, tasting salt. No time for that now. His hands, still strong, still weathered from a lifetime of hunting, gripped the wheels of his chair, turning towards the store room at the back of the small cabin.

He knew what he had to do. He'd come to his decision in the hours before his son died. He knew his useless legs would never be able to carry Tom out of the cabin, let alone drag him to a cave or ice hole where his body could be hidden. If he could not protect his son against his deadly heritage, he could at least let him go to the next world in peace. No scientists would cut him up, put him under a microscope. No one would expose his shame.

Nutjuitok cared nothing for his own life, especially since his wife, Tuva, had walked out into the snow to die. That loss still ached, deep inside, an emptiness that would never be filled as long as he lived. Only one thing he feared: the exposure of his family's secret. He would keep that at any cost, for as long as he lived.

Which, he had decided, would be no longer than noon today. His hands spun the wheels, propelling the chair along the uneven floorboards. He had left the cans of kerosene fuel just outside the door, handy for refueling the heater. He had kept the cabin warm, hoping to make Tom more comfortable. His shoulder muscles bunched as he heaved the full can into his lap. It sloshed heavily as he spun the chair.

Nutjuitok unscrewed the cap and tilted the can. The stink of kerosene filled the air as he poured, hearing the glug-glug of the liquid. Some of it spilled onto his hands as he jerked the can about; its oily feel repelled him. Part of his mind rebelled at this—he thought of Nick and Amaruq. But he knew there was nothing he could do for his remaining children, nothing except protect their secret. If the RCMP checked on him, if a friendly neighbor dropped by, someone might see Tom's body. And then there would be questions, probes, an investigation. The world would know of their secret, the secret that had been kept for generations, the secret that had driven his wife mad and twisted his daughter into a beast.

With a firmer hand, Nutjuitok soaked the floors and the walls, as high as he could reach. The reek of kerosene was suffocating now, but he continued splashing fuel until the can was empty. He thought about Nick.

Should he call his son on the shortwave, let him know

of Tom's death? What good would it do? And Nick would know without the shortwave, would know as soon as Amaruq knew, would know when the subtle, wordless communication among the family was cut. Nick would come back, would bring Amaruq back, and for what? There was nothing here for them any more but a broken old man too weak to care for or protect his family.

Not quite true, Nutjuitok thought. There was one last act of protection he could manage. The fire had to be hot, had to be long, so that when they found bones twisted out of the human normal, they would think it was due to the fire. So Nutjuitok waited, breathing in the fumes, letting the fuel soak into the wood and fabrics, making sure that no quick gust of wind or lack of fuel would kill the fire.

Yes, it was better like this. It was the old way. *Piqujait*, it was called: *what must be done.* To protect his family, to protect their secret, he would take himself and his tortured son into the next world. This way, with the fire, his possessions would go with him, as in the old days. Nick already had the only thing of value—the rifle. Nick could start anew, even go away to the South, as the old man knew he secretly longed to do. And Nick would care for Amaruq no matter what.

Nutjuitok felt warm when he thought of Nick. He had grown into a good man, a man any father could be proud of. He was lonely, but he was strong and smart. Nutjuitok hoped some day his son would find a woman he could love, a woman as strong as his mother, a woman who could love him despite what he was. Or because of what he was. As for Amaruq—the old man fought back tears. For his daughter, he wished happiness, of whatever kind she could manage.

Nutjuitok wheeled over to the bedside. He leaned over, and using the strength that had once hauled walrus across rough ice, pulled Tom's head and upper torso into his lap. One last time, he would hold him. One last time, he could be strong for his family.

Cradling the remains of his son, the old man lit the match.

"This isn't supposed to be here," Nick said. Amaruq flopped down beside him. The three stared into the wind, looking west at the storm streaking their way in an iron-colored front of cloud and rain. But even the clouds could not hide the mirror sheen of almost-frozen water that covered the land below, glinting like aluminum foil across a tabletop.

"I thought you said there was a plateau," Sophia said. She shoved her hands in her pockets, stamped her feet. The wind was like a knife made of ice. Rain began pelting them, almost insolently.

Nick's mouth made a thin, unhappy line.

She looked at him. "Are you sure you didn't take a wrong turn somewhere?"

Nick didn't bother to answer. He knew the ridge under his feet, the horizon marked by a triple cut of broken rock. "I was here, three years ago," he said. Amaruq leaned against his leg; she remembered too, he thought. "Tom and I were hunting, trying to circle round a bunch of musk ox. We came over this same ridge and saw them below us." He turned and looked to his left, at the high, distant shining wall of the ice cap. Was it further away? Smaller?

Sophia followed his look. "Glacial melt?" she said. "That's a lot of water."

"It's July. This is the height of summer," he said. "The ice is melting faster than normal. Something must have dammed the outlet. A rockslide, maybe."

"How deep could it be? Can we wade it?"

"Even if it's shallow, it'll be ice cold," he said. "How long before our feet and legs go numb, even get frostbitten?" He shook his head. "We'll have to find a way around." He turned to study the ice cap to the south.

"You don't mean to go that way, do you?" Alarm freighted Sophia's voice.

"The meltwater streams will be smaller near the foot of

the ice cap, where they come out," he said. "We can go south until they're small enough to cross, then head—"

Without warning, he felt the darkness invade him. The cold of space, the emptiness of grief—*No!*

Amaruq pointed her nose at the sky and howled.

::Tom! Father!::

Nick cried out, choked and fell to his knees, heedless of the sharp rocks.

Tom.

Beside him, Amaruq howled again, an almost human wail of mourning.

::Brother! They're gone! Dead!::

Sophia gasped. "My God! Nick, what's wrong? Are you hurt?"

::Father and Tom—dead! Dead! Dead!::

Nick curled into a ball, hands on his head, despair suffocating him. *Tom*, he thought. *No, no.*

"Nick!" She knelt beside him, put a hand on his back. Amaruq cried again, a low moaning sound that raised hairs on the back of Sophia's neck. "Tell me what's happening!"

Nick hugged himself in misery, rocking back and forth on his knees. "My brother is dead," he choked out. "My father." He reached for Amaruq, who stopped keening and came to him. Man and dog locked in a mutual hug of commiseration.

"Dead?" Sophia looked around wildly. "Where? When?"

He couldn't answer; the thing in his chest was too heavy, too tight. He could hardly breathe.

"They're gone," he whispered. "We can't hear them any more." He took in a long, shuddering breath. "Both of them. Gone."

Then her hands were on his shoulders, pulling him gently towards her. She wrapped her arms around him. "I'm so sorry," she whispered helplessly.

Nick felt the void open up in him, a vast emptiness where family had been, where brother and father and home had been. *How had it happened? Both his father and his brother?*

::Gone. Both gone.:: Amaruq howled again.

He had no home any more. And only Amaruq left, of his whole family. He sagged in Sophia's arms, devastated.

"Nick," she whispered. "We have to get out of this rain. Come on."

Rain? He lifted his face, and the cold wetness slapped him. "Oh."

Sophia helped him to his feet, but Nick felt hopelessness in the pit of his stomach. What was the point? Where to go now? There was no reason to go...home. The word in his mind brought a fresh wave of grief.

He struggled to focus. Sophia wasn't part of this. He should find them some shelter, get her to a place out of the rain, maybe someplace she could warm up.

"Amaruq," he said, his voice a croak. "Find shelter."

The wolf whined. The rain soaked her coat. ::Dead.::

"I know," he said, his voice rough with unshed tears. "But we have to get out of this rain."

Tail down, nose down, Amaruq walked slowly off, while Nick started in the opposite direction. Sophia followed him silently. "Look for some overhanging rocks," he said dully. "Anything that will keep out the—"

Amaruq barked twice sharply. Nick scurried over, then laid a hand on her head. "Good girl," he said. "Good work."

It had started as a couple of slabs of rock leaning on one another like two tired soldiers, but erosion and wildlife had enlarged it into a shelter. It was hardly more than a hole in the earth, but Nick guided Sophia in and followed her. His nose caught the sour scent.

"A fox den," he said. "Some pregnant dug this out last winter, maybe the one before." He concentrated on Sophia, focused on their situation, lest the despair in him bubble out in a howl to echo Amaruq's.

Sophia, white-faced, pressed herself against the wall as he crowded in. At the door, Amaruq stood with water dripping from her fur, her tail and ears drooping. "Come on in," Nick said, scooting over to make room for her.

::No:: The wolf turned and limped away, oblivious to the rain, a picture of sorrow.

He drew up his knees and rested his head in his hands. The empty place left in him burned and ached.

A whisper of sound; he turned his head to see Sophia shedding her parka. She leaned past him, tucking the sleeves into cracks in the rocks. The result was a makeshift doorway that blocked out the worst of the wind, all of the rain, and most of the light. The little den turned into a nest, with the two of them elbow to elbow in the breathing darkness, the first they had known since the plane had dropped them off on Devon Island.

He felt her hand on his arm. "I'm sorry," she said in a low voice. "I don't know what's happened. You say...your family is dead? How do you know? Are you sure?" She laid a hand on his fist.

Her touch was soft, kind. He found his fist opening without volition. He let her hand slide into his, let her fingers twine with his. How could he explain to her? How could he make her understand? She was foreign, even more of an outsider than the people of his own village, who treated him and his like pariahs.

The loneliness and pain crested in him. With a moan, he turned, and she opened her arms, and he was in them. Her arms drew him close, and he smelled her—girl smell and sulfur and sweat and the clean echo of rain. Her skin was warm, smooth, calling to something deep inside him. Seeking oblivion, his hands found the curve of waist, the slope of her spine, ran up her back to pull her close against him as he rocked forward, and then she was under him, warm and comforting, murmuring wordless sounds. He wanted nothing more than to disappear, to fall and to never land, to leave behind all the misery drowning him. He was cut off, cut off, cut off...but here was someone reaching out.

His mouth found hers in the dark, and she welcomed him. Her hands left his shoulders to slip under his parka, tug. He shrugged out of it, felt something pressing on his chest. It was

216

her field scope; he felt her jerk it off over her head, heard it fall on the dirt floor. He kissed her deep and long, felt her response, felt his own senses flare in response. Yes, his body said. Every muscle and tendon in him drew taut, every sense on full alert. She slid her hands up under his shirt, seeking him, and he drew off his shirt. The chill air flowed over his naked skin but had no effect on him, as heated as he was. Then he heard rustling, felt her moving under him, and she was naked against him.

He hesitated only a moment, standing on the ragged edge of need. "Sophia..."

She shut him up with her kiss, sweet and sensual, and he wriggled out of the rest of his clothes, even the clumsy boots that fought him. Hot skin on hot skin sent him into overdrive: hands everywhere, mouth following, discovering curves and smooth planes and soft mounds that said *Sophia* to him, an exploration that mapped every inch of her into his brain.

He plunged and she moaned, then arched. Nick Tonarak stopped thinking altogether, and lost himself in the wild, hot release.

Haughton Crater Research Project, Devon Island, Nunavut
75° 26' 00" N, 89° 51' 00" W

"Dr. Skorjik, can I show you something?"

Skorjik turned, saw Jennifer standing next to a pile of broken crates. "More wounded?"

"No, this is something else." Jennifer pulled a small digital camera out of her pocket. "This was Dr. Beringer's."

Skorjik passed a hand over his eyes. "Yes." His gaze took on a haunted quality. He flicked a glance at Jennifer. "If that's his personal effects, I'll be sure to—"

"No, Doctor. It's something else." She held up the tiny display screen. "This is the last picture he took."

The image was blurry, silvery. Skorjik squinted, and wished for his reading glasses. Which he had left in his office, which was now a smoking ruin. "What is it?"

"It looks like … some kind of flying machine. A … a UFO."

Skorjik scowled. "It looks like a badly exposed rock. Or a Mylar balloon. Or a doorknob. Dr. Roth, is this another of your pranks?"

Jennifer looked startled. "No. There's more than one. Dr. Beringer took them right before he was found dead. Whatever it was, he may have been fleeing from it when—"

"Fleeing?" Skorjik snapped. "From what, a UFO? Dr. Roth, I do not have time to play games out of *The X-Files* with you. This is a serious emergency, we must concentrate on helping our people as much as possible." He controlled himself with visible effort. "Look, I know this has been stressful for all of us, but I need to you to continue helping Dr. Meyers."

"I think this is important."

Skorjik pinched the bridge of his nose. "I have a lot of scared, cold, homeless scientists on my hands right now, Dr. Roth. I really cannot talk about this. And I have to ask you to keep this to yourself as well. I have enough to do without starting a panic among my people." With that, he turned on his heel and walked away.

Jennifer stood uncertainly, holding the camera. She was tired, cold and hungry, and felt the cold shiver of exhaustion creeping over her. Maybe Skorjik was right, she thought. She was too tired to think straight. But the image in that photograph bothered her. She thought about Sophia out there in the cold empty land, with no one but a possible mutant dog or man to protect her from...whatever.

Jennifer looked at the last image, the blurry ball that looked menacing. Whatever that was, Jennifer thought, it wasn't a balloon or a rock. Or a doorknob.

Deep inside, the conviction grew in her: it was a weapon.

Mars Habitat Project, Devon Island, Nunavut
75° 25′ 52.61″ N, 89° 51′ 00″ W

"Something's coming." Bob Courtenay straightened, peering down from the ridge towards the burned camp.

"One of the search teams?" Beside him, Fraser stopped and did the same. Around them, scientists and researchers were stacking crates and boxes to make windbreaks and sleeping shelters. All day the missing teams had straggled in from their searches, all of them empty-handed, all of them wondering why the radios had died, and all of them open-mouthed at the sight of the destroyed camp.

But this was not a returning search party. Distantly, a plane the size of a dragonfly stooped out of the clouds. Fraser watched as it circled the ruins, then lofted in their direction. He saw the red maple leaf on its side. "Rangers!"

Now they could hear the engine, and in seconds the Twin Otter soared over them. Everyone cheered and waved, and the pilot waggled the wings as the plane passed overhead. Fraser's belt radio squawked.

"Rescue One to Mars Hab," came a woman's voice. "Do you read? Over?"

Fraser snatched the radio up to his mouth. "We read you, Rescue One. And we are very glad to see you! Over."

"This is Master Corporal Nan Kallikuk, First Canadian Ranger Patrol Group. Who am I speaking to? Over."

"Constable Will Fraser, RCMP. We are in need of medical assistance, shelter and supplies. Over."

"Copy that, Constable. I can't put down on that ridge. Is the airstrip at Haughton camp functional? Over."

"Affirmative. We will meet you there with ATVs. Over."

"Acknowledged, Constable. Rescue One out." The plane banked north in a circle, heading back to the camp.

Fraser turned to Courtenay. "I'll be taking one of the ATVs. I want Skorjik and you on the other two."

"Are they going to take us home?" a voice asked. Fraser turned to see the tall black man with the broken glasses. "Are they?"

"Yes, but it will take a while," Fraser said. He looked around at the faces—anxious, fearful. The researchers had responded as well as he could have hoped to this crisis, pitching in to haul supplies to the Hab, rotating sleep schedules in the crowded shelter, taking his orders without complaint. But now that rescue was at hand, their patience would grow thin. Nothing whetted the appetite for home like having it within reach. He turned back to the Habitat to get his driving goggles.

By the time Fraser and the two other men arrived at the airstrip, the Twin Otter was parked, tied down, and was being unloaded by men and women in the traditional red jerseys of the Canadian Rangers. A volunteer force, the Rangers were a part of the Canadian Forces Reserve intended to serve as Canada's military presence in isolated areas. Deriving as they did from the local population, they tended to be mostly Inuit. In emergencies, they were the first to respond.

A short figure in red detached itself from the group as the ATVs rolled up. Fraser saw a brown face with sharp eyes under the hood, and returned her snappy salute. "Master Corporal Kallikuk?" he said.

"Sir," the woman replied. "You are Constable Fraser? May I see some identification?"

They exchanged badges, and Fraser noted from hers that MC Kallikuk was older than she looked. While they established one another's bona fides, the crew continued unloading boxes and duffle bags from the cargo hold. Courtenay and Skorjik stood behind Fraser.

"Everything seems in order, Constable," Kallikuk said. "We received a report of a garbled SOS with these coordinates yesterday," she said. "Something about a fire." She put her hands on her hips, staring over at the destroyed tents. "Looks like that was dead on."

Skorjik strode forward. "It was my camp, Master Corporal. I'm Martin Skorjik. I'm the—I was the director of Haughton camp." He hesitated, tears forming at the corner of his eyes. "You heard her," he said. "You heard Verna calling for help."

"We did, sir," the Master Corporal said. "She cut off about halfway through, but we heard the coordinates."

Skorjik brushed at his eyes. "She died at her post."

"I'm sorry," Master Corporal Kallikuk said. "We'll make sure there aren't any more casualties." She turned to Fraser.

"How many dead?"

"Five in the fire," Fraser said. "One of unknown causes."

"I heard something about missing men," she said. "That would be why you're here. Any sign of them?"

"No," Fraser said. "Master Corporal, I think this fire was more than a tragic accident. I think we may have poachers on the island. Or worse."

She lifted an eyebrow but said, "Poachers are your concern. I'm more interested in thirty or so foreign nationals on Canadian soil, apparently in dire trouble."

"That we are," Skorjik said.

A tall man in red stepped up. "Master Corporal, we have no long-range communications."

She turned to him. "None?"

"No, MC. As we flew in, I saw the comms array. It's down."

"Short-range?"

"We're good within a couple of kilometers," he said. "After that, I can't say."

"Do what you can, Ujarak."

She turned back to Fraser, her expression shrewd. "Constable, I think you're right. I think there's trouble on this island." She looked at the sky, measuring. "Snow on the way. We may be socked in here for twenty four hours at least. Not to worry, Doctor. We have food and shelter for your people. After that, we'll evacuate."

"We're grateful," Skorjik said. "Do you have any medical supplies? We have a doctor, but we're running—"

"Ranger Torrell over there has your medical supplies. I'd rather talk about security first," she said. She eyed Fraser. "Are you armed?"

Fraser raised the edge of his parka to show his sidearm. "We have two bear guns—shotguns. That's it. The rest went with the fire or are with our search teams."

"When did they last check in?"

Fraser stared at the nearby massif, seeing the twisted silhouette of the ruined array. "Not for hours. I guess they can't raise us either."

Kallikuk followed his look. "Coincidence? Sabotage?"

"I don't believe in coincidence any more."

She nodded briefly, turned to her crew. "Faraday, break out and deploy weapons and ammunition. And give one of the rifles to the Constable here."

"Weapons?" Skorjik said. "Are you sure that's called for? The fire was an acci—"

Fraser caught the master corporal's eye, and answered for her. "A fire of unknown origin, which killed several internationally recognized researchers associated with the United States' space program. The communications array has been disabled—"

"The storm—"

"An array that withstood winter on this island for many years, and then succumbed to a summer storm? Not to mention your missing men. And a decapitated wolf in the middle of nowhere. No, Doctor," Fraser said, accepting the rifle a young red-clad volunteer handed him. "I'm afraid this is more than bad luck. I think there may be terrorists on Devon Island."

Mars Habitat Project, Devon Island, Nunavut
75° 25′ 52.61″ N, 89° 51′ 00″ W

Ted Meyers grunted as he squeezed through the narrow hatch of the Mars Habitat. The cardboard box in his arms was soaking wet and trying to come apart in his hands. The box held a jumble of instruments, disks, notebooks; the scientists were salvaging what they could from the burnt-out labs. Now Ted lugged the box over to a stack filling one wedge-shaped compartment of the lower half of the Habitat. His knee hit a bench and he cursed, wishing there was more light in this space.

He made sure not to cover up Jennifer's SlimeMaster—a corner of his mouth turned up at the silly name—and shifted a box to make sure it was accessible. As he did so, a door in the front popped open and a tiny vial fell to the floor, rolling under his foot just as his boot came down. The crunch was loud in the small space.

"Dammit!"

He glanced around to make sure no one was watching, then kicked the shards under a stack of equipment. He hoped it hadn't been anything essential to Jennifer's work. He frowned at the dark stain on the floor—was that blood?—then stomped out of the compartment to get more boxes.

Near the ceiling of the compartment, the curve of the wall arced from support to support. A round section of it turned brown, then black, with wisps of smoke rising from it. The odor of charred wood filled the compartment, then the black vanished, leaving a circular hole to the outside. Sunlight poured into the interior, highlighting dancing dust motes, the bare studs and bolts of the supports. The light winked out as the orb blocked it, passing through the hole it had burned. It descended, scanning each box, each crate, until it neared the floor.

Suddenly the globe darted to the bloodstain. It sank to within a millimeter of the floor, strobing silver and blue. For an instant, the image of Nick Tonarak's face appeared in the globe, distorted but recognizable. Then the globe flashed blue-white, and smoke rose from the black char on the floor where the stain had been.

"What the hell is this?" Ted stood in the doorway, staring, his arms filled with another box. He turned his head to shout. "Hey, guys! You gotta see—"

The flare was white and silent. Ted cried out, dropped the box and fell to his knees. "What—?" He tried to bring his arm up to shield his face, but couldn't make it obey him. He tried to shout, but his voice was nothing. Blinded by the glare, he blinked, his eyes watering.

Everything went blue and he felt something in his head, something questioning him, demanding an answer.

Where? Where? Where?

"I don't understand," he cried.

Pain surged through his head as he clutched it. "Stop!"

Wherewherewherewhere?

An image came into his head, of Nick Tonarak and his

dog. He blinked in confusion. Why was he thinking of the bear guard/mechanic? What did he have to do with—

Where?

The pressure in his chest built, until he was fighting for every breath. *What was this thing?* It hung in the air, strobing white and blue, like a Christmas ornament from hell. And for some insane reason, it wanted to know where the ATV mechanic was?

Ted moaned. He didn't understand. Shock and pain disoriented him, warped his thinking. "Lowlands," he gasped. "I think they—"

More pain, so bone deep he could not even scream. Blue fire danced in his head, in front of his eyes. The unbidden image of Tonarak surfaced again, with a sense of agonizing urgency. He focused his thoughts:

Truelove Lowlands. That's all I know, he thought.

An echo, a glimpse of something alien, cold. Ted saw a white, shining cliff, a fissure, a chamber where red light reflected in mirrored walls.

Then everything went dark in his head.

Truelove Lowlands, Devon Island, Nunavut
75° 38′ 13.47″ N, 83° 49′ 21.46″ W

Sophia struggled to breathe. And no wonder, with a man this size sprawled over her in exhausted sleep. His head lay between her breasts, his breathing deep and even. Just enough light speared through the door to show him, copper skin and black hair and long, lean muscle. His big hands lay relaxed and open on the dirt floor beside her. A gust of wind teased her parka where it hung in the doorway, and she felt the icy kiss of the breeze on her skin.

What the hell had she done?

It had been all impulse and instinct and some voice deep in her telling her, without words, that this offered comfort was right and true. Her logical mind told her it was folly to get involved with a man she had met only three days ago, especially when they were lost, stranded, without food or weapons, far from help and possibly being stalked by a hungry predator. She had crossed boundaries not on any map.

The other part of her mind merely whispered, "Nick" in her, and that was enough.

She rested a hand on his head, threaded her fingers through that silken tangle of black hair. He stirred, and his eyes opened. They were the brown of the rock and earth of this land, as expressive as its sky. He blinked, and she felt her breath catch, waiting for his reaction. It had been a moment of sweet madness between them—what would he think?

A shy smile, lowered eyelashes, and then a fervent look. "Hey," he whispered.

"Hey, back," she said. Her heart was pounding.

He shoved himself up to a sitting position. The moment his warmth left her, she shivered. He reached for his parka and spread it carefully over her torso. He looked away from her, a long arm casually resting on his knee, oblivious to his own nudity. "That was...probably a bad idea," he said in a low voice.

Disappointment's sharp edge cut her for a moment. Then his eyes swung back to her.

"But I don't care. I...I'm glad."

She reached up a hand, and he caught it in his, looking down at it. He rubbed his thumb over the back of her hand, his callouses a tiny scrape against her skin. "I'm glad, too."

He brought her hand to his mouth. "I don't...I didn't expect ..." He let go of her hand, shoved his hair out of his face. His laugh was short, bitter. "I don't have a lot of experience with...this." His laugh disappeared and his face took on that sad, wan look. "I don't know why you would ..." He trailed off, lost.

Sophia sat up, wrapping her arms around her knees. "Nick, this wasn't a pity fuck."

His eyes were wide and startled. "Oh. No, I didn't think..."

Sophia smiled. The fact that that had not even occurred to him was endearing. In many ways, he was an innocent. Though not, a smiling part of her mind reminded her, a *complete* innocent. She slid a hand up his arm—hard muscle, warm copper skin flexing under her palm. "Nick, when I met you, I felt... something. I figured it was my overactive imagination."

"I don't have that much imagination," he said. "But I felt... something." He took her fingers in his, looking down at the floor. "Something strong. Something real."

"I know." She had felt it ever since she kissed him that morning. No, before that, maybe when she had seen the man with the melancholy smile who handed her a carving of a legend. "This wasn't a mistake at all, then," she whispered.

"Never a mistake, Sophia." His voice caressed her name, sibilants and hushed breath. "Never."

He leaned towards her and she met him, and they meshed again, limbs and mouths interlocked in a warm tangle. He tasted of her and him and, oddly, coffee. His calloused hands were both rough and tender, an artist's hands, a lover's. This time he slowed down, and she could explore him a little—the planes and tight bands of muscle, the strength in his arms and thighs, the bone beneath the skin.

He rolled, shifted, and something dug into her side. She cried out, fumbled around, and found the little Sedna figurine. He smiled, took it from her, and set it at the door of the den. Then his head dipped to her mouth, and her world contracted down to him and her, the soft slide of skin on skin, the warmth of his body. Somehow he found every point of pleasure in her; somehow she found every place that made him arch and gasp.

She heard herself whispering his name over and over, and heard him reply with her own. His deep voice in her ear murmured words she didn't recognize but perfectly understood. She welcomed him, wrapped herself around him, and let his hands and mouth and body take her down again into that primal darkness, let him overwhelm her until her head fell back, mouth open, giving and taking until it all coalesced in her middle in that sweet, rippling explosion.

Afterwards, they lay knotted together on the pile of their

clothing, half-asleep. The wind gusted, blowing her parka inward, shocking them awake with an icy blast.

Nick yelped and bolted upright, only to crack his head on the ceiling of the den. *"Maudit! Putain! Merde!"* he cursed, rubbing the back of his skull; Sophia bit back a giggle. Gooseflesh pimpled his chest and arms. He reached under Sophia, tugged out her sweater. "Here."

Awkwardly, colliding in the crowded den, they struggled into their clothes. The dirt of the floor had been ground into her pants and socks; all of their clothes still stank of sulfur. Sophia thought longingly of a long soak in a hot tub. They dressed in silence, almost shyly, not looking at one another.

As she tugged on her socks, Sophia thought of Paul and waited for guilt to swamp her. Dead only a few years, and already she was...but no, the guilt didn't come. Instead, there was a feeling of sadness, of wistfulness, of distance, as if Paul was very far away, and receding. She glanced over at Nick, and saw how his hair fell forward to cover his face, and it came to her with a pang that she would miss him very much when she had to leave.

Too much, maybe. What had she gotten into here?

When she finished lacing her boots, Nick reached over and took her hand. He kissed it, held it tightly for a moment, then looked at her with trouble in his eyes. "There's...something I have to say. Something I have to tell you."

A pit opened up in her stomach. *He was married. He had AIDS...*

"It's about...my family." She could see memory flooding back in him, see the pain in his eyes. She tightened her grip on his fingers. "We're...different." He took a deep breath. "Look, just trust me on this. It will sound crazy. I've never...we never tell this to...outsiders."

"This is about your family? You said your father and brother had died. Do you mean, just now?"

He shook his head. "We...have a family curse, I guess you could call it. It's going to sound crazy. It's not crazy, but it is terrible. Terrible. We live mostly apart because of it." He looked at her with a pained expression. "We mostly don't marry outsiders because of it."

A cool feeling crept over Sophia. *What was he saying? A terrible family secret? Murder? Abuse? Incest?*

"Ever since we can remember, as far back as any of our old ones can remember, we—" He broke off, swallowed. Another deep breath. "Sometimes we...change."

Sophia blinked, bewildered. "Change?"

"Into...something else. Something not...human."

"Not *human?*" she echoed sharply.

Nick swallowed. "Animals," he said in a low voice. "To be plain: a wolf."

She jerked her hand out of his. "Is this some kind of joke?"

He shook his head, his hair loose on his shoulders. "No joke. Some of us change into...wolves. Or something like a wolf. And usually die doing it. My brother Tom did." He swallowed. "Just now."

She took a deep breath. "Wow. I've heard some pretty interesting 'get lost' stories from guys, but this one is unique."

His eyes met hers, shocked. "What?"

"This is pretty raw, Nick. And it's not funny. You give me the best sex of my life and then you sit there and tell me you're a *werewolf?* Do I look stupid?"

"Not a werewolf," he said. She shifted away but he caught her hand. "Not like you read about, not like you see in movies. That's...that's made up. Magic. Not real. This is real. This is... genetic, I think."

Sophia felt a trickle of fear. It was one thing if Nick was pulling some sophomoric prank, trying to fob her off after casual sex with some fairy tale. But if he actually *believed* this nonsense...

"Let me tell you, then you can call me names," he said. "For some reason, some reason we don't know, members of our family sometimes change into wolves, or animals very much like wolves. If they're lucky, it happens when they're young enough to survive it. If they're not, it kills them." He stopped, emotion thickening his voice. "It kills them," he repeated. "We don't know what triggers it. We can't stop it. We can't cure it. And it's irreversible." He released her hand, sat back, crossing his arms. "It killed my brother today. In a way, it killed my mother. And it turned my little sister into the wolf you see now."

It took her a moment to understand him. "Amaruq?" It was there at the back of her mind, everything she seen: the observations, the little asides, the way he and the dog seemed to understand one another. Amaruq says. But it was impossible... Sophia shook her head.

"Are you making fun of me? Nick, I'm a scientist. What you say, it's impossible. One species can't just change into another."

Nick shrugged. She sensed a door closing in him. He leaned forward, all intense conviction. "What I *know* is that I watched my little sister go through hell. Her hair fell out, she ran a fever for weeks. Then her bones started reshaping themselves, little by little. Her skin changed, her face. I remember the screaming, I remember my mother crying for hours by her bed, changing her sheets, bathing her face. After months, my little sister ended up as what you see out there. We told everyone she died, we never spoke her name again, the way we don't speak the names of the dead. She renamed herself Amaruq, which is 'wolf' in our language. And she would give anything, anything to be a real human being again." His jaw worked, biting back his anger and bitterness.

"You think this is some kind of joke? It's hell, Sophia. It's hell for her, being a beast with a woman's mind. And it's hell for me, not knowing from one day to the next when it will happen, *if* it will happen, to me."

Another gust of wind blew the parka inward. Sophia hugged herself more tightly. "It's hard for me to take this in," she said. "A human being, turning into a wolf? Can you turn into other things?"

He shook his head. "I've never heard of it. It's not like there are many of us. But sometimes Amaruq says—" He stopped.

"Yes," she said. "I think you need to explain that 'Amaruq says'."

"You really won't believe this." His voice held an edge of humor.

"In for a penny..."

He drew another deep breath, bracing himself. "After we, they change, we can...hear their thoughts."

Oh, that was all she needed, Sophia thought, closing her eyes. *Mental telepathy?* "Do you fly, as well? Or walk through walls? Does kryptonite give you the bends?"

"It's not a comic book," he said harshly. "This is not a joke among us; it *kills* us. I guess it was too much for you to believe. I shouldn't have tried."

"But there's no conceivable mechanism for hearing other people's thoughts."

"And there's one for turning into a wolf?" Nick's voice dripped with sarcasm. "In for a penny..."

"Compared to ESP, yeah, I can almost believe in...changing species. How...?"

"We don't know," he said in a low voice. "We've never known how it works, or what triggers it. But it's not related to the moon, or magic, or spells, or any of that fairy tale crap." He knotted a fist. "God, how I wish it were. Then there would be rules, a spell, something to lift this...this curse. No such luck."

His eyes burned, looking through her. "I think of it like when I shot up a full eight inches in one summer when I was fourteen—think how much muscle and bone my body had to build in that time."

He shifted, restless. "What tells the body to do that? What tells the body what kind of muscle, what kind of bone? I wish I knew. I read and I surf the 'net...nobody has answers. Everything I read about 'werewolf' is some kind of fantasy shit, and they always change back to humans. God, if I could change my sister back, could have stopped the change in Tom..."

She watched him fold into himself, looping his long arms around his knees, staring into the semi-dark. She wanted to touch him, to comfort him, but something held her back.

Was he, really, human? Or sane?

"Do you dream a lot?" he asked in a low voice.

"Yeah," she said, a little confused. "Everyone does."

He turned his head, laying it on his arms, and those brown eyes (so like the wolf's, she now realized) gleamed in the half-light. "We dream. Our whole family, human and wolf, at one time or another dreams *the same weird dream*. Of floating, of being part of a larger whole, of being...something else. I think it holds the key to this, the fact that we all dream it, and the details are always the same. I think it's important." He turned his face into his arms, and his voice came to her muffled. "I think it is. I don't know. I can't find out."

"Have you tried?"

"I wanted to take Tom to a hospital, hoped some scientist might figure it out. But Dad—" He swallowed, swallowed again. "Dad was afraid they'd turn him into a freak show. And why not?" He raised his head and glared at her. "Look at you, right now. They'd all react the same way. Dad was right." He looked away. "I shouldn't have told you. But after we...in case you turn out to be...you should know. You have a right to know."

It took her a moment for his meaning to sink in. "Oh." She shook her head. "It's all right. I'm...protected. I won't get pregnant."

His shoulders sagged with relief. "Oh. Good. I guess." He didn't meet her eyes. "I didn't ask. I should have. It was all so fast..." He bit his lip, nodded. He rolled forward onto his knees, pulling the parka aside and looking out. "The weather's clearing. We should go." He reached for his parka.

Sophia reached for his hand, missed. "Nick?"

"It's all right. We don't have to talk about it again." Without looking at her, he ducked out.

Reluctantly, Sophia reached for her clothing. When she had dressed, she stepped out of the tiny cave.

Outside, the fog had lifted somewhat, but the clouds had sunk low. Sophia zipped her parka and pulled the hood up, staring up at the skyline above the little den. *On the other side,* she thought, *lay the camp and civilization.* People who didn't turn into wolves. Men less complicated than Nick Tonarak and his...pet. Men who didn't think they might turn into werewolves.

She heard Nick whistle for his dog—wolf? She looked at him with trouble in her heart, still reeling from the last two hours, from his story.

What was she to make of him?

VI - CONFRONTATION

Jennifer pushed through the inner "airlock" door into the Hab interior, a stack of charred books in her arms. She bumped the hatch door shut with her butt.

"Hey, Ted, you found a light switch! Good for—"

She tripped, the books spilled out of her arms to thud on the floor, and she tumbled forward onto her hands and knees. Her left knee jolted with pain. "Ow! What—Ted?"

He lay sprawled half in and half out of the wedge-shaped storage compartment, his head silhouetted in the light spilling in through a round hole high in the wall. Cold wind kissed her cheek. She crawled over to him.

"Ted? Ted?" She pawed at his collar, forcing her hand past layers of clothing to find the skin below his ear. Something warm and wet slicked her hand as she felt frantically for a pulse. And there it was, faint and thready, but there. "Oh, my God."

She withdrew her hand, careful now not to move his head. Blood covered her palm, and her heart lurched. Had he fallen? His neck or spine might have been injured. Best not to move him. She glanced up at the round hole, blinked, and looked away. She couldn't understand why it was there, where it had come from. It wasn't important right now.

Reaching the hatch, she jerked it open. "Hey! I need help in here!" she yelled.

People bundled up against the cold stopped their stacking and turned to her. No one answered her. They stood staring at her.

"Anyone! Ted's been hurt! I need Constable Fraser! And a medical kit!" She gazed around at their frozen attitudes. "Now!"

Two men took off running down the hill. In the distance, Jennifer saw ATVs approaching from the north, driven by red-clad people. They were carrying sticks.

No, she realized with a chill. They were rifles.

"I'm not sure what's wrong with him," Ranger Torrell said. He sat back on his heels, his hood thrown back to reveal a weathered face. He pulled the stethoscope from his neck and put it back into the medical kit open beside him on the floor of the Hab. "I can't see any injury. The blood is from his ears and nose. That may mean an intracranial injury, a concussion maybe."

From the doorway, Skorjik said, "So he slipped and fell?"

Ranger Torrell got to his feet. "Most likely. I don't recommend moving him until we can get more medical personnel here."

Kneeling beside Ted, Jennifer looked up. "So we just leave him here?"

"Keep him warm, make sure his airway's open. Make sure someone stays with him until he wakes up," the Ranger said. He glanced up at the round hole. "Probably should cover that window."

Behind Skorjik in the doorway, Courtenay exclaimed, "Where did that come from? That hole in the wall. It wasn't there an hour ago."

Everyone stared at the round little scientist. "It wasn't?" Skorjik said.

"No, of course not. There's only one window in this Hab, and it's on the second level. Why would your doctor burn a hole through our wall?"

"He didn't," Jennifer said. "How could he? What would he use? And why would he?" She looked down at the man on the floor, watching the rise and fall of his torso.

"Whatever," Skorjik said wearily. "Courtenay, do we have anything we can use to block that hole?"

The men moved away, talking in low tones. Other onlookers paused briefly, then went back to work. Someone handed Jennifer a blanket and she spread it over Ted's still form. She picked up his hand and looked at it: there were half-moon marks of fingernails driven into his palms, little crescents of blood. The other hand was the same. What had made Ted clench his fists so hard he had drawn blood? A convulsion? A stroke? She looked up at the hole in the wall, where cold air and sunlight still poured in. She smelled charred wood.

As she shifted to a more comfortable position, something on the floor winked at her. She reached into a crevice formed by two adjoining boxes and drew out a smashed vial—one of her samples. She could still read the number—it was Nick Tonarak's. Her gaze fell to the floor, the stain, the scorch mark. What the hell had happened here?

Ted moaned, shifted. "No!" he cried weakly.

"I'm here," Jennifer said. She bent to peer into his face. His eyes opened, he blinked. Jennifer was relieved to see that his pupils were the same size. "Don't move. I'll get the medic—"

He shoved himself to his hands and knees, head hanging. "Get out of here," he said between gritted teeth. "It's not safe. That thing might come back."

"What thing?" Jennifer said. "You should not be sitting up," she said. "Here, lie down."

He fended off her hand, wincing. "I'm all right. Did anyone else see it? Is anyone hurt?"

"See what?" In the doorway, Skorjik and Fraser stood side by side. Jennifer noted that Fraser held a rifle. Skorjik gestured to someone out of sight. "Fetch that Ranger medic."

Ted rubbed his eyes, his temples. "Shiny. Like a silver balloon, only it changed color. It was here when I came in. It—it flashed at me."

Ranger Torrell elbowed his way into the room, knelt beside Ted. He grabbed Ted's wrist to take his pulse. "How do you feel?"

"Like someone hit me on the head with a planet," Ted said. "It never touched me, though. It just…flashed light at me. And it—" He broke off, glancing from Skorjik to Fraser, their blank faces. "It wanted to know where the ATV mechanic guy was."

Torrell flashed a light into Ted's eyes. He blinked, followed a finger.

"Pupils?" Ted asked.

"Normal," Torrell told him. "No nausea?"

"None," Ted said. "No dizziness, no blurred vision. Head hurts like hell. I'm fine. Who are you?"

"What did you mean, 'it' wanted to know where the ATV mechanic was?" Fraser interrupted. "Who asked you? Did you see his face?"

"It wasn't a he, it was an it," Ted repeated patiently. "I came into the room, and there was a big metal ball just hanging there, in mid air." He glanced from Fraser's face to Skorjik's, frowning at their expressions of disbelief. "It flared out at me, like someone turning on a spotlight. Only it was hot, and different colors…"

He heard Jennifer's soft hiss of surprise, but was watching Skorjik and the constable.

Fraser looked at Torrell. "Could he have had a fit of some kind?"

"It wasn't epilepsy!" Ted said irritably. "That thing was interrogating me!"

Skorjik, Fraser and Torrell exchanged glances. Jennifer put her hand over Ted's. "Tell me what it asked you," she said.

Ted looked into her eyes, confused. "It wanted to know about that guy with the dog, the one who came with you and your friend—"

"Nick," Jennifer said. She thought about the sample tube she'd found. "Someone dropped a vial of his blood on the floor."

Ted looked surprised. "Oh. That was me. I'm sorry. Did I ruin—"

"Never mind that," Jennifer said. She reached into her parka and drew out Beringer's camera. "Did it look like this?" She showed him the image in the camera, of the hovering orb.

"Yeah. That's it. What is it? Where did you get that?"

"You said it was asking about Nick? What did it want to know?" Fraser and Skorjik stared, but Jennifer resolutely kept her gaze on Ted's face, willing him to look at her and not them.

"It...it wanted to know where he was. It..." he reached up, massaging his forehead. "It hurt me. A blinding headache. I didn't know where he was, but it kept hurting me. Then I remembered that you told me he went out with your friend to the Lowlands."

At this, Jennifer's grip on his hand tightened. "You told it where Sophia went?"

Ted blinked. "I didn't say anything. It was in my mind, I couldn't help it."

"It was reading your mind?" Skorjik's tone was skeptical.

"I'm only telling you what happened. I didn't speak. I didn't say anything out loud. But I thought of...what's his name? Nick? And I thought of your friend, and the Truelove Lowlands. And then everything went dark." He turned back to Jennifer. "But there was something else. If it was reading my mind—" He glanced up and caught Fraser and Skorjik's skeptical looks. "I say if it was reading my mind, then I was reading its mind, too. I saw into it."

Jennifer tensed. "What did you see?"

"It's...not human. Nothing I've ever seen or heard of."

"A machine?"

"If a machine could hate, yes. Because it hates. I think it hates Nick."

"This doesn't make any sense," Skorjik said. "With all due respect, Doctor, I think you fell and hit your head, and passed out. This is some after-effect—"

"An after-effect didn't burn that hole in the wall," Jennifer said. She got to her feet, pointing at the wall. "That's not a figment of anyone's imagination. We all see it. It's real. Dr. Skorjik, maybe it's time you realized something is going on here you don't understand. You saw that last photograph Dr. Beringer took. Constable, you're here because two guys went missing. Now, something has burned a hole through the Habitat and tried to kill our only physician." She put her hands on her hips. "Coincidence stretches only so far, Doctor."

"I agree with her," Fraser said mildly. At Skorjik's outraged look, he held up a hand. "Not that I believe some kind of UFO is floating around interrogating people. But we may be dealing with a drone of some kind, programmed for sabotage, maybe. We need to take it seriously."

Ted got slowly to his feet, leaning on Jennifer. He glared at the men. "Listen to me. That thing was here, it was alive, it questioned me. And it wanted Nick, for whatever reason. I saw something in its mind." He paused, swallowed. "It came out of the ice cap. I saw a cave, a hole melted in the ice. It came from that. And it's hunting something. I think it's hunting this Nick person."

Jennifer felt herself go cold all over. "If it's hunting Nick," she said. "It will find Sophia, too."

Mars Habitat Project, Devon Island, Nunavut
75° 25' 52.61" N, 89° 51' 00" W

"What the hell?" Master Corporal Kallikuk growled. "A freakin' UFO? We get called all the way up here for a UFO report?"

Beside her, one of the Rangers methodically unpacked food rations from a box. They were squatting twenty yards from the Hab, looking out over the plain where the remains of the research camp scarred the landscape.

"Well, Torrell did say the guy got hit on the head."

Kallikuk shook her head, slid the action on her Lee-Enfield No. 4 rifle back, checking the load. "Doesn't make any difference with a *qablunaat*," she said, using the Inuktitut term for a non-native. "Their heads are pretty soft to start with, Nattiq."

Nattiq laughed dutifully. "I know, MC," he said. "Tourists get a lot of strange ideas. Remember that time we got called out on a search-and-rescue for some tourists who said a walrus told them—in German, no less—that Atlantis lay inside the Arctic Circle? Got themselves lost, no food, frostbitten, but by golly they were going to find Atlantis or bust."

"Shoulda left them to freeze." Kallikuk tugged her parka closer. She thought of her warm house and her warm husband

and her three kids back in Iqaluit. In two weeks her rotation would be over; she looked forward to seeing them again. She looked forward to being back among friends and family and away from the idiot outsiders who neither knew nor cared to know the land they were walking, flying and boating over. Carelessness was disrespectful. "Talking walruses. Now I've heard everything."

Her assistant yawned, straightened. "Hey, do you think that Mountie is right? There are terrorists on the island?"

Kallikuk snorted. "Oh, yeah. Along with a few Bolsheviks, one or two renegade Nazis, and a Klingon death squad. What does he take us for?"

Nattiq's face was round and anxious, bisected by a thin black mustache. "Fraser's got a good rep. He's been in the North awhile. People say he's got a good head on his shoulders."

Kallikuk shook her head. "Doesn't matter," she said. "No matter how long *qablunaat* live here, they never really get it. You know that. To really know the North, you have to grow up here."

Nattiq looked doubtful, but both military discipline and cultural protocol prevented him from arguing with his superior and an elder.

Several Rangers in their red gear trudged up and squatted nearby. They huddled over their equipment, running checks.

"Hey, MC!" One of the men, a grizzled veteran, called over to her. "Something wonky with our GPS readers. How's yours?"

"Five by five," Kallikuk said, glancing at her GPS monitor. "You forget to change the batteries again, Maurice?"

Snickers at this. One of the older men straightened and came over to her, squatting at a respectful distance. His red Ranger toque was faded from years of exposure. "Did you finish the duty roster, MC?"

"Yeah." Kallikuk pulled a battered spiral notebook out of her pocket. The wind tore at the pages, and she held them down firmly with her thumb as she squinted at the writing. "Okay, your team goes down for rack time in twenty minutes.

Blue and Red teams are on perimeter duty. I'm sending Teddy Qimmiq's team up to that comm array to see if he can get it up and running."

"Copy that, MC," the man said. "See you in four hours." He gestured at a companion, and they stood and walked off towards the Hab.

Kallikuk busied herself sorting rations and handing them out. At one point, she heard the distant mutter of an engine and saw Constable Fraser motoring off towards the burned research camp on an ATV. Distantly, she saw the paired red figures of her Rangers fanning out, rifles at the ready, on their patrols.

"Hey, Pete, get a tarp over these boxes," she ordered.

"Aye, Master Corporal," the young man said, trotting off towards the supply dump.

The sun fell lower in the sky, kissing the rim of the world. The scientists huddled in the Hab and in hastily pitched tents. Kallikuk watched a fog bank gather, watched as it slowly ate the view. First the mammoth Fortress disappeared, then the black smear of ash and ash that used to be the Haughton Crater Research Station. It crept closer and closer, a gray veil. Kallikuk finished repacking the supplies and stood, bending to loosen a stiff back.

Something gleamed in the fog. Frowning, Kallikuk raised a hand to squint at it. A wink, a flash, and it was gone. A trick of the light, she thought, even as a queasy feeling roiled through her. What had that *qablunaat* doctor said attacked him? A floating metal ball?

A blur, and then it was just *there*, hanging in mid-air ten feet from her nose. Kallikuk blinked. It was just as the doctor had described it—a gleaming sphere, silver against the gray fog bank, hovering. The surface of the sphere roiled, changing colors along the spectrum from gray to black to silver. Kallikuk wrinkled her nose in disgust; what was that smell? Nothing natural. She wondered if this was some NASA experiment gone astray. Oddly, the surface brightened for a moment, and she saw a brief kaleidoscope of images: an Inuit man, a wolf, a polar bear. Then the surface blanked again.

240

This was stupid, Kallikuk thought. It was one thing for some tourist to start nattering about mysterious visitors. It was another for her instincts to tell her that somehow, in a way she could not define, this thing was malevolent. Kallikuk found herself raising the Lee-Enfield to her shoulder. "Who are y—"

The reflection of her rifle flashed in the surface of the sphere. Then she cried out as the orb flared red and the rifle heated instantly in her hand, too hot to hold onto. She dropped it with a cry. A flash of white light enveloped her for a microsecond in an aura of intense heat. Then she felt nothing.

"Master Corporal!" Pete Nattiq stood transfixed, the tarp falling from his hand. He stared round-eyed at the immobile figure of his corporal, then shifted his gaze to the sphere. He was reaching for his walkie-talkie when the light flared white, and he crumpled silently.

The ball hovered for a moment, then rose silently straight up, heedless of the harsh winds, and zipped off on a straight line towards two red figures further along the ridgeline.

Half an hour later, an ATV roared out of the fog and came to a lurching stop next to the Hab. Fraser dismounted stiffly, then caught sight of the huddled figures on the ground.

The smell caught him first—a strange, chemical smell. He glanced around, but saw nothing. Probably from the burned camp, he thought, even as he knelt over the bodies. It took him less than a minute to determine that they were both dead. He snatched up the walkie-talkie at Kallikuk's waist and keyed it: there was no response. Cursing, he threw it down and jumped to his feet. He looked around, but the enclosing fog had reduced visibility to a few yards. He cupped his hands around his mouth. "Rangers! Is anyone out there?"

His shouting drew attention: the Hab hatch opened and Ted Meyers stumbled out. "What's going on?" The doctor's gaze fell on the bodies. "What happened to them?"

"Something killed them," Fraser said. He glanced around at the encroaching fog. "The radio's down. You!" He pointed at

Courtenay, who was halfway out the hatch. "Get back inside, and keep your people there." Courtenay ignored him, trotting over to stand staring. Behind him, a dozen people crowded out of the Hab. The last one was Martin Skorjik.

Ted knelt beside the bodies, turning them over gently. "There's not a mark on them," he said. He tugged off a glove and laid his hand on Kallikuk's cheek. "The body's still warm."

On the far side of the Hab, heads were poking out of tents.

Fraser bent down next to the doctor. "Look, I don't know what attacked these Rangers—"

"Are you sure it was an attack?" Courtenay said. "It could have been something they ate before they got here, or some disease..." He trailed off, looking at Fraser's face. The constable's expression made him gulp. "Uh. What do you want us to do?"

Fraser got to his feet. "Get everyone back inside. Even the people who are in the outside tents."

"But there's not enough room—"

"Make room!" Fraser barked, at the end of his patience. "And if there are any firearms among you, deal them out to whoever can shoot. I don't want anyone leaving that Habitat until I get back."

"Get back?" Skorjik's voice was sharp. "Where are you going?"

"I have to find the rest of the Ranger team. I'll take the ATV and patrol the perimeter. Until I return, you are all to stay inside."

Subdued, Courtenay made a helpless gesture and turned to go back in. Jennifer pushed past him and came to stand uncertainly next to Skorjik.

Ted Meyers stood, holding Kallikuk's rifle in one hand. "This is half-melted."

"I noticed." Fraser took it from him, turning it over. His mouth was a grim line. He handed it back silently to the doctor. "Go on inside with the others."

"I'll get my kit and go with you." Ted tugged his gloves back on.

"Me, too," Skorjik said.

Fraser shook his head. "No. No civilians. I—"

"There are no civilians left here, Constable," Ted said steadily. "We're all targets. That thing, whatever it is, did this. I know it. You know it. If it's gone after the other Rangers, you'll not only need a medical man, you'll need another gun. I can shoot."

Fraser glared at him. "You're still on the sick list. I need you to stay here, with the others. They may need you more than I do."

"But—"

"Stop arguing with me, Doctor!" Fraser snapped, control fracturing. "I want you and the others inside, now!"

Skorjik turned resolutely to Fraser, his face drawn. "Constable, this camp is still my responsibility. I insist on going with you. I'll be under your orders, but if you leave me behind I'll follow on foot."

Suddenly, Fraser felt very tired. He felt especially tired of arguing with civilians. "Can you handle a rifle?"

"Of course."

"We leave in five minutes."

Ted and Jennifer stood side by side, watching the ATV roll away with Skorjik perched behind Fraser. Without thinking, Ted's arm went around Jennifer's shoulders. They said nothing, equally troubled. In moments, the ATV disappeared into the all-encompassing fog.

At the bottom of the ridge, where the trail crossed the Lowell Canal, Fraser and Skorjik found two sprawled bodies. Fraser checked them swiftly, shook his head, and climbed back aboard the ATV.

"What killed them?" Skorjik said, his voice a hoarse rasp.

"I don't know," Fraser said. "Same as the others, I think."

Halfway to the burned camp, they came across two other bodies. Fraser left the engine running as he climbed down to check them. As he feared, not only were the men dead, but none of their radios or other electronic gear worked. If he'd needed any further proof that all these recent events were not the work of poachers, this was it. He straightened the bodies and covered the faces as best he could.

He climbed back on the ATV, where Skorjik sat staring. "What about bears and scavengers?" the director asked.

Fraser shrugged and rolled onward. What could they do?

It took them two more hours to find the rest of the Rangers—or rather, their bodies—scattered around their posts. The last pair were at the base of the comm array, flung there like broken dolls.

"That's all of them," Fraser said grimly. "Every single Ranger. All military personnel on this island. The only plane is disabled—you saw what was left of the engine. Tell me now we're not dealing with a military incursion. If I were leading an invasion force, my first target would be anyone wearing a uniform."

"And their second target would be you, Constable."

"Or you," Fraser said. He looked around. "You're the leader of this expedition, as you said. One thing I don't like. Whatever it was that attacked Meyers, it didn't kill him. It killed these men, but left him alive."

Skorjik stared. "You think Ted Meyers is behind this? Or in league with—no. It's ridiculous. Impossible."

"He could have faked that whole 'attack'," Fraser pointed out. "Who better than a medical doctor to fake a concussion? And come to think of it, where was he when the fire started?"

Skorjik stood with his hands on his hips. "No. I'll stake my life Ted has nothing to do with this. And how, or why, would he kill all these men?"

Fraser slung his rifle on his shoulder and straddled the ATV. "It's not just that these men were killed," he said, kicking the machine to life. "It also destroyed their weapons. Doctor, has it occurred to you the point of all this? Someone is trying to disarm us."

Silently, Skorjik climbed back onto the ATV. He said nothing during the ride back to the Habitat on the hill.

The wind had turned even colder as they followed the ridge, and Sophia had to hold her hood closed to keep it from funneling freezing air down her front. Since she had only her left glove, she had to keep her right hand in her pocket, so her balance was off. More than once she only saved herself from falling by a last-minute grab at a rock, which often as not slid under her hand.

Amaruq trotted up beside her, scrambling over boulders. Sophia noticed that she favored her injured leg; she looked tired.

"Hey, Amaruq," she said softly. She stopped, letting Nick go on ahead of her.

The dog, or as Sophia reminded herself, the wolf looked over at her, wagged her tail. Her expression was friendly, even—dared she think it—intelligent.

"Are you really a girl in a wolf's skin?" Sophia mused.

Amaruq stopped short, her tail and ears up, peering intently at her. She yipped once and sat down.

Sophia stopped as well. "You understood me?"

Another yip.

Sophia's heart gave a little bump of fear and excitement. Could it be real? Could it be Nick was telling the truth? But it couldn't be. It was impossible, just not possible. Species could not be combined like that, not even in a laboratory.

Or could they? Sophia considered that forty years ago, no one would have believed that anything could live in a volcanic hot spring, or a lake of acid, or in glacial ice millions of years old. Geneticists had recently fused human genes into mouse brains, and the Chinese were reported to have inserted human genes into rabbit eggs. But who, or what, could have fused wolves and humans? And why? Slowly, she stretched out a hand. "Amaruq? Are you...are you really a, a human?"

The wolf whined, put out her paw and placed it carefully in Sophia's. And then she nodded once, slowly.

Sophia caught her breath. The wolf had *nodded*. Of course, it could have been trained, or it could be some instinct she didn't know, but it looked like the wolf understood her.

"Give her a command," Nick said behind her.

Sophia turned and straightened. His hood had fallen back in the wind, and his hair blew around his head in a wild tempest. His hands were stuck in his pockets. He nodded at the wolf. "In fact, give her one in French. She understands it pretty well." At her look, he cocked an eyebrow. "National language of Canada, remember? We learned it in school."

"I don't speak it very well." Sophia blinked as she realized she was comparing her foreign language skills to an animal's. "Okay. Uh, *s'asseoir!*"

Amaruq snorted, and sat.

Nick smiled. "She says your accent is atrocious, and your verb tense is wrong."

"It's a coincidence," Sophia said. She thought for a minute. "Um. *Tournez autour de trois fois.*"

Obediently, Amaruq turned around in a circle three times.

"She says this is silly. And you forgot to say, 'please'. Ask her to read something."

"*Read* something?"

Nick nodded. "She was in the fifth grade when she... changed. She—" He stopped, pressed his lips into a tight line, then finished. "She used to read the Babysitters Club books in third grade. And Nancy Drew. Mom read her A Wrinkle in Time, when she was changing."

"I loved that book." Sophia searched through her pockets. One of them held a wrapper from an energy bar. Turning her back to Nick, she held it out. Amaruq stepped forward, nose up, eyes on the wrapper. Sophia felt a frisson of ice go down her back as the wolf scanned the label, then sat back on her haunches.

"She says it's her favorite flavor, maple nut. Actually, she's also fond of the ones with chocolate and peanuts, but I try not to give her chocolate. She used to love chocolate, but it's bad for her in... this form."

Sophia rested a hand on the wolf's head and sank down on

her heels, bringing her eyes level. Nick knew she'd been carrying energy bars, she thought. But there were several different kinds. Maybe he'd only guessed right. Her instincts, however, overrode logic. She stared into the wolf's amber eyes. And what she saw broke her heart.

"She can't go back," Sophia whispered.

Amaruq whined and licked her hand.

"A girl who loved Babysitter Club mysteries, pizza and chocolate," Sophia said to herself.

Amaruq nodded, then put her head to one side.

"I wonder if you liked boys, or ever had your hair done, or painted your fingernails."

Amaruq whined, then raised a paw to Sophia's hand. Tears sprung into Sophia's eyes. "God. I take it that's a yes on the fingernail polish?"

"Yeah." Nick's voice was thick behind her. "She liked pink."

Sophia looked at the paw, with its claws, its fur. She looked closer—the dewclaw looked different. Bringing her face closer, Sophia examined it, and felt the hair on her nape stand up. The claw was deformed, flattened, broad like...like a primate's. Like a cross between human and wolf.

She dropped Amaruq's paw. Nick knelt, embracing the wolf. Amaruq closed her eyes and licked her brother's ear.

"If it's not magic, if it isn't an illusion, if it's real..." Her throat was dry, even as she voiced her conclusion aloud. "She can't go back."

Nick shook his head, face still in his sister's fur. "Can you reverse puberty? Can you put a grown man back in the womb?" He stood and faced her again. "Think of it like that. It's not so far off—most of the ones who survive are young, under the age or at the age of puberty. Nauja—that was the name our mother gave her, it means 'seagull'—was only ten. And she was small. She didn't weigh much more than she does now. And it took months, not minutes."

Sophia nodded. It made a weird kind of sense. "Yes, the change in mass alone might be fatal." She winced, remembering Nick's grief. "Your brother..."

"Was twenty nine years old, and weighed more than twelve stone. Nobody survives a Transformation at that age." He hunched his shoulders, staring off into the distance. "Even if it doesn't kill them outright, even if they get halfway and stop, they...they go mad."

"Yes, I can imagine," Sophia said. To lose one's humanity, to be a human intelligence trapped in a beast's body...yes, she would go mad herself. A sudden thought chilled her further. "Nick. Does that mean *you* ..."

"Maybe. I check myself every day. I don't know if it will happen to me. Sometimes it never hits. My father, he never Transformed. And of course my mother couldn't. She was... normal. An outsider who married into the family curse."

Sophia put a hand on his arm, hearing deep grief in his voice. "What happened to her?"

He stared at the ground. "She...she got pregnant, after Nauja changed. She...the babies ..." He swallowed. "They were deformed."

"They? Twins?"

He closed his eyes. She could hear the agony and shame in his voice. "More like a...a litter."

She gasped. A litter? The full horror of it struck her. A human woman birthing *animals?* "Dear God," she breathed. "What...what happened to them?"

His voice turned to stone. "We can't let them live. It's one thing for a human to change into an animal after having lived as a human, but to be raised, from birth, trapped in wolf hide? No. It's too cruel. My father...he killed them, an act of mercy. But it broke him. It broke my mother." His voice dropped to a whisper; Amaruq tucked her tail around her and laid her head on Nick's foot. "It was winter, in full dark with no sun for weeks. Mom snuck out one night into a snowstorm. When my father found her, she had frozen almost solid." He swallowed. "It's why I...I was worried that you might be ..."

Sophia clutched her middle. She knew she was protected against pregnancy, her birth control shots had never failed her. But the idea of...animals growing inside her. She fought the sudden urge to run, to vomit. "How do you live with this?" she whispered.

"Mostly, we don't. Like I said, it mostly kills us. We're all that's left now. Me and Amaruq."

Sophia turned and looked away, her hands in her jacket pockets. "I came all this way to find extreme life forms," she said. "And now I find one I can't believe."

"We're not 'life forms'," Nick said, an edge in his voice. "We're people. We—"

Furious barking interrupted him. They both looked over as Amaruq came to her feet, hackles raised, legs stiff. Her nose swung back and forth, scenting the wind from the north.

"What is it?" Sophia said. "The bear again?"

Nick crouched by the wolf, frowning. "No. Something else. She doesn't know what. But...dangerous." He looked into his sister's eyes, returning her look.

Amaruq's tail went low, tucked under. Her ears flattened, showing fear and defiance. Sophia gazed out over the way they'd come.

The rain had dissipated the fog, so the barren jumble of rock stretched to the horizon, broken here and there by the creeks formed by runoff, or by the deeper cut of the Truelove River. Sophia strained, trying to see the hot spring, or even the cliff they had scrambled down, but everything looked the same: brown and barren.

Nick stood straight, also shading his eyes. "She says she smelled something. There was a scent, something she doesn't understand, at both the wolf site and the camp where Glenn and Leo died. She says she smells it now."

"You don't think a bear killed those men."

He lowered his hand, shaking his head. "There was no blood on the bodies. And that silver stuff..."

Sophia had forgotten about the silver liquid. She patted her pockets, then dove a hand into one. She fished out a couple of plastic sample vials; one of them held the silver-gray mass she had taken from the campsite. "This, you mean?"

Nick eyed it with suspicion. "Let her smell it."

Sophia held out the vial to the dog; she sniffed it carefully, then looked up at Nick.

"She says it's a weird smell, but not the same. What do you think that stuff is? Some kind of parasite?"

Sophia pulled the scope out from under her sweater, held the vial up to the weak sunlight. The image was fuzzy at first; she used her fingers to turn the focusing knobs, making tiny adjustments. Then the image resolved, and she held her breath.

Dull silver specks sprang into high resolution, resolving as angular, geometrical arrangements of smaller elements. Each unit was a geometric spiral, a fractal. The arms spiraled out, intersected, connected, locked together. Some units floated free; she shook the vial to move them into better focus.

"What do you see?" Nick asked. She handed him the vial and the scope, showed him how to focus the instrument. After a long moment, he put down the scope. *"Machines?"*

"Very tiny machines," Sophia said. "The size of bacteria. Or maybe some hybrid form of machine and organic structure. I guess that's how it reacted so quickly when we disturbed it. It was...I think it was building something, maybe using the bodies as fuel or as building material. But I've never seen or heard of anything like these machines."

"Secret NASA research?" Nick asked. He handed her the vial, and she put it away in her pocket. "Some kind of weapon?"

"I don't know. I'm not in that field, but I think I'd have heard about it if anyone was creating machines this sophisticated on such a tiny scale."

"Not if it's black ops stuff," Nick said.

"Black ops?" She looked askance at him. "You watch a lot of *X-Files* re-runs?"

Nick smiled slightly. "No. I read a lot of Michael Crichton thrillers."

"Well, I can tell you this, as someone who works for and with NASA: the government can't keep secrets like this. It's just not that good at it."

"Then what—"

Amaruq rose to her feet with a roar, backing uphill, barking angrily at something below. Nick jumped to his feet and stepped in front of Sophia. "Get up the hill."

Sophia looked back, squinting. Was that a gleam of something in the Truelove cut? A reflection off a mirror, maybe? It came and went so fast she could not be sure.

Nick climbed the slope below her, urging her onward. Amaruq bounded past Sophia, heading for the ridgeline.

"What is it?"

Nick shook his head. "I don't know. But Amaruq says something's on our trail, something she smelled near those dead men. And it's not a bear."

Mars Habitat Project, Devon Island, Nunavut
75° 25′ 52.61″ N, 89° 51′ 00″ W

Jennifer stood staring into the fog where Fraser and Skorjik had disappeared. "What about Nick and Sophia?" she said. "The Constable doesn't seem very worried about them."

Ted Meyers rubbed his temple. "I know. And that's stupid, because that...thing...was definitely after them."

Jennifer glanced down at the bodies sprawled on the gravel. "Are you sure? Maybe it was after these guys. Maybe it felt threatened."

Ted's expression hardened. "I can't imagine anything that would frighten that thing. More likely this was a strategic move to take out any opposition."

The wind whipped a lock of blonde hair into Jennifer's face. She pushed it away impatiently. "You think it will go after Nick?"

"I think it already has."

"How long before the Constable gets back?" she asked.

Ted stalked away without answering. Jennifer had to hurry to keep up with his long stride, then halted when he did, next to the row of parked ATVs. As the search teams had trickled in, Skorjik had made them park near the Habitat.

Ted turned to face her. "I'm not waiting until they get back," he said tersely. "It may already be too late, but I have to make sure."

"You know where they are?"

Meyers shook his head. "I know where it's been. It's...it's in my head. I can't get rid of it."

"The ice cap?"

He nodded. Jennifer straightened, and a hard edge came into her expression. "Get your medical kit. I'll get the rifle."

Meyers opened his mouth, preparing to object. Then he caught the expression in her eyes and closed his mouth. He nodded and walked back to the Habitat; Jennifer followed silently.

Pushing her way into the module after Ted, Jennifer was struck by the heat and noise. Whereas the lower half of the living structure had been cold and drafty when she'd found Ted lying on the floor, now it was hot and crowded. Someone had stuffed several parkas into the round hole left by Ted's attacker, and every light in the facility had been turned on. People stood, sat, and leaned against every possible surface, and every single one of them seemed to be talking. Or shouting. Jennifer resisted the urge to clap her hands over her ears.

"Excuse me, please," she said, shoving through a line that kinked through the crowd, leading to the only working bathroom on Devon Island. "Please let me through."

Haggard faces turned towards her, assessed her as another survivor/victim, and turned away.

"I'm telling you, this is a hoax," one stout woman said loudly to a skinny man Jennifer recognized as a planetary geologist. "This is NASA, trying to shut us down!"

"That doesn't make any sense," the skinny man responded mildly.

"The hell it doesn't," the woman responded, her face reddening. "This is just the excuse those damned politicians need to shut us down. There'll be no space program at all—"

Jennifer pressed on, past a couple of bearded men arguing loudly in Russian, past several people sunk in gloom, and past a grizzled man snoring in a corner. She finally reached the bottom of the ladder leading to the top, only to run into Courtenay fumbling his way down. He looked over her head, and winced.

"Good God!" he cried. "Are you people insane? Turn off those lights! We'll burn out the generator!"

No one paid attention to him, and he stood rubbing his hands together. *Think fast,* Jennifer thought. *Hit him up while he's focused on something else.* What would make a control freak like him give up a rifle?

She tugged at Courtenay's sleeve. When he turned to her, looking distracted, she leaned in and spoke in a low tone. "Dr. Courtenay, someone just spotted a polar bear down near the camp."

He rolled his eyes. "Oh, just what we need. Well, stay inside and we'll—"

"I'm afraid it was sniffing around the bodies."

Courtenay turned pale. "Jesus."

"Let me take a rifle and scare it away. No need to spread panic," she said, glancing significantly at the crowd of frightened, tired researchers.

Courtenay squinted at her. "You've shot a rifle before?"

"Many times," she said with a confidence she did not feel.

"I can't let you. It's too dangerous."

Jennifer leaned closer. "Look around you. What do you think these people would do if they knew you allowed a polar bear to eat their friends?"

Courtenay gulped, fished in a pocket of his overalls and brought out a key ring. "Follow me. Quietly."

He pushed his way through the crowd, Jennifer following. He stopped at a locker next to the hatch. Glancing around at the scientists crowded behind him, he maneuvered himself to block their view. He unlocked the locker and handed a rifle out to Jennifer. "I'm trusting you," he said in a low voice.

"I'll need ammo," she said.

He nodded and handed her a box of cartridges, which she slipped into her parka pocket. "Be careful."

"I will."

He stood back, blocking the view of the hatch, and she slipped out quickly.

Ted sat astride an idling ATV, his medical kit strapped to

the front. He wore goggles and a ski mask against the wind. As she came down the steps, he extended a hand, holding another pair of goggles. Jennifer handed him the rifle, slipped the goggles on, and took back the rifle. She checked the bolt-action, then took Meyers' extended hand. He handed her up behind him with a strong grip, then gunned the engine.

The fog hung over the land like an ethereal curtain. Hunched down behind Ted, Jennifer peered over his shoulder as he headed down the gravel path. He came to the turn, where the path led downwards into the plain where the remains of Haughton Crater Research Station were a black scar. He stopped, turned his head to speak to Jennifer.

"Last chance to get off," he said. "I'm taking a shortcut across the crater."

Jennifer tightened her grip on the rifle stock. "Let's go."

Meyers turned the handlebars to the right, and the little ATV rolled down the slope, crossing the invisible boundary into the twenty-three-million-year-old crater.

Truelove Lowlands, Devon Island, Nunavut
75° 38′ 13.47″ N, 83° 49′ 21.46″ W

Nick shaded his eyes, peering east. "There!" He pointed. Against the dark gray background of the cliffs above the Truelove River, Sophia saw movement. Down in the trench of the river valley, something winked, winked again.

A surge of relief went through her. "They found us! It's probably an ATV." Oh God, she thought. *A shower. A real bed. And a chance to think about what Nick had told her, about what they had done. About what all this meant.*

Nick stepped back. "I'd feel better if we were off this ridge. We're too exposed."

"But don't we want to be exposed? How will a search party find us if we hide?"

"It's not a search party." His mouth was grim. He looked at her, his eyes troubled. "Look, we still don't know what killed those men. And that wolf. Something strange is going on out here. I don't want to take any chances."

254

"Me neither," Sophia said. "But it seems to me we are taking a chance. Look, we missed our call-in already because the radio is dead. So Skorjik or Fraser sent someone out to look for us. That flash you saw is probably the plane, searching."

Nick shook his head. "No, I don't think—"

"Dammit, Nick! If they find the dead men, or our equipment, they'll be looking for us. But they don't know we're up here, and we have no way to signal them. You want to walk away from them?" She looked down the slope, back the way they'd come. "I'm going back down. Maybe I can meet up with—"

Nick grabbed her arm. "No. I mean it."

She met his eyes with a challenge in hers. "Is this more of your mental telepathy?"

He released her. "I knew I shouldn't have told you. My father was right." He hunched his shoulders against the wind, swung on his heel and headed south along the ridge, towards the wall of ice.

Sophia watched him, the wolf at his heels, until the path dipped down an incline and he was lost from sight. She was aware of how cold and alone she was up here on this knife edge of the world, with the sky darkening and the wind bringing the smell of rain. In all that darkening world to the east, nothing moved. It was that very emptiness that had a coil of tension building in the pit of her stomach.

Nick's paranoid, she told herself. She thought of his intensity, the way he'd held her, the slow soft voice in which he'd told her amazing, unbelievable things, testing the limits of her trust and her belief. Back at home in her apartment or her study cube at the library, in the biology lab or hanging out in Jennifer's living room, she would have laughed at his fantastic story, would have rejected the idea. Out here, it didn't sound quite that deranged. And there was Amaruq, a wolf who didn't act like a wolf...

Out of the corner of her eye, she caught movement...*yes*. Something moving against that smear of granite turned black by rain. Something very small, very fast.

Flying.

She wanted it to be the Twin Otter plane. She told herself

255

it was. But she was already backing, turning, starting to run after Nick before she even realized that something in her brain was yelling *no no wrong no.*

The wind screamed at her, moaned over the ridgetop, howled away into the darkening mist. She felt the fear rising in her, still not knowing where it came from, still uncertain—and ahead of her a shape loomed up out of the fog. "Nick!"

He stopped and waited. She swallowed, looked over her shoulder. "Amaruq may be right. There's...something ..."

Behind Nick the wolf was half crouched, ears flat, tail low. Her lips were drawn back in a soundless snarl, her gaze focused behind Sophia. Her head moved as her gaze followed something Sophia could not see.

"Go ahead of me, up the trail," Nick said. He had his boot knife in his fist, the blade naked and sharp. "Keep moving south. Watch your step, but go as fast as you can."

Gusts of wind now alternated with gusts of snow. There was no shelter as they picked their way along the ridgetop, their footing made treacherous by loose gravel. Nick took the lead to lead her along the very edge of the cliff. They moved silently, instinct telling them that it would be dangerous to attract attention. Nick chose a path that put boulders, rises, any kind of barrier between them and their back trail. Amaruq came last, turning every few steps to peer back the way they had come.

The ridge had been angling down for some time, and the white cliff of ice crept nearer, until Sophia could smell it. The ice-wind smelled clean, fresh, without the salt tang of the polar air.

Then Amaruq raced past to take up a stiff-legged stance looking behind her. She turned, and now above the ridgeline she saw it: something moving, something she could not quite see, something that looked like moonlight and silver mirrors. Nick put himself between her and whatever approached.

When it finally came close enough to resolve, Sophia felt a bubble of terrified laughter rising in her. *It's a disco ball,* she thought. A bobbing sphere that bounced slowly back and forth, as if scanning their tracks, its surface swirling like smoke inside a snow-globe. Amaruq gave one fierce bark, backing away.

"Have you ever seen anything like this? Back at the camp?" Nick said in a low voice.

"No."

"It's moving against the wind." His jaw worked, and Sophia saw his fists balled at his side. "I don't like this."

They stood very still as the sphere approached. It made no sound. Sophia stepped closer to Nick, and he took her hand. "Stay behind me," he whispered.

She squeezed his hand. "No." She stood shoulder to shoulder with him, watching the globe bob closer. Her other hand closed around something smooth and cool in her pocket.

When it was about twenty feet away, it stopped. "There's a light," Sophia said.

A faint, pulsing light glowed deep in the center, growing brighter with each pulse. The swirls on its surface spun faster, then halted in an odd pattern that teased the edges of Sophia's mind, familiar and yet not familiar, like a word she could not bring to mind. As she struggled to find it, white light flared from the globe, like a sustained camera flash. She cried out and put her hand up to shield her eyes. There was a sudden blast of cold pain, a burst of heat from her fist, and then the pain vanished, leaving her dizzy.

Both Nick and Amaruq cried out and fell to the ground, writhing.

Mars Habitat Project, Devon Island, Nunavut
75° 25′ 52.61″ N, 89° 51′ 00″ W

"What are they doing?" Fraser said testily. "They're supposed to be inside. I told them to stay inside!"

Fraser brought the ATV to a stop about four yards from the Hab. A small crowd of people milled around outside the hatch. Some of them carried rifles. Fraser frowned and cut the engine. Climbing stiffly off, he lifted the edge of his parka to free access to his weapon. He heard Skorjik climbing off behind him.

As Fraser walked toward the group, they turned anxious faces to him—mostly men, but a couple of women. He recognized the expression on their faces: panic.

Damn.

"Everyone all right, then?" he said, putting his most relaxed tone into the question.

"Two more of our people have disappeared," said one of the men, stepping forward. He held a rifle in his right hand.

Fraser tensed, his hand straying towards his holster. "Sir, I'm going to ask you only once to lower your weapon."

The man blinked, his eyes blue and vague above his dark beard. He glanced down at the rifle, clearly having forgotten it. "Oh. Sorry." He pointed the weapon at the ground. The others followed suit and Fraser relaxed a bit. "Who's missing?"

"Dr. Meyers and Dr. Roth have taken an ATV and a rifle—"

"You let them leave?" Fraser fought the impulse to grab the man and shake him. "Where did they go? How long ago?"

Dr. Courtenay pushed his way through. "They haven't disappeared. I let them leave. They're scaring away a polar bear—"

"A polar bear?" Fraser felt like laughing. In the midst of all they were facing, it was ludicrous. *"A polar bear?"*

"But that was hours ago," Courtenay continued. "Do you think they ran into trouble?"

"You should have stopped them," Skorjik said sharply. "You don't seem to realize how dangerous our position is."

"But the Rangers were out there," Constable said. "Surely they can't have run into—"

"The Rangers are dead," Fraser said. "Every single one of them. And not a mark on them. Now do I have your cooperation, Doctor, or am I going to have to put you and this entire group under military jurisdiction to get you to behave sensibly?"

"Dead?" Courtenay blinked. "But how? Where?" He glanced around wildly, as if invisible attackers were closing in.

"I don't know what killed them. I do know that whoever it is, they also destroyed their weapons. Except for what's here, we are unarmed."

Courtenay went white under his Arctic tan, then flushed. "Who's doing this?"

"I don't know."

The man with the rifle said, "Constable, why can't we all go down to the airstrip and take off in that plane?"

"Good idea!" Courtenay brightened. "Even if we can't get everyone off the island, we can at least relieve the load on our supp—"

"There is no plane," Skorjik interrupted. As Courtenay sputtered to a stop, he said, "Whatever killed the Rangers also took out the plane."

Courtenay looked shocked. "What? How—" He looked helplessly at Fraser. "I don't understand what's going on here."

Skorjik nodded. "No one does, Bob."

A woman with burns on her face shoved to the front. "So what do we do? Sit here while we get picked off one by one? We have to get out of here!"

Fraser set his mouth, prepared to pull rank on each and every one of them, but Skorjik stepped in front of him, holding up a hand. "This is not the way professionals handle an emergency," he said. Every eye was on him.

"We're used to confronting the unknown, right?" Skorjik continued. "So I suggest we stop panicking like a bunch of undergraduates and act like scientists."

Muttering, but some hopeful looks. Fraser stepped up beside the director. "We can't afford to act like scared children," he said. Then he swallowed his pride. "And I can't do it all by myself. I need your help."

Glances flicked among the assembled people. Fraser had their attention. They were tired and afraid and confused, but they were also scientists.

Courtenay looked from Fraser to Skorjik and then back. Whatever he saw, he straightened. "What do you want us to do?"

"Organize," Skorjik said before Fraser could answer. "Get

together and figure out how fifty people can survive on rations for twelve for—would you say a week, Constable?"

Fraser shrugged.

Skorjik turned to his rival. "Bob, these people are tired and hungry and scared. Let's get them organized into teams, set up watches, set up a mess tent and a sleep schedule."

The little administrator perked up. This was something he could do. "You're right. And we can frame it as a simulation, so we can set up and test emergency protocols for a Mars mission. We can rig hammocks to fit more people in, and then set people up in sleep shifts so we don't need as many beds..."

The two strode off, talking, and Fraser yawned hugely. How long since he'd had any sleep? Impossible to tell, with the sun still a hands-breadth above the horizon, if he could have seen it through this fog. He desperately wanted nothing so much as to curl up in a sleeping bag and wake up next Wednesday. Instead, he rubbed his face, wished for coffee, and strode back to the ATV. His bear gun was still strapped to it; all he had to do was hoist himself into the seat and kick the machine to life. He was tired and hungry, but that could not be helped. The longer the doctor and his girlfriend were outside the camp, the more danger they were in. He swung the ATV into the rim road and gunned it.

White spots danced in front of his eyes and he pulled his goggles down over his face. Still they danced, and Fraser realized it was snowing again.

Truelove Lowlands, Devon Island, Nunavut
75° 38′ 13.47″ N, 83° 49′ 21.46″ W

"Nick!" Sophia dropped to her knees.

Nick curled in on himself, gasping. Next to him, Amaruq whimpered, pawing at her ears.

"What is it? What's wrong?" Sophia touched Nick's shoulder but he flinched away.

"Voice...inside me. It hurts..." he gasped.

Sophia looked up at the hovering globe. It continued to

flash, but she felt nothing from it, internal or otherwise. She flung herself on top of Nick, shielding as much of him from the flashing light as she could. Her fist hit the ground and she realized she was holding one of the sample vials that had been in her jacket pocket.

Nick gasped. "No. Get away! I—" He rolled away and vomited onto the path. Amaruq was doing the same thing on the other side of the path.

"What the hell is that thing?" Sophia muttered. She came to her knees, a rock in one hand. "Get out of here!" she cried, and flung the rock at the hovering sphere.

The rock bounced off an invisible shield before it even touched the globe. The hovering ball bobbled a little but remained where it was, above the path. Sophia threw more rocks, to no avail; all they did was make the ball rebound.

The globe turned red and a wave of heat passed over Sophia, as if a tropical sun had come out. She raised a hand to shield her face, the hand containing the vial. The heat stopped and the globe turned silver. Sophia felt a sudden wave of menace, as if for the first time something deeply hostile had noticed her.

Nick gasped. "Oh, God..." Blood ran from his nose and ears.

Amaruq whined. Blood poured from her muzzle. He coughed, a deep, wet sound from his lungs.

It's killing them, Sophia thought. "Can you stand? Maybe we can get away from it."

Nick struggled to his knees, swaying. "Can't ..."

The orb drifted closer, strobing. Too distracted to drop the vial, Sophia bent over and gathered the limp wolf into her arms. She staggered to her feet. "Come on, Nick!"

Taking deep, ragged breaths, Nick stood. Sophia backed away from the sphere, carrying Amaruq. Nick tried to get between her and the hovering globe, but she shook her head. "You go first, so I don't back over a cliff," she said. He shuffled past her, bent at the waist. She felt him grab the back of her parka and tug. Taking one careful step backward after another, they retreated towards the ice cap.

"It's following us," Nick said, his voice husky.

Her stomach sank as she watched the globe bob along behind her, maintaining the same distance, the constant strobe making her blink. She stumbled once, but felt Nick's steadying hand at her waist. Amaruq stirred, whimpering. Sophia could feel her panting.

"Can you see any way off this ridge?" Sophia asked. "Somewhere we can lose this thing in the rocks?"

"Ice ahead," Nick said.

"Is it still...attacking you?"

He drew a deep, shaky breath. "No, it's slacked off a little. I don't know why."

Sophia glanced behind her. The blue-white wall of the ice cap towered above them. A jumble of ice blocks, some the size of cars, was piled at its base.

"Can we lose it in that?"

"Don't know," Nick said hoarsely. He eyed the globe. "Let...me know if it...gets closer."

They continued on; white walls rose to Sophia's left and right. There was no question of hiding their tracks; even if the globe had not been in sight, both Amaruq and Nick were leaving a blood trail. Huge blocks of translucent ice rose on either hand, climbing upwards toward the crest of the great ice cliff. At the same time, the ground beneath her feet grew slippery; she glanced down long enough to see that it was glazed with ice. Her feet slid and she fought for balance.

The globe followed her, and now its flashing light reflected brilliantly off a million frozen surfaces.

"Why isn't it … attacking us?" Nick muttered.

"Can you see a way through?" she asked Nick in a low voice.

"If we can...distract it ..."

"I can throw some rocks at it again," she said, looking about her. She remembered how they had bounced off earlier, and her heart sank even lower. "Dammit, what is this thing?"

She bumped up against Nick and stopped short. Turning, she saw him leaning against a pillar of ice, drawing deep, ragged breaths.

"You should...leave us. Go on." He flung an arm out, gesturing towards the maze of ice before them. "It...doesn't want you."

"What do you mean?"

"Can't you...hear it?" His skin looked tight and drawn over his face. As she watched, he grunted and clutched his middle.

"Nick ..."

He waved her onward. "Go. Take...Amaruq." He gasped and bent over.

"Like hell." She shifted the burden in her arms. "I'm not leaving you."

But Nick was past answering, growing weaker as she watched. Sophia stared at the globe. She felt nothing from it, certainly no pain, no communication of any kind.

"I think...it killed those men," Nick said. "Go, Sophia. Please."

"Not a chance," she said firmly. "I don't feel a thing. You're the one who should go, and leave me to block this...thing."

Amaruq whined and jerked in her arms, and Sophia staggered, wrestling to keep the wolf from slipping out of her arms. She bobbled the vial, just catching it as it was about to fall. *Maybe she should drop it*, she thought. Maybe it would distract that thing.

Out of the blue, it all came together in her head—why the globe was not attacking her, why it was following.

"It's the vial!"

"What?"

She turned the vial over in her hand, watching the globe. Its color stayed silver. "Nick, you say this thing killed Glenn and Leo. If that's true, then it left behind that silver stuff we found."

"Yeah?" His voice sounded even weaker.

"So." She knelt and laid Amaruq on the ice-covered ground. "Maybe it wants it back."

A deep cough racked Nick, but he nodded. Wiping his mouth, he said, "Like a mother bear...looking for her cub?"

"That's why it doesn't attack me," Sophia said. "I'm carrying something it wants."

Nick nodded, took a step towards her. "Give it...to me."

"No. Take Amaruq. Go into the maze and find a place to hide. I can lead it away from you."

"No..."

"Dammit, Nick, this is no time for heroics!"

"Best...time ..." His weakening voice held a ghost of laughter.

Sophia stepped across the body of the wolf and grabbed Nick's upper arm. She felt the deep shudders racking him. "Nick, please," she said.

Light flickered over his face, and she saw that his eyes were bloodshot. His gaze bored into her, desperation in his look.

He started to speak but she cut him off. "Let me lead it away. Save your sister."

She saw his eyes stray to the wolf's inert form where she lay gasping, sides heaving. "Amaruq ..."

"Go on. I'll be right after you, as soon as I've lost it." Sophia put as much confidence as she could into her voice.

Under her hands, Nick shuddered again, deep tremors that shook his whole body. But he pushed himself upright, then knelt to gather up the wolf. It took him three tries to get to his feet, and he stood swaying. "Be careful," he whispered, his eyes intense. "Don't...come back. Keep going."

On impulse, she reached up and took his face between her hands. "Hide." She kissed him passionately, not caring about the blood on his face, on her hands. His response was as ardent, filled with the same longing and fear and promise as her own kiss. Between them, Amaruq squirmed.

She released him, and a hank of his hair came away in her hand. The wind caught it, and it drifted to the icy ground. They both stared at it, and Sophia felt herself go cold all over. She heard Nick's voice: *I watched my little sister go through hell. Her hair fell out...* She turned away, feeling in her pocket for the other sample vial. "Go now," she said.

Nick clutched Amaruq to him. With one searing look into her eyes, he turned away. She heard the crunch of ice under his boots.

Before her, the orb hung as before, still flashing. Could she do this?

As Nick's footsteps receded, the globe advanced. She felt her knees go weak as it approached. The flashing light hurt her eyes, but she kept a firm grip on the vials. Closer it came, rising as if to go right over her. If she'd needed no other confirmation of its target, this avoidance of her would have been enough; the globe was after Nick and Amaruq for some reason.

Sophia held the vials up. The globe stopped and hovered. The vials sparkled as if they held fireflies. Sophia felt a faint wash of heat come and go, and the globe slowly turned blue.

"Yeah, you know what this is. You want it." She clutched the vials tightly, one in each hand. "Come and get them." She stepped to one side.

Whirls of blue-gray swirled inside the globe. She took another step, then another, until she was up against the solid wall of ice to her left.

The orb followed her. The spiraling patterns under its surface grew darker, almost black, and now looked like tar coiling under the transparent skin.

"Come on," she hissed at it. "Come after me, if you want it back." She stepped past the globe, holding the vials high.

The globe flared red. Sudden heat bloomed in her hand and wrist, and she cried out. She snatched her hand against her chest, nearly dropping the vials. "Not working," she snarled. "Is that all you got?"

She was beyond the globe now, backing down the path, back out of the ice maze. The wind whipped her hair into her face, bit at her exposed skin. She smelled rain on the wind, or maybe it was snow. The globe, now as black as polished onyx, followed her, bobbing. Then it stopped, and Sophia raised a vial. She waved it.

"That's right. Come on, follow me, whatever you are." She took another step backwards. "You want it. You know you do. What is this? Your babies? Seeds? Food? Whatever it is, you can't get it unless you—ow!"

The globe color shifted to red. This time it was like fire flashing through her. She gasped, and she was back in the cabin, back in the flames, feeling the hiss and bite of fire, smelling her own skin burning. Her eyes told her there was no flame, but her skin felt like it was melting. Sophia screamed and bent double, but held onto the vials.

"No, it won't work! You can't make me drop it."

Screams. Paul, and the others, and the roar of flames...

"Stop it!" Sophia yelled. Paul was dead, the others were dead, there were no flames. *Choking, fighting for air through the soot-laden smoke. Yells, the pain slamming through her arm and side, the sizzle of her burning hair.*

"No!" Sophia cried. "No! It's not real! *It's not real!*" She took another step backward, another. The orb followed her, and invisible energy like static electricity crackled around it.

Rock under her feet, then gravel. She was out of the ice tunnel. Sophia slid, slipped, but kept moving backwards. The vials in her hands felt like molten glass.

"It's all...in my head," she panted aloud. "In my head. Not...real." In her mind, she knew the vials were all that kept the orb from killing her. Her hand trembled, screamed with pain. *She smelled the kerosene, heard the crackle of flames.*

In her mind's eye, she saw Nick's face, saw blood streaking his cheeks, saw him standing with his arms full of sagging wolf.

Sophia felt her convulsive grasp of the vials weaken. They flared like stars caught in her fist, burning like hot iron. She would not be able to hold them much longer.

Sophia glanced to her right, saw the cliff falling away to the land below. On the horizon, the sun lanced through the clouds, full in her eyes. It lit up the broken, blasted land below, a barren badlands of waste and cold. She looked back at the now-black orb.

"I won't...let you have him," she said through clenched teeth. "Burn me where I stand, but you don't get him. You want it that bad," she hissed. "Go and get it."

Turning, she faced the chasm and flung one vial outward with all her might. It arced over the shattered escarpment and fell away.

The orb zipped silently after it, following its fall down into the shadows.

Sophia did not wait to hear it fall, nor to see what the orb did. She turned and ran for the ice maze as fast as she could.

Truelove Lowlands, Devon Island, Nunavut
75° 38′ 13.47″ N, 83° 49′ 21.46″ W

Jennifer topped a rise and stopped. They'd been walking for two hours along the ridge, having abandoned the ATV when the terrain became to rough for wheeled vehicles.

"What is it?" Ted came around to stand beside her. "Oh."

A red splash stood out against the white/gray rock and pale lichen scattered across the ridgeline.

Ted knelt, touched the red splotch, sniffed. "Blood."

"Sophia?" Jennifer asked, her voice tight with tension.

He straightened, looked her in the eye. "We don't even know if it's human," he said. "Could be a fox kill, or a raptor. We don't know that—"

Jennifer bent down, picked up a shiny piece of paper. She straightened, holding it up. It was the wrapper from an energy bar. "This was Sophia's. I packed it for her."

"That could be anybody's."

Jennifer turned it over. "We bought these in Berkeley two weeks ago. This is her favorite flavor. What are the odds?"

Ted's shoulders slumped. "Okay. So what the hell are Nick and Sophia doing up on this ridge, when they're supposed to be down in the river valley?"

Jennifer looked past him, and he turned to follow her gaze. They stood side by side, looking at the towering wall of white that ran from horizon to horizon across their line of travel, the front edge of the Devon Ice Cap. Silently, Jennifer re-settled the rifle on her shoulder and started forward.

Ted turned his face up and saw the massed snow clouds above him, saw the swirl of heavy flakes. "It's snowing," he said. "We should—"

But she wasn't listening. He glanced up the trail, and she was hunched over something on the ground.

Ted hurried up. "What?"

She pointed. "We're on the right track."

Ted stared down at the bootprint marked in stark red blood. It was headed towards the ice cap.

Ice Cavern, Devon Island, Nunavut, Canada
75° 36′ 44.14″ N, 83° 48′ 09.88″ W

Nick lurched through the ice maze, confused by walls of shining ice. His feet felt like lead, but it was the burning in his bones that weakened him. He wanted to lie down and curl into a ball of misery and die. He looked down at Amaruq. She lay slack and unresisting in his arms, barely breathing.

What the hell was that thing? The pain had hit like a lightning bolt, lancing through him like nothing he'd ever experienced. It was as though his entire body was in revolt. Worst of all was the sound in his head that was like a voice too loud to be heard, speaking a language he did not understand—yet recognized. Confusion swirled in his head. But what scared him, what gave horrified speed to his feet, was the echo he'd caught from Amaruq's mind when it hit her.

::Not again!:: And then the brief memory of fever and pain, and the agony of bone re-shaping.

Somewhere inside him, below conscious thought or memory, his body knew what had happened to him: Transformation. He fought the flare of panic in him, the cold fear of a long and painful death.

He wobbled into blind alleys and dead ends, coming back to the main path over and over in an endless loop of frustration. He could tell he was getting deeper into the ice, closer to the base of the ice sheet, because the light was getting dimmer. Something had melted a bore hole through the ice, but he was too exhausted to think what that might mean. Mechanically, his feet bore him onward, and his mind shut down.

Intrusion. Corruption. The cold intelligence drove relentlessly onward, pursuing that conglomerate known as the Whole. From the moment of their first encounter, the Whole and the Unity were enemies. Ruthless, artificial, driven only by the cold logic of extinction, the Unity revolted against the soft harmony, the easy adaptability of the Whole. Warfare raged across solar systems, fought in the icy darkness between worlds. Slowly the Whole diminished, retreated, sliced apart, unable to withstand the implacable pursuer whose only communication was "Die". At last, the final core remnants of the Whole pulled themselves into one final configuration, resonated a door into being, and fled. But the enemy pursued...

At the edge of consciousness, a Voice. Nick ignored it. Maybe Amaruq was waking up. It didn't matter. He had to get away from the thing, the thing that flashed and hurt. Foot in front of foot, keep moving.

"Nick!"

An echo. Where? Nick stopped, lifting his head. "Sophia?" The thought of her expanded inside him, made him blink and raise his head. Was she hurt? Where was she?

"Nick! Where are you?"

Nick sagged against a wall. She had come back. She shouldn't have. "No," he whispered, and the walls bounced it back again and again, distorted into a hiss.

Inside him, something deep as bone whispered, *Die.*

"Nick!" She sounded closer.

"No," he moaned. "Sophia, no. Get away..."

A scraping sound, and then a hand on his arm.

"Nick," she said, and then she was lifting the wolf out of his arms. "Nick, come on. We've got to find a way out of this."

"No..."

A whimper as she set the wolf down. He closed his eyes and let the wall take his weight, felt the cold seeping through his parka, leaching what was left of his body heat. Then something was pressed to his lips. Water. He swallowed, swallowed again, spluttered.

"Drink it," she said firmly. "You're dehydrated." A hand on his forehead. "And burning up with fever."

"Amaruq..."

"I gave her water, too. Here, I'll take her. You grab my collar from behind, follow me."

He wanted nothing more than to slide down with his

269

back against the ice and let the blackness take him. The burning in his bones, the pounding in his head, the lancing stab of pain were a death sentence. He grabbed at her sleeve, opened his eyes, and found that she was a blur.

"Can't see you," he said. "Listen. What I told you..." He fought for breath, past the constriction in his throat. "That... thing. It triggered me. I'm...Changing."

"What?"

"I can feel it. Like my bones are going...soft."

Sophia crouched down beside him. "What do you mean, changing?"

"Transforming," he said, too weary to explain. It didn't matter anyway. She didn't believe him.

"It's just a fever or something," she said.

He ignored her denial, fighting to stay focused. "Amaruq went through this, not as fast. Something...that thing started it in both of us...Faster ..." He gulped for air as his lungs spasmed. Panicking, he fought for air, fought against the suffocation. He was aware that Sophia had taken his hand in hers. The tightness eased and he could breathe. His head cleared for a moment. He squeezed her hand.

"Sophia," he gasped. "Listen to me. Not kidding here. I'm Changing. She...she went through it, she told me."

"With her mind," Sophia said. He heard the skepticism in her voice.

"Dammit," he said, fighting to get it out before the black fog came back into his head. He summoned all his strength, spoke quickly. "Listen! I will pass out, probably die pretty fast. Amaruq, too. She can't Change again. It's a one-way trip. You have to get out, go. Find your way back."

"I'm not—"

"Sophia! Damn you! Get out...while you can. There's... nothing you can do...for us." The weakness came on him again and he closed his eyes. "Can't...stop it."

Her cool hand on his forehead, the canteen against his lips again. He drank thirstily. He could feel the thickening in his throat. One of his teeth felt loose. He couldn't Transform. He couldn't. It would kill him. Like it had killed Tom, burning him up from the inside out, melting his bones into some surreal shape. Only it was happening incredibly fast, faster than he'd ever heard of.

"It's that thing," Sophia said, staring past him down the alley of ice. "That flying ball. I don't know how, but it did this. I can't believe you both got...sick like this...at the same time just by chance."

Nick didn't care. It didn't matter. The thing he'd feared all his life had happened, the long wait was over. "Got to get you...away," he whispered. Could it Transform Sophia? Was that thing powerful enough to Change a normal human being? He didn't know, couldn't risk it.

Nick opened his eyes. Her face loomed close, but a little out of focus. He remembered the unthinking impulse that had led him to give her the Sedna carving—the serenity in her face, the hidden strength behind it. The spirit that had caught his at first sight. He caught her hand in his. "Don't die on me...Can't lose...everyone ..."

He felt her hands on his face, her kiss on his face. "I'm not leaving you, Nick," she said in a low voice. He heard weariness in it, and conviction. Something else, he thought. Love, maybe. It made the pain a little easier, hearing that. But it made it more urgent for her to get out.

He heard her stand, heard her footsteps moving away. *Thank God,* he thought.

::Nick::

"I hear you, *nukka,*" he said, using the Inuit word for a younger sister. "I'm here."

::Hurts:: A low whine.

"I know...I'm sorry," he whispered. "Maybe it will be... quick." He thought of Tom, of their father. Maybe it was better this way. *All of them together soon.*

Time seemed to stand still; Nick lay quiet, fighting for one more breath, another. The thing inside him was like a voice, yelling too loud for hearing, screaming an order at him in a language that wasn't even language. The meaning was clear, though: *die die die.* Nick figured pretty soon he would do just that.

Footsteps coming back. The shock of ice on his forehead. "Nick," Sophia said.

He opened his eyes, and it seemed there was a red haze in front of him, hanging before her face. She was back. "No," he said in despair.

"There's a passage ahead," she said. "I'm going to take Amaruq into it, and then come back for you. We can rest, and I'll give you some more water."

"No."

"Don't argue with me, Nick." Her voice was firm. "Damn you, I am not leaving you."

"Bitch," he said, hoping anger would drive her away.

Instead, she laughed shortly. "Since your sister actually *is* a bitch, I somehow don't think you mean it."

His fist curled around hers, drew her closer. He found it hard to concentrate, hard to focus, but there she was, anxious eyes and that wonderful, kissable mouth. He remembered kissing it, remembered all the rest. *Loving, strong, smart.* And that curve of chin, the tilt of her eyes, that had caught him by the heart the first time he'd seen her, standing by that display case in Resolute Bay. His breath hissed through his teeth as another stab of pain iced through his bones.

"Negligevapse," he said in a low voice. "It means...it means 'I love you'...Strong Sophia..." His eyes closed, and he heard no more.

Truelove Lowlands

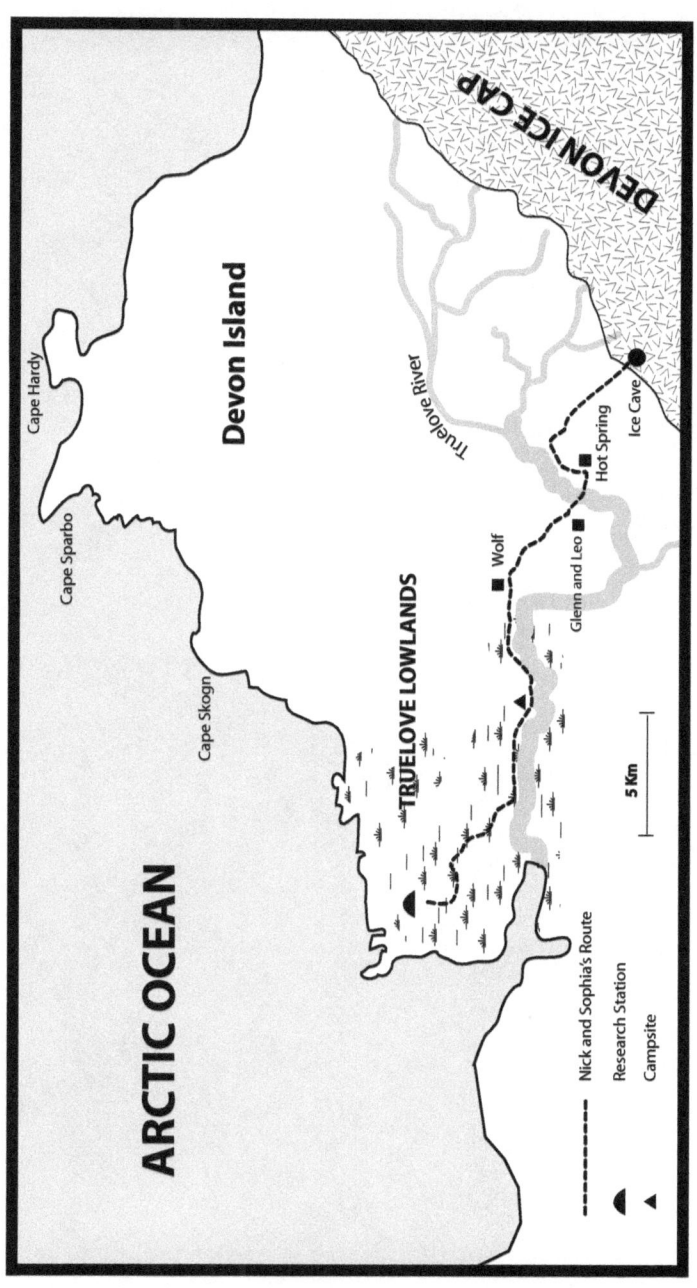

ARCTIC OCEAN

Devon Island

DEVON ICE CAP

TRUELOVE LOWLANDS

Truelove River

Cape Hardy

Cape Sparbo

Cape Skogn

Ice Cave

Hot Spring

Glenn and Leo

Wolf

5 Km

Nick and Sophia's Route

Research Station

Campsite

VII - THE ICE LABYRINTH

Ice Cavern, Devon Island, Nunavut, Canada
75° 36′ 44.14″ N, 83° 48′ 09.88″ W

Sophia took a deep breath to steady her thudding heart. Around her, the thick layers of ice had cut the sunlight to a dim haze, a twilight that grew darker with every step. She was going the wrong way, she knew it. She'd been trying for half an hour to find a way out of this maze, a way that didn't involve retracing their steps into the path of that...thing.

Had she gone left or right at the last junction? It was hard to tell; the ice changed constantly, flickering through every shade of blue and white and grey, sometimes changing color while she stood still. No doubt it had something to do with indices of refraction and the movement of clouds across the sun. It didn't matter; the bottom line was that she could not depend on memory to guide her. Reluctantly, she turned back, retracing her own boot tracks.

Nick's eyes were still closed, but his chest rose and fell more regularly. Beside him, Amaruq staggered to her feet, tail drooping. She faced back the way they had come, towards the sunlight. A low growl rumbled in her throat. She glanced up at Sophia, then back at the tunnel behind them, hackles rising.

"It's coming back?" Sophia looked down at her.

The wolf-girl nodded, an uncanny sight. Sophia glanced back over her shoulder, at the tangle of intersecting cracks, melt tunnels, and crawl spaces she'd just been exploring. They could not go back the way they had come, that would mean another confrontation with the sphere. So they must go forward. She knelt beside Nick.

"Nick, wake up," she said. She shook him; his head drooped. "Nick, please!" She could not carry him, but she would not leave him. Maybe she could hold off that flying thing with the remaining vial. She dug in her pocket for it, but her hand closed on something else. She drew out the little statuette of Sedna.

275

Tears brimmed her eyes. Was it only a couple of days ago she'd first seen it? "Nick," she whispered. "Please wake up." She pressed the carving into his hands.

His fingers stirred, closed over it. Then his fist tightened, and his eyes opened. They looked into hers, confused. "Sophia?"

"You have to get up, Nick," she said. She stood, tugging him to his feet. She slipped his arm over her shoulders and staggered under his weight. "Come on."

He was staring at Sedna. "What? I...I gave this to you."

"Yes," she said. "You have to carry it for me, okay? We have to go."

He stumbled, nearly fell. "Tired..."

"Come on!" Sophia caught a flicker out of the corner of her eye; behind them, the blue-purple gloom of the ice tunnel lit up like with a strobing white flash. "It's coming back! We have to go!"

Amaruq, still facing the corridor, snarled. She turned, nudging at Nick with her head.

"Nukka?" Nick frowned down at her. "Why do we have to... oh." He closed his eyes. "You should leave me."

"I'm done arguing with you." Sophia dragged him a step, another. It seemed like hours, but was surely only minutes, and then they were beyond the point where Sophia had turned back. They reached a junction, where a natural crack in the ice met what looked like a deliberately melted tunnel. But who could have melted a tunnel in the ice? she wondered. "Come on, Nick." She pulled him towards the tunnel. Maybe it led outside again.

Amaruq growled a warning again. Sophia did not need to read minds to know her thoughts; the sphere was close behind them.

Up ahead, a gleam of red light.

"Nick! Look!" she said. Nick limped. She could hear his breath, harsh and ragged. He coughed and spat blood.

"Can't...see," he muttered. She glanced at his face, and was horrified to see blood running from his eyes and nose. His corneas were filmed-over. "Just...shadows. You should leave—"

"Stop it!" she hissed. "I am *not* leaving you! Listen, there's a light ahead. It's kind of...red. Maybe sunset outside, you know, shining through the ice. Maybe we can get out of here."

"No sunset..." he said. "Not...in July."

Sophia's attention was all on the next step, straining to hear sounds of pursuit. She hoped that, if they wound up trapped in here, the vial of silver stuff in her pocket would once again protect them. It was pretty much the only hope she had.

❄

Nick wished Death would hurry up. It could not be long now; his whole body ached. His head pounded with the cease-less *die die die* broadcast by that thing. He didn't know why it wanted to kill him and Amaruq, or why it was chasing them, but he knew it was right behind them, maybe only one turn of the twisted corridor behind. He wanted to fall, to push Sophia out of its path, to protect her but he was too damned weak. He cursed himself.

::Coming fast.:: Amaruq's voice in his head was as strong as ever, but he could sense her strength failing. She would die on her feet, he knew. Which was why he could not give in to the overwhelming impulse to curl up and die on this icy floor in peace. ::Make Sophia go on without us.::

No point in that, he thought. She'd already made it clear she would not abandon him.

::I heard that!:: Amaruq's voice in his head was a bark of surprise. ::Nick, I heard you in my head!::

Not good, Nick thought wearily. It meant the Change has taken hold.

Amaruq's unspoken emotion washed over him—love, sympathy, grief. ::Not long now, Brother.::

He was going to die in this tunnel. He banged a knee on an outcropping of ice, but hardly felt it. It seemed he could feel his bones grinding, changing even as he staggered up a slip-pery incline.

Sophia halted. Before them, an opening in the ice glowed red. "Come on," she said. "It must lead to the outside. That has to be sunlight, some trick of the light." She hauled on him, and he staggered, half-fell against her, and they tottered through the ragged oval of the entrance into a large chamber lit by red light.

"What the hell?" Sophia said.

The chamber they'd entered was a dead end, but clearly was not natural. It was completely spherical, and the sides were lined with...trophies? Heads filled shelves that floated with no visible support, ranging from a bird to a seal to others Nick could not quite make out with his failing eyesight. He fell against the ice wall, scraping his back. He scanned the trophies, seeing the collars each sat on, the strange array of tubes and sacs below each one. The tubes didn't look like plastic or metal, more like something organic...

Sophia stared around the room. "What is this?"

Amaruq snarled, and the sound echoed around the red room. ::Bad. Very bad. Not all dead.::

Nick shook his head, trying to clear his vision. Something on the other side of the chamber shifted and shimmered. The light in the room trembled, like a flame seen through water. Blinking, he saw that the light came from something too bright too look at, a tiny sun hovering above the floor. "What—"

Amaruq whimpered, backing away from the row of heads.

Sophia gasped, and even in the red-tinged light, Nick saw her face pale. She groped for support against the wall. "Oh my God! That's..."

Nick looked where she was looking, and felt his blood turn to ice. The head—the human head—was blinking. As he and Sophia watched in horror, the mouth moved. "Oh my God," he whispered. "It's still *alive?*"

"Nick! It's...it's that guy, I think. Leo. The one whose body we found..." Her voice trailed off in horror.

Sophia stared at the head. "The lips are moving. Could it be some kind of...autonomic reaction? Maybe..."

Across the room, the lips formed the silent words: *kill me.*

Sophia shrieked, then covered her mouth with both hands. "Nick—"

Nick drew in a deep breath, then fought against the urge to vomit. The room stank, a deep, filthy stench of decay and rot and unearthly chemistry. He stumbled forward, lurching across the slick floor. To his right, the row of silent, staring heads—ptarmigan, musk ox, walrus—sat silent, the tubes and sacs underneath each head pulsing slowly, uselessly.

"This can't be real." Sophia stepped up beside him and took his hand in hers. "What...what should we do?"

At arm's length, Nick stopped. Like the other heads in the room, Leo West's head rested on a collar supplied by tubes and sacs of some fleshy material that made Nick queasy to think about. Blood had sheeted Leo's chin and dripped off onto the floor.

"His eyes..." Sophia whispered.

Leo's blue eyes did not track together. One of them stared off to the left, as if studying the wall. The other met Nick's, then Sophia's, with perfect understanding and sentience.

"Can you...understand me?" Sophia said.

The head blinked at Sophia, and the lips formed the word yes. There was no sound.

"No larynx," Sophia said. Her voice was shaky. Nick heard her labored breathing. "And no...no lungs, either. It's...he's being kept alive by those...artificial arteries, I think."

Nick coughed, and felt warmth running down his chin. He wiped it with his hand, and saw blood.

Kill me, Leo's silent lips said again. *Please.*

Sophia shuddered. "I...I can't. Oh, my God, Nick."

Nick stared into the one good eye Leo had left.

Kill me kill me kill me

Nick glanced around the chamber. Now that he was closer, he could see that the shimmering, dancing thing he had seen was a...window? ... of some kind, suspended in thin air. Through the window, Nick glimpsed a landscape that confused him—sand? Broken stone? Two suns in a red sky?

"What kind of twisted mind..." Sophia murmured, horror in her voice.

Not human, Leo's head mouthed. *Ball of light. Kill me.*

"Ball..." Sophia turned, and her shocked gaze met Nick's. "That thing behind us—"

Kill me please kill me kill me

Nick reached down slowly, felt in his boot for the knife. He drew it out.

Sophia caught his movement, opened her mouth, then shut it. Her eyes locked on his, filling with tears, she nodded.

"Go in peace," Nick whispered, and brought the knife up in one slashing move. The keen edge sliced through the tubes and sacs below Leo's head. Something black and wet sprayed out, and an acid stench filled the room. But Leo's eyes locked in place, the pupils dilating, and all movement stopped.

"He's dead," Sophia whispered. "Thank God."

Then something shot into the room over their heads—the sphere. It stopped abruptly, hovering over Leo's head. Its surface roiled like boiling blood, reflecting the fiery red light.

Die die die die die...

Mars Habitat Project, Devon Island, Nunavut
75° 25′ 52.61″ N, 89° 51′ 00″ W

Martin Skorjik was stumbling towards the edge of the drop-off to the Crater when a hand grabbed his elbow.

"Director!"

He stopped, blinking. He stared down at the long drop just beyond the toes of his boots. Carefully, he stepped back twice. "Sorry. Thanks."

The hand released him. It was Courtenay. "Are you all right? You nearly walked right off the cliff!"

Skorjik blinked, then looked past the little man. He was at least a hundred yards from the Habitat, now surrounded by crates, boxes and makeshift shelters. Even now the light grew darker as snow clouds scudded in overhead. "I...I guess I got turned around. I was looking for...I was looking ..." He stopped, confused.

The other man pushed a canteen into his hands. "Take a drink, Martin," he said. His voice was friendlier than Skorjik could remember. "You're dehydrated, exhausted. How long has it been since you slept?"

Skorjik took a long, welcome swallow. "Too much to do. I have to—"

"What you have to do, my friend, is listen to some friendly advice. We're on Mars, Martin. As good as. We're cut off, isolated, in a hostile environment facing unknown dangers. The last thing your people need you to do is play the movie star action hero." He dug into a pocket for a protein bar and unwrapped it.

"Look, I know we've rarely seen eye-to-eye out here," Courtenay said. "But the one thing I've been doing for seven years is figuring out how stressful environments affect people. While you've been doing Big Science, with machines and NASA funding and big-name universities, I've been watching what happens to all these smart people when things don't go according to plan. Let me tell you, Martin, it's not the guys on the bottom who crack first. It's the ones on top."

Skorjik accepted the protein bar and munched unenthusiastically. He wanted to argue with the little twerp, but was too tired. Easier to just let him rant.

"It's the guys with the responsibility who lose focus first," Courtenay said. "It's the ones who have to give the orders, the ones who have to see the big picture who drive themselves too hard and too long. Which means," he said firmly, looking Skorjik in the eye. "That when they go down, they take everyone with them. When you get too tired to literally see where you're going, Martin, when you walk off a goddam cliff in a fog of exhaustion, the whole team takes a hit as well."

Skorjik stopped chewing and blinked. "Okay, I'll take a little break. But then I have to—"

"No," the little administrator said smartly. "You do not take a 'little break'. You come with me back to the Hab, you eat some hot food, and then sack out in my own bunk for a full eight hours. You—"

"Not a chance," Skorjik said. "I'm the leader of these peo—"

A huge shape roared out of the clouds, thundering no more than thirty meters over their heads. Both men ducked.

Courtenay yelled something Skorjik could not hear, waved him to follow, and scuttled back towards the Hab. Skorjik straightened to follow, but was buffeted by a sudden wind as the thing returned—a bright noisy blur against the gray skies.

Then he blinked, and everything came into focus, and he backed away swiftly as the yellow CH-149 Cormorant helicopter descended in a roar. The rotor wash stung his eyes as he bent nearly double, pulling his parka over his face to protect himself from flying grit and debris. He glimpsed the maple leaf flag on the tail section before he had to turn his back on the machine to protect his eyes. Then the roar cut to a muffled whine as the rotors powered down. He heard shouting and turned around, to see a man in an olive jumpsuit and helmet emerging from the hatch. He cupped his hands around his mouth and shouted, "Are you the Martian guys?"

With an inner smile at the irony, Skorjik waved his hands and nodded yes.

Even in his exhausted state, Skorjik was amazed at the swift action that followed. Within minutes, he was seated in a folding camp chair with a mug of steaming coffee in his hands, talking to what looked, to his unmilitary eyes, like a full colonel in the Canadian Air Force. The young man introduced himself, but Skorjik could barely keep him in focus. *It didn't matter*, he thought. Even in his haze, he could see other uniformed men (and one woman) piling out of the chopper, briskly setting up radio equipment, tables, and wind shelters.

He blinked at the young man before him, who was nattering on about something. "Got to get them back," Skorjik said loudly.

"Sir?"

"Fraser. And the others. Dead men, out there," he said, waving his hand towards the crater. He saw that his hands were shaking, and made a fist to stop it. It didn't work, but it helped him focus. He sat up straight and concentrated. "Listen to me," he said. "The last bunch of you guys to come here—Rangers, I think they called themselves—are all dead. Every last one of them."

The young man—a lieutenant, Skorjik now remembered—said soberly. "Yes, sir, so we've been told. My men are on full alert and are armed. My orders are to evacuate this entire island. We heard your SOS. We're based up on Ellesmere Island, at the CFS Alert signal monitoring station. I don't think anyone else north of Iqaluit could have heard you."

Skorjik closed his eyes. "Thank you, Verna," he whispered. And then his eyes flew open. "Lieutenant, we need to find Constable Fraser and our company doctor immediately." He gripped the arms of his chair and rose, swaying a bit. The young man put out a hand to help him, but Skorjik waved him off. "Constable Fraser believed this was no mere accident. He believed that we were under attack by either criminals, poachers or even terrorists." At the young man's skeptical look, Skorjik drew a deep breath, assuming his most authoritative tone. "Your service is charged with supporting Canadian sovereignty claims in the North, are you not?"

The young man blinked. "Actually, we're more of a communications unit—"

Skorjik overrode him. "There may be terrorists on this island," he said. "A foreign power challenging your country's claim to this territory. Are you prepared to defend it?"

The young lieutenant straightened. "Yes, sir," he snapped.

"Then let's get that bird in the air and go find Constable Fraser, Doctor Meyers, and the rest of our missing people. And most of all, let's find out what the hell is going on in this place," Skorjik said.

Truelove Lowlands, Devon Island, Nunavut
75° 38′ 13.47″ N, 83° 49′ 21.46″ W

It took Fraser an hour to connect with the trail of his fugitive doctor and scientist. By now the snow was coming down in flakes the size of his hand. He was grateful the wind had died down, which left him a little visibility. Unfortunately, that meant the temperature was dropping. He was forced to stop every few minutes and slap his hands together. Even with heavy gloves on, the cold was numbing his extremities. He had donned a full face mask and eye goggles but even this was not enough to keep the cold from coating his eyelashes and eyebrows with frost.

The snow was filling in the tracks of the ATV, but by now it was obvious where they were headed. He had expected the pair to head for the Truelove River valley, but it was clear they were headed for the ridge above it. This made no sense to Fraser, but he wasted no time puzzling it out. He came to the bottom of the slope that led up the rocky slope; there in the shelter of a boulder he saw the slewing tracks that showed the ATV had skidded a bit as it started up. Fraser nodded to himself when he saw the faint track. Of course; musk oxen climbed that ridge every summer. He checked his fuel, did a calculation in his head, and then turned his machine up the trail.

By the time he had fought his way to the top of the ridge, Fraser was thinking fondly of the old days, when Mounties used horses and mules. On a slope like this one, a mule or donkey would have been much better than the four-wheeler. Topping the ridge, the east wind hit him full in the face, as cold as a frozen two-by-four plank.

And there sat a red ATV, now coated in a light frosting of snow. Fraser allowed himself a moment of congratulations in tracking his prey so well. Then he wondered where they'd gone.

He scanned the terrain. Below him, the Truelove River valley was now well and truly hidden behind a thick veil of falling snow. Visibility was down to a few hundred meters; he could see about halfway down the slope, he decided. If the doctor and his girlfriend had headed that way...

But they had not. Five minutes of crouching, gently sweeping the snow aside, showed him a double set of footprints leading...south? Fraser stood and frowned into the snow. What the hell were they doing? Had they heard or sighted their missing friends? But what would Tonarak and the biologist be doing up on this ridge?

The track leading along the top of the ridge was too narrow for the four-wheelers. Fraser returned to his ATV, hauled out his emergency pack, and slung his rifle. After one more fruitless attempt at raising someone—anyone—by radio, he turned south and headed up the steep path.

Ice Cavern, Devon Island, Nunavut, Canada
75° 36′ 44.14″ N, 83° 48′ 09.88″ W

Nick drew himself up with his last strength and stepped in front of Sophia.

Not her, not Sophia, he said fiercely in his mind.

Die die die die...

It sounded familiar, that relentless, cold command. As if he had heard it before. In a dream, maybe? But that made no sense. Or did it? No time to wonder now. Nick felt the tide of blood rising in his throat, knew he had no time left. "Sophia, go..."

Then Sophia was standing beside him, the last vial of silver in her hand. She faced the globe.

"Go away, or I will smash this," she said. Her voice was firm, relentless. "If you touch him, I will destroy what's in this vial." She held it up. The vial sparked and swirled, matching the churn and flow of whatever formed the globe hovering in mid-air. Nick saw her hand tighten around the vial, saw the light leaking between her fingers. Her hand did not falter or tremble.

A brush against his leg, and he knew Amaruq was at his side. In his head, he heard her angry snarl. ::Came here to kill us.::

Startled, Nick glanced down. "What?"

::Came here for us. Can't you hear it?::

Nick could. Below the *die die die* that beat relentlessly at his very bones, he heard another trickle, a fearful one: *enemy enemy enemy.* But how could it be his enemy? He had never seen this thing before.

"Nick, back away," Sophia said calmly. "I'll hold it off."

"No..." A coughing fit took him and he doubled over.

285

Amaruq shifted, circling around him and Sophia. ::Won't stop hunting us.::

Nick knew that was true. Better to stop running, he thought, and heard Amaruq's ready acceptance.

The ball hung above Leo's head, motionless, menacing. Colors whorled across its surface: white, blue, red.

"Sophia...!"

She ducked, and the bolt of fire that shot out of the orb missed her head by a millimeter. On the wall behind her, ice vaporized with a hiss and a hole the size of her head appeared into the ice.

Sophia waved the vial. "I'll smash this if you don't leave us alone!"

The globe drifted closer, hovering at the height of Sophia's outstretched hand.

"I...I think it wants the vial," Sophia said. "Maybe it wants to...bargain?"

"No," Nick said. "Don't give it...only reason...we're not dead now."

"I won't," she said firmly. She was looking away from him, concentrating on the orb. "But I can act like I will. You can get away."

::Standoff:: Amaruq's voice said. ::Can't hold out here for-ever.:: Below her bravado, Nick felt the weakness in her, knew she was on the last of her strength.

We'll only get one chance, Sis, he thought, knowing that now she could hear him as he heard her.

An image formed in Nick's mind, like the one Amaruq had imagined to get them onto the plane back in Resolute Bay. He saw the polar bear, saw Amaruq hurtling onto it from behind. Then he saw an image of Amaruq leaping onto the orb from behind, pushing it towards the shimmering window, then the three of them running from the room.

"If you want this," Sophia was saying to the orb. "You have to let us leave. Lead us out of here, and we'll give you this back."

The orb hovered, saying nothing. But now it looked different—clearer, more solid.

On your signal, Amaruq, he thought. *Be careful.*

The wolf was already moving, slinking around behind Sophia, who faced the orb with the vial held high. Nick saw Sophia's arm shaking—with tension or fatigue or nerves. "Keep it...focused on you," he said. The coughing came again, and he spat black blood on the floor.

He was careful not to look at Amaruq, lest he draw the orb's attention to her. *Like hunting with her and Tom again. Distract the prey, separate, flank it, drive it where you want it to go.* He felt all his hunter's instincts rising to the surface. If only he could hold onto the dregs of his strength...

Amaruq was behind the shelves now, behind the head of Leo West. Its unblinking stare did not bother Nick; he focused on the sphere. "Look at...me," he whispered. "You flying piece of shit, look at me."

Sophia turned her head, puzzled. "What—?"

Amaruq leaped, hindquarters driving her up and over the shelf, over Leo's head. She smashed into the globe. White light flashed, but even as he threw up his hands to shield his face, Nick saw the orb swerve sideways, falling, the force of her impact carrying Amaruq with it. And at that moment, he realized she had misjudged her leap.

Together, the orb and Amaruq fell through the window.

"No!" Nick lunged forward, too late.

The orb and wolf disappeared, the window winked out of existence, the spinning object below it went black, and Nick's ears popped with the pressure change.

His scream tore his throat as the room plunged into darkness.

Ice Cavern, Devon Island, Nunavut, Canada
75° 36′ 44.14″ N, 83° 48′ 09.88″ W

"It's...an ice cave?"

Ted and Jennifer stood side by side, staring at the opening in the wall of ice.

"Told you so," Ted said. He felt no sense of satisfaction

staring at the narrow slot among the jumbled boulders. Rather, a growing sense of unease flickered along his nerves. "This is what I...saw."

The faint tracks and blood streaks that had led them along the ridge continued on, mere impressions in the frozen slush of the floor. A thin stream of meltwater trickled along the floor of the narrow slash in the ice.

"I don't want to go in there," Jennifer said.

"I don't either," he admitted.

They stood side by side for a moment, then Ted sighed. "I don't suppose you brought a flashlight."

"No," she admitted. "Silly me. Here I am in country where the sun literally never sets, and it didn't occur to me to bring a light."

Ted rubbed his temples. It felt like someone was tightening a band around his head. "We'll go slow," he said. "We'll have to feel our way along and watch for holes. And we should leave a trail of some kind. Do we have something we can drop like bread crumbs?"

"Let me see," Jennifer said. She rummaged through her parka. "Gum. Cell phone—useless, of course. Candy bar. Lipstick—what the hell did I bring that for? Oh, and my house key. Great."

Ted blinked. "Cell phone?"

She pulled out her smartphone. "Sure. But of course there's no service here. I stashed it in my parka because I use the stopwatch feature to time some of my processes in the lab."

"Is it charged?"

She looked at him oddly. "Yeah."

Ted grinned. "Then turn it on."

Jennifer did so. The screen lit up brightly, illuminating the entire passage. "Why didn't I think of that?" She handed him the phone.

"We're swapping," he said. "You take the medical kit. I'll take the rifle. I go first." She started to argue, and he held up a hand. "Indulge me."

"This is stupid," Jennifer said.

"Yes it is," he said. "And it's non-negotiable. Stay close behind me, and watch your footing." Holding the rifle in one hand and holding up the cell phone in the other, he stepped forward.

The floor was not as slick as he'd expected. The water might be cold but it was still above freezing, and something had melted a narrow passage right down to rock. Pebbles and loose gravel paved the floor as they entered. They had not gone more than a couple of meters before the passage divided. Ted stopped.

"Right or left?"

Jennifer pushed past him, kneeling. "I think they went right."

Ted stepped beyond her and continued down the right hand passage. And there, at shoulder height, was a great long smear of blood, red against the ice. His stomach lurched. "I think you should wait outside," he said.

"Not a chance," Jennifer said. She used her lipstick to mark an arrow on the floor, pointing back the way they had come.

"I thought you'd say that." Ted advanced slowly to the next turn. Again, tracks on the floor showed them that their quarry had gone deeper into the cave.

She did it again at the next divide, and the next. Ted could hear her teeth chattering in the cold. "W-why do you think they c-came in here?" she asked.

"I don't know." The rifle felt cold and heavy in his hand. "We're pretty deep inside the ice cap," he said. He glanced up uneasily. The roof was a series of concave half-bubbles, showing where water had melted down and away. The walls were slick and icy, snaking away in a maze of twists and turns. "Maybe we should—"

The hoarse cry spiraled out of the darkness ahead of them, and then a hot breeze fanned their hair back.

"What?"

Jennifer shot past him, grabbing the iPhone out of his hand. "Sophia!" she yelled.

"Wait!"

But she was gone, pounding down the corridor, and all he could do was follow. "Jennifer! Stop!"

Ahead, the light bounced, and then as he rounded a corner he saw a larger opening, and the glow of the smart phone. It lay on the floor, and Jennifer knelt next to it.

"Jennifer!" He skidded to a stop. "Don't ever—"

"Doctor Meyers?" a voice asked. "How did you guys find us?"

He looked up, and saw two faces in the fading glow from the screen. "Doctor Abenezra?"

"Help me," Sophia said. Her drawn face was painted in chiaroscuro shadows in the light. "He's passed out."

Ted knelt beside Jennifer and saw that the women were bending over Nick Tonarak, sprawled on the floor. Blood covered his face, and there was something odd about the shape of his jaw. Bloody patches on his skull showed where hair had been torn out—or had fallen out.

"What happened to him?"

"Long story," Sophia said. "We have to get him out of here."

"I don't think we should move him."

Sophia picked up a knife lying on the ground; Ted spotted the sheen of blood. "We have to get out of here now," she said. "Now! It might come back!"

"Okay, okay," he said. Had Sophia attacked the Inuit guide? "I'll get his shoulders. Jennifer, can you guide us out?"

He hitched around on his knees to get a good hold, and for a moment the light flashed on the walls of the large chamber they were in. Ted stared, his jaw going slack. Heads... all kinds of heads. And was that a human head? "What is this place?"

"I'll get his feet," Sophia said. "Come on."

Together, they struggled and heaved and finally managed to lift Nick. Jennifer led the way, guided by her lipstick marks. Ted could tell by the warmth of the body in his hands that Nick was not dead, that there was still life in him. But what was wrong with his eyes?

The trio shuffled and skidded, and once Ted slipped on the ice. But just as Jennifer's iPhone battery gave up the ghost for good, they reached the dim, washed-out glow that told them they were back at the entrance.

"Stop!" Sophia said. She lowered Nick's feet to the floor and stepped past Jennifer, signaling her to stay back.

Ted slumped against the wall, taking most of Nick's weight. He stuck a hand under Nick's parka to feel the pulse in his carotid artery. *Dangerously weak.* With his free hand he gently lifted Nick's eyelid; the corneas were red with blood. He couldn't tell what trauma the man had suffered, however. He watched as Sophia crept to the entrance, keeping close to the wall, peering out cautiously. She clutched a sampling vial in her hand.

"Soph, are you—" Jennifer began.

"Hush!" Sophia whispered. In the dim light, Ted saw blood on her parka. He wondered where the dog was. "There's something out there!"

Exchanging glances with Jennifer, Ted lowered Nick to the floor of the ice passage. He'd been carrying the rifle slung on his shoulder; now he slipped it into his hands and stepped up behind Sophia. "Where?"

Sophia pointed; sure enough, something moved among the rocks, a hint of something dark. Was it the dog? thought Ted. He eased the rifle up to his shoulder and sighted it.

And then relaxed. "It's Fraser," he said.

Sophia did not ease off. "Is he alone?"

"Yes."

Jennifer stepped up beside him. He looked from her to Sophia's tense face. He thought about the damage done to Nick Tonarak. He handed the rifle to Jennifer, who met his eyes and nodded, sidling closer to her friend. Sophia's eyes looked haunted.

Ted stepped out of the ice cave, holding both his hands in the air. "Constable?" he called.

"Who's there?" Fraser called.

"Ted Meyers," he answered. "I have wounded here. Can you get us back to camp?"

Will Fraser stepped out from behind an ice boulder, holding his rifle at the ready. "Dr. Roth?"

"She's fine. But Tonarak is badly injured. He needs a medical facility immediately."

Fraser stopped when he caught of Sophia and Jennifer huddled at the mouth of the cave. "What happened here?"

"I'll tell you all about it, whatever I know," Ted said. "But right now we have—"

A sudden roar overhead drowned him out, and everyone ducked instinctively. Ted saw the familiar yellow-and-red blur and felt a weight lift from his shoulders.

Fraser craned his neck for a better look, then nodded. "Search and rescue. Finally. I'll go see if there's some place they can land. Get your man out here."

Ted turned back to the cave just in time to see Sophia collapse into Jennifer's arms, sobbing.

Mars Habitat Project, Devon Island, Nunavut
75° 25' 52.61" N, 89° 51' 00" W

Amaruq. He had to find her. She was somewhere ahead of him, in the darkness. Why couldn't he hear her? Had he lost her? How could he explain to their father, to Tom that he'd lost her? *Amaruq. She had to be here. Couldn't she hear him?*

Nick shot to consciousness, panting. "Amaruq!" Pain seared through his chest and shoulders. He fought for breath, squeezing his eyes shut. *Breathe breathe breathe...*

Something on his face, then air, welcome air. A hand on his shoulder easing him back. "It's okay, Nick," someone said. "Relax."

He breathed deep, again and again. His head cleared, then his vision. He blinked. A face in a surgical mask leaned over him. "You're okay," the voice said.

"Am...Amaruq," he said. His throat felt as though he'd been gargling acid.

"Don't worry about that right now," the voice said. Brown eyes, black curly hair. Nick racked his brain. He should know who this is.

"Nick," said another voice, a voice he knew, and he turned his head, and there she was. Bright eyes above a surgical mask, chestnut hair.

"Sophia," he whispered. Her hand closed on his, and something in him unknotted. "Sophia..." He blinked, trying to focus. What was wrong with his eyes? Everything looked white, pale.

"I'm here," she said. "We're in the Habitat. Dr. Meyers and Jennifer have been treating you."

"He should rest," Ted said. Nick felt fingers on his wrist, taking his pulse. "How do you feel, Nick?"

"Like hell," he croaked. Blinking, his vision began to clear. A colorful blur resolved itself into a poster of...Maui? Then the doctor leaned closer, shining a bright light in his eyes. Nick blinked.

"Pupils react normally," Ted said. "Can you move your toes for me?"

Nick obediently wiggled toes, fingers, and ears on command. He followed the doctor's finger on request. Ted probed his abdomen, felt his neck and made him open his mouth.

"I want you to count backwards from 20 to 1."

"Avatit, arviqtanganit sitamanik, arviqtanganit pingasunik."

"Very funny. In English," Ted said.

Nick counted down in English.

"Can you tell me the square root of 121?" Ted asked.

"Uh. Eleven. Where is Amaruq?"

Sophia's hand tightened on his. He could see her exchange glances with the doctor, saw his small nod. "I'm sorry, Nick. She's...gone. We looked everywhere. She disappeared with that...thing."

Despair filled him. His sister...gone. He closed his eyes, seeing that red room, the open "window", Amaruq hurtling through it, her momentum knocking the globe through ahead of her. And then darkness. "What was that thing?" he whispered.

"We can talk about that later," Ted said. "Right now I need you to rest. You seem to have come through more or less intact, but you've had a hell of a week."

Nick blinked. "Week?"

"You were very sick," Sophia said. "You're going to be all right now."

He turned his head. His vision was clearing now, and he could make out more of the room. He recognized the central dining area of the Hab. It was probably the largest space in the structure. Posters, whiteboards, a few cartoons tacked to the wall. The window, glowing with late afternoon light. A chess board abandoned underneath it, with half the men knocked over.

"I don't understand." He swallowed with difficulty, and Sophia held a straw up to his mouth. He sipped.

"He's not going to rest until he gets some answers," Sophia said to Ted.

"Okay, but make it quick," Ted said. "Now that he's awake, we'll be moving him to Iqaluit."

"What? No!" Nick said. It came out as a croak.

"Doc, can you leave us alone?" Sophia asked.

Ted hesitated, then shrugged. "Five minutes." He stepped away, moving out of sight.

Sophia pulled her mask down, moving closer. "How do you feel?"

"Like crap. What happened?" He lifted his hand, the one that held hers. The sheet slipped off his arm, and he realized he was naked underneath it. The thought made his cheeks go hot. *Ridiculous*, he thought. But there it was. And then his gaze fell on his forearm. "My arm..."

She ran her other hand along his arm, ruffling the dark hair. "I know. You're a hairier guy than you were two weeks ago." She smiled, a little lopsidedly. "Very macho."

A chill ran down him. "Is that...all?" he asked. He locked eyes with her, begging her to understand him.

"You won't be changing any further," she said, her hand tightening on his. "The...transformation, you called it? It's stopped."

"Stopped?" He was stupefied. "It doesn't stop. Not once it starts. Unless I die first."

294

"That was before you fell into the hands of doctors Roth and Meyers," she said. "Not to mention a few dozen extremely fascinated geneticists, surgeons, molecular biologists, developmental biologists, microbial specialists—"

He let his eyes close. "Oh, God." He felt despair wash over him again. His father's worst nightmare. "They're turning me into a science experiment?"

"They saved your life," she said.

He opened his eyes and found hers fixed on him. "Sorry," he said. "I just...what do I look like?" Visions of his twisted brother rose to mind. Did he look like Tom now, a carnival freak, a monster?

"Don't worry, you look pretty much like you did before."

"Pretty much?"

"A little taller, actually. And more muscle."

Nick blinked, then felt slow heat climb his face. "That's all."

She read him right. "Don't worry." She leaned close, whispering. "I peeked. You're the same guy. In every way."

Relief flooded him. Relief, and wonder. "What did they do to me?"

"Well, first of all they spent a lot of time analyzing every drop of blood or tissue you could spare," she said. She smoothed hair off his forehead. Her hand was cool and soft. "The Slime-Master has had a hell of a workout. Jennifer and Dr. Ted put together a gene-therapy protocol based on a co-transfection experiment using 3T3 cells. They used a virus to target homeodomain binding sites on your DNA—"

"Stop!" Nick smiled. "Can I get the Reader's Digest version?"

"They used gene therapy to stop the change. You're stable now."

He lifted his hairy arm. The dark, thick hair ran from elbow to shoulder. "This is stable?"

"Okay, you look a little furrier than you did. But you're within human norms. You should see my Uncle Saul at the beach. He looks like a bear in a Speedo."

Nick felt a bubble of hope in his chest. He took another sip of water. "So...this is it? I won't...change into ..."

She took his face in her hands. "No, Nick. You are going to remain human." She kissed him softly, lingering. He felt a deep hunger rise in him, found his arms reaching for her, pulling her close. *Sophia, beautiful Sophia. Strong Sophia...*

She pulled away, smiling. "Easy there," she said. "Time for that later. When you've rested."

"I love you," he said. He wanted to say it a million times.

She took his hand again. "And I love you. Which is why I want you to come back with me."

"Back?" he said, alarmed.

"Easy," she said. She offered him the straw again. "There's a lot to tell, and my five minutes are just about up." While he sipped, she talked. "First of all, that thing wasn't a terrorist plot or a poacher or anything else we thought of. It was from another world. Maybe another universe."

He remembered the "window", and the two suns in a red sky.

"The physicists are drinking themselves stupid on champagne," she said. "NASA is fighting with the Canadian Space Agency over who gets to investigate that ice cave. The upshot is that the membrane we saw—"

"Membrane?"

"That's what they're calling it, officially. Well, no, they're calling it a 'discontinuity-free density matrix bridge between contemporaneous parallel universes'. The rest of us are just calling it the wormhole."

"Wormhole? Universes?"

"Yeah, I know. *Star Trek* stuff, right?" She put the drinking glass down beside him. "Bottom line is that they think that thing opened up a bridge to another world and came through it. And then disappeared back into it."

"With Amaruq."

Her expression sobered. "Yes. Nick, I'm so sorry."

But he felt the bubble of hope expand. "So she's not dead."

"Well, we don't really know—"

"You didn't find her body. Or that *thing.*"

"No, and there's a hell of an argument raging about that.

About half the scientists are agreeing with Ted, that it came here looking for you and Amaruq. The others think you were randomly targeted..."

"No," he said strongly. He remembered the relentless *die die die* echoing through his head, through his every molecule. "No, they're right. It was looking for us. It came here to kill me and Amaruq."

"Maybe," she said cautiously. "Ted thinks so, anyway. But why would something from a parallel universe even know about you, let alone come looking for you?"

He thought about the dreams, the feeling of being hunted in his sleep. About the long line of his ancestors and the dreams they had all experienced. The One and the Whole, a long war, a chase across time and space. "It was a scout," he said. "A spy. It was hunting us, all of us that are like me and Amaruq."

"Ted thinks those heads were samples, not trophies." Her mouth twisted. "Sort of like my collecting extremophile samples along the Truelove. God, that feels like a million years ago."

"It didn't know what we looked like. That's why it was taking samples." And then the answer was there, right before him. "My God. That's why we change. *We change to escape them.*"

"What?"

He struggled to sit up. "Listen. It makes sense. Our family, all of us, through the years, we've changed. It's a way to hide who we are."

"What do you think you are?"

He thought of the hovering sphere, of its relentless pursuit. "The enemy," he said. "When its voice was in my head, I could tell it was afraid of us. It thought of me and Amaruq as its enemies. I don't know how or why, but I know it...it followed us here." How long ago? And what did that mean about his people?

Nick looked down at his hands and arms, at the dark hair that now covered the backs of his hands. He flexed them, feeling the power in his hands. He wondered if he would ever carve again. Something cool and hard was placed in his palm. He opened his eyes. She had laid the Sedna figurine in it.

"You kept it," he said.

"Of course," she said. "I looked her up. Do you know some of your people used to associate her with shape-shifters?"

"Ijiraat," he said. "But that's not the usual interpretation."

"Ted thinks it may be a way your people explained what happens to your family."

His mouth curled in a smile. "So now I'm a mythological being?" He leaned his head back to look at the ceiling. "If we'd gone through that window, like Amaruq—"

"That door is closed," Sophia said firmly. "And if it opens again, well, there's several hundred guys studying it right now. We'll have warning."

"Do they think it will reopen?"

"No. They took the power source away, that spinning thing. Apparently it's some kind of battery, but it's dead now."

"If...if we're its enemy, if it followed us here, Sophia, maybe that means my people are not from Earth at all. Our people, those of us who change—we're *refugees*. From a long time ago."

She cupped his chin; he felt the rasp of his beard against her fingers. "Maybe. Maybe not. The important thing is that you're going to be all right. You're as human as I am."

He reached up and pulled her down, resting his forehead against hers. "I'm not going to die," he said. It was still hard to believe. *How could they be sure?*

"Sorry," she said, laughing softly. "You only have about eighty years left."

He kissed her, putting all his renewed hope into it. She responded, warm and familiar and sweet. He felt like sunrise. She smiled into the kiss, then pulled back.

He closed his eyes. "Sophia, what happened to my dad? My brother?"

"I'm sorry," she said. "I seem to be giving you nothing but sad news. Constable Fraser went to your house. It had burned to the ground. Your father, your brother—the RCMP found what was left. They say the fire was deliberately set. I'm so sorry."

Nick swallowed. It was pretty much what he'd suspected. Grief welled in him but he forced it aside. Time for grief later, in private. Suddenly he was very tired.

"Nick, you're going to have to make some decisions," she said slowly. "There's no hurry, and I don't want you to feel pressured. But..." She laid her hand over his. "The research station here is out of commission for the foreseeable future. Or rather, it's going to be taken over by a whole different agency, studying that ice cave and what was in it. But I...I have to go home. All of us who were part of the station have to leave."

He felt his gut tightening. *It was always going to end this way. He would stay, she would go.*

"I want you to come with me," she said.

Nick's eyes flew open. "What?"

"Look. You have a...unique...contribution you can make. No, wait," she said as he started to protest. "My university— well, actually, every university in the world, along with quite a few private foundations—has offered to pay you a large stipend to live under their auspices, donate blood and tissue regularly for study, but otherwise live a normal life."

"As a lab experiment—"

"Dammit, Nick, what do you want?" He could see she was fighting tears. "What can you do now?"

He could run away, he thought. But that's not what he wanted. He wanted to go home to his father and Tom and Amaruq. He wanted to go back to...his job? "What do you think?"

She brushed his hair back from his forehead. "I think you're a hell of a nice guy, Nick Tonarak. And I wish you'd come to California with me."

He looked at her, looked beyond her to the window. He knew it looked out over the great crater, over the barren, rocky heart of Devon Island. He thought of his father, his brother, of Amaruq lost to him forever, perhaps. Lost in some parallel universe? That was too weird to get his head around. He felt very tired. Everything was lost or dead or missing. He had nothing left, nothing left at all, only his damnable curse, the body and heritage that made him a freak.

Then he looked back at Sophia, and the little carving in his hand, and something in him chose life. He gripped her hand.

She looked back at him. "We'll figure it out. Together."

He nodded, lying back against the pillow, feeling exhaustion steal over him, pulling him towards sleep and healing. She laid a hand on his cheek. Then she left.

He would go to California. He would be with Sophia. He would let them study him. And in his turn, he would study.

Because he knew, in his bones, that whatever had come through under the ice, from another world, a world with two suns, wasn't finished with him.

It was coming back.

THE END

About the Author

Sarah Stegall is the author of *Deadfall, Deadwater, Farside*, and other stories. She researched and co-wrote the first three *Official Guides to The X-Files*, which spent fourteen weeks on the New York Times bestseller list. She has written for TOPPS, TVGuide Online, and SFScope.com. She has been reviewing science fiction and fantasy movies, books and television since 1994, and her critiques are widely cited in academic works.

After earning a BA in honors liberal arts from the University of Texas, where she majored in drama, philosophy and English literature, she was a stage manager, video editor and technical writer. Sarah lives in northern California. Visit her at www.munchkyn.com.

Colophon

The text for this book was set in Adobe Caslon Pro, a variation of the typeface designed by William Caslon (1692-1766). Caslon is one of the world's most popular and readable fonts. Benjamin Franklin was fond of it and employed it extensively in his printing press. The United States Declaration of Independence and the Constitution were set in Caslon type for their first printings. Adobe Caslon Pro was designed by Carol Twombly.

The section and scene headings were set in Myriad Pro Semibold Condensed. The title pages were set in Final Frontier Old Style.